LAND
OF
ASHES

USA TODAY BESTSELLING AUTHOR
STACEY MARIE BROWN

ALSO BY STACEY MARIE BROWN

Paranormal Romance

Darkness Series
Darkness of Light (#1)
Fire in the Darkness (#2)
Beast in the Darkness (An Elighan Dragen Novelette)
Dwellers of Darkness (#3)
Blood Beyond Darkness (#4)
West (#5)

Collector Series
City in Embers (#1)
The Barrier Between (#2)
Across the Divide (#3)
From Burning Ashes (#4)

Lightness Saga
The Crown of Light (#1)
Lightness Falling (#2)
The Fall of the King (#3)
Rise from the Embers (#4)

Savage Lands Series
Savage Lands (#1)
Wild Lands (#2)
Dead Lands (#3)
Bad Lands (#4)
Blood Lands (#5)
Shadow Lands (#6)

Devil in the Deep Blue Sea
Silver Tongue Devil (#1)
Devil in Boots (#2)

Fairytale Retellings

A Winterland Tales
Descending into Madness (#1)
Ascending from Madness (#2)
Beauty in Her Madness (#3)
Beast in His Madness (#4)

The Monster Ball Anthology
The Red Huntress

**See end of book for
Contemporary Romance
and
Foreign Translations**

Note to reader: Stop now if you haven't read the first 6 books in the Savage Lands Series as reading on will expose you to the horror and distress of those things called spoilers (Gasp!) Also it will be further enhanced if you read the DCL Saga.

Turn back now before it's too late...

Chapter One

Ash

An icy breeze rippled over my skin, as the howl of winter whipped the holiday lights through the Stephansplatz. The nightly festival glittered in the darkness, the lights decorating the wooden huts, Christmas trees, and shops. Music danced on my nerves like fat, bitter sugarplums. The scents of roasting nuts, gingerbread, and mulled wine filled my nose while people laughed and sang in cheerful cadence.

It was sandpaper to my skin. Their joy and lightness felt like barbed wire to my soul.

Burrowing my pounding head against the frosty night, still suffering from the extensive drugs from the night before, I turned down a dark alley, steering away from the festivities and weaving closer to my destination. Glancing over my shoulder, I used my senses to pick up any followers. Anyone with nefarious notions.

To say I've made friends in the last eleven months would be far from the truth. I had created more enemies, even of my friends. It was something the old Ash wouldn't have done, but I wasn't that person anymore. He died almost a year ago and left nothing but hate, vengeance, and rage within these bones I carried.

It was why I hadn't been in Budapest in over three months. I got sick of the looks, the interventions, the judgment. Being told I wasn't "being myself."

There was no self to be. So, I left.

While all of them wanted to focus on the future, I was locked on the past, unable to move on, not understanding how they all seemed to want to forget so easily.

I breathed vengeance and dreamed about death.

Tree fairies were known to be even-tempered and serene, though I had never been a typical one. But even with my composed personality, I could be broken.

Weaving through the streets of Vienna, the influence and protection of Austria being under the umbrella of the Unified Nations was seen everywhere. The maintenance of roads, the advanced electricity system keeping this place glowing even in the darkest of nights. No mass destitution, no crumbling buildings. Not that there wasn't a social divide between fae and human, nor was it even close to perfect, but it was a world away from the decay and poverty of the East, which was only two hours by train.

Checking over my shoulder again, I tugged my hood higher up, making sure my dark blond hair was covered. A couple of people strolled hand in hand down the lane, and a group of college kids laughed and stumbled down the street, singing like drunken fools, oblivious to real life and real problems.

Heading for the buttery light burning inside the pub, I noted the words *Beer Saloon* written out in English on the side of the building. I stepped into the holiday-decorated pub designed with arched white stone ceilings, barrel tables, random beer signage, and dark wood décor. It gave off a distinctive German-but-wanna-be-American-cowboy vibe. A place to relax to live music or get lost in the dim corners lit with dim candles.

A good place to go unnoticed while meeting with seedy connections.

The warm, stuffy air blasted my nose and cheeks with burning heat. The aroma of fried food and beer filled my nostrils while the loud chatter of people hummed off the ceiling and walls, crackling against my ears.

I tended to stay away from people now. I had no patience to be nice, or care about anyone else. The only time I could handle more than one was when I was high as fuck and in a brothel.

Tinsel and lights were strung over the bar, ceiling, and walls. A cheap plastic tinsel tree was propped up next to the bar while a dozen poinsettias were placed around the room, once again harping on the fact the holidays were coming. We should be joyous. Happy. It only reminded me I wasn't.

My reasons for being happy were dead.

For one moment, I let myself be happy, when I should've known better. Even my childhood was a red flag, warning me I was not meant for love. I grew up never having unconditional love, except from one person, and I abandoned her, leaving her to suffer what I could not. Running away to save myself. Until Warwick and Kitty, I didn't understand what true family was.

Shoving the pang of memories, I rolled back my shoulders, strolling for a table. I scanned the place, searching for the person I was meeting here. He had been almost impossible to track down, and it was even harder for him to obtain the information I had been seeking for months.

3

With no sign of him, I tucked myself against the wall in the darkest area, giving me a perfect view of the room and entrance. I nodded at the pretty server as she approached me.

"What can I get you?" She grinned, her lids lowering submissively, the candle on my table flicking over her alabaster skin.

"Paulaner," I answered as I ordered a beer.

Pretending to write it down, her attention stayed on me. "Can I get you *anything* else?" Her blonde eyebrow arched up, her blue eyes glinting with interest. "Even off menu." The insinuation was clear.

"No."

"You sure?"

Shoulders rising, I felt the lash of my tongue, the words ready to break across her in a torrent. Everything about her coy expression, her flirty vibe, crawled up the back of my neck in a storm, taking all I had to barricade it back. I just wanted to be left the hell alone.

"No." My reply punched from my lips, and I turned my head away, staring over the dimly lit room, making it very clear I wasn't interested.

She sucked in at my harsh dismissal, her cheeks heating with embarrassment, probably not used to being rejected, and she retreated.

As a tree fairy, I knew my face and toned body enticed, while the sexual energy was always riding my skin like an electrical charge that drew people in. And at one time, I would have openly flirted with her, taken her to my bed. Smiled. Laughed. Had fun.

That person seemed long ago, in a different lifetime.

Maybe somewhere deep inside I cared that I was being an asshole, or maybe I no longer gave a shit. The nice, easygoing guy who stood most of his life between Warwick and Kitty as the anchor was no longer. I was adrift, drowning in a sea of pain.

Everything changed the night almost a year ago. And I no longer cared that I didn't recognize the person looking back in the mirror.

The waitress placed the pint on the table and disappeared as quickly as she came, not even looking at me. A hint of shame tightened my muscles, but I pushed it away with everything else.

Sipping the cool beverage, I exhaled, the alcohol barely taking the edge off the craving for fairy dust, which still streamed through my blood from the night before.

I barely remembered anything from the orgy except waking up outside on the ground, my clothes in my arms. I was covered in cheap lipstick, cum that wasn't mine, and had a vague recollection of being thrown out by two huge gorilla shifters.

The door opened, pulling my attention to it. A group of four girls and three guys came parading in, a mix of fae and human. Their loud, excited voices and jubilant energy rammed into me with force, my spine bristling as they headed for the bar. The renowned university here had the streets crawling with college kids celebrating finals being done and winter break ahead of them. This displayed another huge difference from the Eastern bloc. There, universities hardly existed anymore, and if they did, they were only for the extremely wealthy. Most sent their children over the borders to the West, while poor kids in the East were stuck working next to their parents in the factories. The carefree college life was not something kids from the East experienced anymore.

My attention on the group, I noticed two of them seemed slightly older than the rest, which had me almost missing the hooded figure settling into the chair opposite me. His quiet movements, nondescript features, and gray cloak turned him into a magic trick, appearing before your eyes.

Not reacting, I regarded the man with boredom, taking a sip of beer and waiting for him to speak first, though his gaze told me nothing got past him.

"Long way from Budapest." Voice low, he leaned his forearms on the table.

"I could say the same for you." I set the glass down.

"My services reach far beyond Hungary, especially now with your new *democratic* president making everything more accessible." The man's lip pulled up.

"Not a fan?" A prickle of protectiveness simmered for Killian. What he and Brexley were trying to create in Hungary was astonishing under the circumstances.

"As you know, my business is a black market of highly sought items. I don't like when they aren't in high demand."

"Then I'm surprised you aren't farther east." Killian was trying to get Hungary on its feet, but neighboring countries like Serbia, Romania, Ukraine, Russia, and Slovakia were fighting against the new wave of democracy, taking their people deeper into authoritarian leadership, straining the thin lines between our countries, hinting at war. *Another one.* It seemed dictators never tired of war, while the people were the ones to suffer it.

"I had business here. Supplies to pick up." He shook his head when the waitress neared, his hood still covering his face. She turned, darting away without hesitation, causing the man's lips to curve up. "I see you have been charming people here as well as you did in Prague."

My shoulders twitched, and I draped my arm over the back of the bench. Not many knew Mykel, Brexley's uncle, had asked me to leave Prague after dozens of complaints about fighting and disorderly conduct.

"You've left a wave of destruction from Hungary to Czech, haven't you?"

"You don't know anything about me." I gritted my teeth. Only one person knew him and knew me and helped set up this meeting, but I didn't think he would tell him anything about me.

"On the contrary." He leaned forward, his brown eyes staring into me. "I know much about you, Ash. Your reputation is starting to precede you. Thrown out of almost every brothel or sex club you enter for breaking property, overindulgence, and having no threshold in your activities. You are becoming known as the man with *very* particular tastes in his depraved orgies." He tilted his head. "Blond, ripped men and blue-haired women, even if they have to wear a wig."

My body jolted back, my teeth crunching down until I heard my jaw crack. I wanted to strike out, to flip the table and pound his face. All reactions I never had before. I had to fight a lot growing up with Warwick in our line of work, but I never craved it the way he did. I never sought it out, always the one in harmony and balance.

Now it was all I wanted to do. All I craved.

He sat back with a slight smile. "With all that rage, I'm wondering why *you* aren't farther east. Seeking what you so desperately want." He clasped his hands. "Like *Romania*."

His words sliced at my chest, making it hard to breathe, nerves twinging up my neck, sitting me up.

"That's where they are? You know for sure?"

The picture of Sonya and Iain flashed into my head, hatred burning acid up my throat. There had been rumors they had left Romania, sailing the Black Sea toward Istanbul, escaping my grasp.

"My sources are *never* wrong. They don't just hunt the

7

seas, they rule them. They know everything going to and from."

"Where?" I leaned in further to him. "Are Sonya and Iain hiding with Prime Minister Lazar in Bucharest?" After months of searching and trying to pinpoint the two people I wanted to kill, I had no actual proof they were hiding in Romania, seeking asylum under Prime Minister Lazar's roof. And with hostile, deadly borders between our countries—and death if I was caught—I needed real, solid evidence.

"Payment first." He smirked.

My hands rolled into balls as I tried to ignore the loud laughs from the coeds at the bar, the hum of patrons talking, the holiday music grinding against my neck. My focus was on the man who could provide the answers I needed. The revenge I craved.

"How much?" I felt for my billfold.

He scoffed, his head wagging slightly. "Not that kind of payment."

My stomach knotted. "You want a favor." I gulped, realizing I should've seen it coming.

"It's how genies work." A perfume of confidence and ego rolled off the man. "You rub my lamp, and I'll rub yours."

"If only you meant this in the dirty way." The need to drink down my beer in one chug, to calm the anxiety rising, almost had me doing it. A sexual advance I could handle, but what he asked was far more serious and dangerous.

Scorpion had warned me.

"As your friend knows, my favors have no time limit. I can call on you at any time, for anything. No matter what it is, you have to fulfill your part of the deal." His brow arched up, almost hiding under his hood. "So, how bad do you want to know their *exact* whereabouts?"

Owing a genie didn't sound much different from a vow, except instead of the vow killing you, the genie had men who would if you went back on your word. Sucking in, I exhaled slowly, already knowing how far I'd go. "I agree to your terms."

A smile curled his lips, and he pulled a manila envelope out of his cloak and tossed it on the table as he stood up.

"Nice doing business with you, fairy. You will know when I need to cash in." He turned, and I watched Dzsinn stroll unnoticed out the door.

Heart thumping in my ears, I reached for the folder. Everything I needed to track them down was inside this envelope. The taste of retribution coated my tongue. They would feel my pain, suffer my vengeance, and experience my wrath.

Sonya and Iain would understand what unbearable agony was. Hell was coming for them.

Fingers grasping for the folder, I started to pull out the contents. Somewhere in my brain, my senses prickled with warning. The air in the atmosphere shifted, the environment telling me something was no longer in harmony, tightening my muscles right as the door burst open.

The room stilled, as if it also could feel the unscrupulous energy.

Five huge, dark-haired men dressed in black clothes, loaded with weapons, and looking like some Mafia-type men, went straight for the bar area. I sensed instantly they were fae, magic curling off them, their movements too quick and subtle to be human. *Were they here to rob the place?* Though there was nothing of value to steal, and the patrons were even less worth the effort. No riches or diamonds, just hardworking people enjoying a Friday night. Not the place to risk getting caught for such little reward.

My hand went to my gun hiding in my jacket, my gaze locked on them as the men spread out. Three of them altered their direction, confusing me when they headed for the group of students instead of the staff, guns drawn on the college kids.

Two of the students who appeared older, a blonde woman and a dark-haired man, reacted, the man fumbling for something in his clothes. Everything happened in a split second.

POP!

The shot went through his skull, blood spraying from his head, his body falling as screams of terror impaled the air.

"Reid!" A petite, dark-haired girl cried after the man. The killer stepped up to the blonde still standing in front of the brunette, his fist cracking across her face, sending her body flying into the corner.

"Eve!" The same girl reached for her friends as her other companions scrambled away, deserting her in their fear. Only one called back for her as they ran for their own lives.

The men ignored them, moving quickly for the brunette, grabbing her arms. A tall, beefy one yanked her to him, wrapping his hand around her mouth, and put a gun to her head, whispering something in her ear.

Panic whistled like a dog call through the room, sparking a resounding terror through the rest of the clientele. Shrieks and commotion exploded under the curved ceiling. A few humans jerked up from their seats, fear tramping them for the only door.

Anxiety twitched as the two men guarding the door shouted at the people to sit back down, their thick accents hard to make out. No one listened. Terror was an uncontrollable response. Some will keep calm, stay logical, and do what they are told. With others, terror takes hold.

Their need to stay alive, to flee from danger, overrides any logic and usually has them run straight into the fire.

"Sit down!" A thick Russian accent ordered. *Bang!* A warning shot went off.

Screams pierced off the walls and people made a beeline for the exit, doing the exact opposite, the room spiraling into pandemonium. When I pushed myself out of my seat, a body rammed into my shoulder, propelling me forward onto the tile with a thud. The envelope flew from my hands, skating across the room.

I watched my only link to my enemies disappear into the stampede.

Panic shuddered through my chest. Scrambling up, more shouts and gunshots echoed off the thick stone, the assailants losing control of the situation as mobs rushed for the exit, knocking over tables and chairs. Pushing against the throng, I searched for the folder. It was my lifeline. My retribution. There was no way I could leave here without it.

A table crashed onto its side, a candle rolling off, my gaze latching on to its destination.

"*Szar!*" I lunged forward to stop it as the flame rolled into the tinsel tree. Flames shot up the fake tree, heat blasting my face, pulling me back. The fire already sprang for the old wooden bar next to it covered in decades of alcohol, drinking it up in a gulp, barking out a deep woof sound as it consumed more.

"FIRE!"

Pandemonium erupted, amplifying the panic to sheer terror, my heart pounding wildly in my ear. My attention snapped around, searching for the folder, the last of my sanity connected to what was in it. *Why didn't I open it the moment he handed it to me?* The information was so close. I had to get it, no matter what.

My eye caught the yellow envelope on the floor, feet from me. Pushing up, I rushed for it as a boot stomped over it, and another kicked it farther under the platform the band had been playing on, the fire creeping closer and closer.

No!

"Let me go!" A girl's voice pulled my attention to see a man in a balaclava pick up the brunette, fighting to keep hold of her as she thrashed in his grip. He hissed words I couldn't hear, shoving the barrel of his gun harder into her temple, dragging her toward the door. The other abductors bellowed to him in Russian over the noise of the fire, waving him to hurry as they ran out the exit. The fire traveled quickly, burning through the wood beams and webbing over the entrance. In seconds, it would trap us in, sealing us in our tomb.

A muffled cry came from the petite brunette, her eyes watering with fear, the kidnapper digging the gun into her head. His grip over her mouth pinned her tightly to his chest, inching her to the door. Her green eyes met mine, filled with a plea. With hope, begging me to help.

For a split second, I debated, the folder only a few feet away, but I knew I couldn't. It was embedded in my DNA to protect, to help.

Darting up, I smashed my fist into the side of the abductor's neck, his body stumbling to the side. Gasping for air, he loosened his grip on her. She used the opportunity to ram the back of her head into his nose with a crack. A hissed cry came from him and he released her, his hand going to his face. I reached out, yanking her away from him as my leg swept out, knocking him to the ground, my knuckles slamming into the spot once again below his chin, striking his vagus nerve. The man's body went limp under me.

There was a beat before I peered over at her. She stared down at him with shock, then found my gaze.

Pop!

Flames crackled around us, drawing my attention to the room thick with smoke. Fire licked at the bottles full of alcohol, and the fracturing glass began to hiss, pressure building in them like kindling.

"Oh fuck!" I yelled.

POP! POP! POP! POP!

Leaping to her, I took her to the floor, covering her body with mine, her tiny frame completely engulfed by me.

Like bombs, the decanters shattered on the shelf, burning liquid and glass raining down on us, slicing at my skin, drenching us in fuel to be consumed by the hungry fire. The blaze surged in howls, clouds of smoke filling my lungs, stealing the oxygen. We had to get out before we passed out and died here.

The folder!

My head popped up, blood and booze dripping down my face, my gaze snapping around, searching. Horror gripped my chest seeing the yellow packet peeking out of the wooden stage being ingested by flames, turning it to cinders.

This was the only copy, and if it was destroyed, so would the knowledge with it.

"NO!" A guttural noise came from my soul. My body clambered across the tile, the scorching heat sizzling my skin like charring beef.

"What are you doing?" the girl yelled at me. "Come on!" More wails from the bottles along the bar squealed in warning, the fire growing bigger.

"No!" I repeated the only word I could utter, my fingers poking and clawing at the blaze, trying to reach the papers. My entire world was within that packet. Everything that held any meaning. It took me almost a year to get the information, and before I could even open it, it was being taken from me.

Just like they were. It felt as though I was failing them again.

"Stop!" The girl tugged on my arm, trying to pull me away, the flames torching the edges of my clothes and hair, my teeth crashing together in agony.

"No!" I continued to blister my fingers trying to retrieve it, black holes burning through the folder, curling the pages, lifting them up in the air when nothing was left but fibers. The information was gone. Lost forever.

POP! BOOM!

A large carafe detonated, spitting spikes of glass down on us, the flames roaring higher. Soon it would overtake this building, me with it.

A part of me wished for it. No more pain. No more grief and shame. I'd be with them.

"You think Lucas and me want your firm, beautiful ass with us?" Kek's bored voice came into my head. A slight playful hint to it, a challenge. *"Please."* She sputtered a dry laugh, dying quickly. *"We want you to get the fuck up, fairy. Fight. Live. Avenge us."*

"Come on." Grabbing my arm, the girl yanked me away, helping me to my feet, her strength surprising for her size. "We have to get out of here."

With a guttural noise, staring one last time at the lump of ash, I let her pull me away.

"Fuck," I whispered. The front door was completely covered in flames, blocking our way out.

"Oh gods, we're trapped," she croaked, coughing and gagging as smoke clouded around us.

"This way." I pulled her with me, heading for the kitchen. Every public building had to have more than one exit. Flames roared, nipping at our backs as I jumped over the unconscious assailant and her dead friend.

"No!" The girl yanked against my grip, grasping for her friend. "I can't leave him." She bellowed. "Where is Eve?" She hacked, trying to find her blonde friend through the smoke. "Eve!"

Sparks and chunks of wood dropped on us. Any window we had to escape was dwindling.

"You have to," I bellowed, wrenching her with me. "Or this will be your grave as well."

She let out an anguished cry but let me tug her with me. Ducking and weaving, we ran through the door to the tiny kitchen, sparks sprinting for us, burning into our clothes, trying to reach us before we escaped.

"Go! Go!" I shoved her out the back door into a narrow, dank alley. The freezing night air rammed down my throat, causing me to choke on the smoky air in my lungs. Eyes watering, my lungs hacking, we stumbled out into the lane, my back falling against the stone wall.

I heaved in air, and my pulse pounded in my ears. Pain throbbed from my bubbling, burned skin, but it was nothing compared to the chasm of grief building up in my hollow soul. Reality settling in. The understanding of what I lost, what was taken from me.

Gripping my head, I let out a guttural cry, my already bleeding knuckles slamming back into the wall over and over. Anguish howled through me like a war-torn landscape. Blood-soaked, charred, and empty of life.

"Stop!" Small, singed hands tried to grab for me. "Stop it!"

Bending over, I let out another bitter wail, my head in my hands. The grief I had locked away for so long wanted to bury me in it. I finally had the information in my hands. My revenge had a focus. In the blink of an eye, it was gone. And it felt as though I was losing them all over again.

15

"Look at me." Her voice was quiet, but it was anything but weak, demanding my attention. My eyes landed on bright emerald-green ones, lighter than my own moss-colored irises. Covered in soot and cuts, it was the first time I really looked at her. Long, straight brown hair hitting the middle of her back, full lips, sharp cheekbones, and freckles sprinkled across her nose. She was stunning. Even my clouded mind could recognize that, but young. Too young. Even though she was certainly fae, she hadn't been on this earth long.

And I had no interest in that or anything else.

Shoving away from her, my safeguard walled back up. Turning down the passage, I ran my hand through my singed hair, my mind started whirling with what to do next.

"Wait!" she called out after me, hobbling in her tall zip-up boots down the cobbled street. "Where are you going?"

They were in Romania. I could at least start there.

"Wait," she yelled again.

"What?" With a heavy sigh, I paused, peering back at her as she caught up with me. Her scorched, short sweater dress was barely covering her now. I noticed what looked like a goblin-metal bracelet on her wrist. The assailants must have put it on her when they grabbed her, stopping her from using her powers.

"You just saved my life… you can't leave me here," she exclaimed. Sirens wailed in the distance, smoke billowing up into the moonless sky.

"Watch me." I started to twist back.

"No." She clutched my jacket, yanking me back.

"What the hell?" I growled, sounding more and more like Warwick.

"Where am I supposed to go?"

My lids narrowed in confusion over her comment—and the fear in her eyes.

"Go home." I threw out my arm. "To your friends, your family. I don't care."

"I don't think I can." She peered to the side, swallowing. A flicker of curiosity popped into my brain. Why couldn't she go home? The men had come after her *specifically*. Put that goblin bracelet around her wrist. Why? Who was she? Who cares? I wasn't getting involved. Any interest in this girl's life was buried under my own concerns.

"Not my problem." I wrenched her fingers off my jacket and proceeded down the alley.

Getting to Romania and through the borders was going to be near impossible, but I would do it.

I had to do it.

The trains didn't start until morning, so there was only one place I could go until then. To forget the past, present, and future. And especially this fucked-up night.

My veins begged for the fairy dust while my feet hurried to numb the pain, to deaden the memories of their voices, the feel of them lying next to me in bed. The happiness.

Turning down the street, I headed for the only brothel that didn't turn anyone away, no matter what horrible piece of shit you were.

And that was exactly what I had become.

Chapter 2
Ash

The whistle of the train punctured my eardrums, stomping across my brain and down my throat to my stomach. Flinching, I pinched the bridge of my nose, sucking in deep breaths. Still drunk and high, my nerves shook with the decline of both.

I didn't sleep anymore. I passed out.

For one moment, a few months back, I thought I could resist the temptation of those vices, fulfill my vengeance like some caped crusader, and become a better man.

It lasted three days.

Sleep became something I avoided. Every time I shut my eyes, they were there. Numbing it was the only way to shut down my thoughts, to pause the endless loop of what I could've done differently. The tiresome scenarios I rolled through my head, how I could've gotten to them earlier, saved them, before nodding off. My mind replayed their deaths every night, and I lost them all over again *every* night. I'd wake up screaming, sweat pouring from me, the horror chilling me to the bone, realizing it was real life and not a nightmare.

They were gone. Forever.

Not strong enough to take it, I left Budapest, feeling free to sink into my depravities.

Dzsinn wasn't lying when he said I had particular tastes and no threshold in my behaviors.

The drugs deadened me from the grief, but it also took away pleasure. I couldn't feel, so I reached deeper and deeper for it, getting more desperate. Like last night…

"Fuck me! Harder!" I barked at the guy behind me, his cock pumping in and out while I plowed into the girl I had tied up and pinned against a dresser so hard the blue wig had fallen off, and tears leaked down her face. She had already come twice, but I didn't stop. The need for pain, for anything, drove me on like a fiend. "Bite me! Make me bleed!" I yanked the blond guy's head down to my neck, forcing him to tear into my flesh. The desperation to experience the bliss of release, to experience anything other than a hollow hole in my soul, had me shaking with violence.

Ever since I walked away from the girl in the pub, leaving the ashes of the folder in the bar, I had been on a mission to forget. A mission to inflict punishment on myself, fury bubbling at the seams, my temper on the edge of sadistic.

My body went through the motions, my release humming at the edges, but that was as close as it got. I stood on the other side of the glass, watching some soulless stranger take over my shell. Observing the cruelty with which he reprimanded them for not being who he really wanted. For Kek and Lucas being dead.

"Enough!" I ordered the guy behind me, pointing at another watching us across the room, stroking himself. "You.

And you." I pulled out of the girl on the dresser, nodding to another woman. "Put that on." I motioned to the wig on the ground. "And get on your knees."

I could picture Kek's coy grin at my demand, the spark in her eyes, lowering herself to the ground, loving when I took charge. The bedroom was the one place I was dominant with them. Kek got off being told what to do, someone daring to challenge a demon, but only in the bedroom. Lucas was the shyer, sweeter one of us and needed someone to take charge. Outside of that, they were more dominant and badass, but not when we shut the doors at night.

No one could say how or why, but we just worked.

The prostitute placed the wig on, lowering herself in front of me. She showed me the fairy dust coating her tongue before taking my cock in her mouth, sucking until I groaned. My hips roughly pushed my dick further down her throat, my skin soaking in the drugs quickly, taking the edge off. My head started to spin, my lids lowering as the other young, pretty fae guy moved around me. His hair was light brown and all wrong, but my drugged-up brain didn't care. I needed someone to break me. To finally take me over, allow one moment I could find happiness.

Peace.

The male whore pushed in and out of me over and over, climaxing hard, his cum dripping down my legs, his loud groans trying to break through my hazy world. Closing my eyes, I pushed the sound of his voice away, focusing on the woman sucking me, pretending it was Kek, until I released down her throat. My eyes fully shut as the drugs took me under, doing what nobody seemed to be able to do.

Give me a moment of serenity.

When a bad dream forced my eyes open, dawn was sneaking through the curtains. My naked body was tangled up with others, and I groaned in irritation and pain. My emotions could stay hidden in the ether, but my bones ached from the abuse. I was still healing from the burns, bite marks, bruises, and soreness of my own making.

As I extracted myself from the tangle of limbs, none of them moved, worn out. They didn't even stir as I stood up, washed myself with a cloth, and got dressed. Peering at the three women and two men in the large bed, I felt a stab of sorrow. I didn't feel satisfied or better.

They weren't Kek and Lucas. Merely cheap versions from my drug-addled brain. A poor man's interpretation of my fantasies.

Drawing my bag up to my shoulder, I pulled out a few extra bills for the furniture damage, leaving it on the table. Slipping out of the brothel and to the street, my lungs sucked in the icy morning air with a bumpy hitch. My legs were shaky, my head pounding as the drugs wore off, my feet traveling toward the train station.

"No direct train?" I frowned at the attendant behind the counter.

The man scoffed, peering at me like I was an idiot. "In the East, you're lucky the trains are working at all."

I knew it, but everything in me wanted to avoid stopping in Budapest. It was too close to everything I was trying to avoid.

"Take it or leave it. It's the only train heading in that direction."

"Yeah, okay. Give me the next ticket to Bucharest."

"Bucharest?" The man's lips pressed, studying me, probably wondering why anyone would be heading toward a hostile country. "Waste of money. I heard it's almost impossible to get in or out of the border of Romania."

My gaze leveled on him, and he swallowed, nodding his

21

head, getting me a ticket. I wasn't used to being intimidating; that was Warwick's job. But when you lost everything, you had nothing left inside, people sensed it. Picked up on the vibe that there were no lines you wouldn't cross anymore.

After being handed my ticket, I weaved through the busy terminal, exhausted and hungover. Grabbing a coffee and pastry, I headed for the train platform. An awareness drifted over the back of my neck, twisting me around, my attention threading over the mobs of people traveling through trying to locate the source, but no one stood out.

Shoving a bit of the flaky apple strudel in my mouth, I turned back, springing up the steps of the train car, proceeding down six full cars before settling into a quiet one near the exit, with single seats across from each other and a small table in between.

A few people settled in at the opposite end of the carriage, a family with two young kids and an older couple, but no one who would warrant alarm. Still, unease prickled over me. Like I was being watched.

Glancing behind me and outside the train window, nothing screamed danger or offered a reason for my jumpy nerves. Maybe my senses were malfunctioning? So tweaked out from drugs, they no longer worked right.

Exhaling, I leaned back in my seat and closed my eyes, feeling the train jerk forward, leaving the station.

Here I go… off to Romania with no plan, no backup, and no idea where they are actually hiding.

I couldn't wait anymore. I would hunt them down and kill them, no matter what it took. Nothing, I mean nothing, would get in my way.

A huff of air and the awareness of someone sitting down across from me at the table popped open my lashes.

I blinked several times.

No. No fucking way.

"You didn't even shower, did you?" Her nose wrinkled, gaze rolling over the charred clothes I redressed in.

"What—" I sat up straight, peering around like something would remedy my confusion. "What is going on? What are you doing here?"

"I guess I can't talk much." She sniffed at her burned clothes. "But I didn't spend all night in a brothel on top of that."

I froze, my lids opening and closing with shock, my intoxicated mind not able to understand what was going on.

The girl from last night, the one I saved... was here. Still wearing the same outfit, her pale skin was healing, showing off more of her freckles that were hidden by makeup last night. Her dark-lined eyes were smudged, but it only sharpened the bright green color. Her tousled hair and disheveled dress gave the impression she had a crazy night.

Annoyance started to overtake my shock. "What the fuck are you doing here?" I hissed again, glancing around like I was going to find a parent or someone who was in charge of this girl standing close.

"Coming with you."

"Wha-aaat?" I sputtered, causing heads from upfront to turn back, my tone hitting a high pitch. Clearing my throat, I leaned across the table, lowering my voice. "What the fuck are you talking about? You are *not* coming with me."

She tucked her dark hair behind her ear, peering to the side, the morning sun glistening off her diamond earrings.

Probably from a well-to-do family, which, getting into a school in Vienna, you had to be.

"I'm not kidding." I reached over, roughly grabbing her arm. "You are getting off now."

"No." She yanked it back, her brows creasing. "And

23

what are you going to do, throw me off a moving train?" She motioned out the window. The train had just passed the city boundaries and was picking up speed.

"Szar!" Shit! I hissed, hitting the table with my fist. "The next stop you are getting off, turning around, and going home."

"I can't."

"What do you mean you can't?"

"It's no longer…" She shifted in her seat, her jaw tight. "Safe for me."

"And what does that mean?"

She folded her arms, not answering.

My gaze went over her again, and it dawned on me that she never went back to where she was staying. Tension and slight fear hinted in her eyes. The metal band, which appeared to have no clasp, was still around her wrist. Goblin metal was fae kryptonite, nullifying our powers. Yet, she was still healing and didn't appear as drained as other fae might be, which tickled the back of my brain.

"The men last night." I tilted my head, nodding at the goblin cuff on her arm. "They killed your friends, but they were after *you*. Why?"

Her jaw tightened.

"Did you know them?" Nothing from her. "By your earrings, I'm guessing you come from a wealthy family." Her silence continued as I went on. "But a pair of earrings isn't enough for five Russian Mafia types to invade a pub. Plus, they never tried to take anything from you or anyone else…" I sat back in my seat. "Which tells me they weren't there to rob. They came purposely for *you*." I paused. "Daddy is more than wealthy, am I right? Use the kid to get ransom money? How close am I?" I chuffed, feeling like I hit the target dead on.

Her dark brow arched up. "It wouldn't be my *daddy's* money. It would be my mother's." She leaned over the table, her lids narrowed. "But it's not money they want."

"Please. Money is the only thing people want."

"What about *sex...*" She purposely slid over that word. "Love? Respect? Power?" Her eyebrow went up, stirring me in my seat with irritation.

"Like you know about *any* of those," I said.

"And you do?"

"I know plenty."

"Right." She huffed. "Was that what you called last night?"

My mouth opened and shut, an irritated a child was putting me in my place. I blamed it on my sluggish mind, but something she said finally hit me.

"I didn't spend all night in a brothel on top of that."

"Wait." I sat up higher. "How the hell do you know where I was last night?" I inclined closer. "Were you following me?"

She shrugged a shoulder.

"What? Why?" I wagged my head in disbelief, my skin burning in my cheeks at the idea.

"I told you, I couldn't go home."

"So you followed me?" Heat crawled up my throat, imagining what she might have heard or seen. I enjoyed leaving the curtains open, not minding an audience to my punishment. "What the fuck is wrong with you?"

A smirk played on her lips. "Are you worried I saw what kinky, disgusting shit you do in there?"

"First, there is no shame in kink." I held up my finger like I was reprimanding her. "And second, I'm more worried about why you are stalking me."

She looked out the window, not replying.

"You don't even know me," I exclaimed.

"I have an instinct about people." She looked down at her clasped hands. "It's something I'm actually good at."

"Oh my gods." I scrubbed my hand down my face with a groan. "You are so fucking naive."

"Fuck you. I'm twenty."

Twenty. Fuck me was right.

"A baby," I scoffed, dropping my hand. "You follow a guy you don't even know onto a train, with no idea of where it's going, because of a gut feeling?" I was throwing stones, though, because tree fairies' powers were about instinct and harmony with the earth. Complete intuition. But I had lived a hell of a lot longer than this girl. Knew far more and had been through a lot more. "You are getting off at the next stop."

"And I said I am not," she challenged. "You can't force me."

"No, but you aren't staying with me."

"Why not?"

"Why not?" I sputtered. "Because you can't," I explained, like that was a rational answer. "Whatever you think, I am not a good guy." Not anymore, anyway. "And where I'm going and what I am doing? It's dangerous. No one can come with me."

"We'll see." She wiggled back in her seat with absolute assurance.

"I mean it."

She grabbed my coffee off the table, taking a drink before biting into my strudel.

The *audacity* of this girl. A scream bellowed inside my head, frustration digging my hands into my head.

"I'm"—she paused like she was unsure—"Scarlet, by the way."

Taking a few huge breaths, a strained laugh caught in

my throat at the sheer insanity my life had taken on in the last twelve hours.

My attention turned to the rushing landscape outside, exhaling with a shake of my head.

"Ash."

Thick, turbulent clouds covered the sky, sinking into my bones like an omen. The moment we crossed over into Hungary, tension pinched the back of my neck, causing my legs and hands to fidget, growing steadily worse the closer we got to the city. I couldn't escape the stop here, needing to switch trains to continue our route southeast, but when we hit the bridge crossing over the Danube, the sight of the newly restored Parliament building and Killian's palace sitting proudly on the hill restricted my airways. Construction and new business signs dotted the skyline. Even in just three months since I had been gone, things had grown and changed.

It was my home. Where my true family was. Though right now, it was my purgatory. A hell I couldn't escape.

Every memory from that night came back with a sharp stab. The sounds of shooting, screaming, clashing of swords, and booms of cannons. The rancid taste of gunpowder and death on my tongue.

Standing there, watching the bullet enter Lucas's brain, his eyes wide with shock and grief. The genuine heartache Lucas felt as Iain fired. Murdered by his own brother. But that was Lucas. Deep down, no matter what, he still believed in the best in people. The glass was always half full.

The agony I experienced, the grief swallowing me whole. I didn't think anything more could be taken from me.

I didn't know that in just one more breath, Kek would join him.

The sound of the blade cutting through her neck, the rage twisting Sonya's face as she took the other part of my soul.

The sick thump of Kek's head hitting the stone, her body following.

I thought I had experienced pain before in my life. The loss of people I loved. But losing those two was like my own death.

Nothing about a demon and tree fairy should have worked. Kek and I were opposites in so many ways, but with her, I felt more alive than I had with anyone else. She challenged both me and Lucas, and without realizing it, I fell for her. Fell for both of them.

Hard.

We brought out the best in each other. The emptiness of being without them had no bottom, a circular nightmare I would never get out of. And a part of me didn't want to.

Here, they were still fresh and vivid, even if they destroyed any humanity I had left. Without them, what was the point of anything?

"Hey?" Scarlet bumped my boot with hers, her brow furrowing. "You okay?"

Jarred by her intrusiveness, I frowned. "Yeah." I twitched and shifted again, becoming aware of how much I was moving around, not able to sit comfortably in my seat. "Fine."

"Sure." She rolled her eyes, glancing out the window. "Been to Budapest before?"

A knot formed in my throat. "A time or two."

"I've never been this far east." She tapped her perfectly manicured nails against her lip, a deep red jeweled ring on her finger with an insignia I couldn't make out, contrasting the dirt and soot staining her hands and face. She was fae,

American, upper class, but had a very subtle, almost Irish melody to her words sometimes, which confused me every time I thought I heard it. She also had this air of being young, naive, and pampered, but at the same time, very worldly and extremely confident in her skin, no matter what filthy, torn clothes she was wearing.

I suspected that her stunning looks and the money she possessed had people bowing to her. And she annoyed the fuck out of me all the more for that. I couldn't wait to get her on a train going back to Vienna. Off my hands.

"It looks like the pictures I've seen of it in the past." Her voice rose with astonishment. "Not at all what my moth— what I heard it was like before. I've heard President Killian is working hard to restore it."

"He is." My answer came automatically, and I cleared my throat, motioning outside. "As you can see."

Killian and Brexley worked their asses off to get this city functioning again. Not that I helped in any way. I was the drunkard getting kicked out of brothels and pubs while my friends rebuilt, planned, and started anew.

My gaze went to where I knew Kitty's reconstructed brothel was. The area would never be fully cleaned up. There was too much money in sex, alcohol, and gambling.

It took us years to become friends, to get over the past and speak again, and I only screwed our relationship up once more.

The train came around, pulling into the grand train station.

"Come on." I stood up, flicking my chin for her to follow. Yanking up my hood, I peered out the door before exiting the train, my eyes sharp as I strolled down the platform, her heeled boots struggling to keep up with my strides.

"So where are we going, anyway?"

"I am heading to Bucharest. You are getting on the next train heading west."

"Bucharest?" Her eyes widened. "Why are you going there? Isn't it dangerous?"

"Yes. That's why you aren't going," I said gruffly, searching the time board and pointing up to it. "There. Next train back to Vienna."

"No." She crossed her arms, moving away from me. "I told you it's not safe for me to go back there."

"Why?" I faced her, taking up the ground she put between us. I used my height to loom over her. "Tell me."

Mouth pinching tighter, she glared back at me, not answering.

"Then I can't help you." I gestured to the platform her train was departing from in only minutes. "Time to return home, *kislány*." *Little girl*. "Call your parents and friends to help you."

Raising her head up higher, she tucked her arms in tighter, burrowing into her stubbornness.

"No, s*eggfej*." *Asshole*. She gritted back fluently in Hungarian, shocking me.

"Teringettét!" Dammit! I hissed out. "Why won't you do what I ask?" I rubbed my knuckles along my scruff in irritation, wanting to strangle her. "You're *not* coming with me, and that's final. You. Are. Going. Home."

"No. I'm. Not." She continued to watch me as if I were the one acting like a child. Moving into her, I leaned close, my voice going low.

"Where I am going is *very* dangerous. Deadly, even. It is no place for a young college girl who hasn't even cut her eyeteeth yet."

Her lids narrowed, a growling sound vibrating in her throat. "You know *nothing* about me."

"And I *don't* want to." I lashed back, needing her to get out of my hair. "Now get on the damn train." When she didn't move, I cuffed her shoulder, yanking her to the platform.

"Hey," she yelped, trying to get out of my hold.

After a handful of steps, my feet came to a stop, my body going still as my gaze landed on a man strolling in our direction, heading toward a cargo train.

Holy. Fuck.

Scorpion.

He and Warwick were the suppliers to many of the businesses in Carnal Row, getting stock shipped in from the West. A few times when I wasn't drunk, I helped them get the products off the trains and load them up.

But it was his connection to Brexley that had me freaking out. He would let her know instantly that I was here, that I had returned, which was the last thing I wanted. None of them would let me do this on my own, and I didn't want any of them to be part of it. Where I was going needed no attachments, distractions, or conscience.

I was going to slaughter with perfect clarity, and I would die doing it.

Dipping my head deeper into my hood, I swiveled around, gripping Scarlet harder, tugging her with me.

"Come on," I hissed, walking faster in the opposite direction as Scorpion.

"Oh my gods. Look." The fear in her tone popped my head up, her attention on the main doorway, her mouth parting in horror.

Szent fasz!

Six familiar men strutted into the building, their thick necks twisting around, scanning the train depot.

They were hunting. For her.

I had no doubt it was the same group of men from the

night before. Somehow, some way, they knew she was here. Had followed her.

Scorpion was almost on us, the men coming the other way. My heart pounded in my ears as I clutched her hand, snaking us down a platform. The need to run bit at my heels, but I kept an even pace, trying not to draw any attention, weaving us through groups of people debarking a train.

"Ash?" Scarlet hissed my name again, her head peering behind us. The six Russian men were spreading out, their sharp gazes searching every person, scanning the crowd.

"Keep your head down," I whispered to her, hating that she had no hooded coat to hide in. She tipped her face forward, her dark, silky locks curtaining around like a shield. Except her long hair was a marker, not a shelter.

"Там!" There! One bellowed in Russian, pointing at us like a tattletale, his buddies jerking toward us, taking off for our platform.

Out of my peripheral, I saw the commotion twisting Scorpion's head in our direction. Ducking into a throng of people before he could see me, I swore under my breath.

"Fuck." Yanking her hand, I tore off for the end of the train, my heart beat ponding in my ears. Though her legs were long, she struggled to keep up. "Hurry up," I ordered. The men were gaining, shoving and pushing through the crowd to get us.

Reaching the last carriage, I stopped at the end, leaping down onto the tracks. Twisting to help her, I blinked as Scarlet jumped down next to me, her form landing with the ease of a cat.

"Come on!" she yelled at me, taking off across the tracks, hurtling over them like balance beams. Her stability on her feet, even in heeled boots, was impressive.

Catching up, I didn't hesitate, gripping her hips and tossing her back onto the plank, her body hitting and rolling onto the cement. Pulling myself up, I scrambled over the ground, getting my feet under me.

"There!" I yanked her up, pulling her with me to a train carriage. Ducking inside, I watched out the window for the men while we ran through the inside of the train. They peered around, searching for where we had disappeared. I could see one pointing back at the train we jumped behind, telling him to check it out. Another one motioned in our direction.

"Dammit." I swung back out of the train and jumped on the one across from us. A whistle rang in the air as Scarlet and I moved deeper into the train.

"Where the fuck did they go?" A harsh Russian accent came from outside the carriage.

Sucking in, I whirled around, grabbing Scarlet and yanking her behind the luggage rack. Wrapping my arms around her, I pressed our bodies together, trying to make us the smallest we could. My head tipped back, and I peered through a crack between the rack and the wall.

My muscles strained, my throat tightening at seeing two of the men step into the carriage. Their jaws locked with irritation, one pacing around, running his hand through his short dark hair, speaking in thick Russian.

"We lose her again, he will be very angry."

"Yes." The other responded coolly. He had a buzz cut, his eyes black as death. "Then I suggest you find them."

"Yes, Nikolay."

Nikolay? As in Nikolay the Bloody?

Fuck me. This guy was notorious within the Russian Mafia—drugs, gambling, and underage sex rings. He was half human, half Vampir, which was nothing like the vampires in movies and books humans love to imagine. They didn't suck blood or turn into bats, but Vampirs did gain power off other people's blood, especially fae's, taking on their powers. They were very similar to Strighoul, though, unlike Strighoul, they didn't consume the corpses of their victims for energy.

Vampirs were mainly in Russia, their power too ingrained in the country to ever leave, but even among Vampirs, Nikolay was known for his ruthless cruelty and assassinations, which no one could pin on him. He was high up in the Mafia and didn't get out of bed for chump change or rich little college girls.

"What the fuck are we going to do?" the other guy asked.

"Check every fucking train until we find that bitch," Nikolay snarled through his teeth. "You take the other train. I will check this one."

His partner nodded, gripping his gun and heading down the walkway.

My lungs strained, my fingers digging into Scarlet, preparing to run for our lives.

"Sir?" A man's squeaky voice swung my head back toward Nikolay. "Do you have a ticket?" A conductor walked up to him, his ticket-puncher in his hand.

"Fuck off!" The Russian turned to him with billowing anger.

"If you don't have a ticket, you can either purchase one or get off." The conductor replied calmly and orderly.

Nikolay glared at him, and I could tell he was about a breath from killing him.

"Sir?" The little man held his ground, his nose rising higher. "Purchase a ticket, or please depart the train."

Nikolay's nose flared, his knuckles white on his gun, about to attack the conductor. Right then, a woman and a child climbed up the steps, backing him off. He had too many witnesses. With a snarl of swear words, Nikolay stomped off.

My lids shut briefly, my shoulders sagging with relief, and I exhaled a jagged breath.

"Oh my gods. That was close." I felt more than heard her murmur against my chest, her body leaning into me, making me suddenly very aware of her. There was not an inch of space between us, her body pressed so hard against mine I could feel her knickers through her dress, her breasts rubbing against me, her hair tickling my skin.

Pushing her away just as the train lurched, I grabbed for her arm again, keeping her on her feet, my throat dry, adrenaline still pounding in my ears.

"Tickets?" The conductor came up to us.

Peering down at her and back out the window where the land started to rush by us, I shook my head.

Fuck me.

"*Two* of the cheapest tickets to Romania, please."

Chapter 3

Ash

I glanced over my shoulder at Scarlet as we made our way down the passage to where the old cattle car used to be. After the fae war, they turned a lot of them into third-class steerage. A place for those who had little means. With my pricey habits lately, my money was dwindling fast, and I had no problem tucking up in some straw for a night. It wasn't as if I was sleeping, anyway.

"Where are we going?" Her words faltered as we stepped into the carriage, scanning over the windowless, drafty cart, smelling of straw, alcohol, body odor, and piss. A dozen men and a few women grouped in sections over the hay, talking or trying to sleep.

Scarlet's eyes slightly widened, her nose scrunching and a frown hinting at her lips as we stepped further in. She tried to hide it, swallowing, making her expression go blank. But not before I could see the shock, exposing her social class.

I would bet she'd never been subjected to this kind of

situation before, nor these people. The lowest of characters and class rode back here, dodgy and either running from the law, poverty, or themselves.

The men's eyes took her in, stopping to gawk where her creamy skin was exposed, her dress barely covering her. Stepping in front of her, I lowered my lids on them in a threat before I turned around, shuffling her off to a corner.

"Gods dammit," I muttered. "Can you not be a problem for just a moment?" Their notice of her pissed me off. She wasn't even supposed to be here, and now I felt like I had to babysit. "You are seriously a pain in my ass," I grumbled. "The next stop, I will tie you to the next train heading west."

Her lids narrowed. "How many times have I told you I can't go back there?"

"And you have yet to tell me *why.*" I gritted my teeth, walking her into the wall of the car, my anger billowing over her. "And can we talk about why the hell you have Nikolay the Bloody, a leader in the Russian Mafia, after you?"

She started to open her mouth.

"And if you say they want a pair of earrings or some money, I will open that up." I nodded to the sliding wooden door. "And toss you out." I leaned in further. "I know it's more than that. Nikolay is infamous. Unless you owe him for drugs or stole from him, I call bullshit."

She squeezed her folded arms tighter around herself.

"Is that it? You take some fairy dust from one of his crew and skip out or something?" A lot of teens got in trouble that way. Not realizing how addictive and expensive their little high at a club would be.

"No," she spat, like I insulted her.

"Then why are they after you?"

She didn't answer.

"And how did they even find us?"

Nothing.

"Tell me!" I growled.

"When you tell me why you are going to Bucharest. Who's there?" she volleyed. "A girlfriend? Lover?"

Fury ground through every muscle, feeling like she peeled back my skin, exposing my pain. I leaned into her face, only a breath away, forcing a sharp inhale from her.

"Revenge."

Her bright green eyes searched mine, and I saw not horror, but pity flicker in them, as though she could see through me. Rage crackled up my spine, weaving through my shoulders.

Moving away from her, I stomped for the carriage door, the open space between steerage and the second-class compartments, needing air. Giving one glance over my shoulder, I saw a group of the men, their hungry gaze still on her, move to get up.

"Fuck," I huffed, whipping around, heading right back for her.

"You don't leave my side." I gripped her arm, dragging her to the farthest section away from them. "You understand me?"

"You think I can't handle myself?" She cocked an eyebrow, a bemused laugh as she fought against my hold. "I could make all of them piss themselves in fear if I wanted?"

"Until I have you safely on a train heading back home." I twisted her to face me, speaking low. "You stay by my side." My gaze went down to the thin goblin metal. "And it looks like you can't do shit until we get that off you."

"Awww." She slanted her head in mocking. "Aren't you just the covert hero wanting to keep the damsel safe? Such the gentleman."

"I swear…" My molars cracked, grinding together. "Sit

down and shut up." Fuck, I was sounding more and more like Warwick.

She smirked, lowering herself into the straw. I was the one being played with.

"And I have a feeling you are anything but a damsel... though you distress the hell out of me." I rubbed my face, taking a few moments before I squatted down near her. The stench of the damp hay had me sighing louder. It smelled similar to urine.

Hungry, tired, and annoyed, I laid back in the straw. My head was aching, my body craving fairy dust like a fiend. The need to feel numb, feel the serenity that came with not giving a shit, pounded between my ears and twitched my muscles. Having to worry about this girl was only fraying the ends of my patience. How the hell did this happen?

"Ash?" Her voice was soft, but not unsure or scared.

"Hmmm?" I muttered, keeping my lids closed.

"I can help you."

My lashes fluttered up.

She tucked knotted hair behind her ear. "I think I could be really useful."

"How?"

She looked off at the wall, staying silent again, though it was as though I could hear her mind buzzing with thoughts.

"Look." I leaned on my elbows. "This might seem fun and exciting at your age, but let me tell you, it's not. You need to go back home. Where I am going is not meant for people like you."

"What the fuck does that mean?" Her voice rose, her brows crunching. "You know nothing about me."

"A twenty-year-old American college student studying at the University of Vienna means you come from a wealthy family. You hold yourself as if you were born with the arrogance of money and no one telling you no. Probably an only child, am I right?"

Her expression pinched.

"Tell me I'm wrong." I flicked my chin toward her ears. "Diamond earrings, which confirms the rich part but also tells me you have no clue of the real world outside your bubble. No one would wear those here unless they wanted them cut from their ears. People kill for a lot less in these parts." I nodded at the room. "Look around. You think one of these people would hesitate to slice your throat so they could feed their family for a month?"

Her fingers went to her lobes, feeling the jewels, quickly taking them out and stuffing them in her pocket. Her cheeks pinked with embarrassment, like she hadn't even thought about it.

"You haven't lived life at all," I chided. "You are nowhere near capable of being *helpful* to me."

"Why? Because I'm small and *look* fragile?"

"This has nothing to do with you being tiny." She was, but Birdie was similar in size. "I've seen women smaller than you fight beasts you can't imagine and handle far more than any man." I shook my head. "It's experience." I doubted she had trained one day in her life outside of yoga and Pilates. "I have lived thousands of lifetimes over your one. Seen and done things you can't possibly imagine. And what I have to do, how far I need to go—there is no line I won't cross."

She didn't blink, watching me closely.

"You will turn around the moment we can and return home." I flopped back down, closing my eyes.

She stayed quiet so long that I thought the conversation was over, my argument finally penetrating her thick skull.

"I'm not an only child," she replied, the backs of my lids fluttering. "I have a brother. And you don't know anything about my life or the experiences I've had." She shuffled back against a pile of hay. "Go ahead if it makes you feel better to think you're doing the right, moral thing by sending me back by myself with trained Russian Mafia men hunting me down. They'll murder me before I can cross the border." She sighed.

"They probably won't *murder* you." I opened one eye.

"At first." She pulled up her knees to her chest. "But I have a way of getting under people's skin."

"Don't I know it," I muttered, rubbing a hand over my face. "Get some sleep."

I heard her moving, settling deeper into the straw. It didn't take long until her breathing evened out, exhaustion taking over and pulling her under. While I lay there wide awake, a sick pit in my stomach.

If I forced her to return home, she might get caught. I didn't know what those men wanted, but I knew Nikolay's reputation well enough to know it wasn't nice. Nor would it be quick. But if she stayed with me, it was certain death. I wouldn't be able to focus on what I needed to do, and trying to keep her alive would probably get us both killed.

She had to return. My goal was the only thing important to me. She was tough and smart. She would get home on her own.

But would you be able to focus on your task? Wondering every moment what was happening to her?

With a groan, I flung my arm off my face and sat up. I needed something to dull my thoughts, take away the voices in my head.

"I need a drink." I stood.

She could stay out of trouble for two minutes, couldn't she? Sound asleep on a train, what could she do?

41

I should have never underestimated her.

The rickety rails rocked the train back and forth like a baby swing. Enough for the sober person to feel drunk and the drunk person to feel sober.

"What would you like?" The human woman bartender moved to me, a steady stream of passengers coming in from the lower-class cars to get refreshments. I couldn't even afford the low-class ticket.

"Anything cheap and to the point," I muttered, keeping my head low. Once, I brewed my own mead and gin at home. When I had a real home. One tucked half into a tree, with a garden and privacy. A tree fairy's dream. It seemed so long ago.

Another Ash, before being a prisoner of Věrhăza, tortured in the House of Blood. When he lost the two people who seemed to understand him, who had been through hell and back, finding peace.

The night Warwick carried in Brexley, laying her almost dead body on my table and demanding I heal her, I should have known everything afterward was set on a different course. Seeing how different he was with her, the connection already there… I could never blame her. She brought Kek and Lucas into my life, and to be honest, a part of me would always be in love with that girl, but there was a niggling section that resented her.

She was why I lost them too.

She and Warwick were my biggest reasons for leaving. I couldn't look at either of them without feeling both shame and rage. Guilt because I loved them more than life, but that didn't stop the irrational anger when they looked upon me with pity and concern.

They had each other. Mates.

I had no one.

They came out of hell stronger, while I crawled out with nothing more than animosity and pain.

I hated who I had become, but nothing was left of me to care.

The bartender set a shot of vodka down, smelling of cheap grain, the pungent fumes watering my eyes.

"Perfect," I muttered, slamming it back. The liquid burned down my throat, making me flinch. "Another," I croaked out, downing it the moment she finished pouring.

The hair on the back of my neck prickled, unease gripping my gut like it understood something I didn't. Standing to my full height, I placed the glass down slowly, my head curving back to the door I had come through, a force pulling me through to the other side. My lungs tightened with anxiety.

"Thanks." I pulled out a few coins and tossed them on the bar, my nerves firing while my boots took me through the exit. My walk became a run, the vodka buzzing in my head, making me slower than I wanted.

My hand grabbed the door handle to the steerage, hoping my intuition was wrong and she was sound asleep just as I left her. When I yanked it open, my gut dropped to the floor.

Fuck.

At least eight men, a mix of fae and human, surrounded her sleeping form. A few had ropes in their hands, and others had knives and guns, circling their prey with their black souls, their revolting intentions clearly marked on their faces. The rest of the passengers looked away, not wanting to get involved.

"Cover her mouth," a bearded fae whispered.

"You touch her…" I palmed my weapon, my nose flaring, moving into the room. "I'll be using the straw to wipe your blood off my boots in a minute."

43

The bearded fae looked back at me with amusement, a smirk tipping his mouth. "You think so?"

"I know so." I stepped closer, my gun pointed at him.

"You are outnumbered." The man stood, pulling out a gun and a knife, nodding down to her. "This little piece of ass really worth you dyin' over tonight?"

"I could ask you the same thing."

"It was her pussy I'm after, though I'm open to you both." He licked his lips.

Fury blazed through me, eclipsing the sound around me, zeroing in on her like a bomb. I needed to get her far away from these men. But he was right; I was outnumbered, and she was too far from me to grab her before they did. *Why the fuck did you leave her alone, asshole?*

Her body lay limp as if she was still sleeping, though a hint of green eyes peered at me through her lashes, and a haughty grin twitched her cheek as her hand balled up.

What the hell are you doing? I felt myself scream at her in my head. These men had weapons; she had nothing.

I saw her move, and in that second, I knew it was all going down, and there was no going back.

What a way to die.

Her fist smashed into the bearded man's face, blood spurting out as he bent over, grabbing his nose. Leaping up, she kicked him hard with her boot, driving the heel into the same broken nose, crushing the cartilage into his brain, a scream of agony ricocheting off the walls. Scarlet reached forward, grabbing his gun as his body hit the ground.

What the hell?

Moving in, I fought my way through the throng, bullets spraying, people screaming, but my attention couldn't be dragged away from her for long.

Something about her was feral, wild, but also trained.

44

She reminded me more and more of Birdie, the way she fought, but also something regal in the way she moved. Animalistic, but elegant. A mix that was lightning to watch.

Ripping off part of her torn sweater dress, she slipped it over another man's head, twisting it until it cut into his neck, obstructing his air supply. The man scraped at the cloth to get oxygen before she spun, breaking his neck.

Another man slipped up behind her with a knife, the blade going for her neck.

"Scarlet!" I bellowed her name in warning, but she didn't respond to my call.

"Shit!" Ramming my elbow into someone's throat, I pointed my gun at the man about to slit her throat, the booms bursting in my eardrums and chest like cannons as I fired one after another until my gun clicked empty, fury growling from deep inside. Brain and blood splattered, the body dropping in a thump behind her.

She spun around, her eyes falling on the dead man before finding mine. It took me a moment to notice no one was left around us. Two men were running for the carriage door, deciding their life was worth more than dying here. The rest were sprawled on the ground around us, blood soaking into the straw.

Heaving in air, I wiped blood from my face, going over the bodies. A few would not be moving for a while, their injuries so severe they'd be in comas for weeks while they healed. Another one sputtered out his final gasps, but the rest lay immobile.

Dead.

The women and men who had minded their own business were tucked into balls against the wall, sniffing and crying softly, staring at us in terror.

My attention drifted to Scarlet, taking in her tiny,

delicate frame. She was covered in blood, bruises, and cuts, hair tangled and messy, now left in only a black lace bra and a scrap of what was left of her sweater dress covering her ass. Brushing hair off her face, she tilted her chin up, her green eyes landing on mine with sureness. "I told you I might be useful."

"Might be?" I stuttered and stumbled, my head wagging, peering around the bodies. "What the fuck was that?"

"What do you mean?" She straightened the patch of clothing she had on, like it was just slightly out of place, not nearly gone. I noticed eyes still on her, their attention on her practically naked body. Fae weren't prudes; we loved nudity and were very comfortable with our bodies, unlike a lot of humans. But something about her had me feeling protective. Like she was too young to be leered at in such a way.

"Don't play stupid," I growled, tearing off my jacket. I marched up to her, trying to plaster it over her body. "How the hell do you know how to fight that way?"

"You mean how did a young, naive, rich girl with fancy earrings know how to defend herself?" She blinked at me, playing innocent. "Guess you don't know everything about me, old man." She brushed by me, swinging my jacket onto her shoulder like she was on a runway instead of covering herself, strolling to an empty area by the sliding door.

"Oh, hell no," I muttered, storming after her. "What you did wasn't just defending yourself." I motioned back behind me. "That was skill. I know people trained in war who don't fight like that."

She shrugged, lowering herself to the ground. "My brother and I were trained young to protect ourselves. We had excellent teachers."

"Where was that wonderful training last night?" I quipped.

"I wasn't..." Shame and deep sadness shifted over her

expression, tears watering her eyes, instantly making me regret my words. Her friends were murdered right in front of her, a gun held to her temple. She fought back more than most would in her shoes and was holding up extremely well under the circumstances.

My friends were murdered in front of me, and I did nothing to save them either.

I waited for her to continue, but she looked away, twisting the red stone ring on her finger, signaling the conversation was over. I could sense there was a lot more she wasn't telling me. A depth beyond the spoiled rich girl. But pushing her to answer would mean I cared to know more, which I didn't.

She was a hiccup in my plan, but she would soon be on her way back home and no longer my problem.

Standing over her like the big bad wolf, huffing and puffing, a strangled cry hummed in my throat, my fists balling. Whipping around, I stomped back for the bodies, grabbing the heels of each one and dragging them to the rickety wood door. The wind howled when I slid it open, thrashing icy flakes and freezing air against my skin. Darkness consumed everything beyond the glow of fire lanterns inside the wagon, the speeding train going too fast to see anything more than thick, prickly brush along the tracks.

Without a word, Scarlet joined me, grabbing their arms. Dead or alive, human or fae, we dumped each man out of the moving cart into the hostile landscape. Tree fairies were usually pacifists. Maybe my childhood with my parents spoke of peace and no violence, but my life had shown me the opposite, especially being friends with Warwick. Everything about him was violence, death, rage, and war.

The one thing I had learned in this last year was that I was no different.

But certainly, rapists didn't deserve any consideration in my book. If they lived through this, then fine, but if these chilling temperatures and the brutal fall killed them, I was more than okay with that.

Not a word was spoken between us, and no one said a thing when we slammed the door shut. The red-tainted hay was the only thing left of what happened. Everyone minded their own business, keeping their heads down.

"Put that on." I nodded at my jacket, noticing Scarlet shiver from the cold. "And try to get some sleep." I found a clean spot and settled in. "I won't be going anywhere."

"Why did you leave, anyway?" She curled herself up against the wall, wrapping my jacket around her, her gaze on me.

Pulling up one knee, I stared blankly out, shamed for needing to get drunk, to be numb so badly it was the only thing I could think of. I left her vulnerable and alone, even when I knew better.

"Doesn't matter. It won't happen again." I shifted, settling deeper in, my gaze not meeting hers. "Get some sleep." I wrapped my arms around myself, leaning into the wall and closing my lids.

Somehow, I could feel her eyes on me, burning into the side of my face as if she was peeling back all my layers and seeing the truth. My heartache, guilt, shame, anger, and agony. Everything I was trying to drown in drugs, sex, and booze.

Squeezing my eyes tighter, I ignored the sensation sizzling at my skin, an awareness of this person who had been a perfect stranger until the night before. I didn't like it. At all.

I had no time to be a babysitter.

"Tomorrow, whatever you need to do or whoever you need to contact, you are heading back." I huffed out with authority.

Scarlet said nothing, but this time, her silence was anything but quiet to me. It was subtle, but I could feel her challenge, her stubbornness, as if it was verbal.

Whatever you say, old man.

Chapter 4
Ash

A high-pitched squeal pierced the air, and my body jerked awake, my eyes cracking open with a jolt.

"Final stop," a conductor yelled, rolling open the steerage door. Dull morning light streamed through, my eyes flinching at the onslaught of cold air. Winter stole the warmth from the bodies curled up in the hay. "Everyone off."

Groaning, I rubbed my eyes, brushing my hair off my face and sitting up. My muscles locked up when I noticed the weight on my leg. Scarlet was curled up in a tiny ball, my jacket draped over her like a blanket, using my thigh as a pillow.

Nature fairies were *highly* sexual. Something as simple as touch usually didn't faze us at all. Touch was the way we communicated, and it could be as uncomplicated and complicated as we wanted, depending on the intention.

This was different.

Any interaction I had experienced lately was under my

control, by my preference and request. It was not *intimate*, no matter if we were fucking or sleeping. It was more of a business transaction. A way for me to disappear so I could breathe.

She stirred in her sleep, awareness hinting on her brow, her lips bunching. She looked so small. Peaceful. Innocent. Even covered in blood and wounds, it was as if no horrors haunted her when she closed her eyes. I stared at her, my fingers a breath away from her skin, consumed with an overwhelming need to touch her, brush the hair off her face, expose her freckles, and feel her serenity. Like I could absorb it, live in her peace for a moment. To not feel any more pain.

"Everyone out now!" The conductor rapped his hand on the wood, the sound thundering through the carriage.

Startled, Scarlet lurched up from my lap with a gasp. I tugged my hand away quickly; my embarrassment at almost getting caught turned to anger and disgust. I was as vile as those men last night. So desperate to feel anything but pain, I almost crossed a line, touching her while she slumbered. And what hurt more was thinking I was doing it so I could forget. Forget *them*. Push away the anguish I *deserved* to feel every moment of every day. Kek and Lucas were worth that. They were worth revenge. Worth mourning for the rest of my days.

"Oh." She wiped at the creases on her face, realizing where she had fallen asleep. "I'm so sorry." She yanked her hand from my thigh.

"No big deal," I grumbled, getting up to my feet, my mood already plummeting. The withdrawal from fairy dust and the little sleep I got had my head pounding again. I really needed another hit. Just a little to take the edge off. "Let's get some coffee." I brushed straw from my clothes and headed for the exit.

Jumping down from the step, I turned and helped Scarlet

to the ground, letting go the instant I could, keeping my attention off her. I needed to find her the first train back to Vienna.

The hazy winter sun could barely be felt along the street of the small village. Places like this twenty-two years ago, before the fae war, would have been normal, little hamlets full of families and retirees. If anyone still lived here now, they had opened shops, inns, and eateries for the weary travelers transferring trains. Besides a menial living at farming in these parts, profit from passengers would be their main source of income.

"You want this back?" Scarlet jogged to catch up with me, holding out my jacket. Her skin was pebbled with goosebumps, her thin lacy bra unable to hide how cold she was, letting nipples peek through.

"Fuck, no," I hissed at her, pulling it back over her shoulders and closing it, peering around to see if anyone caught the view. "Put it on and keep it on until we can find some new clothes."

"Wow." One eyebrow rose. "Didn't take you for a prude."

I exhaled heavily through my nose, my jaw cracking with aggravation. "Don't test me today." I circled around, heading for the ticket booth. I knew the train we were on was only getting us to Békés County, still a few hours away from the Romanian border check. And I wanted her nowhere near that.

Finding the ticket booth, I grabbed for my wallet. "When's the next train to Vienna?"

"Don't have any trains going to Vienna," the older man replied.

"Budapest?" I searched the board above his head for times.

"Not until eighteen hundred."

My shoulders clenched. That wasn't until later this evening.

"When's the next one to Bucharest?" Scarlet scooted up next to me.

"Bucharest?" His eyes widened. "Why would you want to go there?"

"She doesn't," I clipped. "I'll get one ticket for Budapest."

"Two tickets for Bucharest, please," she directed him.

"Dammit." I tipped my head back, trying to rein in my temper. "For the last time, you are not going with me." I peered down at her. "You are heading back home. End of story."

"Vienna is not my home."

"Don't care," I quipped dryly. "And unfortunately, there are no direct trains to America today." I nodded to the man. "Ticket to Vienna."

She held up her hand to the man, and he stopped instantly, looking between us nervously.

Her green eyes met mine, her head going to the side. What was it about women? They didn't have to say a thing. They could slant their heads and look at you, and you felt as though you just stepped onto a landmine. Scared, unsure, and aware you were about to die.

I saw it all the time between Brexley and Warwick, though Kitty was the queen of it. Her staring down people had them pissing themselves. Except this girl meant nothing to me. She wasn't a friend, girlfriend, or lover. Just some person who attached herself to me. And attachments weren't something I was ever doing again.

I opened my mouth to tell her how it was going to be.

Her hand moved from him to me, stopping my words. "I know after all you've seen, knowing who is after me, you wouldn't let a girl go back on her own to be kidnapped and murdered."

"You don't know me very well, then." My words sounded as hollow as they felt.

Her mouth pinched. "I told you I have good instincts."

Snorting, I shook my head. "Clearly you don't."

"When does the train leave for Bucharest?" she asked the ticket agent.

"Sixteen hundred." Four o'clock.

"You're not coming with me." My voice rolled over the ground with grit.

"How about we get some food, a shower, and clothes, and we'll talk then." She patted my arm.

"It's not going to cha—"

"Thank you so much," she read his name tag. "Grego." She smiled at the man with a dazzling graciousness, which lightened the room. "We'll be back."

"I'll be here, miss." He seemed bewildered by her charm, a slight pinkness staining his cheeks.

She nodded and headed out of the door.

What the fuck? I stared between them like I had just lost a game I didn't know I was playing.

"Simply a little advice…" His eyes were still on her form walking out the door before they came to me. "Don't let that one out of your sight for a second." He nodded at me as though I better go catch up with her. "She's too pretty. Trouble will find her."

"You got it backward." I exhaled, rubbing my brow. "She *is* the trouble."

Hands full of coffee and *Lángos*, a fried flatbread we both added sausage to, I escorted Scarlet toward a tavern inn.

"Can I help you?" A heavyset blonde woman called out the moment we stepped inside the place, which was probably someone's house at one time.

"Looking to shower and rest for a few hours." I peered around the pub. A handful of people were at the bar drinking while a few families were eating at the small tables set around. The smell of stale beer and cabbage coiled in my nose.

"Seventeen thousand forints." She waddled up, laying her palm out. "Cash."

A knot weaved in my chest; the prices were robbery, but they knew we had no other choice. There weren't a lot of options around here.

Laying the bills in her palm, anxiety over my dwindling funds dragged sourly down the back of my throat. I counted what was left in my wallet for travel, clothes, and what I really craved. I needed just a hit. A little dust to take the edge off.

"This way." The woman panted as we went upstairs. "Bathroom is here." She pointed to a closed door. "Showers are no more than five minutes. Get in and out. Be thankful we even have indoor plumbing now." She eyed us, her gaze moving over our bloody, torn clothing. "Want to go in together, that's fine, but you don't get double time for that. Water turns off after five, so whatever you're doing? Make it quick."

"Oh...um..." Scarlet started to refute her notion, but the woman had already moved on, pushing a door open down the hall. "This is your room. You get two towels. Want more? You pay. Breakfast and dinner are separate. Extra fee for laundry," she huffed, gesturing us in.

The room was small, fitting in a full bed and two

nightstands, a chair in the corner near the single window looking onto the street. Simple and basic.

"You break furniture—" She nodded between us with insinuation.

"Let me guess… there's a fee for that." I smirked.

Her gaze moved slowly over my body, *humphing* before she slammed the door on us.

"I think she likes you," Scarlet teased, stepping into the room and plopping on the bed.

"I have a way with people lately," I muttered, suddenly feeling the small room close in, the silence wrapping around us, and the natural thought process of being alone in a bedroom with hardly any clothes on.

I felt like a sick fuck for my mind even roaming in that area. My limbs twitched to get out the door.

"Why don't you shower and relax. I'll go get us some clothes."

"I wish I had been carrying money with me that night." She tucked hair behind her ear, looking strangely sad, her teeth nipping into her lip.

"Well, maybe if I hold you for ransom, your mommy and daddy will pay a large sum for you?" I tried to joke, though it fell flat, swallowed up by her silence, her gaze off to the side.

So much was there. The layers weaved in the room, her story not so cut and dry. I wanted to press, to ask her to tell me more. *No.* My brain barked, pushing against my nature. *Remember, she will not be around long enough to care. Don't get involved.*

"O-kay." I placed my palms together. "I'll leave you to yourself. You'll be good, right?" I was slightly nervous to leave her, yet I needed out of this room as if my life depended on it.

She nodded, still not looking at me.

"Do not leave this room or answer the door to anyone but me, got it?"

A nod.

Reluctantly, I made my way to the door, exiting and slipping out quickly to the street.

Not even midmorning, and the lane bustled with activity as another train came into the depot. Vendors yelled out for what trinkets and morsels the weary traveler must not leave without. The scent of fried dough, horse manure, and sausage cooking hung low in the frosty air.

Without my hooded jacket, I kept my head down, my gaze always scanning with multiple agendas. Looking out for trouble, for clothes, and for the true reason I was scouring the streets.

Seeing items of clothing out in front of a shop, my focus went to the building down the street, my arms twitching, my fingers rubbing at my lips like I was salivating.

Bordélyház, Brothel House. The place had a no-frills sign on a shabby two-story house. It wasn't what they were offering up front, it was what they had inside to enhance the experience I lusted for. Fairy dust and brothels went hand in hand.

Physically, I stopped in front of the clothing racks, absently going through them, though everything else inside me was pulling me down the street while my mind tried to be logical. Get the necessities.

Sweat dampened my skin, and my teeth ground together as my hand robotically went through items without seeing any of them.

"*Bazdmeg.*" *Fuck it.* I growled under my breath, my boots picking up pace, jogging toward the brothel. *I mean, it couldn't hurt to see how much for a hit.*

My muscles trembled by the time I stepped into the quiet entry, the craving taking over, as if my body could already feel the high. The tranquility. I knew I would have to quit eventually, but with everything going on, I just needed it to get through for a few more days.

Haven't you been telling yourself that for months now? A voice dredged up, nipping at the back of my mind before I shoved it away.

The time of day had the place quiet, though a few men milled around the bar in the far corner, a few sex workers sitting next to them or strutting around with drink trays. With the trains coming into the depot and an abundance of travelers looking to unwind, places like this were open day and night.

"What can I help you with, gorgeous?" A young fae man winked at me from behind the bar, wearing nothing more than a fitted vest and short, tight boxer briefs, displaying everything.

His gaze devoured me as I strolled up to him. "You can have whatever you want." He made it very clear he was included.

My hands couldn't stop moving, my legs dancing in place, not able to settle, anxiety building up. I needed it now.

His gaze moved over me, noticing me twitch, his head dipping. "I think I know what you want."

"How much?"

"Thirty thousand forint."

"Thirty?" I choked. "That's double the price."

"Look where you are." The man shrugged, a luring smile on his face. "Even harder to get over the border in Romania."

I could not afford clothes, food, train tickets, and whatever other expenses in my future, as well as overpriced fairy dust. My mind told me to walk out, laugh at even thinking of paying that, and buy the items we needed. Yet my legs didn't do as they were told. Panic had me pacing around, the craving rising, melting out rationality.

"Hey." The man leaned over the bar. "You look as if you've had a tough day." He nodded at my filthy, burned, bloody clothes. Peering around as if he was seeing if anyone was watching, he pulled out a tiny baggie from behind the bar. "I'll let you have a taste."

My eyes locked on it; the white glistening powder pumped my lungs in and out frantically. The addiction level was similar to heroin, but ten times that for humans. They had no chance of recovering, while fae were a little more resilient.

Barely.

I could feel the magic in the drug calling me, the dire longing for it howling through my veins. I could sense it was anything but pure, but I didn't give a shit. I wanted it more than air. Without even hesitating, I leaned over, swiping up a little and snorting it down.

Like dousing a fire burning inside, a calm came over me. Closing my eyes, I dropped my shoulders with a huge exhale, relishing how the drug slipped into my bloodstream.

Everything was good again. I could breathe. My mind could relax without the fear of relentless pain rushing in and pummeling me. Though it wasn't enough. The hit wasn't deadening enough of my thoughts.

Kek and Lucas were still there, and now I had this unwanted guilt about leaving Scarlet alone again. The old Ash would've been responsible about getting clothes and returning promptly. Being the good guy.

Unlike this guy, who at ten a.m. was already snorting fairy dust.

All the voices, sounding like my friends, pecked at me, wanting me to do better. *Be* better.

"Fuck off," I snarled under my breath, sick of feeling the heavy burden of judgment. My green eyes opened, locking on the bag full of powder the bartender held.

"That was a free sample. The rest you have to pay for." He started to tie up the top. "I could get fired for even giving you that." He winked, tugging it off the table.

"Wait." I reached over and stopped his hand, my other one yanking out my billfold. "I can pay ten... just need a little more."

The man glanced down at where my fingers held him, his dark brown eyes rising back to mine with a glint. "Twenty thousand, and you can pay off the rest another way, sexy."

Twenty thousand forint was still more than I ever planned on spending, but the back of my throat went dry at the idea of turning it down. I couldn't say no.

My head bobbed in agreement, yanking out the bills and slapping them on the table.

The man's sultry smile curled his lips, his cock hardening when I leaned over, snorting two more lines of dust off the bar he dosed out for me.

The haze came like a wave of blissful fog, the erotic music playing in the room throbbing against my ears. Reality seeped out of my pores, my mind becoming blurry, like everything was a Monet painting, deadening the harsh reality of what I was doing. Details blurred out enough that nothing felt real. Pain fled from my body, and the heavy weight of my lovers' souls lifted off my chest, letting me breathe. My mouth opened in a smile, while my lashes closed halfway, as if they were the only thing that held any weight.

"Here." The bartender placed a drink in front of me, and I guzzled it down as well, not caring what it was.

Fuck. I felt good...

He grabbed my hand, tugging me with him to the back

storage room. My brain didn't think past the moment, nor did it care as long as I could continue to feel this way, barely taking in the racks of alcohol and supplies I stumbled past.

He turned me into a rack, pressing my chest into the shelf.

"You are one of the hottest men I have ever seen." The man muttered into my neck, his hand working my jeans, pushing them down. "You are fucking huge." He groaned as his hand wrapped around my cock, working me.

Elemental fairies—water, earth, fire, and air—derived our sexual energy from nature, and it was so strong we had to have an outlet of release, or we'd go mad.

There were only a few unethical lines, which were, of course, children and animals—and anything by force. Other than that, we had no rules. And I had always been fine with that. Except as he shoved my boxers down, my vision swirling in front of me, it felt off. Wrong.

He rubbed himself before he pushed into me. "Oh gods." He moaned loudly in my ear. "I knew the moment you walked in you would be an incredible fuck."

My body moved with his. A twinge of arousal had my dick stiff, and I tried to enjoy the feel of him thrusting into me, ramming me up into the rack, his hand working my cock like a vice. But my mind was like a gnat, floating and flying back to other things.

Like Scarlet.

This girl was so proper and young. Totally badass in her fighting, but also naive. What would she think if she knew I was getting railed by a prostitute in the storage closet just so I could get high? She'd be disgusted.

She did see you at the brothel in Vienna… so she might know how sick you are, a voice countered.

"I need this massive cock fucking me." The man gripped

my throat, pulling out of me and twisting me to face him. "Gods, you're fucking hot."

My gaze landed on his dark eyes and hair, his stocky body. Everything was wrong. He wasn't who I wanted. I shouldn't be here. My dick seemed to agree.

"This might help." The bartender took some dust from the baggie in his vest, covered his hand in it, and stroked me.

"Oh fuck." A moan grew deep in my chest, my semi-hard cock growing firm in his grip, the drug soaking straight into my bloodstream and pushing me over into euphoria. He continued to rub the dust up and down me, the vein running along the side pounded as it soaked in the drug, aching for relief.

Nothing made sense anymore; reality and time were imaginary flutters of the edges of my mind. Something made up.

With a grunt, I shoved him around, pushing into him, losing understanding and breaking down to my most primal instincts.

I could hear him screaming and moaning as I fucked him without feeling how ruthless I was, disappearing into my dream world, where my mind let me be with Lucas and Kek. I could envision them alive for just a moment, pretend it was us three together here, Kek's pussy clenching greedily around me as Lucas's cum filled me, his soft breath in my ear before he kissed me. Then I would turn to Kek and devour her, pushing in so deep and emptying myself, making all three of us come again.

"OH GODS! *More!*" he wailed, so lost in bliss that he couldn't keep himself quiet. Bottles were falling off the shelf, smashing around us. I could feel him orgasm, his release covering the wall. I wanted so badly to release, to feel that moment of bliss like I did inside Kek. But the harder I went, the more my orgasm retreated. Floated out of reach.

The same as all the times before.

I closed my eyes, trying to grasp for Kek, to feel Lucas behind me. But their images were fuzzy and unclear. They were drifting away from me. As if I was forgetting them. For good.

"Nononono." Panic bubbled under my skin, and I drove into him so hard, trying to pull them back, as I heard the man cry out for me to stop.

"What the fuck is going on here?" A woman's sharp voice turned my head. My wobbly vision saw a woman dressed in some low-neck blue dress with buttons, but it was her matching navy-blue eyes that stopped me in place.

Oh. Gods.

"Kek," I breathed, my heart tripping over itself.

"Fuck," the bartender swore, wiggling out from where I had him pinned and grabbing for his clothes. "Madame Sorina."

The woman strolled in with a commanding presence, two beefy guys on either side of her. Her demon eyes tracked over me, stopping at the powder covering me before she noticed the dozens of bottles smashed over the ground, flooding the floor with wasted alcohol.

The bartender yanked up his shorts, his voice shaky. "It's not—"

She held up her hand. Her expression was stern as she strolled closer, her demon eyes going to me, speaking to me, but all I heard was Kek's voice.

"What are you doing, fairy boy? You look like shit."

"I feel like it too…" I whispered back to Kek. "Gods… I miss you so much."

Her blue eyes narrowed, her mouth moving, but nothing fit. I couldn't understand her.

"Kek." I reached out for her. "Don't leave me."

My body was slammed against the wall, an arm across my throat, a man's face snarling at me. "You do not touch the Madame." His features twisted up, reminding me of a badger. "You will be paying for all of this."

I think I laughed. I wasn't sure.

My head snapped to the side, a pain bursting behind my eye, everything spinning on me. The other man searched my pockets, pulling out my money.

"He only has eighty thousand forint."

A blow doubled over my stomach. My legs could no longer hold me up, and I fell to the ground, more laughter escaping as my bare ass struck the ground, dropping into the pool of liquor and glass.

This time, I saw fists coming at my face and stomach, the boots kicking into my sides, but I couldn't feel anything.

Finally, I felt no pain.

"You better find me another six hundred thousand forint for all this. By tonight. If not…" The woman's face hovered over mine. "Normally I would have you dissected into parts and fed to my hogs, but with you…" She sneered. "I have better use for you." She glanced from my face to my exposed cock, still semi-hard. "You would make me a very nice profit."

Her blue eyes were the last thing I saw as her bodyguards chucked me out, my pants still around my ankles.

Chapter 5

Scarlet

The constant knots in my stomach and the tension riding my muscles only grew with each hour that passed without Ash's return.

Still wrapped in a towel, my hair drying down my back, I paced the small room, tugging at the goblin metal circling my wrist, rubbing the skin raw.

He was supposed to go get clothes and come right back.

Four hours ago.

My intuition was always something I trusted. I had it fine-tuned with all the fake smiles and bullshit in my life I had to see through. A person can come across as sweet and sincere to those who don't look past the first layer. I had seen the kindest smiles attached to the cruelest of intentions.

Something felt off with his absence. Not that I knew him. At all. Yet the moment our eyes met two nights ago, I felt this strange connection. Like I understood him. The pain and grief he tried to hide, the sense he was lost.

Alone.

I understood it. You could be in a room filled with people who loved you and still feel absolutely alone.

Grief, guilt, regret, and fear were isolating. They detached you from others, especially when you had very few people you could trust. And those I did, I couldn't turn to. Not now. I couldn't put them in a bad position because of what I did.

Another death weighed on my soul now. Grief squeezed my lashes together. A sob vibrated in the back of my throat as I recalled the bullet going into Reid's head at the bar. His life vanished in a second. I couldn't stop thinking about his family. What they must be going through. He was such a good guy. The best. And he was dead because of me. And Eve… I had just left her there to die.

I came to Vienna to start anew, to get away from the heartache and loss from what I had done. Now I realized it all followed me here. And I deserved it.

Twisting my ring around my finger, I fought against the natural urge to contact my family, especially my brother. But I *couldn't*. It was too dangerous.

Huffing in aggravation, I rubbed at my face. So many would be aghast if they knew the pretty picture they saw on the outside, so put together and charming, didn't make you any less of a disaster on the inside.

"Fuck it." I reached for the slip of sweater I still had, the need to go out and track Ash scratching at every muscle.

Covering myself as much as I could with no underwear or bra, both items far too dirty and burned up to wear again, I used the strip of sweater dress as an ultra mini skirt. Wrapping his jacket around me, I crammed my feet back into my painful heeled boots and ran out the door.

Clouds had moved in, covering the sun, the midday light

already heading for the horizon, forcing me to pull the jacket tighter to me. The streets were quieter than the morning hustle, the shop owners waiting for the next arrival of trains.

Skirting through the lane, enough eyes fell on me, and I hurried quicker, pulling Ash's hood up higher.

I poked into bars and shops, but Ash was nowhere to be found. My stomach twisted into a ball, fear pumping my heart faster.

What if he left me? What if something happened to him? What if they killed him? *Calm down.* I ordered myself, taking in the lessons I learned about stopping my panic from taking charge. Controlling my emotions. Breathing in and out, I closed my eyes, inhaling a deep breath. The bracelet cut off a lot of my magic, but my senses were still excellent.

Taking another deep breath, I sucked in, searching for his scent, tasting it on my tongue. When I caught a whiff, my lids bolted open, and I moved to it. Heading to the far end of the street, it grew stronger and stronger, pulling me around a building into a back alley.

"Holy shit!" I jerked, seeing the back of his blond head, his body lumped next to some dumpsters. "Ash!" My heels clicked the cement as I ran to him, shock and terror shrilling my voice.

"Ash?" I shook him. "Please, Ash, wake up." *Please don't be dead. Don't be dead.*

A pained moan came from him, letting me breathe out a gulp of air.

"Oh, thank the gods." I started to roll him to me and gasped. His face was bloody and bruised, his T-shirt torn, his jeans around his thighs... and holy fuck. His cock swung toward me like a bat as he rotated to me. "Holy. Shit." I gaped.

I had hooked up with guys; I wasn't a total prude, but

he made my cheeks heat. Struggling to swallow, I tried to not stare, but the man was exceptionally huge and thick. *Stop looking.* I forced my eyes away, noting white dust on him.

"What is covering you?" A chalky film coated his cock. My nose wrinkled, smelling another man's cum, alcohol, and some kind of magically enhanced substance.

A sick feeling splashed around in my stomach, recalling the brothel sign out front. My throat tightened at the understanding of exactly what he had been doing.

Fae were more open to sex and sexuality, but maybe that's why he looked at me like a nuisance. I was clearly not his type, and I didn't want to be.

Though I know I spotted blue-haired women, with him at the last whorehouse.

"This whole time, you've been getting high and laid?" Irrational anger spat down on him, my hands shaking him harder. "Wake up."

Another groan came from him, his lids struggling to open, his half-lidded, mossy green eyes finding mine. I couldn't stop the sharp inhale he produced from me. When Ash looked at you, really looked, he made you feel like you were the only thing in the world.

"Heyyyy…" he slurred. A happy smile pulled his mouth, splitting open his cut lip, blood leaking down his chin. His hand reached up for my face. "It's youuuu." He went serious, his gaze rolling over my bare face, his thumb sweeping over my cheek, forcing me to suck in. "Freckles."

He dropped his hand, his lids closing, going back to sleep.

"No." I shook him. "Wake up."

His lids pried open, a grin showing back up. "Hey, it's you again."

"Yeah. It's me," I snipped. "You are a mess." I stood, turning my back on him, not wanting to see his enormous cock flopping about, covered in someone else. "Get up."

He groaned and huffed behind me.

"I should've known you'd be at a brothel." I folded my arms, trying to block out the memory of watching him through a window in Vienna. I hadn't seen it all, the curtains blocking some, but I had seen there were more than five of them with him, loud cries seeping through the glass to me across the alley. "Seems to be your go-to."

I don't give a shit who he is with or what he does. I reminded myself, trying to shake off the foul mood I was in. *You don't even like him that way. You can't even get over your ex.*

Fierce pain surged up, and I shook off the image of the boy I had been in love with all of my life, focusing back on Ash. It was the fact that Ash left me waiting alone in our room. He was supposed to get us clothes and come back hours ago. It was rude.

The rustle of him trying to stand had my eyes drifting back subtly over my shoulder. Not able to look away, he stumbled and weaved, trying to tuck himself back into his pants, his deep V-line keeping me locked on him even after he zipped himself up.

Of course Ash was perfect in *every* category.

"*Szar,*" he mumbled, falling against the wall, his hand rubbing at his ribs, his head dipping back into the brick wall.

"Why are you beat up?" I turned back, my arms still crossed.

He squeezed his eyes shut as if his head was going to explode off his body.

"Did you not pay or something?"

His head jerked up, his hand fumbling to his back

pocket, then to all his jean pockets. "Fuck!" He continued to search, though I could tell they were all empty.

"Wait." I put up one hand. "Are you telling me you lost all the money you had?"

"I think it's a lot worse than that." He peered at the back door, suddenly more lucid. "Come on." He gestured me away, his hand going to my lower back, pointing us out of the alley. "We have to get out of here."

"We need clothes before we go back to the room." I motioned down to myself.

"No, I mean we need to get the hell out of this town." He limped down the street, glancing over his shoulder.

"What? Why?" I tried to keep up with his pace.

"Because."

"Ash." I stopped him, my head wagging with confusion. "What the hell is going on?"

He shifted his weight between his legs, his bruised face starting to go down a little. "I fucked up."

"You couldn't have possibly fucked up more than I have. No one has." The comment came out unfiltered, my teeth driving into my lip to shut me up.

His forehead wrinkled, taking me in.

"Plus," I rushed on. "There are no trains until later. You need a shower." I waved my hand in front of my face. "I'm not kidding. You smell like dirty sex and booze."

Instead of laughing, he looked away from me as if he was ashamed, his throat bobbing. "We don't even have money to get food or clothes."

Reaching into the pockets of what was left of my sweater dress, I tugged out my diamond earrings. "Yes, we do."

"No." He shook his head. "I can't let you do that. I'll figure something out."

"*What?*" I sputtered, glancing around at the quiet village. "There's nothing here. And look at you." I motioned to his wounds. "Whatever you did didn't go too well for you last time. I'm part of this; I can pay my fair share."

"You're part of this?" He tipped his head, and a crooked smile hinted on the side of his bruised face.

"Yeah." I swallowed, feeling oddly nervous at this insubstantial exchange, though it felt anything but.

"Then." His voice was low, his figure stepping into mine. "You will be spending some of the money heading back home."

"Ash." I exhaled in exasperation.

"I *need* you safe." His green eyes narrowed.

My breath hitched at his intensity. It was as if I was seeing a hint of another version of him. It shifted my feet back, needing air.

"And I need you to take a shower and wear something that doesn't smell like prostitutes and blood."

I rubbed at the worn cotton fabric of my newly purchased pants. In the States, they would've been found in an unwanted donation pile, something discarded as rags. And I would have been one of the guiltiest for wrinkling my nose at them, calling them cheap and basic. Now, I was just grateful to have warm legs. Adorned with a thin black sweater and hooded wool coat, I felt more protected, blending in with the people around me. The secondhand boots were a size too big, but my feet didn't ache in them.

I had no makeup, my hair was stringy from the lack of conditioner, and I was covered in slow-healing cuts and bruises. If my friends could see me now. *They would walk right past, never believing it was me.* But I was clean, dressed, and warm.

The door swung open, and I looked up to see Ash stride in with only a towel around his waist, droplets of water sliding down his skin from his hair.

Holy. Shit.

As if a club thwacked me in the lungs, air ceased to move, and I was stunned by everything my eyes were taking in, unable to look away.

I wasn't blind. Ash was striking with his clothes on, but almost naked? I wasn't prepared. His body was *epic.* Like the gods picked him out as their mascot, a poster boy to represent them. Stamped him with an approved logo and sent him out into the world to stupefy the public.

Chiseled, with a slim waist, he had an intricate tree tattoo inked up his side and wrapped around his arm. The man didn't have an ounce of fat; his arms and chest were toned. Not so overly muscular that it was gross, but enough that my pulse beat loudly in my ears, my throat going dry.

Then my eyes picked up the deep black and blue marks across his ribs and stomach.

"Oh my gods." I leaped up, rushing up to him, my hands tentatively touching the vivid bruises. "Are you okay?"

His stomach sucked in where my fingers grazed, his body stilling.

"Yeah." His voice came out low and gruff. "Probably a few fractured ribs." His throat bobbed. "I'm fine. I heal quickly."

I peered up at him, realizing how close I was, how intimately I was touching him.

"Oh. Right." I dropped away, back peddling. "Of course. Sorry." I folded my hands, my words bubbling with nervous energy.

He stood there staring at me, causing my cheeks to burn. Why was he staring at me? Was he going to kiss me?

He flicked his chin behind me. "Need to get my clothes."

"Oh." I glanced at the pile on the chair by the window, a rush of embarrassment flushing me. "Right."

I tried to move at the same time he went for the chair. The room was so small I had nowhere to go, forcing my body to bump and slide against his as he angled himself around me, feeling his wet skin and his cock under the thin towel drag across my stomach.

Gulping hard, my body flamed to life, dropping a bead of sweat down my back, halting me in place as he carried on, totally unaffected. My teeth drove into my lip as I turned away from him, feeling, for the first time in my life, completely unsure and awkward. Why was I so discombobulated? What was wrong with me?

I had never been shy around men, or anybody for that matter. Raised to stand toe-to-toe with power and authority, I was born confident and fearless. Nothing spooked me. Until... well, everything had changed lately.

My gaze lowered to my boots, my fingers playing with the toxic bracelet around my arm, a stab of pain thickening my throat.

"Hopefully you can get someone to get that off you." Ash nodded his head at the band on my wrist before pulling on a vintage black band T-shirt over his head, drawing attention once again to the deeply carved V-line at his hips.

Whipping my head away, I rolled my lips together, fiddling more with the bracelet.

"Yeah." I barely heard my own voice.

"Goblin metal is a bitch." He shucked on a pair of jeans, letting the towel drop. "Though you are handling it really well. It made me lethargic and achy. Completely useless to fight or stop anything…" Darkness creased his brow, his jaw twitching. It was as if I could feel his memories seep around him, feel them like tangible objects.

Sensing my gaze upon him, he shook it off, shoving his feet in his boots. "We still have plenty of money to get some food and train tickets."

The earrings I pawned gave us a nice little chunk of change for basics, but if anyone actually knew the worth of the one-carat diamonds they possessed and who gave them to me, they'd probably pass out. I was raised to understand and appreciate my family's standing and be humble enough to feel for those who had less, but it never registered as profound until here. Ash had called me out on the train, and now I saw how oblivious I was to money. I never had to worry about it. The earrings were such little trinkets to me, I'd never imagine someone killing me to get them. To be able to feed a family for a year or more from them.

"And enough to hire someone to get you back to Vienna."

"Hire?" I snapped, my lids narrowing.

His green irises met mine with determination. "You're right. It is risky for you to head back alone."

"So I go forward with yo—"

"No. It's ten times worse going forward," he talked over me.

"I don't care." A rush of anxiety came out of nowhere, forcing out my words. The thought of being alone knotted under my ribs.

"This is no longer up for debate." He stood up, using his height against me. "Not only is Romania extremely inhospitable to anyone not from there, but their own people are being murdered daily. This is not a cute little adventure. It's no place for you."

74

"But—"

"Don't you get it?" he shouted. "I don't *want* you here. I've *never* wanted you here."

Hurt stuck like a lightning bolt, the harshness penetrating deeper than it should have. I usually persisted until I got my way, and I had thick skin. Not much fazed me, but this felt like a dagger. My teeth locked together in an effort to hide any emotion.

"It's not personal." Ash pinched his brow, lowering his voice.

It felt as though it was.

"If it's so dangerous, why are you going in?"

"There is something I have to do."

Revenge. It was what he told me on the train. "If it's so *inhospitable*, isn't going in by yourself pretty much suicide?"

His lips quirked in an almost cruel smile. "I wasn't planning on coming back out."

"What?" Air lashed through my lungs, my chest pulling in sharply at his confession. He was going to Romania with full understanding he would die there? The idea of him no longer being in this world had me dizzy and panicked, though it made no sense. I barely knew this guy. We had only met, what, two days ago? Yet the notion crashed into me like a wave.

"No." I shook my head. "Nooo."

"You don't have a say." He brushed by me, grabbing for his jacket.

"Whatever it is, it can't be worth your life."

He stopped like I had laid down the deepest insult, his muscles locking up. Outside the room, I heard branches from trees cracking, scraping at the window, his magic fuming out of him, connecting with nature, confirming what I already thought.

Tree fairy.

Slowly he turned his head back to me, his moss-colored eyes dark with anger. "They are worth *more* than my life." He grabbed his pack, filled it with supplies, and marched out of the room, not looking back.

Exhaling, I snatched up my bag, following him out the door, suddenly wishing for the nap I didn't get to take.

The sunset was already kissing the cloudy horizon, dusting the quiet streets with deep grayish-blue shadows. Icy air slipped through my coat, and I peered longingly at the few pubs that glowed with warm fires inside. The scent of cooked cabbage and sausage made my stomach growl, letting me know it had been hours since I had eaten.

A clock chimed in the distance, declaring it was only fifteen minutes to four.

"*Szar*," Ash swore under his breath, peering between the train station and the pub, realizing his train would be departing soon.

"Let's hurry." He started to pull me toward the pub. "There is probably someone in there I can pay to take you back."

"No. I'd rather go by myself." I stopped at the curb, crossing my arms. My infamous stubborn streak was setting in. Determination and persistence usually ended up getting me what I wanted.

"Oh, no." Ash flipped back for me, his head shaking. "You made it clear it was too dangerous for you to go back by yourself, remember?" He threw my argument back in my face. "And I concur. I would feel much better knowing you had someone watching you."

"Watching me? I'm not an infant." I hated how he couldn't seem to see me as the grown woman I was.

He cocked a brow, burning more irritation up my back.

"And if you recall," I reminded him. "I can take care of myself."

"Not against the Russian Mafia."

"Why do you even care?" I gripped the handle of my bag. "You didn't even want me here."

"You're right. I didn't, but it doesn't make me a monster." He glared at me with vexation. "I don't want you to get hurt."

"Too late for that," I spat, slamming my shoulder into his and marching past. He had hit on a deep insecurity, an open wound still bleeding from the last person. Someone I had loved with all my heart. And I hadn't been enough.

"Hey...stop," I heard him say right as two burly men stepped from the alley, dressed in dark clothes. They moved in front of me, one pressing the muzzle of his gun to my head. The resonance of the hammer clicking back, ready to fire, echoed through the air, and a cry stuck in my throat.

"Looks like you were skipping out on us?" The one with the gun to my head spoke. He had a white streak going through his short, dark hair like a mohawk, his face reminding me of a honey badger. The other one resembled a boar, with wiry brown hair, thick nostrils, and teeth like tusks.

"Not at all." Ash came to my side, trying to put himself in front of me. "Actually, I was heading to the pub. Try my hand at gambling. Get the rest of the money for your madam." He pulled out the bills we had left over from pawning my earrings. "I got this much."

Boar swiped it from him, counting it. "This isn't enough."

The barrel pressed harder into my head.

"Don't!" Ash kept trying to take my place. "Please don't hurt her. It's me you want."

"We *want* the rest of the money you owe," Badger grunted.

"And I'll get it to you." Ash tried to bump me out of the way, but the gun dug into my skin. No emotion showed on my face, but every muscle shook. I was scared, but I was also fighting the instinct to protect myself. The need to fight howled under the goblin metal, crashing around inside, demanding to inflict pain. *Death*. "She had nothing to do with this." Ash's voice pulled me from my single-minded thought, focusing on him. "Take me."

Boar stuffed the money into his jacket pocket, laughing. "Why choose one?"

"Plus, she seems like the perfect bait to play hostage." A malicious sneer hooked Badger's face, and he stepped closer to me, his gaze on Ash. "Young, beautiful..." He leaned in, his nose dragging up my hair, causing a chill to shudder through me. "And innocent enough, it would be fun to corrupt her. They're so easy to shape and mold at this age."

"You touch her..." When Ash growled, a few branches creaked overhead.

"You'll what, pretty boy?" Badger huffed, tapping his gun against my head, his mouth close to my ear. "You know your boyfriend here was fucking a male whore, high on fairy dust earlier."

"Yeah? So?" I shrugged with indifference; the need to show how little I feared them had words rolling off my tongue without much thought. "Sometimes I watch. Sometimes he does." I smirked at the man. "But most of the time, I join in with him and our plaything. I enjoy being in the middle."

The two men chuckled darkly, and out of the corner of my eye, I saw Ash's reaction, felt his surprise spike from him, not ready for my response.

I hadn't been ready for my response.

"Oooohhh... not so innocent, then. Looks like you already molded her to what you want." Badger grinned. "I think Madame might have a place for both of you. You'd make a great addition to her menagerie."

Ash jerked out of his stupor. A low rumble emanated from his chest, a dark cloud sliding over him, turning him from beauty to beast. Clouds before a torrential storm.

A branch snapped off overhead, dropping near us, turning the men's heads and distracting their attention for a moment. It was enough, and I didn't even need to look at Ash to know what he wanted.

My hand knocked into Badger's wrist with a burst of energy. The gun popped out of his hold, sailing across the pavement onto the road as my boot snapped into his gut, bending him over. Twisting, I knocked into Boar's arm, the gun firing up in the air instead of at Ash. His gaze darted to me in appreciation before we both jumped back in.

Ash and I moved in a strange dance, somehow keeping an eye on each other while fighting our enemy. Kicking, spinning, punching, we dropped and moved similarly to the fight on the train. Except these guys were trained. Very well. Their shifter animals were deadly opponents.

Feeling the threat of their attacks, my muscles itched, needing to act, to protect. A noise vibrated in my throat, and I plowed into Badger, knocking him back on his ass. A fist slammed into my cheek and again into my ribs. Feeling a crack, the force tossed me to the ground. I froze for a moment, pain almost numbing me, but in the distance, I heard a train whistle its departure.

The train to Romania.

A screechy animal noise came from Badger as he launched for me with teeth and claws. Kicking up, I rammed my heel into his crotch, buckling him over with a yowl. Flipping over, I scrambled for the gun left on the ground. My nails pushed me toward it, my ribs throbbing as my arm reached out, my fingers brushing the handle.

A hand wrapped around my ankle, yanking me back over the gravel, burning the side of my face.

Noooo!

I was trained to fight. Trained to fight dirty. But I was still much smaller and weaponless. Even worse, with the bracelet, I was magicless.

"Curvă." Whore/bitch. Badger seethed over me, his fingers wrapping through my hair, gripping it and yanking me up, pain shooting through my nerves. "I'm gonna enjoy watching you become a slaved whore." He got right in my face. "Or maybe I'll slit your pretty throat here." He yanked a knife from his holster, the blade pressing into my neck.

"Nooo!" Tree limbs rained down on us with force, hitting with a loud *thunk*, somehow missing me. A howl of pain rang out, and the knife at my throat disappeared. Sweeping my gaze behind me, I saw Badger's unconscious body on the ground, a huge branch over his body. He groaned, starting to wake up.

My attention went to Ash, Boar sprawled on the ground at his feet.

"Come on!" Ash rushed to me, his fingers circling mine, yanking me with him. I stopped, Ash's head snapping back to me as I swiped up Badger's disregarded gun, digging into Boar's jacket and taking the money before the pig-shifter could stop me.

"Hey!" Boar yelled, rising to his feet and waking up his partner.

Biting down on my lip, my hand holding my ribs, we ran for the train station.

Bang! Bang!

Ducking behind a bush as Boar and Badger came shooting at us. A whine of metal screeched in my ear—the train pulling away from the platform.

"Hurry!" Panic gripped my body. The desperation to be on that train, to escape, had me darting for it. If we missed it, we were fucked. These guys knew this town, owned it, and we would not be making it out alive.

Ash's voice bellowed behind me, but I didn't stop, my little legs pumping, my sights locked on the last car, picking up speed, sensing him catching up behind me.

POPPOPPOP! A haze of bullets zinged past us, one so close I felt the heat lick at my cheek.

The train hooted, making me go faster, my legs burning, my ribs screaming in protest as I tried to keep up.

"Grab on!" Ash's hand went to my ass, lifting me with a boost, flinging my body up. My bones hit the top of the step, exploding pain over me as I rolled onto the platform. Lifting my head, my gaze caught the tracks coming up, thick brush before it dropped off into a river.

"Ash!" I belted in fear. Every second, we got closer. "Now!"

Ash leaped for the step, my hands grabbing onto his arms, helping to pull him up. He crashed down next to me right as the train went over the bridge, swooshing by the low rocky river below.

"*Szar.*" He leaned his head against the railing, gasping for air. He peered behind us. No sign of the men, the village shrinking further in the distance.

We did it. We were safe.

For now.

Sitting next to him, my hand on my ribs, reality began to set in as the train hurled itself toward Romania. Twilight clawed in deeper, the turbulent clouds ahead warning us what was coming.

He didn't want me here, which was clear, but I had no choice anymore. I could only go forward.

I was going with him into the land of no return.

Chapter 6

Ash

The train swayed and bumped over the tracks, my heart still beating wildly in my chest, sweat cooling on my skin. I stared forward, not wanting to accept how, in ten minutes, everything flipped on me. What I fought against had happened anyway. Like I had no say in the matter, no matter what I did. Except my own folly was what led to this. My actions biting me in the ass. Punishing me. I felt I had marked this girl for death. Dragged her down into my darkness because she dared to get near me. A gravitational pull that smashed everything around me to dust.

Kek and Lucas had suffered the same fate.

Curving my head, I peered at Scarlet. The train picked up speed, blowing her hair around. Her lids tapered in pain, her hand on her ribs as she took in slow, shallow breaths.

"You're hurt?" I sat up straighter.

"Just a cracked rib." Her teeth ground together, disguising her discomfort as the icy winds turned her cheeks and nose a reddish pink.

My attention dropped to the bracelet, realizing why she was still in so much pain. It was blocking her powers so she couldn't heal quickly.

"We need to get that off you." Especially because of where we were going. Standing up, I scowled at the metal. "You can't fight or heal properly with it on." I took her free hand, helping her to her feet. I could sense the intense magic in the cuff trying to siphon mine too. A familiar nausea pooled in my stomach. It was one I had experienced in prison. Not as much as Killian or Warwick, but enough to make me want to throw up just being this close to it again. The nightmares of that place lived freely in my head, tormenting my soul.

Something was different about hers, a magic weaving with the goblin magic I couldn't decipher, something that made the hair on my arms prickle.

"Come on," I muttered, my arm around her, helping her walk. I moved us through the door to the stock cart, sitting her against the wall in the only free space left. This carriage was narrow and filled with crates on one side, giving us third-class steerage with little space.

"Just rest." I pinned my lips. Something twisted in my chest at seeing her hurt. A need to take it away, heal her. Tree fairies were nature's healers, working with Earth's gifts to help others.

Instead, I got her hurt.

"A shot of whiskey will help ebb the pain, but..." I looked at the door and back at her, scanning the room for potential threats. No one stood out, but I didn't want to leave her alone again.

"I'll be fine." She nodded to the door. Seeing my hesitation, the fight going on within me, her voice became firmer. "Go." She pulled out the billfold she stole back from the henchmen.

"You sure?" I took it, glancing around the cart again, a mix of women and men, muttering in groups or trying to sleep.

"Yes." She flinched, adjusting her ass on the hard floor, her lids squeezing together. "Please."

Her agony was the only thing that made me decide to leave her.

"You have the gun?" I muttered.

"Yes," she huffed. "Now go before I shoot *you*."

A snort choked up my throat, my head shaking. "Okay, I'll be just a few minutes. Please, stay out of trouble."

The amusement died rapidly as I exited the steerage, heading for the snack cart, shelving all the terrifying thoughts about her being on this journey into Romania with me. There was no choice now—unless I tossed her off a moving train, which might be a better option. Not only was she too young and inexperienced for what lay ahead, but now she was hurt *and* crippled by the goblin metal. Basically, a baby fawn in the jungle.

She could fight extremely well, but that's not what would protect her.

It was odd; I couldn't sense what she was. Most of the time, I easily could figure people out, their energy buzzing around, their mannerisms or attributes giving them away. With her, I ran into a wall, but I sensed a darkness behind the barrier, a wildness I couldn't explain. It seemed to go against her sophisticated, refined demeanor.

The refreshment cart was rundown, barely anything there, yet it was filled with people. No one was really speaking, just quietly drinking. A heaviness blanketed the room, all of us very aware in less than two hours, we'd be in hostile territory.

"Two double whiskeys," I told the bartender. *You*

shouldn't drink. You need all your wits about you. I yelled at myself, wanting my mouth to open, to just get the one for Scarlet. Yet the words never ventured out before the server set two cups on the table in front of me. It would be fine. Plus, I was feeling the crash from the drug this morning starting to hit. I needed the filter to lessen it.

Downing mine, I turned, going back for steerage.

My lungs eased when I stepped back in, seeing her alone in the exact spot I left her. She seemed to attract trouble as much as I did.

Strolling up to her, I stopped at her boots. Her lids were shut, her knees up to her chest, her head tipped against the wall. I stared down at her bare face. Bundled up in fabric, she looked so tiny. Freckles dusted her nose and cheeks, her porcelain skin not yet clear of bruises and cuts. She was young, but she didn't seem *as* young as when I first met her. I could sense grit and strength in her.

My soul might be dead, but I could still see. The girl was stop-in-your-tracks stunning. Breathtakingly pretty. Though looks meant nothing to me. I'd lived way too long to care what was on the outside and not the inside. Humans put way too much praise and worship on pretty people, like only caring that your house had a nice exterior while the inside was crumbling and rotting.

She shocked me at every turn, messing with my head just when I thought I had her pegged.

"Sometimes I watch. Sometimes he does. But most of the time, I join in with him and our plaything. I enjoy being in the middle."

Her statement flashed through my head, forcing me to suck through my nose, my cock twitching. I quickly shoved out the thought, my shoulders rising.

"Here," I grunted and shoved the cup at her, her lashes

flying open in surprise. Her bright green eyes lifted to mine, and they felt like they were looking through me, seeing every fucked-up thing inside me.

"Drink it."

She lifted her hand, taking the cup from me. "Thanks."

Rubbing the back of my neck, anger lashing out. "I guess you got what you wanted." I tossed out my arms.

She watched me, sipping down the whiskey, causing my blood to stir more.

"You think I planned it that way?"

"Might as well have." I sounded irrational to my ears, but I couldn't stop. "You wanted to come to Romania with me *no matter what.* Thinking this is what you do. Push and push until you get your way."

"Ash—"

"Do you get what might happen to you?" I growled, not caring that I was causing a commotion. "What it's like there? Your fight training doesn't matter there. You live in a rich little bubble, thinking nothing really can happen to you. And now I'll have to carry your death too."

Her shoulders went back, a realization blinking across her face. My mouth slammed shut, knowing I had said too much. Awkward silence hung between us for a few moments.

She set her empty cup to the side, her hand reaching up for mine, her cheek twitching from the stretch. "Ash. Sit." Her fingers laced with mine, tugging me down with her.

Giving in, I let her pull me down, my shoulders lining up with hers against the wall. I pulled up my knees, laying my arms over them.

"Unless you want to toss my ass off this moving train,,," she muttered, her voice sounding exhausted. "We're in this together."

That was what I was afraid of.

Romania was now enemy territory under a violent military dictatorship. After the battle with Istvan, where power fell back into Killian's hands, Prime Minister Lazar secured the border, taking up even more control and power of the country for himself. To the point, the people of Romania could not even utter a criticism of their leader for fear they would be murdered. It was hostile land for locals and fatal for outsiders.

Deep down, I doubted it was Lazar who had taken this on himself. The man was smart, but the extremes he was going to made me think he was just a puppet in this. It was Sonya who was the shadow ruler. I had no doubt wherever she was, Iain would be, which was where I would be too.

"I'm sorry you're mad at me." Her lids fluttered, her body wanting to sleep.

"Get some rest," I said. "We have a few hours."

"Okay," she muttered, her head falling on my shoulder.

My lungs hitched. Slowly, I let out a hefty breath, settling against the wall so she was more comfortable.

"And I'm not mad at you," I whispered, my cheek brushing the top of her head. *I'm scared.* Scared meant I cared, which was something I promised myself I would never be again.

Especially heading in with the notion I wasn't returning.

A slam jolted my eyes open, voices barking into the carriage, my brain trying to make sense of everything.

"*Documente de călătorie!*" A man shouted, his tone booming with anger and power, jerking my body fully awake and pouring fear into my bloodstream. A handful of figures stomped into the carriage dressed in dark pants and jackets with red and gold Romanian flag patches on their sleeves. They each carried a rifle, with a handgun and blade hooked to their jacket belts.

"Hey." I nudged Scarlet, pulling her up with me, her body still wanting to sleep, to heal itself. "Get up." I tucked her in close, our hoods covering our faces. I wanted to put her in my backpack and keep her hidden.

"*Documente de călătorie!*" The man bellowed sharply again, demanding our travel papers in Romanian, putting everyone on edge. Soldiers moved to the first grouping, their rifles down, but their fingers on the trigger ready to act, as the man in charge snatched documents from a couple, purposely intimidating and creating fear. Another man stood to his left with a clipboard, his mouth pursed, his eyes like an eagle. His sharp gaze moved over each person, lingering on the men longer, as if he was trying to pick apart their features.

"Ash," Scarlet muttered, a flutter of panic in her tone.

"Stay quiet. Give them your papers and do what they say."

"But..." she croaked under her breath, the guards moving up the line to us. "I don't have travel papers."

"What?" I breathed out in a hiss, my gaze shooting to hers, anxiety ramming up my throat.

"We don't need them in Austria. It's part of the Unified Nations. I didn't even think about it."

Of course she didn't. It was something she probably never thought about or carried in her life.

"Fuck." My brain circled with what to do as the guard moved down the line. "Okay. Stay calm. We'll say they were taken from you." It happened all the time. Travel documents were a hot commodity on the black market. People were robbed of them constantly. "Say as little as possible. The more you explain, the more you look guilty."

The guards came to the family next to us, my heart pounding in my chest.

"Ash…" Dread colored her tone.

"It will be okay." I gripped her arm. I wasn't sure it would be.

"No." Her voice was low, but the emotion screamed through me. "Isn't that you?" Her chin flicked to the man with the clipboard. His back was turned to us, displaying his notepad.

Blood drained from my body, the ground tipping over as I stared at a photo… of me. It was grainy, but there was no denying it. Especially when next to my mugshot was Warwick, Brexley, Caden, and Scorpion's photo. The word *Wanted* was written in big letters, and below it was *Shoot to Kill.*

Oh. Holy. Fuck.

Scarlet's missing papers were the least of our worries.

"What do we do?" She peered at me, gulping. I knew she could feel my terror, because I could feel it battering against me like a windstorm.

My throat was dry, panic trying to steal any rational thought from me. I peered around. The train was congested with travelers and crates, but behind the jammed carriage, I narrowed in on the door we came in when we boarded. There would be a camp of soldiers outside, loaded rifles, barbed wire fences, roadblocks, trained dogs, and trenches.

It was suicide, but it was our only chance.

"The back door." Looking like a loving boyfriend kissing her temple, I spoke into her ear. "You run. No matter what happens." *Even if I'm gunned down.* "You don't stop for anything. You understand?" I wouldn't let the notion of her getting killed tonight even enter my mind. I wouldn't let it happen. "On my word. You run." My lips pressed against her head again. For good luck… or maybe it was a goodbye.

The guards were handing back the papers to the family next to us, still preoccupied with them before they moved to us.

"Now." I grabbed her hand, yanking her with me, threading through the throng of people.

"Stop!" Voices shouted as we shoved and pushed to the door. Ripping it open, Scarlet darted through. Taking a second to glance over my shoulder, I saw guards ramming through the crowd only feet behind us.

Sprinting out the door onto the platform right as Scarlet jumped down, her hand touching her ribs, but adrenaline was pumping too high for her to feel the pain.

Leaping down next to her, my brain tried to map out the lay of the land, decipher a path with the least threat. The darkness swamped the rural farmland, stretching out into nothing but night and obscurity. No nearby houses or towns glinted in the distance; only a few stars peered through the thick clouds above. The immediate area was lit by fires and battery-charged spotlights, which dotted the guards' encampment.

"This way!" She motioned me to follow, her nose sniffing in the air, running into the darkness.

"Get them! Shoot!" A man's voice rang behind us, setting off an alert throughout the camp. Dogs started barking, loud car engines turned over, and men shouted as a spotlight from a tower flashed on, pointing in our direction.

"Shit!" I hissed, tugging her out of the beam of light. With every step we took, it felt like they gained ten, a rogue wave about to crash down on us.

"Watch out!" Scarlet tugged me to the side, narrowly missing a low barbed wire trap, ready to wrap around ankles and dig in until you went down. I hadn't seen it at all.

Fae had far superior vision than humans, but nature fairies weren't especially known for having exceptional eyesight, especially at night. We were more in tune with what people would call our third eye, not the two in our head.

Scarlet moved with confidence, as if she could see as clearly in the night as in the day.

POP! POP! Gunfire reverberated against the cloudy sky like a bomb, vibrating my bones as the bullets zinged by us. Trucks sped over the terrain, the glow from the headlights bouncing, trying to laser in on us, the howl of dogs chilling my blood.

Leaping over more barbed wire traps, I grabbed Scarlet's hand, stopping her, my gaze going to what was right next to us. "There." I tugged her toward a muddy trench. Climbing down, I sank into the muck. Reaching up, I grabbed her hips, lowering her next to me, hearing a small cry grunt from her lips, her arm cradling her side.

"Come on." Hunching low, we scurried quickly, following the ditch, heading east. Shrieks boomed around us like shrapnel, their voices getting closer, fire torches glowing in the night air.

A beam came down on us, reflecting my shadow across the dirt.

"They're here," a guard screamed. "I found them."

Fuckfuckfuck.

Pop! Pop! Pop!

Bullets spit off the earth near our heads, cascading clods of grass, brush, and dirt on us. Panic filled me, forcing my legs faster. Scarlet tried to keep pace, her strength amazing me as she trudged through the mud. But I could sense her energy waning, her cracked ribs draining her, her feet stumbling through the sludge.

"No." I lanced my fingers in hers, gripping so tight, dragging her along, willing my energy to transfer to her somehow. "Don't stop!"

Losing them as the trench cut right, I knew this was our only chance to escape. Or hide.

War trenches were crudely designed within the land. The walls were full of holes and overhangs, with parts of them crumbling in.

Dropping onto my back, I rolled in the thick, freezing sludge.

"What the fuck are you do—?"

Before she could finish, I jumped up, wrapping my arms around her, slamming her up against the muddy wall, right under an overhang of roots and bushes. I pressed my body so hard into hers that a gasp huffed from her, probably from pain.

I knew I didn't have to tell her not to make a sound. Our hearts slammed in sync together, my face buried in her hair, feeling her pulse against my lips. I kept still, hoping my muddy back blended us into the side like we were part of it.

A squeal of tires stopped overhead, a car door slamming.

"Where are they?" A thick Romanian accent pitched overhead. "Where did they go?"

"I don't know. They were just there, Captain Dumitru," another answered, his timbre younger and faster.

"You useless fuck," the older man, Captain Dumitru, snapped. "Get the dogs. We will find them. Search the fields and out toward the road. They are probably heading that way."

"Yes, sir." The younger one rushed out; the only sound was his feet running off.

My hand went to Scarlet's mouth, nodding up, telling her not to move or speak. She nodded, not looking at me.

Stillness surrounded us, the shouts and dog barks now in the distance. The silence stretched on. I knew what Captain Dumitru was doing. Watching. Waiting. For us to feel we were safe with all soldiers turned away and try to run.

Scarlet's heartbeat wailed against mine, nails digging

into me, her body starting to shake and twitch. I drew my head back to see her face. Her lids were closed, her pale skin dripping with sweat like she had the flu. Fae didn't get sick, but we did get metal poisoning.

Like iron to high fairies, goblin metal tore through all fae, consuming our magic similar to a Strighoul.

Watching her, I realized it was more. Tiny, almost insignificant changes were fluttering across her face, her nails growing sharp, her bones popping.

Her body was trying to change, fighting against the goblin magic, which was painful and making it useless. Like crashing against jagged rocks over and over. She was a shifter, but I still couldn't figure out what kind. Her aura wasn't anything I'd felt before.

Seeing her struggling, grappling for air, making tiny noises that could be heard, anxiety took over. I had to calm her down. My thumb rubbed back and forth against the pulse in her neck, trying to ease her. I drew her in closer, encouraging her to use my body as an anchor as I ran my thumb over her skin, feeling her heart slow.

Feet scraped the dirt above, both of us stiffening. Dumitru's boots hit the soft earth over us, causing the ground to dip overhead, barely holding his weight.

A torch flashed on, igniting the ground near us. The smell of cigarette smoke wafted over.

Not even daring to breathe, I watched the light move across the ground, revealing every nook and cranny along the sides. The light glinted at the edges of my muddy boots, my mind wishing us to become one with the earth.

Click.

The torch turned off.

He took in a heavy inhale of his smoke, exhaled it out, then tossed his cigarette down next to us. Gravel grated under his boots as he twisted around and walked away. A car door slammed and the jeep engine fired up, squealing as he pulled away, leaving us against the muddy trench.

My shoulders lowered in relief, though we were far from safe. Leaning back, I stared down at Scarlet, my hands cupping the sides of her face, forcing her to look at me.

"You okay?"

"Yeah." Her gaze fluttered, not landing. "Fine."

It wasn't a lie, but it certainly wasn't the truth either.

"You're okay to keep running?"

Brows knitted, her eyes finally met mine in irritation.

"Making sure." My fingers brushed dirt from her cheek, my knuckles dragging down her neck, noticing she had bitten down so hard into her bottom lip that blood dampened it. My thumb slid over the wound, wiping the red stain from her mouth.

She went still, and it was then I realized what I did and the fact I was still fully pressed against her. Not even air could get between us. My body took notice of the heat coming off her, the rush of adrenaline pumping through my veins.

I stepped back, skating my fingers back through my hair.

"I know you're in pain. But we need to get out of here as fast as we can. Staying off the roads."

"I don't need a pep talk." She pushed off the dirt, annoyed with me. "I can keep up just fine."

The howl of a dog pierced the air, snapping both our heads back toward the camp. It wouldn't be long before they would be scouting this area again, and we needed to be long gone.

"Come on."

Climbing out of the ditch, we got over a barbed wire fence and started to run.

And didn't stop.

Heading deeper into the perils of Romania.

Chapter 7

Ash

We trudged across the flat farmlands and rolling hills, the smell of snow hinting in the night air that cut briskly through the fabric of our clothes. Walking for hours through abandoned villages and dense shrubs, we stayed off any major road, impeding any real progress we could've made, but I would not risk being caught. With each passing hour, Scarlet's energy waned, her stumbling steps getting smaller. Wrapped up in her coat with her head down, she stubbornly pushed forward, yet her body was starting to protest. She would not be able to run or fight if we were found.

The desire to snap the goblin metal from her arm so she could heal splintered and sizzled in my chest as if my sheer will could make it so. Every time I turned back, the color had drained from her face even more, her brow pinched with pained determination. I felt the memory of *Věrhăza,* the torture from the House of Blood, wash over me with an icy-hot sweat.

If it wasn't the nightmare of Kek and Lucas dying before me over and over, I woke up to the screams of dead prisoners, the wails of agony, the suffering still deep in my bones. My heart pounded, thinking I was still there and getting out had been a dream.

Watching Scarlet endure the goblin poison daily itched at every fiber of my being. It was in my nature to take care of people, to heal, to want harmony and well-being, especially for those I loved. I was the emotional protector of my found family, the one who provided comfort, stability, and reason.

Three things I didn't have as a young child.

My blood family was so deep into the practice of "Earth's harmony" that they failed me and my sibling on every level.

Though I couldn't say I was the poster boy for comfort and stability anymore. Case in point staggered behind me. Allowing this young girl to get this far with me emphasized that very idea.

Scarlet tripped over her shuffling boots, nipping at my last thread of patience.

"We're finding a place to settle for the night." I peered around the dark night. Only the glow of the moon through the clouds gave the rolling farmland any distinction.

"We can't." She gritted her teeth, anger lining her forehead, peering behind us as if the Romanian guard would come around the corner right then. "We're not far enough away."

"Another three or four miles isn't going to help. And you..." I tipped my head, feeling irritated for some reason. "Aren't going to make even that."

"I'm fine."

"You're not."

"I said keep going." She shot daggers at me. "I. Am. Fine."

"And I said…" I stomped back to her, getting right in her face. "You. Are. Not."

Rage bloomed from her, and for a second I thought I saw something in her eyes, an orange tint to her green irises, and then it was gone.

A few more beats passed before I stepped back on my heel. "Look at you. You're about to fall over."

Her chest puffed up.

"Anyone would," I instantly combated, motioning to her wrist. "Believe me, I understand what it does to your body. I would be on the ground right now."

She stared down at the bracelet.

"And there is something extra about that one."

Her head jerked up, swallowing. "What do you mean?"

"I don't know, but it has another magic I can't place." My hand hovered around the metal, trying to sense it through the thick layers and complicated magic. It was right there, yet I couldn't reach it. The tips of my fingers grazed the vein down her wrist, stopping at the metal. She stared down at where my hand was on her arm, her body stiff.

Stop touching her. I took a step back, clearing my throat.

"We need to find someone who can take it off." I moved back more, my tone matter of fact.

She didn't respond, her silence creating even more unease.

My mouth opened to speak when snowflakes started to float down, the temperature dipping low enough for winter to start shedding its skin. Scarlet was already shivering, and the night was only beginning. The temperature would plummet. Turning around, I headed down the one-lane road in search of shelter.

The night was so silent, but the sound of her boots scraping the pavement, her breathing labored because of her cracked ribs, her teeth chattering from the snowy air, pummeled my ears like spikes.

For the next mile, I flopped between blaming myself and blaming her for being here. Analyzing every incident that led us to this point. I tried to get her to go home. I demanded it, yet here she was. Wounded, exhausted, broke, and far from her friends and family because of me.

And what I had to do… the lengths I needed to go for my revenge? They did not entail a wealthy exchange student as my sidekick.

Up ahead, through the trees, I spotted a puff of smoke billowing from a chimney, a barn sitting to the far side of the house. The snow was getting thicker, the flakes padding our shoulders, soaking into our clothes. I needed to get her somewhere warm. Quickly.

"There," I whispered, motioning for her to follow me. I would rather both the house and barn be vacant, but at this point, we couldn't be fussy with lodging.

Fae might not die of hypothermia, but it was still extremely painful and took a huge toll on our bodies. I didn't have time to sleep for a month to heal. Or have her go into a fae coma on me.

Sneaking across the field, I crept up to the old wooden barn door. The structure looked like it had been there for a century. Yet as fragile and decayed as it appeared, it probably would still be standing longer.

Making sure all was clear, I opened the door, peeking into the space. The strong scent of hay and wheat was absorbed into the wood, as if it was only yesterday the grains had been moved out, leaving just their scent like perfume. Old-fashioned wagons were stored on one end; the rest held equipment and some decaying straw left from the harvest.

Getting Scarlet in, I shut the door behind us, setting us

in complete darkness. It was still cold, but it was ten times better than outside.

"*Szar.*" I tripped over something, stumbling to regain my footing.

"Stay there." Scarlet's voice slinked through the darkness, my ears picking up her confident footsteps, moving easily through the room. I heard a crank of something before a flash of light flinched me back. My eyes adjusted, seeing Scarlet by a side table, an ancient lantern blazing in her hand.

"You can see that well in the dark?" It came out more as an accusation than a question, the curiosity of wanting to know how she was overtaking my rule to not care.

She shrugged a shoulder, placing the lantern down onto the table, giving off enough glow to move around the room, once again not answering my question.

My hands rolled up in balls as I descended deeper into the room. Asking a fae what they were was an intimate question. Similar to asking a stranger how many sex partners they've had. Some answered easily, and some found it offensive. In the Otherworld, when it still existed, secrets were power, especially when the humans didn't know about us. They were traded, bought, and killed for. Many fae still lived by this code, though with each new generation, the old ways were starting to die out now that Earth and Otherworld were one.

"Not going to tell me?" I said nonchalantly, checking out the room and pocketing a curved knife on the workbench.

"Tell you what?" Her response was as blasé as mine, her fingers trailing over the wall of hay rakes and pitchforks.

My jaw worked. I never lost my patience more than I had with her. "We're gonna play this game?"

She peered over her shoulder, reading me before she looked away. "It's complicated."

Growling, I rubbed at my head, feeling a scream building. "You are such a pain in my ass."

"And you aren't in mine?"

"In yours?" I scoffed. "You're the one who followed me. I've been trying to get rid of you since Vienna." My voice rose, my arms going out as I marched up to her. "And complicated is who you are, but not *what* you are. That should be pretty cut and dry."

Her head tilted, her attention going past me.

"I know you're some kind of shifter."

"Shh." Her head slanted more, listening for something.

I went still. "What?"

"I thought I heard something," she whispered, concentrating on noises outside.

I heard nothing at all except the creaking of the ancient barn and the patter of snow on the roof. Ten seconds went by, the sound of my pulse striking the time like a bell, but nothing broke in to get us.

"It's probably nothing. Just the barn making noises." She shook her head, closing her eyes for a moment.

Her focus off me, I became very aware of how close she was. Her features were stunning, but I could see the pain, exhaustion, the bruises still marking her face, wanting so badly to heal, but unable to.

"You need to rest," I mumbled, her lashes popping back up. "There's some straw over there you can use as a bed." I flicked my chin behind her. Too tired to fight me, she shuffled over, lowering into the moldy cushion with a groan. Following her, I took off my backpack, squatting in front of her, helpless as she held onto her ribs, blinking back the tears. "You should eat something." I rustled through the pack, pulling out a stale granola bar.

To a tree fairy who ate only organic and grew his own

veggies and herbs, this shit was garbage, though it was the only thing that could really survive on the road like this.

"I'm not hungry." She turned away from my offer, her nose flaring with nausea.

"I don't care. You need to—"

The door to the barn slammed open with a loud bang, jerking me up and around.

"Nu vă mișcați!" Don't move! Behind the rifle pointed at us, a small, dark-haired man stood in the doorway. *"O să te omor!" I will kill you!*

"It's okay." I spoke in his native tongue, trying to soothe him, standing in front of Scarlet. The fact she didn't get up told me she was far worse off than I thought. "We're just here for shelter."

"Don't take me for a fool," he seethed in English, easily picking up that we weren't from here. I could feel a little magic coming off him, but it so insignificant he was most likely a half-breed. "You don't think I know who you are?"

My muscles locked up, panic curling through me. He knew who I was? Was my picture distributed so widely through Romania that I didn't even have a chance of getting close to Bucharest?

Lazar may have put the order out for me and my friends, but I had no doubt who was actually behind it.

Sonya.

"We're just trave—"

"I heard it over the walkie-talkies." He kept his finger heavy on the trigger, stepping in farther. His appearance suggested middle age, though it was hard to tell with fae. "You're the two who escaped from the border patrol, aren't you?"

Air trickled out of my lungs with a little relief.

"Look." I tried to call on my abilities to soothe and calm

someone. "We're not dangerous. We just need a place to rest, and then we will be gone."

He peered around me, taking a better look at Scarlet, his bushy black eyebrows pinching together. He nodded at her. "She looks familiar. I've seen her someplace before."

"No," I scoffed, shocked it wasn't me he pointed at. "Definitely not." I glanced back at Scarlet, pausing on her for a moment. Sitting on the hay, her back pressed to the wall, arm around her torso. Fear whisked over her features slowly enough for me to catch before her walls went up. It tasted odd; a strange mix of alarm and fear slid over my tongue. She dipped her head, her hair curtaining her face, her lungs laboring.

"Please." I went back to the man, my palms still displayed toward him. "She's hurt. She needs a place to rest and heal. We will not cause you any problems."

"Seems like you already have," he mumbled, moving around, getting closer to Scarlet. I moved with him, keeping my body between them.

His mouth twisted, concern worrying his brow. "What's wrong with her?"

"Cracked rib."

"She's fae. Why isn't she healing?" He nodded at her face, the bruising and cuts from our fight with the bodyguards still vivid.

"Goblin metal." I pointed at her wrist, sensing only truth would work with him.

He cringed, stepping back, but his gaze stayed on her. Completely transfixed. Whatever it was about her, it seemed to disarm him. He sighed, lowering his gun.

"Why are the guards out searching for you?"

"She lost her travel papers." It was true, just not the full truth.

"So you ran from them? And got away?" He blinked at me in shock, really asking, *You were willing to die for not having documents?*

"It's *complicated.*" I shot a glance at Scarlet, using her phrasing from earlier.

"It must be." He huffed out a clipped laugh. "The fact you escaped from them and got this far?" He truly looked awed. "Guess you deserve a drink for that."

"Yes." I practically melted in his hand, the need slamming into me, my mouth watering.

"Well…" He blew out. His attention traveled back to Scarlet. I could sense his skepticism rising when it landed on her, yet he seemed even more inclined to help her despite it.

Odd.

"Just my wife and me." He made his way back to me. "We don't have much, but you can come in and have some *ciorbă rădăuțeană* she just made." A soup named after the town of *Rădăuți* where it originated. A staple, especially during the holiday season. "And I have some *tuică.*" A plum brandy that was similar to *pálinka.* Though each country considered theirs the one far superior.

"Thank you."

His dark eyes met mine, and I could see the threat in them. If I did anything to make him regret this decision, he would kill me himself.

Dipping my head in agreement, all I cared about was to get Scarlet somewhere warm and some actual food in her belly.

"Okay." He still seemed hesitant. "Follow me." He clutched his gun and headed for the door while I turned for Scarlet.

"I'm fine out here." She tucked tighter into herself. "I'm simply gonna go to sleep."

"I'm not leaving you out here." I crouched, cupping her face and tilting it up to me. "You need to get warm and have something to eat."

"I'm fi—"

"You're not. If you think you have any chance of keeping up with me tomorrow"—I forced her chin higher—"you need to get your strength back."

She rolled her lips together, knowing I was right.

"Come on." I wrapped my arm around her, slowly helping her to her feet. A cry squeaked out before she bit down on her lip.

I adjusted my hold on her body, helping her to walk out. My mouth pressed against her head, trying to tease her. "You're as fragile as a human right now."

"Shut up." She smacked my arm, which only made her flinch more in agony.

"We can't afford not to take his offer." My mouth moved closer to her ear. "But don't let your guard down. Okay?"

She nodded against me.

I couldn't feel any ill will toward us, but with her, I wasn't willing to trust anyone.

Not when the border patrol was out hunting us, and I had a price on my head.

When we entered the one-story house, smells of garlic, chicken, and onions cooking in a warm, creamy broth crawled down my throat, strangling my stomach with hunger. My mouth watered, but deep down, I knew the food wouldn't satisfy my appetite. My body was starting to crave something no food or drink could satisfy, causing my muscles to twitch.

"Dragostea mea?" My love. The man rambled deeper into the small house, the floors creaking under his weight. My head skimmed the low beams as I stepped inside with Scarlet, giving me a better view of the simple home. A kitchen lined the far wall, hutches and cupboards crammed in on the other two walls. A table and chairs sat in the middle, leaving a little space by the door for a sofa and two chairs across from a fireplace, which had several pots cooking in it. Colorful handwoven rugs and tapestries draped the walls and lined the floor to insulate the interior, creating a cozy vibe.

"Sotia?" Wife.

A stout woman stood in the kitchen, slicing into steaming warm bread. Her short black hair was pulled away from her face with a headscarf, some gray hair poking out, letting me know she was human and aging rapidly compared to her husband.

Fae could definitely get old enough to get gray hair, but they would be so ancient that magic would plow through your senses and dissolve any doubt they were old.

"We have some guests." The man motioned for us to come further in.

The woman twisted to face us. Wariness straightened her, trepidation in her gaze quickly disappearing when she saw Scarlet holding on to me, barely able to stand.

"Oh!" She wiped her hands on her long skirt. *"Te rog intra!" Please come in.* She waved us in while she moved for my companion, her gaze latching onto Scarlet's face. She went still, her eyes widening in a perplexed reverence. Her hand went to her mouth, her eyes going even bigger, like some deity had entered.

"Anca." The man said her name, jolting her from her stare.

"Oh. So sorry. You remind me of someone…" she babbled, swishing her hand. She spoke to Scarlet in English, though it was noticeable it was not as natural for her as it was her husband. "Oh, dear, you look frozen to death." She noticed the way Scarlet was holding her ribs. "Are you hurt?"

"Cracked rib." I spoke for her, knowing small talk would take even more energy from Scarlet. She was fighting goblin metal while being half-starved and frozen. She had watched a friend get murdered, was beaten up, burned up, almost kidnapped and killed—all in less than three days since meeting me.

"Oh no. Please sit down." She gestured to a chair at the table, then rushed for the cramped kitchen, pulling out a glass and bottle from the hatch. "We do not have medicine, but hopefully this will help, my dear." She poured the plum brandy for Scarlet, making my mouth water.

Lowering onto the chair, Scarlet winced, her nails digging into my arms.

"Thank you, ma'am." I nodded to the woman as she handed the cup to Scarlet.

"Anca." She pointed at herself. "My husband is Vasile." She nodded to where he stood at the end of the table.

"We are so grateful for your hospitality." I rubbed Scarlet's hands around the mug, trying to warm them up. "But it is better you do not know our names." Standing up fully, I looked into Anca's dark eyes. "I swear, we mean you no harm."

Anca's lips pinched together, and she dipped her head in understanding, as if this was not the first time they catered to lawbreakers hiding in their barn. "You both must be starving." She went to the fireplace, grabbing a potholder to get the soup out of the flames.

Almost twenty-two years since the fae war, and this part

of the world still functioned without the simple modern conveniences the West had re-adapted to.

Vasile strolled to the table, grabbing the bottle of *tuică and* pouring himself and me a glass.

My head bowed in gratitude, and I downed the brandy, barely tasting the hints of vanilla and citrus hitting the back of my throat. It wasn't until I swallowed it down, my muscles easing, that I realized how tense I was. How frantic I was to take the edge off, no matter how it came. The taste of liquor only intensified what I really wanted, the sweet alcohol a poor substitute.

Vasile poured more into my empty cup, probably believing my anxiety came from the night we had. To be fair, that was part of it, but being in a life-or-death situation was part of daily life when you had a brother like Warwick. The only time I had peace in my life, living a more standard tree fairy life, was when he was in the fae prison, *Halálház*.

Was I content and happy during those quiet years? I thought so. Tending to my herbs, growing food in my garden, sipping tea, and meditating with nature. It was what I was born to do. Yet when Warwick stepped back into my life, dropping a wounded girl on my table and flipping my life from peaceful to chaotic, I felt myself come to life again, especially when Lucas and Kek weaved themselves into my world. I wasn't a normal tree fairy. I was never at peace when life was quiet and tranquil.

"Please sit." Anca bade me, bringing the pot of soup to the table and grabbing the warm bread while Vasile placed down bowls and spoons for us.

I heard myself mutter my thanks again, realizing this was the most I had uttered that word in a very long time. The notion had me dropping back another mug of brandy, hoping to clear out my conscience, kill any thoughts that connected my brain to it.

Ladling warm soup into our bowls, Vasile passed the bread around, pouring me another cup of *tuică*.

Anca hummed to herself, getting the little food and drink they had to share with us. She motioned for us to dig into our delicious meals.

The creamy chicken exploded on my tongue, the homemade food causing a groan to bubble up. The brandy and soup filled my chest and stomach with warmth.

Pausing, I watched Scarlet eat, her cheeks flushing with the heat of the fire, her lids crushing together with delight as the flavors slid down her throat to her empty stomach. An overwhelming wave of protectiveness for her overwhelmed me, along with gratitude for these people who took us in without caring about our crimes.

Without thinking, I brushed back strands of Scarlet's hair that had fallen in her face, tucking them behind her ear. Her eyes darted to me and I felt them pierce me, jerking my hand back at the intimacy I felt between us.

"You good?" I cleared my head of any thoughts going past me, being courteous. Tree fairies were very touchy people, so it didn't mean anything.

She swallowed, nodding her head. I could see exhaustion creeping up on her, preparing to take her.

"Eat." I pushed the bread to her, turning my attention back to the couple, not liking how her green eyes bore into mine.

Once again, I noticed it wasn't only me whose attention she captured. Anca's eyes kept darting to her throughout dinner, an odd expression fluttering over her features.

Aware of my gaze, Anca dropped them from Scarlet, shaking her head.

"Scuze." She blushed at being caught. "I can't get over how familiar she looks." She leaned on her elbow, her focus back on Scarlet. "Doesn't she, Vasile?" His mouth full of

bread, he bobbed his head in agreement. She tapped at her lip, her eyes brightening. "*O da...* You look so much like—"

"I have that face." Scarlet pushed her mostly eaten bowl away. "This is delicious, Anca. Thank you. But do you have a bathroom I can use?"

"Oh, yes!" Anca leaped up, as if she couldn't believe she didn't think of it first. "I'm sure you'd like to get cleaned up and into something warm to sleep in. I can place your clothes by the fire to dry." She talked quickly. "This way."

I got up, helping Scarlet to her feet.

"I'm fine." She moved away without looking at me, tottering after Anca down the small hallway.

Lowering myself back into the chair, my attention still on where Scarlet disappeared, a sensation I quickly shoved away prickled at my gut.

"She needs to get the goblin metal off her arm so she can heal." Vasile leaned back in his chair. "Otherwise she is going to get sicker and sicker." I could hear the implication. The warning.

"I know." I clutched my mug, taking another deep sip. "I'm thankful to you and your wife that she is fed and warm." I directed my sentiment at him.

"Anca and I are taking a huge risk."

"Yes. I know."

"What is happening in this country... we are against it. We feel helpless. So maybe this is my way of fighting back." Vasile nestled deeper into the chair in contemplation. "Helping those running from the regime. And there is something about you two..." He sighed heavily. "My land has fought the perils of dictators before, and we have persisted, even with the rise of authoritarianism after the fae war. Though this time feels different. Lazar's cruelty is different."

"It is." I nodded. "Because I don't think it's Lazar who's in charge anymore."

Vasile looked at me, no surprise in his features, as if I was confirming something he might already have known.

"I believe he is used as a puppet by a powerful fae. Sonya."

"Sonya?" Vasile's eyes widen. "The fae leader who tried to take Budapest?"

Anger and guilt burned in the back of my eyes, picturing her face slicing through Kek's neck, the glee as blood sprayed over her. My lover dropping to the ground.

"And her son." I gulped down the rest of my drink, refilling it instantly, trying to block Lucas's bloody face.

"If that is the case." The wood chair squeaked as he shifted. "Then Romania will get harsher, more volatile. Deadly." His chin flicked to the hallway. "And she will only get sicker and weaker from fighting the goblin metal. You know she has no chance of making it across this land. She will die here."

My reaction to his sentiment was instant. I blamed it on the alcohol affecting my emotions, but a panicked ferocity barreled through me, stealing the oxygen from my lungs for a moment. It was violent. Brutal.

No. No. No...nothing can happen to her. I will destroy everything if she dies.

Shaking my head, I tried to clear my irrational thoughts.

"Calm down," he uttered, and I jerked my head up to hear the trees outside cracking and scraping the roof. My fingers clawed into the chair, my teeth grinding together.

He spoke only the truth, and I was the one to bring her into this mess.

"We can't turn back now," I muttered low, inhaling and exhaling. Uncurling my fingers, I sat back in the chair.

Vasile nodded as if he understood that was not an option for me.

"Then you got to get the metal off her."

"Finding a goblin or someone who has the magic tools to cut through it is not an easy feat. Practically impossible."

Vasile took a drink, his brows pinching.

"You don't happen to know anyone, do you?" I scoffed, thinking the chances were nil.

Vasile's lips thinned, his gaze distant.

"Do you?" I sat up further in my chair, tracking his expression.

"Know?" He shifted uncomfortably again. "You could say at one time I did." His dark eyes darted to the hallway his wife had gone down, the house small enough you could hear her helping Scarlet prepare a bath. "Way, way before I met Anca, when this world was a different place, when I was a *different* man, the simple life did not suit me." He paused, getting lost in his thoughts for a moment. I tried to stay calm, to let him tell his story, my need to know if he could help Scarlet crawling up my body.

"I was deeply involved in black-market mining. Things like gold." He cleared his throat. "Metals."

My chin lifted, my complete attention on him.

"I became unbelievably wealthy, no one understanding how I had so much luck, how easy I seemed to find the treasures others mined decades for." Sadness watered his eyes. "The secret was, I didn't find it on my own. I had help... a mining *Vâlve*."

"Vâlve?" I coughed out, setting down my mug in surprise. Vâlves were known in Romania as female spirits. Protecting, helping, guiding. But if someone got too greedy, stole, or used their treasures foolishly, the spirit would cruelly and relentlessly seek atonement for those crimes. I had heard

111

of them, but they were rare, so rare some fae thought they were a myth.

"My own Vâlve of the mines," he whispered. "She was in love with me. And there might have been a part of me that loved her too." He blinked several times. "But my greed overtook any feeling I might have had for her." Grief flickered over his face. "Talyssa took everything from me, made me suffer for a century with nothing. And had me fall in love with a human so I could suffer watching her slowly die. She wanted to make me feel the pain I made her feel." He glanced around. "But I can't resent her for it. I enjoy the simple life now, found peace and tranquility in it. Found my heart, even if it's temporary." His eyes glistened, staring in the direction his wife's voice could be heard. He took a few moments before he cleared his throat.

"The point of this story." His contemplation fell on me. "Vâlves of the mine have no reaction to metals—whether to iron or goblin."

"Wait." I straightened. "You mean... they can touch it."

"They're spirits, so the metal has no real effect on them." He shrugged. "And Vâlves have the power to take it away from you. Make all the gold and metals you have disappear."

Take it away. Disappear. Like off Scarlet's arm.

"Where?" I leaned into him. "Where is this Vâlve?"

"Talyssa." He said her name as if it would conjure her. "She was in the caves of Valea Cetatii." He leaned on his forearms, a guilt still hanging over him. "Between Bran and Brașov."

That was on our way to Bucharest.

"The caves are closed now. Been cleaned out for decades. I don't know if she is still there."

"It's worth a shot." We had no other options. "Thank you." I realized he didn't have to tell me any of this.

112

He clasped his hands together. "Be careful. Vâlves are *extremely* emotional, and if you make them mad or hurt them, they will come after you with everything they have. They will make you pay dearly." His personal experience hung heavy on his brow; the memories he wouldn't share, what she did to him, could be felt in the air.

He may be happy with where his life was now, but her vengeance no doubt took a toll. Not only changed his life, but him fundamentally.

"Ummm... I'm sorry to interrupt." Anca's voice jerked both of our heads to the entrance of the hallway. "I'm afraid your *iubit*." *Lover, sweetheart*. "Fell asleep in the tub, and I can't get her out." She motioned for me to follow her.

"Oh." I stood. "Of course." Giving Vasile a grateful nod, I trailed after Anca to the washroom.

My alcohol-soaked brain was still mulling over what Valise had told me, not even thinking, when Anca opened the door for me. I stepped into the tiny bathroom, hearing it shut behind me.

My boots went still on the rug, my muscles stiffening, my eyes rolling down the completely naked figure in the bath. The water only reached her torso, exposing her breasts.

My cock went hard, aching and straining my pants as my eyes rolled over her tits, her stunning features soft in sleep, her cheeks flushed.

Fuck.

Energy zinged around me, pulsing my cock. Sex was our default. Nature fairies were like steaming pots, needing to constantly relieve the overflow so we didn't explode. Too much magic from the environment thrummed our nerves like guitar strings.

The desire to fuck stole my breath for a moment. To feel that bliss, the utter release I never felt anymore, no matter who I fucked or how hard or "good" it was. My eyes squeezed together at the onslaught of need, my hand squeezing my cock more to cause pain than anything else.

Stop it, you sick asshole. I barked at myself. *You are drunk, desperate to get high, and horny. It has nothing to do with her.*

Naked figures never bothered me before. Fae loved being nude. It was natural, normal, and, most of the time, not even sexual. What the fuck was wrong with me?

Taking a heaving breath, I berated myself again before I opened my eyes. Grabbing a towel, I leaned over and pulled the plug on the tub. *She's like a little sister.* I repeated in my head, turning to my clinical healer side. *You mean like the one you let die?* A voice nipped at me.

"Scarlet, wake up." I draped a towel over her front as the last of the water disappeared down the drain. "Scarlet?" I shook her. "Come on."

Her lashes batted, her green eyes barely hinting through her lids before they closed again.

"You're not going to make this easy, are you?" I grumbled, getting my arms under her frame and lifting her out of the tub. I disregarded the way my hands glided over her ass and bare back, the way her body curled into mine, her wet skin soaking through my clothes.

The movement pushed a moan from her throat, sucking in the pain from her ribs, but her eyes stayed closed.

"Scarlet?"

She tucked deeper against me, muttering.

I sighed, wanting nothing more than to put her down and get far away.

Making sure she was covered, I awkwardly opened the door with her in my arms. Anca stood right outside, waving to me to follow her to the room across the hall.

"I'm sorry, we only have the one bed in here." She scurried to the nightstand, turning on a kerosene light. "And we're trying to save as much energy as we can." Her throat bobbed in embarrassment. "It hasn't been good for us farmers lately."

Authoritarianism never was. It wasn't good for anyone except those at the top.

Settling into the room, it felt small and chilly, holding a twin bed against one wall, a nightstand, a chair, and a clothes cabinet. "But I brought extra blankets and some clothes to sleep in." She waved to the pile on the chair.

"You have been so kind." I spoke quietly, not wanting to wake Scarlet.

Anca's gaze hopped between us, a loving smile warming her face, and I could sense what she was thinking, her thoughts voiced loudly with her unshielded human emotions. She thought us so in love. A beautiful couple.

"If you need anything, don't be afraid to ask." She stepped out, shutting the door before I could respond.

Turning, I lowered her to the twin bed, the towel pulling away from her.

My teeth ground together, and I twisted to grab some of the clothing Anca brought.

"Scarlet?" I needed her awake enough to help me. "Sit up."

She moaned something.

"Scarlet." My patience was thinning as my willpower to not trail her body with my eyes started to disintegrate. "Help me out. You need to stay warm. Put this on." I helped her sit up, pushing a sweatshirt over her head. Her lashes started to flutter open, and she stirred enough to wiggle her arms into the sleeves before curling back onto the pillow. Good enough.

Covering her with the blanket, my fingers brushed through her damp hair.

"Goodnight, Scarlet."

"Scarlet?" She murmured the name sleepily, her brow furrowing, like she was confused. She muttered again so low I wasn't sure I heard her right. "That's my grandmother's name..."

Chapter 8
Scarlet

Only skimming sleep, my mind became more cognizant of sound and movement around me. The words I mumbled as if they were from some dream, so delicate it popped like a floating bubble.

My weighty lashes pried apart, blurry vision catching a tall, broad figure standing in the dim light across the room, his profile facing me. Exhaustion had me slow to catch up and figure out where I was, but it didn't take me long.

Ash stripped off his wet shirt, his tattoo flexing over his muscles, his pants riding low on his hips. I stayed absolutely still. It didn't seem to matter that I had already seen Ash almost naked. It did nothing to stop the heat from pooling between my legs at the complete awareness of him. Ash was hard not to be conscious of.

This time, the way the candlelight reflected off him, I could see his skin was marked with multiple scars along his hip and lower back.

"Where did you get those?" I croaked.

His head swung around to me, his eyes catching mine. I sensed a second of something I couldn't place before he looked away, hanging his shirt over the chair to dry.

"*Now* you're awake," he huffed, ignoring my question. He grabbed some blankets from the chair, laying them down on the floor.

"What are you doing?"

"Getting ready to go to sleep," he replied dryly. "Something you should be doing."

"Yeah." The response barely made it out as I watched him make a bed on the floor, his ass to me. Funny enough, I was wide awake now.

"I feel bad you're sleeping on the floor."

He snorted. "I have slept in *far* worse places. Having a rug underneath me is luxury."

"Oh." I wasn't sure if it was a question or statement. My mind was looping with all the places he had probably laid his head down. "No luxury in whorehouses?" It slipped off my tongue before I could stop it.

Ash's mossy irises slid up to mine like he could see right through me—hear the twang of jealousy flushing my cheeks.

I wasn't jealous, though. I mean, he was hot. No one could deny it, but I didn't feel that way about him. Not when I was still in love with someone else.

Someone who loves someone else.

The influx of agony I had gotten used to burned up my esophagus before I could stomp it back. Thinking about him, what I did because of my pain...

"Judging those who weren't born with money?" He lowered himself to the floor, unlacing his boots. "Some have no other means to survive, to keep from being homeless. And some enjoy it."

"I wasn't judging." I lifted my head, frowning.

"Yes, you were." He flapped out his blanket, laying it over him. I noticed he kept his loosened boots on. Probably in case he needed to run. Clearly without me, since I was pretty much naked. Maybe it was his plan. Find me a home he could dump me in, like some pet rescue.

"Maybe I wasn't criticizing them," I snipped. "Maybe I was judging *you*." I turned my head away from him, angry at his assumption. There was truth in it, but more than anything, I felt his judgment of thinking I was so insipid and uptight.

He let out a sigh, his body shifting. The light next to me on the table was extinguished, the rustling of him getting comfortable on the floor breaking up the silence.

My words sat heavy on my chest. I wasn't someone who ever spoke without thinking. I couldn't. Too much could be taken out of context. But it wasn't natural for me. My temper, even as a child, always got the better of me, and while my brother continued to play, I was put in time-out a lot. Time-out was a good description of my entire semester abroad in Vienna.

Tucking my pillow under my head, trying to find a comfortable position, I couldn't lay still. All my thoughts, what I just said, looped in my head. I could hear my mother's reprimand, telling me I was better than that.

Fighting internally, I finally exhaled. "I didn't mean that."

"You did." His tone had me flipping around to face him in the dark. Between my sight cutting through the dark and the outline of light streaming from the door gaps, I could make out Ash on the floor, one arm under his head, staring blankly at the ceiling.

"I probably deserve it." His brow furrowed, a guilty expression flittering over his face. "You're not the first to say or think it."

119

Curiosity bubbled out of my mouth. "What do you mean?"

He blinked, seeming to get lost in his thoughts. After several minutes, he muttered, "I used to be someone better than this." He readjusted his arm under him. "I used to be the person people turned to. Counted on."

"What happened?" I whispered, afraid even that would make him stop talking.

His features darkened, his throat bobbing. I think he forgot that I could see him in the dark, probably thinking he was hiding behind the shadows.

"I lost people I loved, and in that, I lost more people I cared about."

My mouth bunched together, feeling his pain as if it were my own. Our situations were probably totally different, but I could relate to the sentiment profoundly.

"You know the saying, *'Tis better to have loved and lost than never to have loved at all*?"

"Yeah."

"It's bullshit."

"One hundred percent," I agreed.

His head twisted toward me, and I could feel his curiosity zinging. "You're far too young to be cynical like me."

"I guess it's what happens *in* those years, isn't it?" I tucked damp hair behind my ear, feeling a strange intimacy and freedom in the dark. "You could live a thousand years and never know the pain of heartbreak, or you could live twenty and have it destroy you beyond repair." Emotion watered my eyes, the raw pain unexpectedly still hitting like an open wound.

Ash curled more on his side. "What happened?" There wasn't an ounce of condescension, belittling the idea that at my age I could experience anything truly deep.

"He was my first love. My best friend...I thought he was my soulmate." *I loved him with everything I had.* I blinked back the tears wanting to gush out. Anguish hung there like residue I could never get rid of, but the worst part was that deep down, I still hoped I could be the one. That he'd wake up and realize it was me he really wanted, though I knew it would never happen.

He had always looked at her the way I looked at him. Hope was a fucking horrible thing. It gnawed on you until you were nothing but bones of worthless dreams.

"We were each other's firsts, and I thought he loved me too." I swallowed, reliving what we had shared together and then the collapse of everything. "He was in love, but not with me."

I went silent, getting lost in the trail of pitiless memories. And regrets. That's what destroyed me the most. The night everything changed was because I couldn't handle the grief anymore. My pain had lashed out, anguish painting the walls, anger in shredded pieces on the floor.

And now I would be paying for it for the rest of my life.

"I'm sorry," Ash replied, returning to his back and staring at the ceiling. "Whoever he is, can I say, he's an idiot."

"I wish it were the case." How easy it would be if it was so simple. But he wasn't. He was a good person. He just didn't love me, and I still couldn't deal with it. I would never be the one he wanted—the bed he crawled into at night.

Not wanting to fall down that rabbit hole too far, I turned back to Ash. "You spoke of revenge?" I licked my lips. "The person you lost... you were in love?"

Ash was quiet for so long, I wanted to take it back, stepping too far over the invisible line I didn't see.

"Persons," he said low. "There were two."

"Two?" My brows shot up. Fae were open to all of that,

121

but I had never thought about being with more than one person. I didn't want anyone to be okay with sharing me, and I was too jealous to share anyone I loved.

"A man and woman. That surprise you?"

"No." I swallowed, though I think it did a little. I couldn't imagine anyone wanting to share him. Though I now understood his blend of women and men in the brothel. "You're doing this all for them?"

"Yes." His jaw clenched. "They were murdered in front of me. Retribution is all I have left."

"Is it, though?" I asked. "What about your friends back home? Family?"

"They understand."

"You think if they lose you, they will understand?" I exclaimed, my head swinging. "Let me tell you, they won't."

A nerve in his jaw twitched, and he shifted on his bedding. "They'll have to."

"Ash—"

"Go to sleep," he ordered, trying to put an end to the conversation.

I wasn't born to be ordered around.

"It's selfish. You might not care, but they will suffer every day." I would know. It wasn't the dead who endured the loss. It was the living. "Don't you care about them?"

He moved in silence, his speed like leaves blowing in a tornado. He whipped over to me, one hand pinning down my arm, the other pressing the base of my neck to the pillow, capturing the gasp in my throat at his sudden movement.

"Selfish?" His mouth was so close I could feel his anger spitting off his lips, his eyes glowing with fury. "You have the *audacity* to call me that?" He pushed his hand firmer into my throat, and the trees outside crackled with his energy, adrenaline spiking in my veins. "When all you've done is forcibly insert yourself into *my* life and *my* business. Causing mayhem in it all. I should already be halfway to Bucharest, instead I'm sleeping on the floor in a farmhouse, running from border patrol." He leaned over more, his chest bumping mine, his knee braced between my bare thighs, making me hyperaware I had no underwear on. "Who the hell do you think you are? You don't know me. And I certainly didn't ask for your opinion," he seethed, his thumb pushing down on my sternum.

No one had ever spoken to, treated, or touched me this way. No one would have dared. Air heaved through my nose, my blood pumping wildly.

"Maybe it takes a stranger to tell you the truth," I speared back at him. "That your head is so far up your ass."

"You think you're the first?" he growled in reply. He dragged me up the bed, tugging up the sweatshirt I was in. "And what about you? You don't think you're being selfish? Does your family know where you are? Didn't you just leave them without a word?"

"I had to." I tried to break from his grip, my ribs protesting. "But I didn't leave hellbent on killing myself for some stupid revenge."

"Stupid revenge," he sputtered.

"Do you really think the people who died would want you here? Dying for what? An idea of their honor? It won't bring them back."

Ash tipped back, ire shaking his limbs.

"How are you honoring them by treating *your* life like nothing?"

"Why do you give a shit about what I do with my life?"

I couldn't answer that. I didn't know.

"If you cared anything about your own, you'd get the hell out of this country. The hell away from me."

"I can't," I belted out. My emotions curled into me, making the monster inside salivate, itching my wrist. It wanted freedom. It craved violence.

"Why?"

His eyes darkened when I didn't answer.

No one could ever find out.

"Why?" His fingers pinched down on my neck. "Tell me, why?" His knee moved up, spreading my thighs, his thin pants rubbing into my pussy.

A sharp inhale tore through me, hints of a moan threading around it, my hips automatically rolling against the pressure. His body went still, freezing in place, his eyes going back and forth between mine.

The world stopped on a dime.

Desire dripped from me, my wetness soaking into his pants, burning into his skin. I fought against the overwhelming need, the craving for him to choke me harder. I wanted him to push his fingers into me, feel his cock stretch me. My body yearned for it. Pleaded to be fucked into sedation.

His nose flared like he had plucked those thoughts from my head, and then horror widened his eyes, jerking him away. Ash moved across the room, turning his back to me, his hands shoving through his hair before stalling on his hips.

Humiliation rained down, stealing my breath and heating my skin. It rolled around and around in the silence, growing like bacteria. I could still feel the imprint of his fingers, the need still pulsing between my legs, while shame crawled up from the trenches, twisting my yearning into disgust. Yanking down the sweater, I sat up, pulling the cover back over me, peering down at my hands.

Sex was never an uncomfortable topic for me before; it couldn't be in my world. I had always been forward, going after what I wanted. But what had happened the last time, even before that, caused things to change.

I hadn't felt *anything* sexual lately for anyone… and to be turned on by him yelling at me, gripping my throat…

"I'm sor—"

"Nothing to be sorry about." Ash rushed away, running his hand over his face, shaking his head. "I'm the one who should be sorry. I shouldn't have touched you like that. It was wrong."

But I liked it. I crushed that thought like crackers in my hand, scattering it like dust.

We both were tensely quiet for a few minutes, the room suffocating, before he spoke.

"We've got a long day tomorrow." He lowered himself back to the floor, settling in. My eye caught the wet spot on his thigh before he covered himself with the blanket. "Get some sleep."

Yeah. Right.

Laying my head back on the pillow, I turned away from him. The silence was thick, allowing the flesh of my past to crawl out from the black depths and sink its claws into my mind. Reminding me of all the things I had done to get myself here.

Time ticked by, what felt like years, before I eventually drifted into a shallow slumber. My consciousness skimmed the surface, aware I was asleep but prisoner to my mind. Trapping me in it, holding me down so I couldn't look away. It always started out the same, a voyeur to my dreams, a bystander screaming for it to stop before it forced me to relive it through my eyes again. Experience the power, the high taking over my pain.

The monster could not be contained. It whispered, it hunted, and then it devoured.

Blood.

Screaming.

Nooooo! Stop! Please...

Was it my pleading or theirs? I didn't know anymore.

"Scarlet?" A figure was next to me in the dark. My lids were open, though my brain still struggled to know if I was awake or dreaming. It didn't feel any different. Still trapped, my lungs fought to grasp air, my limbs fighting to break free.

"Shhh. It's okay." Fingers touched my face, brushing them soothingly through my hair. "It's just a dream."

As if his words released me from my prison, I gasped and gulped for air, the threads of my dream vanishing under his touch. But without the shield of sleep, the pain of reality punched a hole through my gut, pushing a sob up my throat.

"It's okay. I'm here." Ash spoke softly. It was like he had a direct link to my brain, calming me in an instant, though my body still quivered, my skin coated in sweat, my heart in heaviness.

His hand slowly stopped, pulling away when he thought I was falling back to sleep again.

I couldn't help but stare at him—his strong bare chest, his blond hair loose, his green eyes seeing nothing but me. And I felt something I hadn't in a long time.

Safe.

He started to rise.

"No." I had no control over my actions, impulse driving me. I grabbed his wrist, my head wagging, though my eyes wouldn't even meet his in the dark. I didn't want to think about it. I didn't want to acknowledge anything.

I was scared. Alone.

Tugging his arm, I turned onto my side, away from him, trying to pull him down next to me. He didn't move for a few moments, cutting deeper into my shame, and I curled into myself.

Ash blew out his nose and scooted down next to me on the small twin bed, his arm staying around me, his body pressed firmly into mine, his mouth nestling close to the back of my neck.

"I'm here." His voice barely made it to my ears. "You can sleep."

And for once, I did.

Safe and dreamless.

Chapter 9

Ash

Warm. Relaxed. Peaceful.

My body hummed with each sentiment, snuggling deeper, craving more. It was bliss, a feeling I hadn't experienced in a long time, yet against my will, my eyes cracked open, spilling milky light between my lashes. Awareness slowly dragged me out of my slumber, the smells of fried eggs and smoked ham drifting into my nose.

I sighed with contentment, feeling serene everywhere… except my cock, which was pushing hard against the zipper like it wanted out, wanted to sink into the warm body I was curled around.

My lids flew open, oxygen halting in my chest, last night flooding back.

And the awareness of a naked ass curved into me.

Long, silky brown hair pooled on the pillow I was sharing, Scarlet's head facing the wall. Her small body was tucked tightly into mine, her sweater pulled up to her hips.

128

My arm was wrapped around her, my hand halfway up her sweater, grazing her ribs right below her tits.

I waited for panic to take over, to leap away from this girl and berate myself for letting this happen. My heart slammed against my ribs, but I couldn't move. Or maybe I didn't want to.

I hadn't slept this soundly since I lost Kek and Lucas, and for once, I didn't wake up drenched in sweat, screaming... or coming off a high, smeared in dried cum and tangled with faceless whores.

Scarlet was so warm against me, her figure cuddling into mine like a security blanket, and for one second, I wanted to live in this moment. To have serenity. To not suffer endless sorrow.

As much as I wanted to tuck into her hair, close my eyes, and fall back to sleep, I became too aware of the fact she was pretty much naked against me. My mind strolled back to how her pussy soaked into my pants last night, how close I came to forgetting everything, unbuckling my pants, and fucking her hard. I could sense how turned on she was, how responsive.

Scarlet wasn't the type you fucked once and walked away from without a thought. Especially since we were stuck on this journey together. And that was all I could offer anyone. My heart was dead, my soul was empty, and my cock was unbiased about who it sunk into. Except right now, it felt anything *but* impartial.

Groaning, I rolled over, placing my bare feet on the ground. I scoured my face, my dick throbbing. I tried to breathe through the need to fuck, hoping to force my body to relax.

It wasn't working.

This had been normal for me at one time, but since Lucas and Kek died, I only got hard when I was drugged up in a brothel, taking my anger out on the world. And when I came, it left me empty. Unfulfilled. Searching for something else to take my pain.

This isn't because of her. I just need to let off some of this excess energy. Take the edge off.

The craving hit like a brick—my mouth watered for fairy dust, to feel it trickle into my veins, alleviate the tension… and then fuck this energy out of my system with someone I didn't care to know.

My fingers twisted into my hair, the need for at least one of my vices ripping away my tranquility.

"Hey?" Scarlet's husky morning voice slithered around me. I glanced back, watching her stretch, still sleepy and hazy. I quickly turned back, my knuckles turning white.

"Wow. I slept so good," she muttered.

"Yeah." I bounded up, grabbing my shirt and yanking it on. *Me too… the best sleep I've ever had.*

The shift in the room was instant, coldness lapping up the silence behind my comment, Scarlet clearly sensing my mood.

She sat up, one hand tugging at her sweatshirt, the other holding her ribs, staring down. The blissful expression she had a moment ago had darkened. Insecurity, shame, hurt? I couldn't tell; I just knew I had put it there. And all I wanted was to have her smile back.

"Buna dimineata." *Good morning.* A knock softly tapped the door, Anca's voice coming through the wood, whipping me around to it as if I was caught doing something bad. *"Micul dejun este gata."* *Breakfast is ready.* "Also," she switched to thick English. "And *dragă*, I have your clothes clean and dried for you." She addressed Scarlet.

Opening the door to our hostess, I nodded my head. "Thank you."

Her gaze went from me to Scarlet's barely dressed form on the bed and back to me, doing well to not look down at my massive erection carving through my cargo pants. She dropped the clothes into my hands, and a knowing smile shyly curled her lips.

"I'm sure you both are starving." The double meaning felt like she left a grenade in the room when I shut the door, something we had to avoid, or it would detonate.

Scarlet got up, her eyes not meeting mine, taking the clothes from my hands. Pushing past me, she left the room, going to the toilet and shutting the door.

Sighing, I dropped onto the chair, retying my boots.

All I wanted was for Scarlet to be safely back home with her family so I could continue on with my quest. I didn't have time for distractions or to worry about people. That was why I left Budapest.

I knew Brexley, Kitty, and Warwick would've stopped me, or knowing Warwick, he'd have come with me. And I couldn't have that.

This was my mission and mine alone. I couldn't forget that. This was about Kek and Lucas. Retaliation for their lives and for what was taken from me. I had sworn to them I'd track Sonya and Iain down and make them pay.

It was a vow I would not break, no matter the costs.

I could hardly savor the cold ham and fried eggs, the food skimming past my tastebuds in a hurry to get to my stomach. The night before, I had been too tired to really appreciate Anca's home-cooked meal. This morning, I scarfed the organic, farm-raised food into my mouth like it was the last meal I would ever see. With my luck, it might.

131

Sensing Scarlet's gaze on me, I peered up while guzzling coffee. "What?" The cup clinked on the table as I set it down.

She wagged her head, cutting her egg into small pieces as if she were being graded on her manners.

"Did you chew?" She huffed.

"No, I swallow." Our gazes locked on each other. The response had popped off my tongue absently, but the moment I noticed the pink in her cheeks, I realized what I had said. My chest and throat tightened. A rush of emotion heated my skin, and I stared down at my plate, my appetite lost.

I sounded the same as the old me. The happy me. The one before I lost everything and became bitter and angry.

Kek and I used to love to tease Lucas with innuendos in front of people to see how long it would take him to turn bright red, hiding a shy smile.

Gods, we were incorrigible.

That part of me had died with them. And I was okay with that. It felt right because how could I feel joy without them, especially so soon? To laugh and tease again with someone else?

The egg in my throat fought to go down, my bones uncomfortable under my skin.

"There is plenty more." Anca pointed to a plate of cheese and pickled veggies they had stored from the summer months.

"I'm stuffed." I forced a smile, pushing my plate away. "Thank you."

Anca frowned. The need to fill my belly until I couldn't move was baked into hospitality here. She quickly hopped up, taking the plate toward the kitchen area.

"I will pack this up to take with you."

In the light of the early morning, I could tell Vasile was

a lot more restless with our presence in their home, as if the murky rays of sunlight were pointing right down on the house, telling everyone he was harboring fugitives. I understood his unease and told him we would be heading out immediately, though Anca demanded we eat first.

"You can take either one of these paths." Vasile stubbed his finger on a map he had laid out. "But once you hit Sebeș, keep southeast to get to the caves. They are here." He circled with his finger. "Bran or Râșnov is the last place to get any supplies. But be careful. I've heard there is a big military presence around that area now. Might be where they are training recruits." His thick brow flatlined, his lips twisting.

"Military? There?" I asked curiously, sensing unease rising in him.

"There are strange rumors being spoken of that land again." He stared at the map. "Things people don't want to talk about." He went quiet, then shook his head, rubbing his chin, chuckling darkly. "But I guess that's nothing new for Transylvania."

To humans, Transylvania had become almost this cartoonish stereotype of vampires who slept in coffins, with peak hairlines, capes, and a cliché Dracula laugh.

The castle was famous and funny enough, but the man who made it so, who wrote the book, had never stepped foot in Romania. Legend blurred the lines of reality and fiction. The castle became famous for this story that people treated as real, and it had nothing to do with vampires.

Not to say it didn't have its own dark, haunted history, but what lured people there, feeling the magnetic vibes of something they couldn't explain, was fae magic. It had been a fae stronghold during the first battle between humans and fae, before we had to go into hiding for centuries.

"I appreciate your help." I rose from my chair.

"Here, take this with you." Vasile rolled up the map, handing it to me. "The mountain area still might have spells, keeping people away. Just stick to the path."

"And here." Anca placed food wrapped in newspaper in my hand. "There are also some herbs in there to ease her pain."

The gratitude I felt for these people scraped against my skin, not liking the emotion it stirred, leaving me speechless.

Scarlet got up like she sensed my struggle, speaking instead.

"You don't know how much your kindness—" Her shoulders stiffened, instantly pooling anxiety into my gut, when her attention went to the window. I didn't even have time to ask her what was wrong when I heard the motion from the road.

Crappy magic-adapted car engines whined noisily as they hit the gravel. Vasile darted for the window, peeking out of the curtain, and I could see two familiar old jeeps filled with border officers bouncing down the road for the farmhouse.

They found us.

"Dracu!" Vasile hissed, whipping around to us.

"Do you have a back door out of here?" Anxiety pitched my voice as I moved for Scarlet. From what I had seen, there was only the front door, and all the windows were too small to climb out of.

The brakes on the jeeps squealed as they came to a stop in front of the house, dosing my veins in terror.

"Anca…" He and his wife shared a look, and she nodded.

"Come with me." She waved me to follow. "Hurry."

Nudging Scarlet, we darted after her. The sound of engines turning off, car doors slamming, and men's voices pierced the back of my spine. We followed her back into the room we stayed in. Anca yanked back the rug I ended up not sleeping on, showing a hidden door in the wood boards. Yanking it open, stale dank air laced with smells of grain and dirt hit my nose. It looked like an old storage to keep things cool, an ancient refrigerator before electricity.

A pounding hit the front door while I heard men's voices circling the house. They were ready for someone to come leaping out the window.

"Go," I ordered Scarlet, shoving the wrapped food into her hands while I grabbed our bags, not wanting to leave any remnants behind.

"Grabă!" Hurry. Anca muttered desperately over and over as another knock rattled the entrance, a voice demanding entry.

Crawling into the small dark space after Scarlet, I had to tuck in tight against her. Anca's fearful eyes met ours as she lowered the hatch, shutting it. I heard her shuffling, placing the rug back over the crawl space, sealing us in.

Boots hit the wood floor from the living room, and strong, muffled voices knocked against my pounding pulse. I could easily pick out Vasile's timbre compared to the others, but I struggled to hear exactly what they were saying, my panic hazing my senses.

Fingers laced through mine, squeezing tightly, calming my erratic heartbeat. I exhaled at Scarlet's touch, focusing on my other senses, picking up on their words.

"You sure you haven't seen or heard anything out of the ordinary?" The guard's voice was booming with intimidation. It was the one from the other night, Captain Dumitru. "Nothing in your barn?"

"No," Vasile responded. "Me and my wife here. We went to bed early, and as you see, we just had breakfast."

"Just you and your wife, huh?" Slow and methodical, boots thudded across the room. "That's a lot of plates and silverware for two people." Scarlet's hand crunched down on mine. "Looks to me you had guests."

"We were so tired, I didn't clean up the dishes from last night." Anca's voice had a slight tremble in it.

There were heavy footsteps and then the echo of skin being slapped.

"Don't touch my wife," Vasile yelled, sounding strained, like he was being held back.

"Your wife has no manners. She clearly has not been properly trained. She should speak only when spoken to," Dumitru barked. *"Caută în casă!"* Search the house! he ordered his men.

The reverberation of feet moving, the clatter of dishes crashing and breaking, and furniture being knocked over swelled to a crescendo. The guards moved through each room, purposely destroying what little these people had.

The door to our room squeaked open, air holding in my lungs, my body ready to react. The floor creaked overhead.

"Bed's been slept in," one muttered as metal squealed over the floor. I heard the bed frame being flipped over, shaking the space below it.

My pulse stuck in my throat. All it would take was one kicking the rug just enough to see the outline of the hatch. To open it and look. We'd have nowhere to go or hide from gunfire. We'd be killed in seconds.

Anxiety cut each breath like a scalpel, dotting my vision. I gripped Scarlet's hand tighter when I realized she was shaking violently. And somehow I knew, like the night before, it wasn't in fear. Her body was withering against the goblin metal, instincts demanding her magic to rise and protect her while the poison curbed her from doing so. Convulsing, her spine hit against the foundation, a low growl in her throat.

Fuck.

Not able to speak, I blindly grabbed for her, pulling her to straddle my lap, my arms encasing her against me, willing her to slow her breaths in the same rhythm as mine. Her heart thrashed against my chest, her body still wiggling. I stroked her hair, plastering her to me. Her face dug into the curve of my neck, her mouth against my skin like she was trying not to be heard, a few words I didn't understand escaping.

And then her teeth sank down.

My hips jerked, a groan catching in my throat as my cock hardened, engorging under the sliver of pain. I clutched the back of her neck, holding her in place, swearing her teeth were sharper than normal, hitting a core nerve.

For a moment, everything came alive. I could taste the eggs and coffee I had, smell the dank earth and her perplexing scent, see the flecks of dust sprinkling between the floorboards, hear the men above us shuffling around, her breath in my ear, feel the weight of her body on mine, the movement of her chest matching my rhythm.

Yet something hovered on the edges, a darkness, which scared me. I had never felt it before, something unnatural, but still ancient and old as time.

Then it was gone.

"Find anything?" Dumitru stomped in, his boots once again pausing right over us.

"No, sir. Nothing."

"The dogs picked up their scent not too far from here," he grumbled. "Have the canines go into the fields. They can't be far."

"Yes, sir." Three men replied in unison, and a train of footsteps departed the room. Voices rose and lowered, and then the front door slammed. I sagged back into the wall, my hand stroking Scarlet's spine, her pulse easing, her tremors drifting away.

It wasn't until the sound of the jeeps roared away that Scarlet lurched back, her eyes wide like she now realized what she had done. Her gaze dropped to my neck, the sensation of her mouth still lingering there.

"I'm so sorry," she cracked, her fingers swiping at the spot tinted with red. Raw pain circled her green eyes, which almost looked stained with orange or something in this light.

"It's fine."

"No." She shook her head, agony still in her eyes, but she had a faraway look, like she was stuck in another time.

"Hey." I clutched her chin, forcing her to look right at me. "It's okay." Going by my cock, it was more than okay.

Her gaze tracked mine, seeing the truth there.

The hatch above us whipped open. Anca peered down at us, her lids blinking before a small smile hinted at her mouth. "Looks like you guys are just fine. Got cozy in there?"

Scarlet scrambled off my lap, standing up and climbing out, her expression strained with embarrassment. I followed behind, taking in the red mark across Anca's cheek as I shut the trap door behind me.

"Are you all right?" My impulse to help heal her, to get herbs to ease the pain, rocked me on my feet.

"I'm made of tougher stuff than that." She batted away my concern. Her lips pressed together as Vasile stepped into the room.

"You guys need to get far from here."

Scarlet looked around, her arms out. "But what they've done to your home. We can't just leave you—"

"Yes, you can," Vasile replied sternly. "You must."

I agreed. They had already put themselves out for us. Their house was trashed, and Anca was assaulted—all because they helped us.

"Someday I will find a way to repay you," I promised

Vasile and Anca, bearing both of our backpacks, wanting Scarlet to carry no other burden but her cracked ribs.

"We help people because it's the right thing to do. The harsher the world is, the more help should be given." Anca kissed both my cheeks and went to Scarlet.

She took Scarlet's hands, her head wagging, one hand reaching up to touch her cheek. "I can't get over how similar you look to her."

"Yeah. I get that a lot." Scarlet leaned in, kissing her cheeks. "Thank you for your hospitality. I will make sure you are compensated for the damage here."

I tipped my head, peering at her. Her speech was very formal, almost rehearsed.

"There is nothing to worry about. All old stuff anyway." Anca and Vasile walked us to the door.

Saying goodbye, we stepped out, heading quickly away from the fields and main road and toward a trail.

"What was that?" I nudged her when we stepped on the path.

"What?"

"I don't know… you sounded very courtly."

"I'm rich, remember?" she replied flatly. "It's how we speak."

"And I guess how they bite too." I winked, touching the small wound on my neck. "Though that seemed a little less proper and more feral."

She picked up her pace, not responding to me.

"Scarlet?" She didn't react. "Hey?" I grabbed her arm, turning her to me. "I was just teasing."

"Don't." Her lids narrowed. "Don't tease. Let's not even talk. We have a lot of ground to cover, and we need to get away from here." She strode down the lane, furious at something.

I was about to call after her when howls from dogs came from the distance, and I quickened my step behind her.

She was right. We had to get far, far away before they locked onto our scents and I had teeth sinking into me in a very different way.

Chapter 10

Ash

We slogged down the hill in a laborious cadence. Spires of human churches and buildings crested the dusky horizon, lights guiding us through the fields to the town of Sebeș. The idea of a warm place to sleep and hot food in our bellies motivated me to keep going.

Barely.

Snow swelled the clouds overhead like pregnant sheep, baying in discomfort and ready to give birth. The contradiction of sweating under your clothes and being so cold you could no longer speak hadn't lessened in the last thirty hours. Not that Scarlet seemed keen to talk to me anyway. Her answers to everything since we left had been short and curt.

Exhaustion coated Scarlet's features. Her pallid complexion highlighted her pink cheeks and nose, rosy and runny from the freezing temperatures.

We had only slept a few hours in some dilapidated

abandoned house the night before. At least it gave us shelter from the icy temps as we nibbled on what we had of Anca's leftovers. Sleep came fast, but it didn't keep me long—an endless loop of nightmares surging me awake with fitful gasps.

Scarlet pretended to be asleep, but I could feel her wide awake along with me, both of us suffering silently in the freezing night.

Silence had never bothered me before; it was where I used to find comfort and meditate in my thoughts. Now I found death. Not just in myself, but in the villages and hamlets we had passed through. Twenty-two years after the fall of the Otherworld, these places had become forsaken. Most had given up a long time ago, moving into bigger cities to try to survive, leaving these places derelict and lifeless.

Scarlet's muteness bothered me the most because I could feel her thoughts battering loudly, though I couldn't hear them. I felt her shutting down more and more, yet I couldn't seem to stop it.

And why did I even care?

Of course I cared about her as a living, breathing person, but I didn't need her to express herself to continue to do that. I could see her drifting off to dark places, the vacant stares at the wall as we ate last night, getting lost in a past I knew nothing about. It made me want to pick at her. Find a thread and pull until she unraveled.

The old Ash would have. He was interested in people, curious about their lives.

This man no longer did. He used up all his empathy. His humanity. He only craved finding a brothel to fuck and get high in.

My teeth sat on edge at the idea of fresh powder riding through my veins. To not feel anything anymore. To not care about her silence.

Between a river and two major crossroads, Sebeș had become a booming town. Even more than it probably was before the fae war. A hub for trade, travel, transporting, and, of course, titillation.

Firelights flickered from the signs down the strip, trying to gain notice over the identical business next door. Various styles of buildings were crammed together, and in some I could feel German/Dutch influence from its first settlers, even though they had been taken over many times since then.

Horses, wagons, and a few derelict motorcycles filled the narrow street, assaulting the air with manure and battery acid. Music and light streamed from the pub's windows while women and men of the night stirred in the rooms above, their day just beginning.

Looking at Scarlet again, noting the exhaustion on her face and the way she held her ribs, I knew she needed a bed tonight.

"We still have some money left." I nodded toward a tavern. "Let's get some food and a place to sleep."

She didn't fight me, but neither did she respond in any way. Aggravation ground through me, strangling my nerves. Was it the goblin metal? The pain?

Was it me?

I took her non-response as a yes, leading her to a door. The sign *Bordel* danced in red lights above our heads. Her gaze went to it, her mouth flatlining.

"Brothel," she huffed under her breath.

"Cheapest place in town." I shrugged defensively, feeling like she knew exactly why I picked this place instead of others, my craving showing through. Brothels were usually the cheapest for food and booze. They wanted to get you gambling, drunk, high, and paying for whores.

Warmth blasted me when we stepped in. The packed

143

place steamed like a sauna, transmitting the stench of body odor, cigarettes, cheap perfume, and sex.

One half was dedicated to gambling, the other was more for food and liquor, the bar on the far wall. Traveling men and women—fae and human alike—filled the downstairs while prostitutes wormed their way through both sides, working the room and finding their latest mark. The prostitutes were mostly human women, with a sprinkle of men in the group.

"How can I help?" A woman with a red wig came up, reminding me of a very cheap version of Rosie, though there was no comparison. This girl was a tacky shell of my friend.

The whore's gaze rolled down me. "You look weary and tense." She winked, peering at my crotch. "I'd love to help you with that."

"I'm sure you would," Scarlet grumbled, her eyes rolling to the side.

"No need to get jealous. For a little extra, you can watch. Or you can join in, *prinţesă.*" *Princess.* "Or maybe *he* can watch."

I could feel Scarlet's hackles rise, her chest puffing up, her lids narrowing like she was ready to punch this girl.

"Just food." I curled my finger into the back of Scarlet's belt loop, tugging her back into me. "And a room."

The woman's gaze went between us before she waved us to follow her further into the room. The buzz from the gambling area tapped at my skin, the thrill of the win or loss as alcohol poured freely, opening the guests' pockets further. One man blatantly snorted powder off a prostitute's bared breasts, licking and sucking them dry.

My hands knotted, my cock twitched, and a muscle in my jaw jumped. Sex always turned me on, whether watching or participating, but that wasn't what had my pulse dancing along my neck. Forcing my head to turn away, I followed the redhead, who sat us at an empty table. "I'll tell the madam you want a room later." She winked and strolled off.

My weary legs and feet groaned in happiness as I sat, while my knees danced under the table with energy. I swung my head back around to the man, knowing what was dropping in his blood system.

Yearning for a small taste had the back of my mouth watering. We had been through so much in the last few days. I just needed a little hit to relax.

"Here." The prostitute/server dropped a plate of *mici*, fries, and a bottle of cheap *tuică* onto the table with two glasses. She leaned over, letting both of us see her breasts almost fall out. "I will be back to check on you. Let me know if you need anything." Her hand grazed my leg under the table, her fingers drifting almost up to my cock. "I'm here to help." She squeezed and strolled off.

Scarlet snorted sardonically, her head shaking as she grabbed for a napkin, laying it across her lap like she had been trained since birth to do.

"What?" It was the first real reaction I had gotten from her in a day.

"Is that how it always is?" She looked toward the red-wigged woman.

"How what is?" I poured our glasses full of liquor, shoving one to her before plucking a *mici* off the plate and shoving it in my mouth. The food looked awful, and I was certain the grilled meat was neither pork nor beef, but I was so hungry I didn't care.

"That." She motioned out while her other hand properly scooped up fries and meat onto her plate with a utensil. "Always being hit on. Being looked at like they'd pay *you* to hump your leg."

A laugh barked from my chest, not expecting her

statement. She was such a mix of unpredictable and formal, and I never knew what would come out.

"What can I say? It's hard being me." I smirked, observing her try to fight a smile, only making me want to put a full one on her lips. "Plus, if that was the case, I'd be a *billionaire*, and we wouldn't be sleeping in an abandoned home with no heat or food." I slammed back the entire glass of plum brandy, my eyes watering from the cheap liquor.

"No, but you'd probably still be in a whore house."

My spine stiffened. "What does that mean?"

"Just means you seem *very* at home in them."

"Well, my friend, Kitty, owns one, so I've been in one enough." *And she's kicked me out and banned me from ever coming back.* I chugged down more alcohol at the memory of the night she barred me from returning. I thought disappointing her would make me be better, wake me up… it didn't. Failing her and the rest of my family ended up causing me to dig deeper into my hole.

"I love that they welcome all walks of life, no matter who you are." I watched her cut into her *mici* like it was a steak, sawing it into bite-size bits and gracefully placing it in her mouth. I waited for the grimace, the acknowledgment of crappy-tasting food, of a meat substance I couldn't even place. She probably ate gourmet food, had a chef prepare her meals, but she said nothing. "You can be anyone here."

She popped another piece into her mouth, taking a swig of brandy. Chewing, she stared around the room, looking at everyone. "There were… social events my mother had to put on." Her gaze still danced around the room. "I would get so bored." Her eyes rolled back. "Gods, I hated them. Especially when I was young. My brother was better at faking it, being charming. Though, don't get me wrong. He was a terror too." A genuine smile lit her face. "But he was better at acting innocent and wiggling out of trouble."

"Not you?" I tipped the glass to my lips, my gaze locked on her.

"No. I was the troublemaker. I couldn't control my emotions as easily as him. And because I was a girl, most thought I should be sweet and pretty. The quiet, well-mannered one." She finished off a fry, wiping her hands on a serviette. "My best friend... he..." Pain cut over her stunning features, telling me it was the boy she had talked about. Her first love. "He started this game to distract me when I was close to losing it. He would point to someone and make up crazy stories about the people in the room." She laughed to herself. "Affairs, murders, blackmail. Gamblers and thieves, pirates and spies. The older we got, the more gruesome and torrid they would get." She batted her lashes, her eyes clouding over. "What's funny is these people..." she glanced around. "They would be the lives we would give those stuffy types. It's like I got dropped in one of my stories."

"You mean, you never thought you'd be on the run in Romania with cracked ribs, eating mystery meat in a whorehouse, while that man gets a blowjob under the table?" I nodded to the booth behind Scarlet. Her head snapped around, seeing the male prostitute under the table sucking the man off while he ate his dinner.

Her head swung back to me, her eyes wide, her cheeks pink, a nervous laugh coming from her. "Wow."

"Guess they're both getting sausage packed with mystery meat."

A burst of laughter bubbled out of her, spreading warmth through my chest like a numbing agent. Our eyes connected, and I felt something tug inside me, and I realized I was smiling back at her. An authentic, genuine smile. Something I thought had shriveled up and died.

"Tell me." I leaned back in the chair, peering at her with

a heavy gaze. Each sip of brandy heated my frozen limbs, relaxing my muscles. My legs spread wide under the table. "What story would you give me?"

"You?" She lowered her cup, her attention not able to stay on me. She licked her lips, her voice low. "*You are* the story."

Fire speared from my chest, moving out. "Okay, then give me the opposite life." I could think of no good reason why I was playing this game, but I couldn't seem to stop.

Her emerald eyes finally met mine, and they contemplated me, her nails tapping on her lips.

"Banker?" She shook her head. "No, substitute teacher."

Liquid caught in my throat as a laugh snorted out of me. "Substitute teacher?"

"Sadly." She shook her head. "Your lack of confidence and the inability to speak in public because of your shyness keeps you from getting a full-time position or a date. You have no friends because you smell like curdled cheese."

Pounding at my chest, I choked out more laughter.

"And because of that, you have to live in your mother's attic, practicing origami and abstinence."

My head tipped back with a roar, amusement aching my stomach muscles like they hadn't been used in a long time.

"Wow." I wiped my eyes, tipping my glass to her. "Some imagination there."

Her eyebrows wiggled, her mischievous smile matching mine. "If you only knew."

Once again our eyes caught, staying on each other far longer than they should have. I could feel the shift, see the smile drop slowly from her full lips, her throat sucking in.

Something in my gut clenched. Completely bare of makeup, dirty, sweaty, bruised, and still probably half frozen, she glowed with life. With depth I had not seen before. Her beauty shined through, striking me in the dim light.

A groan came from the table behind her, pulling her attention away, and her breath hitched. The man's moans puffed out quicker, a bite of food pausing on his lips as he groaned out a long huff, releasing into the prostitute's mouth. The whore's throat bobbed as he swallowed him down.

My cock stiffened, need tightening my balls, my mind flickering with memories of Scarlet's teeth cutting into my neck, her wetness soaking into my pants.

A surge of guilt, anger, and disgust shot me up from the table, desperate to get far away from here. From her. She was a child compared to me. I could not think of her that way.

"Let's get a room so you can clean up and rest."

I picked out the madam at the bar. Dressed in finer clothes, she was about five-three and of Turkish descent. Nothing about her features suggested danger in any way, but she had an aura around her. A power. Her yellow eyes watching and noticing everything.

They tracked me as I strolled up to her.

"You need a room," she stated before I could even open my mouth.

"Yes." I flicked back at my companion. Scarlet was occupied with watching the debauchery happening around her. She tried to pretend she wasn't affected, but I could see the discomfort, the shock in her eyes. "Just the one for her," I said to the madam.

"You have *other* needs?" Her golden irises studied me.

My head dipped just enough for her to notice.

"This way." She motioned for us to follow. I glanced back, Scarlet's focus on the rowdy gamblers.

"Scarlet?" I called her name.

She didn't react.

"Scarlet," I called louder, trying to get her attention.

Not even a flinch.

"Scarlet!" I huffed, stomping the few feet between us, her gaze finally snapping to me. "I've been calling your name."

"Oh." She blinked. "I didn't hear you."

"How could you not?" My brows furrowed. "Come on." I motioned her to follow me, catching up with the manager of the brothel.

The woman took us up to the top floor, the lower ones being used for their "clients." Vulgar moans and the creaking of metal beds followed us all the way to the top, tensing every bone in my body. The madam opened the door to the tiny room with low arched ceilings. The only other items besides the small bed were a side table with a water bowl and a few thin towels.

"Bathroom down the hall," Madam stated.

"Thank you." I let Scarlet go in.

"That's 200 lei. For room and food." Madam put out her palm, not letting me pass.

I dug into my bag, pulling out a few notes and placing them in her palm.

She folded them up, tucking them into her bra, her laser eyes on me. "Let me know your preferences downstairs," she said quietly to me and then glided down the hall, disappearing from view.

Not once in my life had I ever felt shame for using prostitutes, for enjoying sex with various partners, paid or unpaid. But something pinched in my gut, itching underneath my skin at the notion, the bite mark I could still feel throbbing against my pulse.

Stepping into the small room, I bowed my head slightly to avoid hitting the low curved ceiling. Scarlet dropped her bag on the single bed in the corner, her back purposely to me. I could feel a defensive barrier, her spine so perfectly straight, and I knew she heard the *doamnă*.

The silence between us bloomed like blackthorn while the salacious noises from below streamed into the room, scraping the devilish thorns down my spine.

"So." I cleared my throat. "You have everything you need?"

No answer.

"O-kay. Get some rest. We'll leave early tomorrow." I turned to go but stopped, annoyance nipping the back of my neck, glaring at her as she didn't respond to me. Did I want her to stop me? "What's wrong?" Irritation coated my question.

"Nothing." She dug into her bag, pulling out some clothing we got at the shop in Hungary.

"Scarlet…" I exhaled.

"Nothing's wrong," she snapped and turned around. "Go get high or laid… probably both. I don't care."

"Really?" I scoffed.

Her lids tapered, a haughty expression as if I were some lowly peasant on her face.

"Really." She folded her arms. "Go run and hide from your issues in drugs and sex. Seems to be your default."

Anger blazed, curling and toiling like a current through me, dropping my feet across the floor before I even thought, getting barely an inch from her.

"You *don't* know me." I curled my hands into fists, fighting the temptation to grab her neck, curl my fingers into her spine.

"Am I wrong?" She held her ground, tipping her chin up at me, glowering back at me.

"Don't think being around me for a handful of days makes you understand me at all. Comprehend what I've been through."

"You act as if you're the only one who has lost someone.

Who has also suffered." She spoke through clenched teeth. "You're not!"

"Breaking up with your little boyfriend doesn't count."

Her skin flushed red, and for a second I thought I saw her eyes flash the same color, but it was gone so fast, I was sure I imagined it.

"You don't know me or what I've been through either," she seethed.

"You're right. I don't." I stepped in closer, a breath from her face. "And I want to keep it that way."

"Me too."

"Good." I took another beat, realizing how fucking close I was to her. The sounds of someone climaxing below us strained the air like static. "Try to stay out of trouble." I whirled around, heading for the door.

"That's rich coming from you." I heard her yell as I slammed the door.

A scream caught in my throat, rumbling from me in a low growl as I trudged down the hallway, scouring my face with aggravation.

No one, and I meant no one, had ever aggravated me so easily. I had some pain in the ass friends, but nothing fazed me much. I let it roll off my shoulders, laughing because usually it was some other guy's or girl's problem. Like, I could enjoy Brex because deep down, her ability to get in sticky situations fell on Warwick.

Even Kek and Lucas never pissed me off. They were so easy to be around. Did I lose all my patience, or was it just her?

"Fuck." I hissed, stomping down the stairs to the gambling room. What infuriated me even more was that I was doing exactly what she accused me of. Drowning my pain in drugs and sex.

Chapter 11

Ash

I laid my head on the back of the booth as the room hazed into a softer backdrop, the hum in my veins peeling off the weight I carried, the heart that laid dead and buried in my chest.

The chemical-to-magic ratio in the fairy dust was off, my body sensing the low-quality substance. The twitch in my brain from some synthetic compound was already making my pulse pound and my eyes dart around in paranoia.

Normally I wouldn't care as long as it hushed my guilt, quieting the voices in my mind and filling up the hollowness in my heart. Except tonight, my vexation with the girl three floors above me still nipped and bit at the back of my head, not allowing me to fully relax. Enjoy what I had been craving for days.

"Go run and hide from your issues in drugs and sex. Seems to be your default."

Her accusation bounced around in my brain and down

153

into my gut like a pinball. It wasn't the first time someone had said something like this to me. Warwick, Kitty, Scorpion, Brexley. They all pretty much told me the same thing, yet Scarlet's disappointment felt even worse. And all I wanted to do was forget it all.

"Madam said you were seeking a specific sort of fun tonight?" a voice spoke, my eyes popping open when I hadn't even realized they had closed.

My vision zeroed in on the girl from earlier, standing there with more lines to snort, now adorning a blue wig per my request. This color reminded me of mold.

Next to her was the male prostitute I saw giving a blowjob to the man eating.

I could feel the frown contorting my face, my irritation growing.

"Let Zahăr and I help you relax," the man purred, sliding over into the booth with me. "We can make you feel so good before we head upstairs for some real fun." His hand ran up my leg and over my cock. I felt nothing as I watched him try to get me hard.

The girl, Zahăr, meaning Sugar, slipped on the other side of me, pushing the tray of dust closer. It was the only thing that looked good to me.

Leaning over, I inhaled a line, hearing my zipper lower. Then a hand clasped around me, starting to work me. "Well, hello, *big* boy." The man's eyes twinkled.

"Let me help." The girl leaned over as he tugged out my dick, working my base as her mouth slid over the tip, sucking.

The room went even hazier as I watched them both work my semi-hard cock, feeling almost like I was no longer in my body, not able to get fully hard.

The need to release, to let off all this energy, to finally feel something more than pain gurgled in the back of my throat. Anger huffed through my mouth as she took me deeper, sucking hard. Not even noticing him anymore, I stared at the blue hair, trying to force myself to imagine Kek, to make her the focus of my fantasy. To let myself for one moment believe she was alive again, it was real, and I was happy.

I let myself believe, my drugged mind placing Kek with me, yet my body didn't respond. It wasn't working.

Fury bloomed under my skin. "Suck harder," I gritted, the girl doing exactly what I asked, gagging on my size. I could feel a prickle in my spine, a possibility of release, making me frantic.

I grabbed her wig and ripped it off, tumbling her brown hair around her shoulders and over my lap. My cock surged as my fingers laced through it, my brain flickering with images of teeth digging into my neck, the memory of spread legs, heaving chest, and wetness soaking through my pants, burning my skin.

My cock pulsed. I pushed her down harder, her lips and tongue strangling my cock, seeing another brunette working my cock with her mouth, her green eyes peering up at me, her cheeks flushed pink.

"Oh, fuck…" A groan clawed at my chest, my cock down this woman's throat. My eyes shut, feeling her swallow, my mind picturing someone else choking my cum down like the good girl she was, her bright emerald eyes watery with the abuse, her gaze filled with heated desire.

Serenity popped like a balloon, dropping me painfully back to earth, realizing what had just happened. Who I had thought of. Burning shame and disgust launched me into nothing but cinders, making me feel sick.

"Get off." I pushed the girl away, scooting out of the booth and away from them. The drugs plunged into my system the moment I stood, spinning the world around me like a merry-go-round. Stumbling and banging into walls, I came to the third-floor landing and stopped.

Air lunged in and out of my lungs. My thoughts were like wasps I couldn't catch, but I could feel each sting.

I didn't want to be downstairs, but I couldn't go into the room with Scarlet either.

Falling against the wall, my blurry gaze lowered. My cock still hung out of my pants, the girl's saliva coating it.

Repulsion. Guilt. I felt them all again, but this time for different reasons. It was the first time I had ever felt dirty for what I did, making me want to crawl out of my skin, scrub my body down, and block the memory.

I wobbled to the side, not able to stand. I was itchy. Gross. And smelling like a whore. I tore off my clothes in the hallway, staggering to the shared bathroom.

The water trickled from the showerhead as I washed my body and hair, things tweaking around me, the chemicals brashly echoing through my system, tilting reality on its side. Normally I craved this feeling, loved not being tied to reality, but tonight it made me want to peel my skin off.

As if I could still smell the cheap perfume from the whores, I scoured harder, needing to wash it all away, including my own thoughts. Though my mind was set to torture me, recalling the times the three of us showered together.

Gods… we were so fucking happy.

I leaned under the stream, a cracked noise rising from my soul. I was so lost without them, and even though they were gone, I could feel them leaving me again. Their memory, their presence, laughs, smiles, voices… losing them felt like I was losing myself.

"I'm so sorry," I muttered, as if needing their

forgiveness for thinking about someone else. Like I was replacing them, which terrified me. "I miss you both so much."

Fuck. I was tired. So fucking tired.

Stepping out of the tub, I noticed the door wide open. A woman gasped as she darted by, a door slamming behind her.

I barely recalled where I found a towel, staggering down the hall toward the thing I knew could provide what I wanted.

I need to sleep.

With the drugs taking out all logic or understanding, forgetting any shame I felt earlier, I almost fell into the room at the end of the hall.

A form lurched up from the bed in the corner, her bright, wide green eyes illuminating the dark. The same eyes I imagined earlier peering up at me.

"Ash?"

"Shhhh." Tottering over to the twin bed, I crawled onto it.

"What are you doing?" Scarlet watched me, her voice pitching.

"Sleep," I mumbled, wriggling in behind her.

"You can't sleep here,"

"Shhhh." My eyes closed, my arm wrapping around her waist, pulling her down.

"Ash…" she warned.

"Sleep." I tucked her into me, my whole body relaxing into hers, feeling warm and comfortable. The contentment I had been searching for. A life raft. Hearing and feeling the exhale coming from her, I nuzzled my face into her silky brown hair and let go.

Falling happily into chemical-induced slumber.

Sleep took me so wholly, I didn't stir once. Not one nightmare or panic attack. I drifted quietly from sleep, not hulled out like a shotgun. Groaning with satisfaction, I stretched my limbs, memories of the night before trickling back to me. Getting off. Shower. Getting into bed with Scarlet.

My lids popped open, realizing I was alone in bed—and naked. I crawled in with Scarlet with just a towel on, hadn't I?

Dull morning light streamed through the attic window, my attention landing on Scarlet, sitting in the single chair, facing me, her knees tucked up to her chest, her arms wrapped around her legs.

"Hey." I grabbed the sheet, tugging it with me as I sat up. The towel I went to bed with was in a ball at the end of the bed.

Her eyes drifted away, her throat swallowing. The energy in the room shifted, becoming awkward and tense.

"We probably should go." She dropped her legs down. "It's late." She stood up. "Your clothes were in the hallway when I got up earlier." She motioned to the pile of fabric on the nightstand. "I'll let you change so we can leave." She turned for the door.

"Hey." I lunged forward, grabbing her hand and tugging her back to face me. My knees on the bed, I covered my lower half, denying how my dick hardened at the touch. "Wait."

"What?" She shifted on her feet, annoyed.

"What's wrong?"

"Nothing." She fidgeted, and I knew she was lying. "We need to get on the road."

"What's your hurry?" I tipped my head, scanning her.

"I thought you were the one who wanted to leave early." She tucked a strand behind her ear, the hair I knew smelled like the almond shampoo Anca had. I'd been inhaling the scent all night.

"I did." I frowned. "You're just acting weird."

She fidgeted again, twisting her ring as she always did when she was agitated.

"Are you mad at me?"

"Mad?" She huffed out in a strange laugh.

"Then what?" I waited.

"You left me in this room, as though I were some twelve-year-old, while you went downstairs to get your dick sucked," she spat.

I jerked, almost dropping the sheet, sharper memories of the night streaming back to me.

"Were you spying on me?"

"Spying?" She huffed. "I didn't need to. It was out for all to see." She waved an arm around. "I can leave the room if I want to. I'm not a child."

"But you saw..." My throat grew thick, recalling tossing that harlot's blue wig to the ground, and getting rock hard at her brown locks, the hazy notion it was *her* sucking me off instead. Did she see that? Did she figure out what I was thinking?

My tongue slid over my bottom lip, her focus drifting to my mouth. I dropped the arm I was still holding, peering down at the bed we shared.

What the fuck was happening to me? I couldn't stop fucking up. Touching and being inappropriate with her. I crossed lines.

"Do what you want, I don't care, but to come in here after and climb into bed with me?" She gestured to my naked body.

"Fuck." I ran my hand down my face, my stomach knotting at my actions. "I'm sorry. I completely overstepped boundaries here." I wasn't thinking beyond my need to sleep next to her.

"No, that's not…" She tapered off, shaking her head. "It's fine. It's nothing." She grabbed her bag, wincing at the pain in her ribs. "Let's go."

"Let me carry that." I tried to reach for the bag, but she slipped for the door.

"I'll meet you downstairs. Who knows, I might find someone to entertain me while I wait." She walked out, shutting the door.

Darkness billowed up, tinting my eyes with anger. My head started to pound from the shitty drugs, and I felt the peaceful moment when I woke up evaporate into smoke.

The idea of one of those common whores touching her sparked fury in my blood. It felt wrong in every way. She was too good for that.

Dressing quickly, I grabbed my bag and hauled ass downstairs. My ire escalated at seeing her sitting at the bar, the bartender leaning over the table into her, a salacious smile on his face as his eyes roamed her.

"You are a stunning thing." He touched her cheek. "I wouldn't mind having you for breakfast."

Oh. Hell. No.

"Dziubuś." The pet name fell from my lips, a term coming deep from my past, from another life. Strolling up to her, I lifted my hand to her face, my thumb dragging over her bottom lip, hearing her suck in at my touch. "I've been looking for you. You ready to go?" I shot a look at the bartender.

"I don't think so." She pulled away, glaring at me. She turned and smiled at him. "I was just offered breakfast."

"To *be* breakfast." The man's gaze rolled over her with lust.

A growl I wasn't expecting stabbed in my throat, my hand squeezing hers as I yanked her off the stool. She hissed

160

at the pain in her ribs, but I continued to drag her out of the whorehouse and into the freezing day.

"What was that?" She yanked out of my grip.

"You don't want that." I nodded back at the place, indicating the sleazy prostitute. "Believe me."

"Don't tell me what I don't want. I can decide myself." Her fingers wiggled as if she wanted to strangle me. "Gods! Stop treating me like some kid."

"Then stop acting like one," I shot back.

"Oh yeah, you're the semblance of a functioning adult." Her voice rose with mine. "I might be young to you." She stabbed a finger in my chest. "But at least I'm not a coward."

I saw red. I saw blue. I saw black. Anger exploded behind my temples. "Coward?" I bellowed. "You think I'm a coward?"

"Yes," she screamed. "You don't face your pain; you live in it. You use it as a shield. As an *excuse.* You hide in the numbness of your drugs and the shallowness of the whores, because there you don't have to feel." Tears sprang into her eyes, and I felt this went deeper. "There nothing touches you, but you don't realize how much it hurts all those around you. You're a selfish coward."

Scarlet pushed by me, striding for the path, leaving me standing there. Speechless and knocked on my ass.

The fact this girl, a stranger, could shred through me, call me out, and leave me gutted was distressing.

But she hadn't lived through what I had. Hadn't lost both her heart and soul. *She knows nothing of real life. Of true pain and loss,* I told myself, stomping after her.

But something in my gut told me she did.

She had seen darkness.

Chapter 12
Scarlet

Snowflakes clung to my lashes, blurring my vision as I ambled down the road behind Ash. It had been hours since we had even mumbled a word to each other, which pecked at me like a chicken. The silence was only broken by a rare motorcycle or horse and buggy going by. Even though we were far out of the border patrol area, Ash still had us hide every time someone passed, his face recognizable.

My curiosity about why border patrol had his picture ate at my thoughts. What had he done? How did they know who he was? Was I with some criminal?

The questions sat on the tip of my tongue, ready to jump off, but I couldn't seem to actually ask them. The events of last night and this morning slammed my lips together in annoyance. I couldn't seem to shake all the emotions streaming through me, along with the nonstop loop of what I saw last night.

Under my jacket, heat bloomed up my cheeks at the memory. When he left the room, I couldn't sit still, pacing and restless. All my life, I had fought between holding up this image, doing and saying the right thing, and wanting to tear it all to shreds. I was split in three—me, the monster, and the darkness.

The monster won last night. It wanted out, to shed the pristine, perfect image. To let down my guard for a moment. But what I found instead... Ash in a booth, with the whore's mouth around his cock. The way Ash threaded his fingers through her brown hair as she sucked his cock, his head tipping back in pleasure. The man next to him gripped what the woman couldn't get down her throat while he jerked himself off, staring hungrily at Ash's cock. The woman choked as Ash pushed her down farther, her nails digging into his thighs.

A pulse throbbed between my thighs, and I imagined it was me instead. The vision was so sharp, I swear I could taste him on my tongue, feel him down my throat. It made the room spin around me, stealing my breath.

I ran back upstairs like the little girl he accused me of being, out of my element. Feeling unsure was a new thing for me. Confidence had never been a problem. Now all I seemed to feel was fear and insecurity.

I tried to not think about it, but the picture of what he'd been doing gripped my chest and divided me into pieces all over again. Embarrassment flooded me for even remotely wishing it was me, but the worst was jealousy. And on top of that... desire. Curiosity.

Laying in the dark room, the sounds of a bed pounding below me, along with the moans, took over my body. Slipping my fingers into my pussy, I imagined my ex over me, like I had so many times before, but it was Ash's image that kept infiltrating my mind, taking me hostage. His green eyes were bright, his mouth in a sexy smirk as he opened my legs wider, pumping his fingers in deeper, whispering what a good girl I was. I had never been into praise kink, but maybe it was because I never had anyone do it to me. Wetness dripped from me as Ash took control in my imagination, my back arching, my teeth driving into my lip, holding back a cry as my release sang through me.

Heaving, I sank back into the bed, humiliation creeping in when the door to the room burst open. The man I had secretly imagined getting me off stood there wet and only wearing a towel.

Crawling into bed with me after probably fucking both whores, he made me feel nauseous, as if I was the little woman waiting at home while he fucked around on me. I wanted to fight him to get him far away from me. When he shushed me and wrapped his arms around my body like we had just had sex, my brain struggled with truth and fiction. It was too much.

Neither of us wanted this. Our hearts were somewhere else. It was just because a warm body was next to us. But when I finally fell asleep, I didn't dream of my heartbreak or the sins I had committed. It was peaceful and sheltered, like I was cocooned away from all the nightmares dragging me down into the pits of hell.

I woke up safe. Happy... and with Ash's cock pressing against my opening, only my underwear keeping him from entering me.

A wave of need bubbled a moan up my throat. Yearning to push back into him, to feel him enter me in the hazy half-dream, where neither of us was fully awake, our bodies acting before our minds caught up.

The problem was he might be asleep, but I was wide awake.

Jolting away, I scrambled to the chair, watching him reach out for my absent body, a frown creasing his forehead.

What the fuck is wrong with you? I screamed at myself. It took everything I had not to just let it happen. Hell, not to instigate it. What would he have thought if he woke up already inside me? It was a line we couldn't uncross. *You are acting out because you miss him. My best friend. The boy my world had revolved around since I was born.*

My heart was still breaking. I couldn't take it out on Ash. *Yeah, remember what you did last time.* I drew my knees to my chest, palming my face, tears burning my eyes.

I left Vienna because I had to, to keep people safe. My friends who died were just a sample of what would come. But also because I could no longer pretend I was fine. I felt trapped in a prison of my own making. Running from my crimes. From my life. Except I felt even more lost now.

Looking at Ash sleeping, I once again was divided. I should go. Leave him to continue his journey the way he wanted without me as a burden. All I seemed to be was a burden. Too much when I tried to be me. Too many parts pulling me into the dark. He shouldn't have to take that on. And I could never let him find out the truth.

Yet, my ass wouldn't get out of the chair, sneak out of the room, and leave him. I knew the day was coming. I never should've gotten on the train to follow him in the first place. But I'm not sure I could have stopped myself if I tried. The tree fairy had something that drew people in, a moth to a flame, burning you to ashes, just like his name indicated.

Ash's head swung back to check on me as we traveled down a snowy pass, snapping me back to the present. He had to stop and slow down the last four hours, my steps getting shorter as my energy waned, matching the daylight draining from the sky. My legs ached, and blisters burned the back of my heels. My ribs throbbed and my teeth chattered.

His lips were pressed together, and I could tell he was fighting the urge to say something, grating on me even more. Last night was on me, but the way he acted this morning with the bartender? What was that? Did he think he was saving me or something? As if I were some damsel needing his help?

A scoff came up my throat at the thought. He had no idea what I was capable of. Most didn't.

"What?" Ash turned back to me again, his shoulders tense, the snow piling up on the road, making it harder to walk.

"Nothing." The response was a struggle to get through my teeth, my joints stiff with cold. Fae felt everything humans did, like cold and heat. We just didn't die from them. Though our bodies would shut down if we needed to heal. And with goblin metal, I was even more vulnerable, more susceptible to the elements and slower to recover.

Ash pinched his nose, inhaling slowly. "I swear…" he muttered under his breath.

Now it was my turn to ask, "What?"

His eyes darted to me, his head shaking.

"No, please continue. You've been huffing and puffing for the last six hours, glaring back at me. Just get it out." Finally catching up to him, my boots stopped in front of his.

"I'm the one huffing and puffing?" He laughed dryly. "You've been sighing every thirty seconds."

"No, I haven't."

"Yes, you have."

"I'm simply *breathing*." My hands tucked tighter under my armpits. "Maybe that's what's *really* bothering you."

"*May-be*," he gritted back, our eyes locked in battle.

It was in that moment I really wondered what I was doing. He certainly didn't want me with him. So why was I still here? One call and I could be home. Safe and warm.

166

You are not a clinger. You don't need anyone. I railed at myself, embarrassed I let it go this far.

"Fuck this." I turned, ready to walk back to Sebeș, when a rumble vibrated the pavement under my feet. We were on a bend in the road, not able to see what was coming, but it sounded closer than it should have—and heavy.

"Ash," I whispered his name, panic bristling up my neck, intuition scraping my stomach, The vibration and noise escalated with every second.

"*Szar.*" His arm came around me, hauling me back with him into the snow-covered field. "Get down," he ordered. Following me into an irrigation ditch, he pressed us against the side closest to the road, hoping no one would see us.

The ground shook with weight, the sound of machines tearing through the snow to the asphalt. Peeking up, I felt a hammer come down on my chest.

Tanks.

They were dated, as if they were resuscitated from some war way before my time, but the size and number of them stilled my lungs. An exhibition of ten tanks paraded along with a dozen large, covered trucks carrying more unseen items, moving in a procession line down the road.

"Military convoy," Ash muttered.

"They're traveling west." I swallowed, knowing what it meant.

"Yeah." Ash's throat bobbed. "But that's not to protect their border. That's laying down a threat to Hungary, and our country is too fragile to handle a war right now. And they know that." Emotion and fury lit behind his features. "That bitch. I know she's behind this… I'm going to kill her. I promise both of you that." He muttered so low I barely heard him, like he was talking to someone else. He wagged his head with a huff, still talking to himself. "Gods, Killian, don't take her bait. Don't do anything stupid."

My heart shuttered when the convoy came to a stop, brakes squeaking in the evening air. Men climbed out of the cabs, yelling and talking to each other, their speech too quick and convoluted for me to understand perfectly.

Ash stiffened with dread.

"What?"

"They found our footprints in the snow."

"So?" My mouth dried. Many people walked these paths—except I hadn't seen any prints but ours. They would stand out in the fresh, clean snow.

My heart was pounding as I watched a man look at the ground and point in our general direction, noting where the footsteps stopped and headed into the field. A man barked out something, and three soldiers started turning our way.

We had nowhere to go. Nowhere to hide.

"Scarlet." Ash's chest started to rise and fall, his tone filled with all the things he didn't say, but I heard them anyway. Run. And don't stop.

His eyes went behind us, across a huge field to another tree line, the darkness making the leaves blur together in one painted canopy.

Adrenaline poured into my veins, though my body shook from weakness, the metal around my wrist biting into my skin, keeping me from being able to protect myself. Protect Ash.

The men stomped toward us, searching. His eyes met mine one more time, feeling like they punched through all the cobwebs and exhaustion, giving me life. "Run!"

My legs took off, stretching as far as they could go.

"Stop!" Bellows hummed in my ear before the encroaching night was filled with gunfire.

Bullets zipped near me. Any one of them could embed into my spine or go through my brain. Game over.

Ash had warned me. Told me this was no place for me. That Romania might be the land I die in, far from my loved ones. I was used to being protected. Nothing too dangerous. But as each bullet brushed by me, missing its target, there was a strange sort of high—I had never felt more alive than I did in the hands of death.

Even when the bullets quieted, we did not stop, breaking through the tree line and jumping a stream before crossing another field. Ash weaved us through a small village several miles away before we slowed down, catching our breath.

"Think we're safe?" Sweat pooled under my clothes, my lungs heaving.

"A convoy like that can't easily turn around or come after anyone." He bent over his knees, sucking in breaths. "Plus, their order is the mission, not chasing two vagabonds. To them, we're not worth the effort."

"But if they knew who you were?" *Or me.* I lifted an eyebrow.

A devilish smile hitched the side of his mouth, his gaze finding mine, making the beat of my heart stumble. Ash wasn't just hot or gorgeous. He was sensual in his confidence, radiating a guarantee, a sultry promise of what he could offer, something which made both women and men shiver with desire.

We watched each other for a few moments before he broke our gaze, glancing away. "We need to find shelter." Ash stood straight, dragging a hand down his face. "You need to get warm and eat something."

"You too." I looked up at him as a few flakes swirled down around us, the night quiet with everyone in the village tucked in their warm homes. "You tend to be the caretaker, don't you?"

"What makes you say that?"

169

I shrugged one shoulder. "I can tell. You put everyone else before your needs."

"No, I don't." His eyes tracked mine, his expression serious, like he was actually looking at me for once. "Don't be fooled. I'm the worst of them all."

"Why do you say that?"

"Because." He loomed over me, heat crackling off him. "You'd be safely back with your family if I did." He swung around, walking into the village, leaving me a buoy in his wake.

A low firelamp flickered between us as we finished off the watery tripe soup and day-old bread. I wrapped a heavy, smelly blanket around my shoulders, the chill still finding its way into my bones, though it was ten times better than outside the storage room.

The village was small, and everything was closed. The only thing telling me people lived here was the flickers of light in the windows from their fireplaces.

Ash had stopped at a general store, noticing a light on in a flat above. He knocked on the door, a man's face peering suspiciously from the blinds upstairs. Ash reached out, taking my hand and pulling me into him.

"What are you—?"

"Follow my lead." He wrapped an arm around me as the door cracked, a chain opening just a few inches. A small dark-haired man with a mustache looked out, smoking a hand-rolled cigarette.

"Buna ziua." Hello. Ash spoke to him in Romanian.

"We are traveling through and have nowhere to sleep and nothing to eat."

"Nu problema mea." Not my problem. He was about to shut the door when Ash's voice rushed on.

"My mate is pregnant." He touched my stomach, rubbing it tenderly as if a real baby was growing there. My muscles locked up. The heat and size of his palm caressing me, the possessive way he hovered over me. "Please. It's freezing out here. I need to get her indoors and a little food for our baby."

The man's eyes moved over us, noting my shivering frame and exhaustion. Grumbling under his breath, he pointed to the back. "There is a storage room you can stay in for the night."

The man was skeptical, which I understood, but he gave us blankets, soup, and bread, waving his hand when Ash said we could pay him a few coins.

"At least we have a roof overhead." Ash dropped his spoon in the bowl, laying back on his blanket. The room held staples like huge sacks of wheat, corn, and oats, overwhelming my nose with the smell of grain.

Leaning against one of the sacks, I pulled my legs into me, setting my bowl to the side. I could still feel his hand imprinted on my flat stomach.

"Think he believed us?"

"Probably not." Ash snorted, glancing at my body. "But at least enough to ignore it."

"I could be." *I won't ever be.* "Just not showing yet."

Ash didn't reply, the firelight flickering off his eyes as he stared absently at the ceiling.

"Did you want kids?" The question blurted from me.

A scowl dug into the space between his brows. "No."

"Why not? You'd make a good father."

"Really?" He laughed, motioning around. "Yeah, great role model." He stared off again, his arms folding behind his head. I didn't expect him to continue on, startling me with his next statement. "I would never want a child to go through what I did."

"Like what?"

He drew in a long, choppy breath, letting it out in the same way.

"Before I met the people I call family, I had run away from the people who gave me life, who were supposed to be my family."

I didn't dare speak, afraid he'd stop.

"My parents were of the mindset that love and nature were above all, and to truly experience it was to give oneself over to the tree deities..." He tapered off. "Mind, soul... and *body*." His words were clipped at the end. "No matter what it meant to your blood family, the goddesses were more important. Needing a parent was being selfish, even at three." My stomach knotted at his claim. "They were the air you breathed, the food you ate, and you had to serve them every moment for this great honor." He shifted his arms, still staring above. "They found others similar to them, and they started a commune. Back then, villages had to rely more on each other to survive, but this place was different."

My throat thickened. "It was a cult."

He flinched at my words, but his chin dipped.

"And like every cult that may start off with good intentions, it twisted into something ugly. The vile side of nature and love." His throat swallowed roughly. "Orgies, switching partners, blood rituals and sacrifices."

I jerked at that. I had heard about them—blood rituals and sacrifices from the old world were sordid, explicit, and demented. Mostly illegal nowadays. Many people died or murdered others while living in them.

"That became common among the adults in the community." He went quiet for a moment. "I woke up many times to the neighbor fucking my mother or five neighbors along with my father. I watched the leader of the cult fuck my father religiously while his wife watched when my mother was on a monthly retreat," he said emotionlessly. "Our home was a one-room hut. We saw and heard everything."

"Oh gods," I whispered. Whatever freaky shit adults wanted to do, the kids shouldn't be subjected to it also.

"They'd tell me it was all in thanks to our deities. The least we could do to show how grateful we were." He rubbed at his scuff with his knuckles. "And of course, when I started to grow up, this really fucked with my boundaries and sexual understanding." He swallowed again. "The older I got, the more the elders took notice, especially the leader. He wanted me to start joining in these rituals." His voice got more distant, like he was walling up his emotions. "I was only eight."

Tears and bile thickened my throat, feeling such heartbreak for him and vile disgust at his parents and this leader. How could they let this happen? They should've protected him.

"It was almost a year of being included in these rituals when I ran away." His voice dipped, showing the emotion underneath. "I didn't understand how something, which made my parents so proud and appeased the gods, could make me feel so terrible. I knew deep down it was wrong, and I couldn't take it."

"Gods," I muttered, trying not to cry. "You shouldn't have had to. No child should go through that."

"No, but…" He pushed his fingers and thumb into his eyes. "I was selfish for leaving."

"No, you weren't," I declared. "They were the selfish

173

ones. Ash, what they did, what they let happen to you, was wrong."

"Yeah, but when I ran... I left my baby sister behind."

Oh. I could see the torment, the guilt he carried for years leaving her. "You were what, nine? A child. That is not on you."

"She needed me, and I walked out on her. *Myszko* needed me. To protect her." *Myszko*. It meant mouse in Polish.

The name he called me earlier made more sense. *Dziubuś* was Polish for *'little beak'*.

"You're from Poland?"

"That area," he replied. "Borders and territories have changed since."

"How did you get to Hungary? I mean, you were only nine."

His head turned to me, his brows lowering in question, wondering how I knew he ended up in Hungary.

"Besides some of the phrases you use, it's the way you spoke of it earlier. You called it *your* country." I shrugged one shoulder. "I figured it out."

His attention went back to the ceiling, his mouth twisting.

"Nine was seen as much older then." He sighed. "I traveled with a merchant who picked me up. He was heading back to Budapest for a trading market. He had me doing odd jobs, brushing pelts, cleaning the wagon, to pay my keep. I got off and decided to stay. It was where I found my real family."

Tugging on my lip with my teeth, I pressed for more. "Do you know anything about your biological family? What happened to your sister?"

"Most likely, she wasn't even my full sister. The

174

chances of her belonging to any male in our village are just as likely as my father." His lashes fluttered faster. "But yes, I know what happened to her. For a while, my found family and I traveled around." He cleared his throat, setting his head back on his arms. "Our journey led us close to my old village once, and when I asked around about what happened to them, someone said they had all committed suicide in a ritual, thinking the world was coming to an end. All of them were found dead. My sister was an adult by then, but I guess she had a child. A boy. My nephew died with her."

"Oh gods, Ash," I croaked. "I'm so sorry."

His lids blinked faster, his tongue sliding over his bottom lip.

"Neither my sister nor her child should have died for their beliefs—or suffer the abuse I know they probably turned on her because I wasn't there. They brainwashed her. I should have taken her with me."

"How old was she when you left?"

"Two."

"Two?" I shook my head. "There is no way you could have. You were a child, but she was a baby. You can't blame yourself."

"Why not?" His words spat out sharper. "I could have gone back for her, at least. Could have protected her." He sat up, pulling his knee up, laying his arm over it and brushing his hand through his hair. "That's why you shouldn't be here either. When anyone gets close to me, I fail, and they die."

I had no doubt that remark went deeper than just his sister.

"What was her name?" I asked softly, trying to keep him from plunging into his dark thoughts.

"Hazel."

"Well." I wrapped the blanket tighter around me. "I

175

would tell Hazel that her big brother is amazing. All he's done is protect me."

His eyes flicked up to mine, watching me for a long time.

"Think we need to get some sleep." Gravelly and low, he cleared his throat, looking away.

I nodded, knowing the topic was closed. Sinking myself onto the blanket, I curled up in a ball, my limbs frozen, my ribs aching.

Ash lowered the fire in the lantern, covering the room in thick shadows. We didn't want it completely off, as it was our only source of heat. I could hear him settle, the room going quiet and still.

"Ash?"

"Hmmm?"

"Thank you for telling me."

A long stretch of silence went on and on, and I was sure he wasn't going to respond. Tucking my head deeper into my arm, I let my lids close.

So quietly it was a murmur rumbling over my skin, he said, "You're the first person I've told the whole story to."

This time I didn't open my mouth, feeling the hiccup in my lungs from his claim, the thrill I didn't want to acknowledge of being the person he confessed to.

The old confidence I used to have, which owned me without any doubt, burned up my spine and into my brain, prompting me to act. Rising, I didn't let myself second guess as I crawled over to his blanket with my own.

"Scarlet, what are you—?" He jerked at my approach.

"I'm cold, and I want to sleep, okay?" I cut him off, not wanting to overthink or analyze my actions, my tone almost a plead. "*Really sleep*."

His green eyes caught the light, and I could tell he

understood. Knew exactly what I meant. No nightmares. No panic attacks. No ghosts haunting us. A time-out, where he and I seemed to battle back the devils wanting to take us.

He scooted over, turning on his side as I burrowed into his warm body, my back to his chest. Stretching my blanket over us, he wrapped his arm around me, tucking tightly around me, and I fell asleep, Ash protecting me from the biggest monster of all.

Myself.

Chapter 13

Ash

The farmland gradually gave way to snow-covered green forests as the elevation began to rise. The temperature dropped even more as thick trees blocked out any dim sunlight the day brought.

This was where I was happy… among the trees. My magic bristled down my skin, causing everything in me to feel more. Absorbing so much energy, I twitched with it. It would need to be released soon, or I would start to lose it.

Scarlet and I had slipped into silence again as we plodded through the snowy paths, as if last night was just a pause in our discord before the tension resumed. Sanctioning a night of sleep we couldn't seem to find anywhere else.

For most of the day, I was lost in my thoughts, my revelation last night trudging up old memories of the past. The family I left behind, the decisions I made, the regrets I carried. But it was the fact I told *her*, of all people, my full story. Warwick and Kitty knew most of it, but I never told them what my parents let happen to me, the truth of what transpired when I was barely eight years old. What I had witnessed from the age of three, when my parents joined the cult.

It never even came up at all with Kek and Lucas. Not much talking ever happened with us, though, unless it was bantering and playful.

Sourness lined my stomach at the realization of how little I knew about their lives, or them about mine. We didn't talk much besides about what we were going through at the time. We shared the connection of Věrhăza, the sense that death could take us at any time. Even when we got out, we were fighting a war, a high-stakes game that had us living on the edge. We never spoke about anything serious because we were living it.

Yet the stakes were still high, and I opened up to her. Why? What made it so easy to spill my past to her? Sharing something like that created an intimacy, a bond. I did *not* want that. Not with her. Not with anyone. We were never supposed to be that to each other.

Sliding my gaze back to her, her cheeks and nose red, her breath puffing like smoke from her lips, something twisted in my chest, and I snapped my head back around, inhaling a breath. The recollection of waking up this morning came back to me, warm and comfortable. My body had cocooned hers while my dick pushed once again against my zipper, insisting to be let free.

We were both acting as if the morning in the bordello never happened. Even in my sleep, I was aware my cock would've been inside her if she wasn't wearing panties.

A groan vibrated in my chest at the thought, my hand shifting my dick in my pants where it throbbed with need. The energy from the trees, the indecent thoughts of my mind, were like a pressure cooker.

Stop it, Ash. She's just a kid.

Did I even believe that anymore? How the hell was I in this mess?

She was some random college girl who stumbled into the same bar I was in, and now it felt like our paths were so intertwined I couldn't see straight. I needed to untangle them. To get the goblin metal off her wrist and get her home before it was too late. I could feel it—the foreboding in my soul, the sense nature was warning me through the thick shadows. Darkness was ahead.

Coming down from the mountain, I saw the outskirts of a city below, the town building up around the center. The hums of motorcycles and smells of pollution from a packed-in population lapped at my senses.

Braşov was once the sixth largest city in Romania but had risen since the fae war. Its proximity to Bucharest and centrally located between Iaşi, which bordered Moldova, and Craiova, which was close to both Serbia's and Bulgaria's borders, made it a perfect trading post, with people exporting and importing goods.

Trading hubs brought in the worst types of people. A once beautiful quaint town boasting holiday markets and tourists, with cobbled streets and painted shops, nestled between mountains, rich with history, was now bogged down with thieves, sleazy peddlers, con artists, and debauchery.

Many had moved here after the war to find work, to survive the catastrophe that happened when the fae barrier broke and magic flooded in, bringing the two realms together. And with people and the need to survive comes corruption and licentiousness.

Pulling my hood up, I tried to keep my face hidden, thankful for the darkness of night. No one would hesitate to turn me in if they recognized me from a wanted photo, knowing they could get a reward. There was no loyalty amongst thieves.

The number of people mulling around and crowding the narrow lanes between buildings had me tense. The smell of vomit and piss was heavy in some areas, while others held a rotting food odor. Homeless, drunkards, and a vast amount of off-duty military had me moving closer to Scarlet, my gaze darting around as we came to the square.

"Is it me, or does there seem to be a lot of soldiers here?" Scarlet leaned into me.

"Yeah." My attention went to all the men in guard uniforms milling around, drinking and laughing in groups, like they had a night off and no longer cared about the shady things happening around them.

This had never been a military base. Not before or after the fae war. So what were they all doing here now? Everything about it had my shoulders rolling back. Something was off.

"Stay close." I seized my hand in hers, snaking through the throngs of people. I would walk right out of this town if we didn't need supplies, but this was the last major town to get anything before we hiked up to the caves. Plus, I knew Scarlet was chilled to the bone, hungry, and exhausted. "Let's find a place where we can get some dinner and sleep." *And I can release some of this energy.*

The cheaper places were a few streets off the main square, the women and men in the windows conveying exactly what they were selling.

My feet stopped, and a pang in my gut swiveled my head to look for a simple pension down the lane. It would be more money, but taking Scarlet into a brothel suddenly seemed inappropriate.

"What's wrong?" She glanced around, her nose sniffing like she was looking for the reason for my abrupt halt.

"Nothing," I replied. "I thought you might want to sleep somewhere else tonight." My gaze went up to the women wiggling their fingers at us to enter and taste a sample.

"Somewhere else?" Her eyes danced around us. "This is the cheapest, right?"

I nodded.

"We can't spend what little money we have on a more expensive bed."

For some reason, hearing her say bed had my mind placing us in one, except we weren't sleeping.

Shaking the thought out before it settled, I shifted my weight. The energy I had absorbed earlier was making my brain malfunction. I needed to expel my excess vigor, and soon, before I did something stupid.

"This is what we can afford." She squeezed my fingers, calling attention to the fact I was still holding her hand. "Plus…" A coy smirk pursed her full lips. "They're starting to grow on me." She let go of my hand and disappeared inside.

Fuck.

I stood there for another beat, trying to pretend my dick didn't just perk up with both ears, my skin tingling with lust.

No-no-no-no-no! I yelled in my head, drowning out any other response. *You're horny. Take it out on a stranger, not her. Most of all, not her.*

All I could offer was meaningless sex; I had nothing else left. My life was only to avenge Kek and Lucas. I would not let myself think about the fact I could only orgasm the other night because I imagined her. A brain glitch when I was high.

A noise worked up my throat, my fingers scouring my temple. I needed a drink… and just a little dust to calm me down, my magic tapping at every nerve, turning my mind into a swamp of lust.

Following Scarlet in, the heat of the low-ceiling packed

room burned at my cold skin. The setup was similar to the one we stayed in at Sebeș, with gambling and music on one side, the bar and tables on the other.

A beautiful, dark-haired fae man strolled up, his features so delicate he could be mistaken for a woman. He highlighted his face with a lot of makeup and fake jewels around his eyes, a bright silk robe, and slippers.

"Welcome, my loves, to my casa. I'm the procurer here, Maestro Silk." He spoke good English, his arms swinging flamboyantly. His gaze took in both of us. "Well, aren't you two the *gorgeous* pair? My goodness... *Hell-o!*" His eyes ignited with interest, but it felt harmless. "Dirty and in need of a bath, but some of us like that, right?" He elbowed me with a wink. "And you!" He went to Scarlet, cupping her face. "Look at those cheekbones, lips, and eyes. People would die for those, including me. Oh, I'm so envious. You are stunning." He tilted her face, peering at her longer. "You remind me of someone. Who is it... Why can't I remember?" he berated himself.

"Do you have a room available?" Scarlet stepped from his grasp.

"Dragă." Sweetheart. His voice went low, like he was spilling a secret. "We have many availabilities. It's all what you want. An hour, a night, a room with extra toys, a room with equipment, a *party* room." He winked at her, biting his lips when his gaze stopped on me, making a playful growl sound at me. *"Whatever* you want."

"Just a room for her," I spoke. "Nothing else."

"Gotcha." He pointed at me. "Not the sharing type. That's fine. We welcome all here."

A laugh wedged in my ribs, wanting to bust out in hysterics at the statement. Me? Not the sharing type?

Kek and Lucas might have been the only real

"relationship" I was in with two people, but my entire sex life, even now thinking about my childhood, had been "sharing." I never imagined having just one person, not for a tree fairy. Our sex demand was way too high, and I got bored easily.

About to correct him, something kept my mouth shut, okay with him thinking Scarlet was off the table for anyone else.

"Why don't you have a seat at the bar, get something to eat, and I will go shuffle things around to get you a room." Maestro dramatically waved his arms toward the bar, new customers already pulling his attention to the door.

"Why do I have a feeling we're gonna be waiting for a room for a while?" She watched him flutter around the new people entering, probably already forgetting about us.

"Then we drink here until we pass out on the sofa over there." My hand went to her lower back, moving her to the bar. The simple touch, even through layers of clothing, shot a zing up my arm.

"Ugh, can you imagine what is on that sofa?" She shivered, climbing on a stool. "The amount of bodily fluid?"

"You think the bed we slept in the other night was any better?" I straddled the one next to her, our eyes catching in the low light, my humor dropping away at the slight blush on her cheeks, knowing what she was thinking about. Because my cock didn't forget, reminding me every moment of the heat and wetness it sought like a missile and was blocked from.

Breaking the contact, I cleared my throat, calling over the bartender. "Whiskey for me."

"Same." Scarlet nodded in agreement.

The fae woman nodded, her boobs spilling out of her bodice as she poured our drinks from a brandless bottle and slid them over to us.

184

"Oh gods." Scarlet eyes watered at the potent smell. "This is whiskey?"

"Probably made in the back there." I picked up my glass, aware this was a bad idea, yet still not stopping. *"Noroc!" Cheers.* I tapped my glass into hers, downing a huge swig.

A backdraft of flames scorched up my throat, forcing a loud huff from my lips.

Scarlet started hacking next to me, tears running down her face as she rubbed her chest. "Fuck," she sputtered, tapping at her chest. "That's pure alcohol."

Her swearing always pulled my focus. She was so elegant and prim, but at the same time, it fit her. Fit the rawness I could see in her. This darkness.

The homebrew went instantly to my head, and I was already making stupid choices as I asked the bartender for another round.

"What's on the menu?" I asked when the woman placed more drinks in front of us.

"Tripe soup."

"Oh, goodie." Scarlet finished off her first drink. Last night's soup was so watered down and salty, it barely took the edge off our hunger, but the man had been kind to feed us at all.

"Two of those, please," I ordered. We needed food, and options were slim nowadays.

Turning more to her when the bartender walked away, I felt the room blurring at the edges. "So, Scarlet…"

She didn't respond, her attention on her glass.

"Scarlet?"

Her head jerked up. "What?"

"You okay?"

"Yeah, was just spacing out." She twisted on her stool more to me, pulling off her outer jacket and brushing back her long hair. She really was stunning. Without any makeup, she looked younger, but at the same time older. More comfortable in her skin, like she didn't need to put on an act.

"Why are you here?"

"What?" She sat up higher.

"Don't you miss your family? Aren't they freaking out because you aren't home?"

"Yes, and most definitely yes."

"Then why aren't you with them?" I rested my head on my hand, the booze leaning me more into the bar. "Why are you here… with me?"

She rocked on her stool, her eyes falling on me before she looked away. "Because I have to."

"Why? Why do you have to be here with me?" Why did it sound like it meant more every time I said that?

She took a drink, tucking hair behind her ear. "For their safety and mine."

"That's not telling me much, *dziubuś*."

Her emerald gaze lifted. "Little beak." She swallowed. "Why do you call me that?"

I hadn't even realized I had just called her the name again. "Not sure." Shrugging, I gulped back whiskey, everything becoming warmer and fuzzier. "Fit, I guess." I hadn't spoken Polish in a century, so I had no idea why the old nickname came back to me.

The barkeep set down our dinners, sliding more drinks our way. In any of these places, the drunker you were, the wider your wallet would open.

Neither of us went for our food. We watched each other, continuing to drink.

"Question." I licked at my lip. "Are the people after you the cause or the reason you're running?"

"They are the result of my own actions."

"Hmmm." My head ticked down, wondering what this girl could've possibly done that was truly bad. "Interesting." A smile curled my mouth, the alcohol lowering my guard. I could hear the drag of my voice, the unintentional salaciousness of it, the tease. "So Scarlet is a naughty girl after all."

She sucked in, her neck and cheeks turning a pretty rose color, something in her eyes flashing. Wild and raw. Every fiber in my body responded to it, the hum around her charging the air between us.

She sipped, her gaze sliding to me. "What makes you think I was ever a good girl?"

Warning. Warning.

My knuckles cracked around the glass, my body so keyed up from our journey through the forest that I was vibrating with need. Even something playful and cheeky from her had me about to explode. I needed to shut this down, or I was going to do something we both might regret.

"I can just tell. You're good," I replied nonchalantly, almost insultingly. I swiveled the chair to face the room, scanning the workers' faces, hoping to find an outlet, maybe a few. My mood was telling me I'd end up in the party room tonight, except my dick didn't respond to any of them.

Her glare seared the side of my face. Ignoring it, I drank instead, drawn to the gambling room where drugs and alcohol were freely flowing. A jump of excitement leaped to the back of my tongue, instantly craving the dust they were all passing around to each other.

"Of course." A derisive snort came beside me, bringing me back to my travel companion. She scooped in a spoonful of broth, her head shaking.

"What?"

"Nothing. I don't want to get between you and your true love." She gracefully sipped in more soup.

187

"What the hell does that mean?" I turned fully to her, my forehead creasing.

She glanced back at the gambling tables, picking up exactly what had caught my attention.

"As if you aren't sitting there thinking of getting high." She placed her spoon in the bowl. "I'm surprised, though. I've heard it makes men limp."

I leaned my elbow on the counter, my voice low. "Not me." Her jab seemed to do the opposite of what she suggested.

Her gaze swung to mine, her throat swallowing. Our eyes met, and the room seemed to haze around us, blurring every line I had put in place.

"And it wasn't the only thing I was thinking about."

"Oh?" She twisted to fully face me, leaning on her arm as well, her face not even a foot from mine, her eyes smoky from drink. "What?"

My focus dropped to her mouth. Her full, wet lips suddenly felt like a taunt. A trial I might willingly fail.

Fuck. *I wanted to kiss her.*

Inhaling sharply, I pulled back, looking at the bar, my tone back to being impassive. "You should get some sleep."

Something was wrong with me. I had never acted this way. Flirty, cheeky, touchy, yes, but my control had always been in check. I played up to the line, granted, but this felt different. And I didn't like it. Kek and Lucas hadn't even been gone a year. They deserved my full focus. My promise to them. To honor them.

I downed the soup in a few gulps, finishing off my drink, numbing the constant pain behind my ribs, the fatigue being drained from me.

"My darlings!" Maestro came up behind us. "I did not forget you. Like anyone could..." He bounced between us. "You two are impossible to forget. So pretty. Mmmmmmm." He wiggled, making a happy noise, his gaze once again sliding over me. "I got you a room upstairs. It's a double bed." His eyebrows went up and down. "Figured you could make it work."

"Great." I hopped off the stool. "I'm sure it will be fine. *For her.*" I felt my next sentence roll around on my tongue, aware of what I was doing. "I will be needing other accommodations."

"Oh?" Maestro's head snapped between us, looking confused and slightly upset, as though his favorite couple had broken up.

"I will be heading to the party room." I was making my point clear. To her or myself, I wasn't sure.

"Oh..." He peered at her, almost asking if she was okay with this. She folded her arms, staring off, appearing bored. "Okay. Just you? Because I can take off the room if you both want to go."

"No." It practically came out a growl, my teeth grinding together. "Just me."

I was not sexist in any way. Women could enjoy those things with no judgment from me, but Scarlet was not the type. She had loved that idiot boyfriend her whole life. She was a one guy kinda girl. Someone you loved, married, had a kid with. She needed a man who only craved her. Whatever shit I was into, she should not be lured in or made to feel priggish because she didn't.

"Of course." Maestro nodded, waving his arm, forcing a smile back on his painted lips. "Follow me."

Sensing her eyes on me, feeling her burning anger, I could not look at her.

I didn't want to see what kind of guy I was in her eyes.

Chapter 14
Scarlet

Pacing back and forth in the room, the wood floor squeaking with my heavy stomps, I twirled my ring around my finger, a scream building up in my throat.

How fucking dare he…

I had never been treated as a child, not even when I was one. My parents always treated my brother and me with the full respect of an adult, making our own choices, whether they were successful or failures. They let us grow and experience that. Granted, I always had a role I had to play, and even when I was young, I was expected to live up to that responsibility. So to be treated like a baby who couldn't make her own choices?

He had no idea who the fuck he was dealing with…

"Aaaahhh!" I let out an aggravated cry.

At the bar, for one second, I thought he wanted to kiss me, then the next, he was patting me on the head and sending me to bed with a bottle.

"Asshole," I muttered. I didn't even want him to kiss me… I didn't. It was just the fact Ash was acting like the very idea of me joining him was unthinkable. That I would never do such a thing. Or he wouldn't allow such a thing.

My lids lowered, a wicked smile growing on my face, my brother's voice coming into my head.

"Oh, no… I know that look." He shook his head. *"It usually means I will get grounded also."*

"Come on, little brother." I smiled. *"Live a little."*

Stripping off my sweater and jeans, left in my knickers and tank, I fluffed my hair around my shoulders, still buzzing from the homemade whiskey.

My brain was not thinking past showing him up as I made my way up to the attic where the party room was. I wanted him to be aware I had the right to be there too. I was almost a twenty-one-year-old woman who made her own decisions.

He couldn't tell me what to do.

My stomach fluttered as I neared the door. Music slipped out, but it didn't cover up the moans coming from the room.

My feet halted for a moment, fear tapping at my drunken mind. It wasn't too late to turn back, run back to the room, and pretend this never happened.

Don't be a fucking coward.

Rocking forward, I twisted the handle with a shaky hand, taking another breath before I opened the door.

Whatever I was expecting… I wasn't ready.

The floor was covered in pillows and cushions, and two swings hung from the ceiling. Various whips, handcuffs, and toys were on a table, while a few smaller tables were loaded with trays of drugs and alcohol. Music played in the background, giving a backdrop to the cries throughout the room.

191

Over twenty people filled the space in different sections, and no one was wearing a bit of clothing.

A woman right near the door was getting pummeled as she sucked a man off while another man fucked him. The swings were filled with women getting eaten out by what looked like two snake-shifters while a man jerked off to them. A human man wearing a collar was being whipped by two fae women in the middle of the room. A group of five were at one end, doing things I tried not to watch, but couldn't stop.

I had messed around and been to parties, which had gotten kind of wild. Or so I thought. It seemed like kid stuff compared to this, and it made me embarrassed and insecure, far out of my element. But I couldn't deny the flip of that, how intrigued I was. Energy skimmed over my body, my nipples hardening, pleasure drenching the room until all you could do was breathe it in. The need to let go, to orgasm, trembled through my body, hunting for one. My gaze searched the room, stopping on the man I was looking for.

Naked, Ash bent over a tray, snorting in a line of dust. With his back to me, I watched his movements, the way his perfect ass flexed, his muscles moving under his taut skin, his broad shoulders, and those two indentations on his lower back.

My gods...

You'd have to be dead not to notice him, perfectly aware he was absolutely one of the most beautiful and sexy men you'd ever know in *any* lifetime.

Wetness soaked my underwear, my breath hitching, wanting him to turn around. See me standing there. My need to see his response to my presence was irrational, like I actually cared that he found me attractive. That he wanted me.

A blonde woman came behind him, her hand sliding down his back, running over his firm ass. She whispered something in his ear before her voluptuous body dropped to her knees behind him. Her tongue licked down the crease in his ass, sliding her tongue across his balls. He gripped the table, his body pushing back into her, his head tipping forward.

Red flashed over my eyes, a growl climbing my throat, my magic battling at the seams, something deep wanting to spill off my tongue. I wanted to tear her away from him. To shred into her. He was not hers to touch...

Kill her. The voice bubbled up, whispering the words in my ear, showing exactly what I could do. Oxygen snapped up through my nose, my body jolting back as I slammed back the dark thought, the desire to act on it.

"Wow. You are the most stunning thing in here." A pretty fae man strolled up, his hand sliding across my belly as he came around me. "Think we need to take these off." His other hand went under my tank, skating over my healing ribs, the tips of his finger brushing under my breasts, tingling my skin. "Way overdressed."

My head felt foggy, my reactions slow, as if my limbs were too heavy. The alcohol in my system blurred the fear, and the room's energy was like an aphrodisiac. And I couldn't stop staring at Ash and the woman, terrified of what I had felt, both in fury and turned on.

"Unless this is what gets you off?" His voice was heavy in my ear, his teeth nipping at my neck, sliding one hand between my thighs as the other caressed the underside of my boobs. "You like watching?" He followed where I was staring. "Ahh, yes. I enjoy looking at him also." One hand dipped into my knickers, brushing over my pussy. "Watch him while I get you off, beautiful."

I couldn't seem to say no, letting his fingers dip lower, parting me. My throat hitched. He groaned in my ear, slipping in deeper. "Gods, you're wet. You feel so good, *Zânǎ*."

As if Ash heard him, could sense me in the room, his head snapped back right as the man's fingers pushed inside me, shaking me violently. My mouth parted as Ash's green eyes landed on mine.

The entire world stopped, halting on a pinpoint. I felt nothing but Ash, his gaze embedding into me, *his* fingers sinking in me, *his* lips at my throat, his breath on my skin. I could feel him so acutely, as if it was the only thing he wanted as well.

The man groaned in my ear, pushing two fingers inside me, his thumb rubbing over my clit, dropping Ash's gaze to the man's hand pumping deeper into me.

Then, in a blink, the world started moving again, and everything changed. Fury exploded across Ash's face, his frame puffing up. His jaw slammed shut as he pushed the woman away. My gaze couldn't help falling on the huge cock swinging between his legs, hardening as he strode for me.

"Get your fucking hands off her." Ash shoved the man, stumbling him back.

"Hey, man. She was enjoying it." He held up his hands, then licked the ones that were inside me.

Ash turned red, his arm swinging out to strike him. "Fucking piece of shit."

"Ash!" I grabbed for his arm. "Stop."

"Listen, if she's your girl and you don't want to share, you shouldn't be in here." The man huffed and walked off.

Ash tipped on his feet, ready to go after the fae man.

"What the fuck was that?" I exclaimed.

Ash's head snapped to me, his nose flaring. He swiped his clothes from a hook on a wall and hauled me out the door.

"Hey." I wiggled against him. "Stop!" I broke away, facing him. "What are you doing?"

"Me?" He yanked on his briefs furiously. "I could ask

you the same thing." He stepped closer, looming over me. I'd seen Ash mad before, but now he vibrated with rage. "Why were you in there?"

"Because I wanted to be," I shot back, not backing away one inch, though he continued to use his height, his body practically touching mine. "I can do what I want, when I want. You have no say over that."

His chest heaved, his voice going low and tight. "You don't want to be in there."

"Why not?" I folded my arms. "Because you think me a child? Too innocent to enjoy sex?"

A nerve in his eye twitched. "No."

"Then what, Ash?" I was ready to fib through my teeth. "I left you alone to do your thing. Why couldn't you have the same respect for me?"

"Left me alone?" His hand flattened between my breasts, shoving me. My back slammed into the wall, sparking fire up my spine. Ash dipped his head down close to my mouth, ire pumping through him. "All I could feel was you in that room like a fucking spell." I sucked in. "And don't tell me you weren't there for me. You wanted *me* to see you getting off by some stranger. You wanted me to know you were there."

My chin lifted, ready to deny the claims.

"And you shouldn't have been in there because you're too good for shit like that." He snarled. "You deserve better." He pushed away from me and disappeared down the hall.

Staying pinned against the wall, I couldn't move, my body still throbbing, my breath catching as my mind caught up.

He was right. I did want him to see me. For him to know I was at his level. Not some sheltered girl who lived in a privileged bubble. And I did like when he watched me, loved how his eyes darkened with desire, his cock hardening when he came for me. That I could affect him. As he did me...

It was loneliness and lust. That's it. We were stuck together. It was perfectly normal to feel this way, right?

Sliding down the wall, I put my face in my hands.

Nothing about Ash and me felt normal.

Plumes of vapor puffed from my mouth, the freezing temperature seeping through every piece of clothing, infiltrating my skin. The sun's slow rise deepened the shadows where I leaned against the outside of the bordello, hoping the fresh air would pull me out of my contemplations.

I had slept horribly. Every noise, every footstep near the door, had me holding my breath, wishing it wasn't and was Ash returning to the room.

He never came, allowing my mind to play out the scenarios. He was the one who was making a woman scream down the hallway multiple times that night, the one causing the bed to squeak above me, or making the man moan in the room next to mine.

Covering my ears, I tried to push thoughts of Ash away and *purposefully* think of my ex. That used to be effortless. His eyes, his laugh, his ghost of a smile, the way his large arms would wrap around me, making me feel so safe. Gods, I had been so in love with him, so sure we were meant to be. I truly believed he would get over his crush on her and see what was before him the whole time. I ignored the way he watched her, the same longing in his eyes I held for him.

Maybe I could've continued to ignore it because she

waved him off, denying she felt anything for him, pretending he was a child to her, but the moment she stopped lying to herself, I had no hope. He was completely hers.

It wasn't just an axe to my heart, but to my ego. I wasn't told no often. And I was never without a stream of admirers. I had men of all ages from all over the world telling me how stunning I was, how incredible I was, and how they'd give anything to be with me. I hadn't cared about any of them. I only wanted him. Only thought about him. Built my fantasy future around him.

When he ran to her, my world, real and fantasy, crumbled. What I did in retaliation, trying to cope with the pain, would leave a scar on my soul and blood staining my hands.

"There you are." Ash stomped out of the front door, pulling on his jacket, his attitude still full of vinegar.

He appeared exhausted, with bags puffing his red eyes, but the asshole still had the audacity to look hot as hell. How fair was that?

"I was looking for you," he grumbled, pulling back his hair into a knot.

"I was right here." I folded my arms, gazing down the cobble path.

"Guess my mind-reading skills are lacking today," he quipped, his brow pulled down, staring off. Neither of us was fully looking at the other, pretending last night didn't happen, which was harder than it should've been. Images of his sculpted ass, powerful thighs, and muscles rippling down his back haunted me. The way his cock swung between his legs like an elephant trunk, stiffening as he walked to me.

As if Ash sensed the turn of my thoughts, his eyes snapped to me. Inhaling, his gaze traveled the bloom in my cheeks, stopping on my lips.

Heat flourished under my skin, my core squeezing with need. I had no doubt last night, in that moment, in that room, I would have let the fae get me off and then let Ash fuck me while the man watched. The thought overwhelmed me, the barest truth, and I was stunned by how turned on I was at the idea.

Ash snapped his head away from me as I looked the opposite way, both of us moving on our feet, glancing everywhere but at each other.

"We need to get supplies." He took off down the lane, not needing a response from me.

Hitching the bag onto my shoulder, I followed behind, purposely keeping a distance between us.

Striding down the passage out to the main square, I saw vendors setting up for the day, holiday decorations draped above the unloaded wagons, and people milling around the minimal Christmas tree. I had no idea what day it was, but I knew Christmas was close.

My chest squeezed with thoughts of my family at this time of year. The love, laughter, warmth, and craziness the holidays brought. But even before Ash, I had not planned to return home this year. The memories were too raw, my heart weak, and my darkness was too volatile. I was not ready to face it or face them being together. Face what I had done.

By now, I had no doubt my parents realized something was wrong, were worried, and were looking for me, but it was better for no one to know where I was. I needed to keep everyone safe.

The sweet smells of *gogoşi, kürtöskalács,* and other various pastries being sold by vendors wafted into my nose, my stomach rumbling. I knew Ash couldn't have heard my stomach protest, but he veered toward the stands as if he had, sensing my hunger before I could even speak up.

"Two coffees, donuts, and a chimney cake," he ordered in Romanian, pulling a few coins out of his pocket.

The man behind nodded, getting our order.

"Here." Ash handed me a black coffee. In the West, you could get it with every type of milk, flavoring, or sugar, but in the East, those extras were luxury items. Something so simple as sugar, all my friends would take for granted.

I blew on the hot beverage, ignoring the watery brew scalding my tongue as I sipped it down.

"Thanks." Ash nodded at the vendor, taking the parchment-wrapped fried goods, the steam curling into the frosty morning. I followed Ash like a puppy on a leash, the scent of the pastries making me prance behind him, begging for a taste.

Sitting on a step, he waited until I was settled, then handed me a couple of Romanian donuts.

"Oh, fuck," I moaned around the hot, crispy dough, fanning my hand at my tongue, swallowing it before I chewed. I popped in another small bite right after as I tore off a piece of the chimney cake, already stuffing it in my mouth.

A snort came from Ash, drawing my eyes up to his. He sat on the step above mine, his coffee between his feet, a donut pinched in his fingers, his head wagging. A smile hinted at his mouth as he watched me.

"What?" I muttered, gulping down a bite.

"Did you chew, or did you just *swallow* it all down?" A brow lifted.

Pink flooded back into my cheeks, not for the embarrassment of eating like a scavenger, but for the dirty places my mind went at his query. I didn't trust my response, my tongue and mind at war.

"It's the first time I've seen you eat as if you enjoy food instead of treating it like a duty." He popped a *gogoși* into his mouth, engrossing me in the way his mouth moved.

I huffed, putting my focus back on the chimney cake. "I enjoy food."

"Do you?" He tugged a piece of *kürtöskalács* from the one I was holding in my hand, regaining my attention. "Usually when someone is ravenous, they consume everything, not caring about the mess."

I held the air in my lungs, not sure if he meant the double meaning, but I felt it slide down between my thighs. Everything this man said or did this morning seemed to invoke dirty thoughts and images of last night.

And I hated it.

My one act of defiance changed everything. A desire I could ignore before blossomed under my skin, itching my muscles and making me restless and irritated. I was aware of him before, but now I couldn't seem to shake the sensation of him swathing me, not letting me breathe or think clearly. Thus the reason for blurting my next words.

"You should see how ravenous and messy I get when I'm hung—" *Shut up!* My teeth slammed together, realizing what I was about to say.

"What?" His brow furrowed.

I shook my head. "Just when I'm *really* hungry." I shoved another piece of fried dough into my mouth, shutting me up.

I knew Ash didn't buy it, like he could feel the untruth coming off me.

Feeling his gaze burn into me, my eyes lifted to his mossy green stare. His hand reached out to me, a thumb sliding over the corner of my mouth, forcing air to hitch in my lungs.

"Crumbs." His voice came out gravelly. His eyes tracked mine with a reserve, as if he was also being dragged into this force field against his will. His throat bobbed as he slowly trailed the pad of his thumb over my bottom lip, his touch sparking energy through my veins, clipping my breath.

What the hell were we doing?

But I didn't stop him. In fact, I did the exact opposite.

My tongue pushed against his thumb, tasting the cinnamon still coating it. A noise rumbled in his throat, only enticing me to do it again. Air funneled through his nose when my tongue licked purposely around his finger, getting every speck of sugar.

A nerve in his jaw jumped, and he barely rumbled out my name. "Scarlet—"

"Raven!"

The name pierced the quiet morning like a bullet, automatically jerking my head toward the voice.

Ice filled my veins, terror screaming through my bones as my entire world tipped over, spilling out my worst fears. They found me.

But my body froze seeing the familiar face call for me, disbelief at seeing her alive. About to sob in relief, rising to run to her, I noticed the men walking with her.

Dread stopped her name on my tongue. Relief and joy soured and turned to fear and dread.

And then utter betrayal.

Chapter 15

Ash

Hearing her moan, her eyes fluttering closed when she bit down on the fried donut, everything in my body went taut like the strings of a violin. Thoughts of the night before flooded back, though I had spent all night trying to exorcise them from my mind. Normally, I would have gone downstairs and drank until I passed out, but my limbs were very restless. A need I would not identify had me running out of the brothel, getting as far from her as I could.

I had walked almost all night, wanting so badly to enter the next whorehouse I found and find release from my edginess. But I didn't. Something kept stopping me from going in and kept pulling me back to the one she was in.

Now, watching her devour the pastries in front of me, a moment of seeing the untamed side of her had my hand reaching out like she was someone I could touch freely and intimately. My brain jarred to a stop, spinning in reverse, while my body did the exact opposite. Leaning into her, addicted to the feel of her skin, the curve of her mouth, the way the sugar sprinkled over her full bottom lip, slightly chapped from the cold.

My gaze locked on her lips, last night fucking with my head.

Seeing her in that room, in *my* element, changed something I didn't want altered. Now all I could see was her standing there in her underwear, her cheeks flushed as his fingers pumped into her pussy, getting off while she watched *me*.

She didn't belong there. Yet to my complete dismay, my cock turned painfully hard the instant I saw her. Making it even more clear, even with the woman on her knees sucking my balls into her mouth, my body hadn't responded as it should have. It responded to the person it shouldn't have. Like it was now.

Stop touching her.

I was about to listen to myself when her tongue swiped over the pad of my thumb, licking the cinnamon off my skin and sending shockwaves through my system. Need plowed through me like a blizzard, spinning everything into a blur. Branches from the Christmas tree snapped, my molars grinding together as I tried to contain the magic suddenly snapping from me. The impulse to kiss her, to slide my cock down her throat, to taste her...

My voice barely made it above a whisper, a question and a demand in one.

"Scarlet—"

"Raven!" a woman yelled.

Scarlet's head jerked to the side, her eyes widening, her mouth parting. Alarm dropped into my gut, my head swinging, following her gaze.

What. The. Fuck.

A familiar tall blonde walked toward us, her eyes a violet-blue, telling me she came from a family of pure seelie fairies. Her hair was tied up in a high ponytail, wearing all black and a long coat, her younger face and high cheekbones finally registering in my brain who she was.

The friend of Scarlet's who had been shot the night in the pub in Vienna. She should've been dead. The fire alone should have killed her.

My attention jumped to the five men who came up next to her, one smiling smugly at us.

Oh. Fuck. Nikolay the Bloody.

A gasp came from Scarlet, hurt and anguish overflowing from her eyes. I could feel the betrayal slice through her, the understanding her friend was not who she seemed.

The Russian men lifted their weapons, pointing at us.

"Raven, don't run," the girl spoke to her. "I don't want to hurt you."

An anguished cry came from Scarlet, her head wagging like she still couldn't comprehend what was going on.

All I saw was the guns, the danger. Nothing else mattered.

Bolting up, letting the coffee and pastries spill at our feet, I grabbed Scarlet's arm, yanking her with me, seeing the men raising their weapons.

"Run!" I ordered her, both of us taking off across the square.

Bullets penetrated the air, sending innocent civilians screaming and ducking for cover. We had been shot at many times before, but a deeper panic wound around my lungs. The idea of one of those bullets going through her, ending her life… taking her away…

A flash of recalling a bullet going between Lucas's eyes, his life gone from mine forever in scarcely a split second.

No.

Shoving her in front of me to get her out of reach, I was ready to feel an iron ball sink into my skin. The bullets flew around us, embedding into the storefronts as we sprinted for an alley.

"This way." My hand wrapped around hers, tugging her down a passage. We weaved around trash bins, wagons, and drunks still passed out in their own urine. In sync, we moved together, zigzagging through lanes, hearing boots strike the cobbles behind us and barks of Russian growing louder.

Turning down a lane, I realized too late it was a dead end. The path backed up to an old human church.

"Fuck!" I hissed under my breath, my eyes searching for a way out as the men gained on us. I reached for a door handle, and it popped open. "Come on." Rushing Scarlet in, our feet hit the creaky wood floor.

"Stop!" A stout, shorter man in a robe held up his hand, trying to slow us down.

"Sanctuary!" Scarlet blurted out, running by the man as I herded her toward the confession booth.

"Think it's time to start confessing your sins, *mroczny*." *Dark one* in Polish.

"Why not you?"

"If I started on my sins, we'd never leave here." I prodded her through the door, cramming in behind, shutting the door right as I heard Russian voices come through the back door. I turned to face the opening, her front against my back. The space was only designed for one person, so my body pressed firmly into hers. My hand tugged out the gun in my harness, ready to shoot the first person who opened the door.

"Stop! This is a house of God," the clergyman boomed.

"Not my god," one of the Russians snarled.

"No violence or blood shall be spilled in here."

"Then you better tell us where they went." I recognized Nikolay's timbre. "The girl and guy who ran in here."

"Who?"

"Do not play a fool, Reverend," the woman said, her accent American. I felt Scarlet's body jolt at the voice, her nails digging into my thigh where one hand gripped my pants, the other held her knife. This girl had been at the bar with her that night, a friend, so why was she here with the Russians? Especially because they shot her. It made no sense.

"I have many men and women coming in here," the clergyman replied calmly.

The sound of a gun being cocked clicked off the high ceilings. Boots clipped over the wood floor, sounding like two were circling him while two others were searching the church. My finger rubbed over the trigger, my body tense against Scarlet's, feeling her heartbeat slam against my back.

"You disappoint me," the girl replied.

"Please. There is to be no blood spilled in here," the man pleaded, though he still kept calm.

"Then answer us," Nikolay threatened.

The handle to the confession booth rattled, my muscles locking up, my finger pressing firmer down on the trigger. It wouldn't be terribly hard to break the lock.

Fuckfuckfuck.

"I spotted a man and woman exit the door over there," the priest exclaimed loudly, the rattle at the handle stopping.

"Go," the girl ordered someone, the man at the confession booth moving away.

Two pairs of feet scuffed over the wood floor, the creak of the side door opening and closing.

"You better have spoken the truth, Reverend," she warned. "Though I've seen far too much hypocrisy and lies from your kind to truly believe you."

"Believe or not, I spoke no lies." Technically he probably did see a man and woman exit there at some point, just not us.

There was another long pause.

"Raven?" Her voice rang off the stone, bouncing back. Hearing that name again, my neck craned back to my companion. A prickle that had been nagging the base of my spine for a long time was growing louder. "If you are here, know you won't escape me again. I know you too well. I know how you think. You will pay for your crimes. And so will your family."

"You cannot threaten in the place of worship."

The woman laughed. "Right. Centuries of greed, debauchery, gluttony, and rape, and I'm the bad one?"

"I think you need to leave now," the reverend stated.

"And here I thought you were open to everyone." She laughed again.

"Go."

"If we find out you are harboring them, Reverend…" Nikolay spat. "I'll have no qualms about slitting your throat."

Sounds of their feet moved across the floor, the door slamming behind them, leaving silence in their wake.

Scarlet exhaled, her lids shutting for a moment before reopening and finding mine still on her, searching her face. Anger started to fill my chest and take over my mind, my gut screaming with a truth I seemed to know.

Her eyes tracked mine, seeing the fury and confusion in them, but before we could utter a word, the door to the confession booth opened, the clergyman standing there with a key in one hand, waving us on with the other.

"Come on," he hissed. "Follow me. I know a secret exit."

Jerking away from her, I pushed my thoughts away, following him down steps into the crypt.

"Keep going down, and it will take you to a door." He waved us on. "That door will lead you out to the street on the back side of the church."

"Thank you." I nodded at him, waiting for her to proceed before me.

Together we ran for the exit.

But I knew the girl I ran in with, the one I met at the pub, wasn't the girl running out with me now.

Slipping across town, we ventured into the more desolate area, the block housing built in the communist time, when the government, not necessarily the people, was aligned with the Soviet Union. It was a grim and dark time in Romania, showing how strong the people were to battle through and fight for their country.

Someone like Scarlet, growing up in America, could never understand what it was like living under true repression. The people in the East understood the darkness of starvation, misery, grief, and cruelty. And since the fae war, many countries that walked the line of democracy fell back over the line, sinking into the impoverishment of totalitarianism again.

My companion stayed right on my heels, not uttering a word, though I could feel her need to say something to me. She seemed to grasp I was walking a tightrope, my body vibrating with adrenaline and anger, keeping myself on the task of getting us safely off the streets before I let anything leave my mouth.

Finding a room to let, which had skinny children, flea-bitten dogs, and bony chickens wandering outside, I handed over more of our dwindling coinage. I recognized we'd soon have to find a way to get more money for supplies before we headed up to the caves.

The old man happily took our money, showing us to the sparse one-room in the old apartment building, which probably violated every code—if they had any of those here.

A single rickety bed was pushed against the wall by a window, with two wooden chairs and a table.

"*Toaleta pe hol*." The man pointed down the hall to the toilets before shutting the door on us.

Silence rang in my ears as I set down my backpack. The awareness of being safe for now only let my fury seethe to the surface.

"Ash."

Hearing her voice snapped any illusion of calmness I had. Moving in a blink, my hand grasped her collarbone, shoving her against the wall with a thud. A gasp parted her lips, her eyes wide as I loomed over her, twitching with fury.

"Who the fuck are you?"

"What are you talk—"

"I'm not stupid," I seethed. "You think I didn't notice when sometimes I call your name, and you don't respond?"

Her jaw ticked, lips pinning together, her eyes lowered.

Flattening her firmer into the wall, tipping her head up to mine with my thumb, forcing her gaze to mine. "Your name isn't Scarlet, is it?"

Her eyes were defiant, her silence shattering any calmness, drying up my patience and allowing my fury to take control. I let it.

"Tell me," I roared. "Who the fuck are you?" I pinched her chin between my fingers. "Because the Russian Mafia wouldn't go this far to track you if you were merely some rich kid. And I recognized the girl with them. She was with you at the bar that night. They shot her…" But now I realized they shot her in the hip. Something she could heal from. But they put a bullet through the other man's brain. The Mafia isn't compassionate toward women. They should've killed her also. "Who is she? Why is she with the Russians?"

My companion sucked in through her nose, but she tried to quickly cover it up, her jaw tightening.

"Baszd meg!" I slammed my free hand against the wall by her head. "Tell me! Because it's my life you are risking here as well. I have a right to know."

"Oh, now you give a fuck about your life," she spat back, trying to push me away, flinching at the ache it caused her ribs.

Re-gripping her chin, I tapped her head back into the wall, getting about an inch from her mouth, feeling her breath lick against my neck.

"My life is for *me* to sacrifice or give, not for *you* to decide." My voice was low and gritty. This unfathomable urge to offend her, make sure she knew her place, propelled my mouth. "Lucas and Kek are worth my life… you are *not*."

My words slapped like a whip, making her flinch. She shoved me with more power than I was expecting, stumbling me back.

"Yes, I get it. They were the only reason worth living." She fumed, her arms wrapping around her fractured ribs. "You've made it perfectly clear how you feel about me."

"Are you sure?" My jaw was tight, my feet stepping back for her.

"I know you don't want me here. You've never wanted me here." She strode for the bed, grabbing her backpack from it. "So why don't I give you exactly what you want." She marched for the door, causing a strange panic to spike my heartbeat.

"Ooohhh, no no no." I moved in front of her, blocking her exit. Grabbing her arm, I shifted her back farther into the room. "You don't get to walk away now."

"Why? It's what you want."

"Tell me what the hell is going on." I ignored her claim, getting in her face again. "Who is that woman? How are you involved with Nicolay? I heard her call you Raven... is that your name?"

Her head jerked to the side, her lids blinking, her tongue sliding over her bottom lip.

"Is it?" Though I already knew.

"Yes," she replied quietly.

Backing up, a sense of betrayal rolled my hands into fists. A part of me wasn't surprised at all, like the whole time I knew the other name didn't fit her.

"Scarlet is my middle name. It was my grandmother's name." She shifted on her feet. "My first name is Raven." With her long dark hair and beautiful, refined features, it was as though the moniker was made for her, was her in every aspect. And I recognized it as if I identified before I actually knew...

Dziubuś—my little beak.

"So you lied to me?"

"Like you haven't lied to me." She flung out her arms.

"I have never lied to you."

"I didn't know who I could trust."

"Are you kidding?" I motioned around the room, tapping at my chest. "You are the one who stalked me. Followed me all the way here."

"I know." Her cheeks colored, and she turned away from me.

"Why was that girl who was partying with you in the bar now with the Russians? I thought she was your friend."

211

"I thought so too." Raven brushed her hand over her face, pacing in the tight space, a devastating truth reflecting on her features. "But this whole time…" She wiped her eyes. "I thought she was someone I could trust. My family could. Someone I called a friend." She cleared her throat. "I feel so stupid. How could I not see the truth?"

"Do you know her connection to them? Why are they after you?"

Raven's head lowered, her long hair curtaining around her face.

"Scar—Raven?" I corrected myself. Her name sparked off my tongue, feeling natural and commanding. Names held power with fae, and now that I knew her real one, I could see the effect it had on her when I uttered it, feel it hum in my bones.

A shiver ran down her spine, her breath catching. Her head shook as she moved farther away from me, staring out the window.

"What happened?" Alarms were warning me that this young coed wasn't as innocent and sweet as I thought. "Raven…"

Her body jolted at my commanding tone, importance wrapping around her name.

"I…" She folded her arms. "I did something. Unforgivable."

"What?" I moved closer. "What did you do?"

She stared out the window, her voice thick. "I killed someone."

To most, it might be a frightening declaration to hear. To me, the life I had lived since I was born, and even more so when Warwick and Kitty were running a city, death was often something we dealt with daily. And many deserved it.

"Did you do it out of necessity?"

Her head shook, her lower lip trembling. "No," she croaked.

"Tell me what happened."

"I-I was in a bad place." She fought back her tears, her gaze locked on something outside. "I had just found out about my ex that they had slept together the night before. I was a mess, and this guy was there flirting with me. He was hot, and with a lot of wine… He was perfect to take my hurt out on." She wiped quickly at her eyes, gaining control of herself. "It was supposed to be revenge sex. A night I could pretend I wasn't hurting." She gulped. "But I lost control. And he died."

"Lost control?" My brows rose. "He died while having sex with you?"

She nodded.

"Like in the act?"

Her head bobbed again.

Damn…

Agony flooded her features, making me wish I had kept my mouth shut. But holy shit. The refined princess here was more feral than I gave her credit for.

Gazing at her, I couldn't help but look at her differently, the innocent view I had of her before rubbing off. But what did it say about me that I found her more fascinating?

"O-kay." I kept my voice soothing. "We'll get back to that, but can I ask what it has to do with the situation we are in?"

Her head twisted to me, her green eyes bright with unshed tears, her expression severe.

"He was the son of someone *very* important, who secretly controls the Russian Mafia."

Oh. Fuck.

"Az istenfáját!" I ran my hand through my hair. "That's

213

why you're running? They're after you because you killed one of their own?"

"His family isn't really Mafia, but—"

"It doesn't matter. Even if they are hired… they won't stop coming after you." I ran my hand down my head, rubbing my neck. We were fucked. "And your friend? She works with them?"

"I guess so." Raven lifted her shoulder, her head bowing, and I could feel the hurt and betrayal. "I didn't know. Eve was someone I trusted, my family trusted. Someone I thought cared about me. Cared about Reid. Now he's dead." She swallowed back a sob. "I can't go home. I can't put my family in that situation."

"They'll go after them anyway." I shook my head. "Especially if they can get to you by going after them."

"It's more complicated than that." She twisted her ring around her finger, staring down at the red stone. "I've already been such a burden to them. I've caused so many problems. More than you know."

"That's what family is for. I'm sure they'd rather have you home. Safe."

"I'm sure your family would say the same about you."

Touché.

"It's better I'm not there. For now," she said adamantly. "As I said, it's really complicated."

"Looks like we have time for complicated." I plunked down on the bed. We needed to lie low for a bit, find a way to get money, and come up with a plan.

She fully turned to me, her arms wrapped around her stomach. "You first. Tell me about Kek and Lucas."

My spine went rigid, my defense walling up at hearing their names come out of her mouth. They didn't belong there; they were mine to speak of, to think about, to possess. Her uttering their names dropped guilt into my gut, making them feel more distant, like I was losing them. Letting my vow to them drift away.

The sudden need to escape the sharp pain, the craving for fairy dust, urged me to my feet, heading for the door.

"Where are you going?" She jerked from the window, traveling to me.

"I'm gonna get us some food," I muttered. And alcohol.

Slamming the door, I stomped out of the apartment building, my head rolling with everything I had discovered and the severity of our situation. Going after Sonya and Iain was going to be dangerous enough, but now we had the Russian Mafia after us.

I held my head low, drops of rain splattering down on my hood as heavier clouds promising snow rolled in from the horizon. I trekked across the wet cobblestones, my body edgy and alert. Though I wasn't sure if it was for the right reasons. Watching out for any threat, my mind kept slipping back to what Raven had confessed.

I should've been more upset she lied about her name, but in truth, I was kinda proud. She was smart enough to realize names had power, and she hadn't known me enough to fully trust me. Which made me the idiot. I hadn't even contemplated she was anything more than what she presented. A young, naive college girl who got in way over her head. Not a threat, and certainly not someone who had a marked history.

Not someone who killed a guy during sex.

A flash of her riding someone, her head thrown back,

her breasts bouncing, losing complete control, invaded my mind.

Fuck.

I adjusted my cock as the image put me under her instead, my hips snapping into her just as hard, sweat covering us, moans filling the room.

My dick hardened, pushing against my zipper. It had been happening a lot more lately, like my sex drive was waking up out of a coma after losing Kek and Lucas.

Waking up for her...

A growl came from my throat as I tried to shove the full movie happening in my mind back into the archives.

Did she give this guy a heart attack? How old was he? Human? Fae? Good enough for her? Clearly not worthy enough to handle her. How wild was she in bed?

I had so many questions, but they were all for something I shouldn't care about. Should have no interest in finding out details to. That was her personal life.

I didn't care.

But everything that had happened this morning, running from one of the most feared Mafia groups, and all I kept thinking about was her and this guy. She fucked a guy to death...

What a way to go out. Sounded good to me.

The need for sex, need for fairy dust, need for something I couldn't even put my finger on prickled over my body as I walked into a pub. It was busy for a midmorning, the cold weather driving people in for warmth, getting it from either fire or alcohol.

I needed a drink, and I could get hot food to take away for us. Two birds, one stone kind of thing. Though the craving to release some of my tension was what propelled me through the doors, wishing for more than liquor to be found here.

A mix of fae and human, women and men, milled around the small, dark bar. Debauchery covered the room in an oily film. Some of the clientele appeared as if they had just gotten off a shift at the factory, some preparing for a day on their back—or up against a wall.

I respected brothels. At least they were regulated. Workers got wages, security, and room and board. Freelance prostitution was the bottom of the barrel. You had no rights, no protection, and barely got enough money to get your next meal, forcing you to work round the clock. And every client might be your last. The murder rate was the highest with hookers, who usually had no one to even notice they were gone.

This pub was full of sex workers, which brought in the upper-class men looking for a very cheap, quick time before going home to their wives and kids.

"Whatever you have that's strong." I straddled a bar stool, addressing the bartender. A stocky human man with a sharp nose and thick mustache and eyebrows, nodded back, pouring me something from a clear bottle. He slid it over to me, and I didn't hesitate to take a gulp, my eyes watering over the cheap brandy, the burn choking down my throat.

"Another," I requested, thanking him when he refilled my cup. It had been a really bad day, and it wasn't even noon.

"You have takeaway?" I asked.

"Tripe soup and bread."

"Great," I muttered dryly, the alcohol not working fast enough. "You have anything *stronger*?" I tapped my nose, the sign for dust.

"We don't have that here," he huffed, a disapproving frown on his face as he wandered to another customer.

"I could help you with that." A man in a nice suit slid onto the stool next to me, a drink already in his hand. His groomed appearance and ensemble suggested he was doing well in life. He turned a smile on me, his brown eyes rolling over me with interest. His graying temples and creases around his eyes defined him as human, probably in his late forties, early fifties. Handsome enough to be called it, but not so much you'd notice him in a room. It was the confidence in his position that drew any notice to him, screaming he had money, which was a very attractive quality to have here.

"Free of charge." He winked.

"*Nothing* is free of charge."

A grin pulled his lips, understanding my meaning.

"Wise words." He took a sip of his drink. "Then think of it as an enticement."

"I'm not a prostitute if that's what you're thinking." I scoffed, peering around at the men and women who undoubtedly were. They were moving around the room barely dressed, while I was dirty, sweaty, and looked like I had been out trekking for a month.

"*Everyone* is for the right price." He smiled at my disheveled appearance. "Do you have a price?"

I opened my mouth to protest, this human's ego pissing me off.

"Don't respond yet." He spoke first. "Let me say, I am a man with very particular tastes and inclinations, which my dear wife would not approve of. When I find something which intrigues me..." He gave me a nod, indicating I was that thing. "I go after what I want. And I pay *handsomely* for it." He dug in his pocket, pulling out a tiny clear bag of dust, barely enough to get one hit. My gaze dropped to it, blood pumping in my veins for a taste. "This evening, around seven, I will be upstairs in room 105, if you feel inclined. Bring a friend. I would love the company." He slipped off the stool, pulling on a heavier jacket. "Think about it. I will pay half up front if you wish." Without another word or glance, the man strolled out of the pub.

Sitting there, not sure if I was insulted or disgusted. Normally, I had no problem with being propositioned by either gender. Sex was sex. Especially if you were pretty and fit. Though I felt repelled instead of turned on or intrigued like I normally would have been. The idea felt wrong and made my skin crawl for some reason, Raven's disapproving expression sticking in my head. Maybe it was because I was the one usually paying, not the other way around. Except he was offering the one thing we needed more than anything. Money. We had no other means of getting it. Nothing more of hers to pawn.

But I could sell my body.

Just for one night, Ash. You've done it a million times before. What is the big deal? You've fucked groups of people at a time, being so high you couldn't recall one of them. Why is this any different? My fingers played with the small plastic baggie, the yearning to sniff it down dripped sweat down my back. *You are both getting something out of it.*

We needed money. We couldn't get supplies, lodging, or even food soon if I didn't do something.

Clutching the bag, I shoved it in my pocket, knowing I would need it later.

"Two tripe soups to go," I ordered, placing down the last few coins we had.

For the first time since I was a child, I was doing something I didn't want to do but knew I had to.

Raven could never know.

Chapter 16
Raven

Hours passed before Ash returned, dumping a bag of lukewarm tripe soup and a stale piece of bread on the table.

"All they had," he grumbled, kicking off his boots. He climbed on the bed, facing away from me. He barely said a word, but I could feel his mood shading the already dim room, dividing us.

Sitting in the chair, I stared at his back, fighting the urge to cry. His response was what I feared, what I got from so many after they learned what I did, and none of them even knew the full truth. That had been covered up.

He couldn't even look at me, and I didn't blame him. I was a monster.

Gazing out the window, watching the snow fall, I wrapped up in a ball, missing my family fiercely.

Maybe Ash had been right from the beginning. Maybe I should've gone home, left him alone. All I did was drag him into my mess, and all he wanted was to be left alone to avenge his lovers.

A knot formed in my stomach at the idea of him and these two faceless people who still haunted this room. It wasn't jealousy, exactly, but the way he talked about them, the fierceness he had for them, willing to forfeit his life for their memory…

Irrational as it was to me, who didn't want that kind of love? No one had ever felt that for me. I was the girl men wanted to obtain, to brag they had been with, but they never cared to know me. Probably wouldn't even like the real me. They liked the pretty package, the affiliation, not the one spilling tripe soup down her sweater.

"Ugh," I groaned, standing and brushing off the liquid, the oil from the soup staining my top. I let out another exhale. At one time, a sweater with a stain would've been put in the trash, not even good enough to donate. Now my old ideals seemed arrogant and spoiled. Who I was even six months ago wouldn't recognize me now.

Having Ash back calmed the craziness inside me, and after I finished my soup, overwhelmed by the day, I crawled onto the bed next to him. With the heat of his body and the sound of his steady intake of air, it wasn't long before I succumbed to sleep as well.

When I woke up again, Ash was sitting on the chair, pulling on his boots, his expression pinched, his movements aggressive. Something stopped me from speaking, but I curiously watched his arms flex and his brow furrow while he spoke under his breath with sighs as if he was battling with himself about something.

Leaning on his legs, he scrubbed at his head with a heavy exhale. He sat like that for a beat before he plucked something out of his coat, a tiny clear bag filled with white powder. He stared at it for several minutes, rubbing at his forehead, before he ripped it open, snorting the dust.

Standing up as if the battle had a victor, his choice made, he glanced over at me, and I closed my lids, pretending to be asleep. I could feel him watching me, hear a heavy exhale before his boots hit the floor. The door opened and shut.

Scrambling out of bed, shoving my feet into my shoes and pulling on my jacket, I didn't hesitate, not able to fight the urge to follow him, instincts telling me something was going on. I slipped out after him. Even blocked from my magic, I was excellent at shadowing someone without their knowledge. To be on them without them even knowing I was there.

The snow slapped against my skin when we stepped out into the darkness, the clock in the distance ringing with the hour of seven p.m. A handful of people moved through the neighborhood, heading home or out for something to eat. Bundled up, it was easy to go undetected, following Ash to a pub underneath a three-story building. Light glowed from inside, the chatter of voices slipping out every time the door opened.

Expecting him to go in, needing to get his next high, was a lackluster end to my undercover stalking. But instead he went for the door leading up into the building.

Why was he going in there? Was he meeting with someone? For sex? Drugs?

Curiosity pushed me forward, especially when I noticed him hesitating at the door, his head shaking before he yanked it open, stomping in.

I could not pinpoint or ask why I didn't end my pursuit then and go back to the room, disappointed he wanted to be anywhere but with me. My legs carried on, jogging to the door and sneaking into the empty entry. It smelled like mold.

Activity through the building and the noise from the pub echoed off the barren walls.

Tiptoeing up the stairs, I followed Ash's scent— a mix of crisp leaves in the afternoon and a musky, woody smell, which I swear was an aphrodisiac to my strong senses, leading me forward as if I were on a leash.

The top of Ash's head could be seen walking down the first-level hallway. Ducking, I stayed low enough on the stairs, creeping up just as he rounded a corner.

This was another chance to turn around, to leave him to whatever he was doing, but I didn't, my curiosity impelling me.

A cry of a child bellowed from down the hall, dishes clanking from another, a woman moaning out someone's name as loud bangs tapped the wall, the building a jumble of opposing sounds and smells ramming into my ears and nose.

Skulking down the hall, I peeked around the corner, my chest deflating, seeing an empty corridor. He was gone. I had missed where he was going. Dammit.

Huffing, I started to turn around when one hand came around my mouth, the other around my stomach as my body was yanked back. A shocked cry stabbed at my throat as I felt lips graze my ear.

"Think you can sneak up on me?" Ash's voice licked up the side of my neck, his tone harsh, sending shivers through me. His body pressed into the back of mine.

Yes. I thought. There was no one I couldn't slip up on. So why not him? How did he know I was here?

Ash jerked away from me, whirling me to face him, his expression a map of rage and impatience.

"What the fuck are you doing here?" he snarled, his green eyes burning bright, his shoulders tense.

"I followed you."

"Yes, I noticed."

"I was curious where you were going."

"It's none of your business," he snapped, glancing quickly to a door near us, room 105. "Now go back."

"No."

A strangled cry gurgled in his throat, his hands going to his head. "Raven."

"What are you doing here?" I motioned around in confusion. It wasn't a brothel, though I could hear people having sex in a few rooms along the hallway. "Meeting your drug dealer?" I spat, shaking my head at him.

"It doesn't matter what I'm doing here," he gritted through his teeth, once again glancing at the door like he was nervous someone inside would hear. "You need to go."

"No." I balled my hands. "If you need to get high so badly, do it with me here," I challenged, hoping he'd choose to leave with me. Fairy dust could be addictive, and I was afraid he had already tumbled down that road.

"I'm not here for drugs," he hissed at me.

"Then why are you here? Sex?" The burst of anger through me was hard to disguise. "Another orgy party?"

"No." He blew out.

"It's complicated."

"Sex is complicated?" I scoffed. "Pretty straightforward to me. You stick your cock in whatever hole."

"Raven." He pinched his nose. "Go. Home."

"You brought a friend as I asked. Good." A man's voice jarred me, shooting my attention to an older gentleman standing in the doorway of 105, wearing a silk robe. His hair was dark and short, silver painting the areas near his temple and sideburns. He was of average height and lean, his hands looking like he had never done a hard day's labor in his life.

"Wow. She is a true beauty." His gaze took me in

hungrily, then to Ash, his lust still apparent. "You both are perfect."

"No." Ash's head shook fiercely, a defensiveness to his stance, almost blocking me from view. "She's not part of this."

"Really?" The man tipped his head. "I can pay handsomely for her also."

A rock sunk in my gut, everything feeling off.

"Pay?" The word came off my tongue with confusion. "What's going on?"

Ash swung back to me, shuffling me back, his voice a demand.

"Leave. Now."

"Ash…" Confusion lined my forehead, though I was pretty sure I already knew in my gut.

"Please." His voice broke, his eyes pleading with mine now.

"Two thousand leu for you both," the man stated, his self-assurance lifting his mouth in a smug grin. He knew what he had just laid out. "It is a lot of money."

It came to around five hundred dollars and could cover our expenses for a long time.

My head turned back to Ash, understanding flowing down on me.

Oh my gods…

Ash was prostituting himself to get money. To get *us* money.

He wouldn't look at me.

"Ash," I whispered his name.

After a few moments, his eyes finally met mine, his shoulders rolling back, his expression detached.

"Go, Raven."

My heart ached because I knew this wasn't something

he wanted to do this time. This was out of necessity, not for pleasure. And he was doing it for *us*.

"No. I'm not leaving you to do this."

"You are," he replied. "It's not a big deal."

But it was. I could feel it. Ash might be open with sex, but that was when he could give it freely, his choice. This was because we needed income. To become a prostitute was very different from choosing to sleep with them.

Staring up into his green eyes, my heart slammed in my chest, adrenaline pumping in my veins, emotion swirling in my gut. I couldn't walk away knowing what he was doing. I knew what I had to do.

"Two thousand leu." I pulled away from Ash and journeyed closer to the man. "Each."

The man choked out a surprised laugh as Ash grabbed me, hustling me back.

"Don't listen to her." He started to push me down the hall.

"Ash."

"Raven." He shook his head. "You are not doing this."

"Why not?"

"Why not?" he sputtered. "First, because I said so." My eyebrows hauled up to my hairline from his response. "Second, you are not meant to be part of any of this shit."

"What does that mean?"

"You are not a whore." He bit down. "You are *better* than this."

"So are you."

"I'm not."

"Either we both leave, or we both go in."

"No." He shook his head. "*I'm* staying. We need money."

"Then we both go in." I tried to brush by him, ignoring

the absolute terror I felt at what I was agreeing to and what it might entail.

Ash grabbed for my arm again, dragging me into him. "We'll find the money somewhere else."

"Where?" I motioned around. "We have nothing left to sell. We don't even have enough to gamble. We are out of options."

"I'll figure it out—"

"I agree to your terms," the gentlemen stated. "Two thousand leu *each*. But it's both of you or nothing."

Ash sucked in, understanding how much that was in an area like this.

Nerves thickened my throat as I nodded. "Agreed."

What the hell was I doing? This was so far out of my comfort zone I couldn't even figure it out. This was not at all where I thought this evening would lead.

The man grinned at me and stepped aside, indicating we should enter his room.

"Raven…" Ash's low tone was a blend of fear, anger, and panic.

Terror sloshed in my stomach, my head spinning as I ignored him and stepped into the room, crossing the threshold, the decision made.

The room was simple, but a lot nicer than our room. It housed a queen bed with two nightstands, an armoire, and a desk with two comfy side chairs. This room even had its own bathroom.

The armoire was open, revealing his suitcase. A briefcase was on the floor next to the desk, and on it were two bottles of alcohol and lines of fairy dust. He was probably here on business, coming through for just a few nights, looking for fun between meetings.

"Please, help yourself." He poured a glass and placed it in my hands, gesturing to the dust. "It will help you relax."

I had tried fairy dust and ecstasy a few times at clubs, but it wasn't something I did regularly at all. My parents would've killed me if they found out I'd even tried it. And as much as I was a rebel, alcohol had been more my thing than drugs. But as my hands shook, anxiety almost crippling me, I stared at it with need.

Ash came into the room, his anger covering up the distress I felt coming off him. He looked like he was about to grab me and run, his eyes jumping around, his feet not able to stand still.

"As I promised." The gentleman nodded to the drugs and alcohol. "It will help." He leaned down, sniffing a thick line of dust, his head going back as he let out a light moan.

"You can't touch her." Ash's voice was clear and concise.

"What?" The man's head jerked up.

"Touch me. Do whatever you want, but not her."

"I'm the one paying a lot of money for the both of you." He poured another drink, handing it to Ash. "I get to do what I want. And I will be touching her… and you." He took a huge swig of the alcohol. "But I think you have me mistaken for someone who cheats on his wife."

"Huh?" He was married? I wasn't even sure where he and Ash met, but I figured it was when he disappeared earlier.

"I'm confused." Ash lowered his lids at him. "Why are we here?"

"I'm as faithful to my wife as I can be, but it doesn't mean I don't have *particular* interests she would not approve of." His head danced between us. "I can touch, and I can play, but I don't fuck anyone. What I really enjoy is *watching*."

Shock knotted my stomach when realization tricked down my esophagus.

"And the little scene you gave me out there?" His hand

228

stroked down his robe, his pupils dilating. "There is so much heat and passion between you. I would've paid more."

"You said half up front," Ash spoke.

"Of course." The man pulled out a wallet from the desk drawer, took out some bills, and handed them to Ash.

"This isn't half."

"I need to see more of what I am getting." The man took a drink. "But if you please me, I will pay every penny. I am a man of my word."

Staring down at the cup in my hand, I downed the liquid in a gulp. The alcohol burned my throat, but it was still an upgrade from what we had been drinking before.

The gentlemen held up the tray with the lines. My chest heaved with fear, but what freaked me out more was a sense of exhalation. Anticipation. Not wanting to think, I inhaled the powder, needing anything to calm my nerves. Forget I was whoring myself out for money.

The man walked the tray over to Ash, but Ash's eyes were on me, his stare trying to penetrate my mind, pick out my thoughts, sense what I was feeling. And I felt paper thin under his gaze, like he could read every one, sense my secrets, even the ones I didn't want to acknowledge.

His attention finally lowered to the platter, his jaw working as if he was trying to fight the call of the drug, but it was a losing battle. He bent over, doing two lines and then swallowing down his entire drink.

"This should also help." The older man turned on a small device sitting on the desk, music streaming out of it. Radio had made a huge comeback, a device easier to adapt to the magic in the air, and it could get the news out wide again. TV screens were fully back in the States, but they were still not common here.

Sexy jazz music crooned in the background.

"Take another." He divided up more powder. And I inhaled the line, my shoulders dropping, everything becoming a little hazier and less important. The music swirled in my ear, and I twisted my hips to the melody. My clothes started to scratch at my skin, feeling very hot and heavy.

"Yes, take those off." The man came behind me, helping tug off my coat. "Shoes too."

I kicked off my boots and socks, my gaze going to Ash. He looked as if he was ready to charge over, but the gentleman held up his hand. "Stand there and watch her." His hands slid under my sweater, tugging it over my head, my hair tumbling down my back. My chest was only covered by the cheap, see-thru sports bra I had gotten in Hungary.

The man sprawled his fingers over my stomach, trailing my skin like it was silk. It felt good. My skin tingled with sensitivity.

"Exquisite." His finger curled under the bra, drawing it over my head, baring my breasts. The drugs were taking away more and more of the fear, shifting it into something else. I craved to be touched.

Ash's eyes lowered to my tits, a nerve in his jaw jumping as the man's hands slid over them, cupping them, his thumb rubbing my nipples.

"So young and beautiful." I felt his erection hardening against me from behind, but I kept my gaze on Ash, like he was my anchor, my oasis while everything blurred around me.

The gentleman unhooked my pants, letting them slide down my legs, leaving me in my underwear.

Ash's chest heaved. His face stayed emotionless, but I could see him almost vibrating, his hands in fists.

"So possessive." The man continued to knead my breast, causing small huffs from my throat, his attention on Ash. "Stay there."

He moved to Ash and slowly undressed him. The dust was heating my veins, but Ash being stripped in front of me ignited my blood. His physique was unbelievable, his face so fucking hot and beautiful it melted me. I couldn't seem to control my reaction to him.

His eyes locked on mine as he shrugged off his shirt, dropping it to the floor.

The older man undid the buttons on Ash's pants, dropping them to the ground, sliding his hand over his erection, causing a small moan to hum in my throat, wishing it was my hand. My pulse pounded in my ears, wetness seeping from me.

"You two are so stunning." The man moved between us, his hand skating over our bare skin. "I can feel the friction coming off you both, and it's making me so hard." He reached over to the table and picked up a bottle of liquor, trickling it down my tits.

The sensation felt like satin gliding over my sensitive breasts. I gasped when he dipped his hand in the dust and coated my nipples with the substance.

"Suck them." He ordered Ash. "I want to hear her moan."

Ash didn't move for a moment, his focus drawing up from my nipples to my face. He almost looked as though he wanted to refuse, but his cock twitched, lust breaking through from his gaze.

Like a panther hunting its prey, his eyes stayed on me while he came for me. His toes bumped mine, his frame towering over me. I could feel my muscles trembling, heat curling up through my core.

His hand slid softly over my hip; his touch had me biting down on my lip. Ash's nose flared as he leaned over, his breath sliding from my ear down my neck, tickling my breasts. His tongue swiped across my nipple. A noise dragged up my throat as his mouth covered it, his tongue flicking and sucking.

"Oh gods..." The groan belted out of me without my consent, my lids closing as he moved to the other one, sucking it clean. Fuck, this man was talented. My pussy pulsed painfully as his teeth nipped at my nipple. Both his hands moved to my hips, sliding over my ass, pulling me into him.

Panting and moaning, I tipped my head back as he went back over each one, making sure he got every speck of dust. Just this had an orgasm blazing between my legs, making me desperate for more.

I had sex with my ex while on ecstasy before, and I thought that was mind-blowing... but *nothing* had felt like this, like Ash's touch, his mouth, the groans I heard coming from him. He had barely touched me, but my need for him to be inside me overpowered everything, and it scared me how much I liked someone watching him do these things to me.

Only a small voice kept screaming in my head. *What the fuck are you doing?*

"Okay, stop. It's her turn." The gentlemen instructed. Ash continued to suck on my breasts, his tongue flicking and lapping at my skin, sucking the spot between my breasts, his hands moving up to cup my boobs, his thumbs rolling over my nipples, working them as he dragged his tongue up my breastbone.

"Gods... Ash." I was about to come; I could feel the throbbing, the pain of needing him. I wanted him to kiss me, to push down my panties and drive into me.

"Stop," the guy said again, pulling him back. "I don't want her to come yet."

Ash reluctantly pulled back. His focus was hazy but

stayed locked on my chest, his tongue getting the tiny bit of powder on the corner of his mouth. The older man poured alcohol down Ash's torso and sprinkled it with powder. "You'll be sucking his cock soon, but not until I tell you. You'll come when I say. And you will be fucking her until we *all* come." He sat in a chair, letting his robe fall open, displaying his lean, soft body, his uncircumcised dick standing straight up.

But he no longer was of significance.

"Lick it off him. Every inch." He pointed to Ash.

Ash watched me stroll up to him, my tits wet from his mouth, the drugs sinking into my skin, making everything tingle more. I didn't care about anything but him, craving him, needing him to slip inside me. To taste every inch of this beautiful man. Every scar, every tattoo… every bit of his skin.

"Raven." My name was so low and so deep it was barely a word, but I could feel he was still trying to give me an out, saying without a word that we could leave if I didn't want to do this. Except I did. Badly. The drugs made me bold, fearless. I just wanted, which was all that mattered to me.

My face level with his chest, I leaned in, my tongue gliding up his pec, nipping at his nipple. Ash heaved in through his nose, his frame jolting as my mouth followed the trail of dust across his torso, licking and playing with the other before I lowered, tracing down his sternum. His breathing stuttered, growing heavier, as he watched me kiss and suck along his body. The brandy and fairy dust slid down my throat, emboldening me, decimating any barriers my mind might have put up. The taste of his skin, the feel of his incredible physique against my lips, was bliss. My tongue dragged down through his deep V-line, cutting across the waistband of his boxer briefs where some of the drug dropped too, where the tip of his cock pushed out of his shorts.

My mouth watered, seeing pre-cum seeping from him, and I swiped my mouth over him, letting my tongue curl around his erection.

A guttural groan tore from him, his hand dragging up the back of my head, gripping my hair tight, fighting between holding me back and pushing my mouth down on him. Either it was the drugs or him, but the last little voice died away, and my lips covered the tip of him, sucking off his pre-cum.

"Fuck…" he moaned, his head tipping back, his fingers digging into my scalp, igniting more desire through me. I slid my mouth fully over him, my tongue wrapping around his engorged cock, tasting him. Another long moan pulled from his lungs, sounding like pure ecstasy. "Raven."

The power of my name, the way it moaned from his lips, throbbed between my legs so hard I almost dropped to the floor.

"No. I told you not yet." The man ordered, his legs open, the effect we had on him out on full display. He stood up, sauntering over to us. "I want to taste her first."

Ash's shoulders hitched back, a threatening growl in his throat.

"Someone is overprotective." He winked, taking Ash's hand. "Don't worry, you'll be assisting." He moved Ash's hand to the waistband of my underwear, sliding them under. The man's dick leaked as Ash's fingers slipped between my folds, parting me.

A loud, long noise whined from me.

"Yes. Like that." The man's voice got more excited, his hand still covering Ash's. He pushed them to move deeper, rubbing through me again. My nipples ached, my hips widening for more.

"Finger her pussy hard," he ordered, letting go of Ash. "Make her beg and plead for you to fuck her."

Ash's thumb circled my clit as his finger sank into me.

"Oh gods." A haze of pleasure consumed me, my body succumbing to the smoky dream as I felt Ash's fingers pump in deeper. The room filled with moans, and I no longer knew who they were coming from, nor did I care.

"*Szar*." Ash hissed under his breath. "You are so fucking wet and tight."

My lips parted in a choke, our eyes meeting as his thumb kneaded my clit again, feeling already the hint of an orgasm. "Oh gods... harder," I spoke softly, not able to catch my breath, my hips bucking into his hand, begging him for more.

"You want him to fuck you, don't you?" The man provoked me. "You want him to spread you open and fuck your pussy. It's dripping for him, isn't it? So wet..."

The truth was there, and there was no filter for me to deny it. No thinking, only feeling. And this felt so unbelievable.

"Yes." My head nodded, my hips pumping into Ash's hand, the sound of my wetness obvious. "I'm so wet. Please... fuck me."

"I can't wait anymore." The man yanked Ash's hand away from me, putting his fingers into his mouth, sucking my taste off Ash's hand, his own hand rubbing his cock. "Oh god... You taste so fucking sweet."

Ash's attention went from me to where the man sucked on his fingers. I couldn't decipher his expression, but I felt the confusion, the mix of rage and longing.

"God, you two are getting me so hard. I've never felt this much magic. I'm about to break all my promises to my marriage." He strangled his cock, taking a deep breath. "I never wanted to fuck two people more." He stepped away from Ash, licking his lips. He stumbled over to the tray, taking another hit of the dust, his pupils fully dilated and blown out. He fell onto the chair, his legs open, his hand moving up and down his shaft. "I want to watch you fuck her hard, but first eat her pussy. Get it all wet for me. I want to hear her screams echoing for days in my ears."

I heard a voice, deep below the fogginess of the drugs, an alarm telling me this was too far, but the voice was quickly drowned away.

Ash's gaze was cloudy, and I knew we were both past the point of rationality.

"Take off your underwear," the man ordered, settling back in his chair and stroking himself. "And sit on the bed facing me."

As if I had no control, I did as he said, peeling down my knickers, my wetness dripping from me as I sat down on the edge of the mattress.

"Spread your legs."

My thighs parted, my attention completely on Ash, almost like the man had a script and was giving us directions, telling us what to do, but held no other power.

Ash made a noise, his eyes dropping to my pussy, his tongue dragging over his lip, making me even needier.

"Jesus, her young, wet pussy." The man groaned. "Feast on her! I want to hear how wet she is."

Ash dropped to his knees, his gaze locked on my pussy, desire burning in his eyes as his hands gripped my thighs, spreading me wider. My nails dug into the bedsheets when he leaned in, his lips brushing my inner thigh. Softly, his tongue parted me, licking slowly through me.

"Oh gods... fuck!" I rolled my hips into him, need shaking me.

With a loud moan of his own, he gripped my thighs, roughly putting them over his shoulder before his mouth consumed me, kissing my pussy deeply, his tongue sliding through, hitting every spot, tearing out a cry from my soul.

My back arched, my hips rolling with every stroke of his tongue, everything I understood or knew shattering around me.

"You taste so fucking good," he growled against me, devouring me as if there was nothing else in the world he craved. "Like nothing I've ever tasted before, and I don't ever want to stop."

Don't. Ever. But I couldn't form the words, my moans echoing off the wall, and I didn't care who heard me. I liked this. I liked being watched. I wanted more.

"Yes, that's it!" The man yelled, his hand moving faster. I could hear him jerking off, but I didn't focus on that. "Fuck her pussy harder with your tongue."

Ash took his words as a command, licking, sucking, and nipping until I lost complete control. Gripping his hair, I rode his face with unrelenting demand, pleasure making me feral. I could feel the monster roaring inside, needing out, needing to fuck. Needing blood. The sounds of him feasting on me grew almost grotesque.

"Yes! Yes!" I could hear the man baying in the distance. "Fuck... yes!"

"Oh gods!" I belted out, an orgasm sizzling through me, my nails digging into the back of his head, producing a moan from Ash. He pushed his fingers into me, his teeth nipping at my clit as he rubbed my bundle of nerves. "*Ash!*" My spine jackknifed, a guttural cry wailing from me, my pussy strangling his fingers as I came hard on his tongue, my vision going dark.

Ecstasy blasted within me, and I floated in a bliss of drugs and absolute pleasure, his finger and tongue fucking me all the way through it, ripping another climax out of me. It was several minutes before I could catch my breath. My body shaking so violently I couldn't seem to find any ground to secure to.

Holy shit.

Ash's mouth pulled away, making cool air rush through my slit.

Limp and sedated, but at the same time elated and wired. I wanted more. Craved it more than the drug in my system, excited to hear the man order Ash to fuck me.

Except the room was quiet besides our heaving breathing.

Too silent.

My gaze went to the older man. Passed out cold, his hand was still fisted around himself, cum pooling across his chest.

Ash sat back, his tongue sliding over his glistening mouth. His head was down, his hand scouring the back of his neck. Following his gaze, I spotted his semi-hard cock, thick cum coating his stomach and boxers.

He came too. But he didn't look happy about it. At all.

Reality started to seep in, and I pulled back, closing my legs, my pussy throbbing with what he did to it.

What the fuck just happened?

"We should get out of here before he wakes up." Ash cleared his throat. Wiping his mouth, he stood up. Using the bedsheet, he wiped his cum off his stomach and snatched up our clothes, tossing mine to me. He wouldn't look at me. His demeanor was colder, like he hadn't just whispered how good I tasted, as if this was simply a role he was playing and he no longer had to pretend.

Still buzzing, I got dressed, feeling regret and shame ooze in as he got more and more distant. I had forced this. Ash didn't want me here, and now it would be awkward because I wouldn't walk away.

His tongue had been in my pussy. We both came. Hard.

Maybe to him, it was no big deal. A normal Wednesday night, but to me?

Ash grabbed the man's wallet, yanking out the rest of his cash.

"How much?" Please don't say he was lying to us about having the money.

"Five thousand total." He flicked through the bills before stuffing it all in his pocket. "Think we were owed a bonus for making him come so hard he blacked out." He replied evenly and took off out of the room.

I followed him, my legs so wobbly I could barely walk.

My body was humming, already craving more. I hoped to the gods it was fairy dust I was addicted to and not him.

Chapter 17

Ash

Fuck. What the hell did I do?

Slamming down every thought trying to bubble up, I tried not to think. *At all.* But with every step I took through the snow, I could feel the stickiness in my briefs, remnants of my cum smearing over my abs. I could still feel her mouth on my skin. Her taste coated my tongue.

Glancing briefly back at her, she trailed a few feet behind me as we ventured to the flat, her legs wobbly, her cheeks flushed, and her eyes blown out.

The drugs still roared in my system, but I felt incredibly sober now. Reality drummed on my walls, trying to infiltrate my consciousness, wanting to analyze and understand what happened. And how I let it.

Not that you can stop Raven when she wanted to do something. But I could have made her leave. I could've fought her. Chosen for us to find another way to get money. But I didn't. Not really. Why didn't I?

Entering the building, I stomped up the stairs, going into our room. Raven slipped in behind me. Silence descended on us, screaming into the void of our indiscretion.

The two of us alone in this room felt like a hundred were crammed in, with no air.

We could play this two ways—ignore it as if it never happened or act as if it was no big deal. We did what we needed to do to get five thousand leu from a man who had a voyeuristic kink.

So what? We didn't even kiss. We were just doing what he told us.

But nothing about it felt like *no big deal*. I didn't want it to stop. I wanted to fuck her on that bed. I wanted to kiss her, drive into her over and over, make her climax a dozen more times, feel her strangle my cock... with him awake or asleep.

But I stopped myself.

Peering at her through my lashes, I watched her take off her jacket, her expression closed off. When only ten minutes ago, she had been on fire, desire burning behind her eyes, body fully alive, screaming my name as her nails dug into the back of my head.

At the memory, my cock stirred in my pants.

I gritted my teeth together, needing to get away.

"I'm taking a shower," I grumbled, grabbing some clean clothes and hauling down the passage to the bathroom.

Sex was nothing to me, pretty much like breathing and eating. It was part of being fae. Even more so to a nature fairy. And I had sex with so many—friends, strangers, men, women, single, committed, married couples, groups—always with kink. So why was this any different?

Standing under the shower head, I let the weak water pressure trickle down on me, trying to ignore how hard I was again, trying not to think, but all I could hear were her moans, how warm and wet she felt, what her tits and pussy tasted like… what it was like when she came on my tongue.

How easily I came…

My hand wrapped around my cock, anger crackling up my spine as I stroked myself, pissed at myself. Pissed at her.

That was never supposed to happen. Raven wasn't even supposed to be here. She drove me crazy. She wasn't supposed to be anything more than a girl who happened to be at the same pub that one night. But somehow this girl had become part of my journey… my life.

Tonight was a mistake. As though she changed everything with a moan, coming on my mouth. As if she marked me.

I didn't even want to admit this to myself, but this was the first time—*ever*—I had come just from eating pussy. I had the stamina and control to pleasure and fuck for hours. After I lost Kek and Lucas, I couldn't seem to get off, and when I did, it definitely wasn't easy. That's why I ventured to so many brothels, needing so many people… but still struggled.

Tonight, I had orgasmed effortlessly—and so hard that I lost consciousness for a moment.

Since she had joined me on this journey, I had released without difficulty down the prostitute's throat—when I imagined *her*. Tonight, I was so turned on, so in tune with her, I came when she did, as if I could feel her orgasm as well as my own.

"No." I leaned into the tile wall, forcing myself to think of Kek and Lucas. They were the ones I loved. Who I missed.

Not. Her.

My heart started thumping, feeling no spark as I put them in the shower with me, pretending it was them getting me off, trying to recall Lucas's dick inside me, Kek's mouth around my cock.

Teeth clenching, I stoked harder, demanding I get off to them.

But my climax faltered, staying level, needing release but not letting me have it, like so many times before.

"No!" I hit the wall. "Fucking come," I demanded my body, yet nothing triggered me, no matter how much I evoked Kek and Lucas.

My mind went where it needed without letting me have a say. The picture of Raven spreading her legs, her hair tumbling over her breasts, the feel of her tongue wrapping around the head of my cock.

A groan bubbled out of me, imagining her taking me all the way in her throat, my fingers threading through her dark, silky hair. Her moaning around me as she took me deeper.

"Fuck. Fuck," I hissed, my balls tightening, my hand aching as I rubbed harder. Then I pictured my tongue sliding through her pussy again, hearing her cry out, and my body jerked hard, ropes of my sperm painting the wall and gushing over my hand. A loud moan came from me as I emptied myself.

Catching my breath, my mind cleared, and everything hit me. A truth crushing me from the inside out. My frame sagged, falling back into the tub, the water spraying down on me. I curled over myself and broke apart, a sob hitching in my lungs.

Ruthless emotion flooded out of me in harsh swells, tearing across my chest and heaving from my soul. The pain was so severe I couldn't catch my breath.

Because I knew deep down...

I was starting to move on from Kek and Lucas. Loving them differently than I had.

And I was not okay with that.

The morning brought the haze of sun, but darkness hovered over Raven and me as we walked back to the old part of town. We had barely spoken more than a few words to each other since last night.

While she showered after me, I had run out to get food, which she barely touched, saying she wasn't hungry. She curled up on the bed, her back to me, and pretended to sleep.

We needed to talk, but my mouth wouldn't form the words, lost in my own angry, resentful, and muddled thoughts.

I contemplated leaving, giving her half the money for a journey home, and walking out, ending this torture for us before it was too late. But I couldn't get myself to do it, finding every reason to stay. I mean, the Russian Mafia was after her. And now that I understood why they were, she was not safe. Putting her on a train alone? She'd be dead by the time it hit the border.

With their threat on my mind, I was on high alert, slipping us through alleys, trying to stay off main roads on our way back to old town. We weren't the only ones. People clogged the lanes, bustling with a strange energy, shuffling forward in a wave as if everyone in town woke up at the same time and headed for the plaza.

"What's going on?" Raven muttered against me, her brows quirked, peering around at the hordes of civilians moving together toward the center.

I shrugged, having no clue. "Is it Christmas today? Some holiday gathering?"

"Oh, I think it is." Raven's brow knitted, an edge of sadness to her voice. Probably realizing she was here with me and not home with her family. That her gift this year was me eating out her pussy for Christmas Eve.

A noise caught in my throat, my cock responding instantly to the memory and the need to do it again. I shoved the thought from my mind as soon as it popped in, but an itch already drove over my body. The craving for her taste overpowered any yearning for drugs.

The closer we got to the square where the supply shop was, the more warnings started to tingle through me, telling me it was more than some holiday event.

Hundreds of military men milled around the marketplace, congregating in units and holding sentry with a stillness that poked more tingles at the base of my spine.

We had seen a lot off duty here the first night, but these men were completely the opposite. Marching around in perfect sync, loaded with weapons, their movements crisp and intimidating, herding the masses into the middle of the plaza.

A sickness rolled into my stomach.

"Seriously, what the hell is happening?" Raven hissed next to me as we peered around a corner, frowning as an endless stream of people knocked into us, trying to get around.

"Not sure." Though I noticed some kind of stage was set up near the Christmas tree. "A holiday event?" I hoped.

"Do they need armed forces for a holiday event?" Raven's mouth pulled down. "This doesn't feel very jolly. Here, kid, sit on Santa's knee while a soldier holds a rifle to your head."

"They are very serious about who's been good and who's been *naughty*." My eyes swung down to her, my chest clenching, realizing that was the last thing I should've said. Her cheeks flushed pink before she turned away from me, probably thinking the same thing I was. How deep my tongue had been inside her last night.

We'd be very much on the naughty list.

Clearing my throat, I surveyed the crowd, the guards a

complete change from the ones partying here the other night. They were almost...

My throat tightened, and I shoved back the thought. *No.* I wagged my head against the notion. *There's no way.*

Yet so many alarms were going off inside, taking me back to a place I never wanted to think about again. A hell that still haunted me. Guards who were turned into perfect mindless soldiers.

"I need to get closer," I said to her. "Keep your hood up and head down," I instructed Raven, adjusting my head deeper into my hood. Slipping out from around the wall, I grabbed her hand in mine, weaving us through the throng of villagers standing compactly in the square.

Inching closer to the stage, I kept a tight hold on Raven, the prickle on the back of my neck growing more intense. Eyeing a soldier near me, his expression blank, his body stiff, I tried to find a hint of what I feared, what I had experienced and seen before.

No. It's not possible. But was it? I had helped destroy the labs, ending all new clusters of fae/human interfusions. Even though many had escaped after the battle with Istvan, I knew their quick decline from robotic to feral. They wouldn't be this way so long after the battle a year ago.

You are just seeing things, Ash.

A guard barked out orders, the rest stomping their feet, grabbing for their rifles, and tightening in around the mass they funneled into the middle.

"Ash?" Raven said my name nervously right as car engines thrummed over the chilly morning air, rolling in on the outskirts of the plaza, where more guards held watch.

The motorcade comprised two huge army trucks, two army jeeps, and two sleek black cars, the windows tinted black.

The pit of my stomach fused into a knot.

"This is so exciting. I can't believe they are visiting us on Christmas Day." A woman next to me bounced on her toes, trying to get a better view.

Her husband huffed. "They're taking over this area anyway."

"Oh, hush." She batted at him. "They've done so much for us here. You should be excited. You have a job at the castle because of what they're doing."

"Yeah." He bobbed his head with very little enthusiasm.

"Who?" I twisted to her, my voice like a whip. "Who is visiting?"

She blinked up at me as if I were the most clueless person in the world, her hand motioning toward the convoy.

"Prime Minister Lazar, of course." She motioned to the short, dark-haired man getting out of one of the black cars, his son Sergiu being ushered from the other side.

My heart drummed against my ribs. Seeing them again, especially Sergiu, brought me back to that night. He had helped them escape. He had been part of it. Had been the man Brexley was supposed to marry.

"But even more exciting… is our new queen is here." The woman squealed, pointing to the other black car, where two more were being escorted from their vehicle.

My heart stopped.

The only sounds I could hear were the remnants of Lucas's body hitting the ground, the swing of a blade, the crunch of bone and flesh slicing off Kek's head. My scream hollowing out my ears and emptying my soul until I was nothing but a corpse on the ground with them.

That night rushed back in full color, forcing me to experience it all over again.

My heart came back to life, banging in my chest so loud everything buzzed around me.

I felt Raven squeeze my hand. She might have even been talking to me, but I heard nothing.

All I heard was the woman next to me shriek as the four figures stepped onto the stage.

"Queen Sonya and Prince Iain."

Chapter 18
Raven

The crowd buzzed around us, clapping and screaming as Prime Minister Lazar, his son, and a woman and man I didn't know stepped onto the stage.

"Queen Sonya and Prince Iain," The woman next to us cheered, her hands going to her mouth as if she wanted to cry.

Queen Sonya and Prince Iain?

Romania didn't have a queen.

My head jerked back to the four standing on the stage, waving at their subjects. The woman was beautiful, tall, thin. Her blonde hair was wrapped in a bun bound in jewels, her lips bright red. She wore expensive fabrics and an immaculate white fur coat.

Fae normally did not wear animal skins, being one with nature instead of hurting it, especially when so many fae shape-shifted into animals. It was against our code. It was wrong, like humans wearing human skin clothing.

She didn't seem to abide by that rule.

Her son, who looked so much like her, stood in rich finery. His chiseled face and lean frame suggested he never had to work very hard for anything he was given, though he had soldier badges draped on his lapel and arm of his coat like Christmas decorations. They were a stunning pair. Everything you'd picture a queen and prince to be: tall, blond hair, and bright green eyes with their fae beauty. And it was in contrast to Minister Lazar and his son Sergiu, who were short, dark-haired, dark eyed, human, and extremely unhappy looking. As if they were being forced to be here, to swallow a pill they didn't like.

Sonya's high-heeled white shoes stepped past Lazar to the microphone, as if he was of no consequence, a secondary character to her presence.

"Romania!" Sonya's beautiful voice curled out from the speakers. "It is so good to see you all here this morning. Generations to come will envy you being here to witness this historic day. A day when Romania became a country envied by others for its strength and power." Cheers went up in the air at her declaration. Her red lips curved into a smile while she waited for the applause to quiet. "How long has it been since you could hold your head high, feel pride for your country? It is time to go back to when Romania was formidable. A leader in this world." More claps and calls whooped at this. "It has been almost a century since you were led with true strength. A devoted leader who puts you first." My attention jumped to Lazar at her clear insinuations, the insults she was saying without saying—he was not the man for the job. Prime Minister Lazar's expression was stone, though I noticed his jaw twitch, his hands fisting tighter into a ball at his side.

"You need someone who can see you through and win the war coming to these borders—a monarch who can bring you back to greatness. It is time for a change, do you not agree?" She held up her arms, the cheers rising louder. "I am that change. Your queen!" The audience hailed at her words, most not realizing—or not caring—that she had just declared herself their ruler. No vote, no say, no choice. And they all seemed besotted, willingly handing their freedom to a regime with pretty words and possibly false promises.

"I don't understand." I shook my head, peering back at the prime minister again. "Lazar is clearly letting this happen? Romania hasn't had a queen since 1947. What is going on? Who are they?" I turned to Ash. My stomach dropped in fear, taking note of his demeanor. He was next to me but was no longer with me.

"Ash?" His frame was rigid, his chest pumping up and down, his nose flaring. "Ash?" He didn't respond, his gaze locked on the two fae with wrath I could feel shaking through his limbs. "Hey." I retook his hand, turning to face him, but he seemed to not even know I was there. Following his gaze, mine went back to Sonya and Iain, his focus also on them, stalking their every move.

I could taste his rage, the need to kill, like it was my own. It only incited the darkness inside me, stirring it up, craving death more than anything. It howled against its barrier, chanting at the back of my tongue.

"What's going on?" I tugged his hand harder, needing him to stop, to look at me. "You're scaring me."

"All hail the queen!" her son Iain roared into the microphone next to her, dipping his head.

"All hail the queen!" the people regurgitated back in a chant, bowing down, sliding a chill down my spine.

Ash's body vibrated. A rumble lodged deep in his throat.

"Ash?" My gaze ticked to him and then to the hundreds of soldiers surrounding us, the guards on stage, their weapons ready to fire at any hint of protest. Their stiff, alert forms almost begging for it, eager to spill blood in this square.

Ash stepped forward, his hand reaching for the gun under his coat.

"Ash. No." I tried to step in front of him, but he pushed by me, not even seeing me. He'd get only one shot off before he'd be gunned down. "Ash! Please. Stop!" I grabbed the sleeve of his jacket.

He didn't.

Panic infiltrated my veins, needing to stop him. The thought of him being murdered in front of me, his life taken… *from me.*

The thought skimmed my mind, a howl echoing deep inside my bones. My hands seized the back of his hood. Adrenaline pumped through my muscles, yanking him back with a grunt. He stumbled back, almost falling on his ass, finally cutting his attention off them, giving me time to get in front of him.

"Stop." Grabbing his chin, I forced his face down to mine.

The urge to slam my mouth on his, to break his trance, to let him feel all the emotions swirling in my gut, almost overpowered me. I craved the feel of his mouth, the taste of the tongue that was inside me just last night. I felt an intimacy there now, as if I had the right to kiss him, to touch him.

"Ash. Look at me," I ordered, the demand in my tone giving no argument. "Now." His eyes finally snapped to mine. He blinked like he finally saw me, his nose flaring. "Don't you dare leave me." *I can't be here without you,* I thought to myself, realizing how scared I was of him leaving me. Being without him.

His throat bobbed, his jaw clenched, but he didn't move.

"Don't be an idiot. Not now. There are too many guards

around them. *Please*. Wait." I licked my lip nervously. "If not for yourself, do it for me. I can't… do this. Be here. Alone."

He watched me for a beat.

"Please," I begged softly.

His lids clamped closed in agony. Several moments passed before he reopened them. Swallowing roughly, Ash dipped his head in agreement.

Exhaling, my shoulders lowered in relief. I grasped his hand, leading him away from the crowd.

"How disrespectful to walk away when your queen is speaking." A man's voice spoke from the stage, whipping my head to see the self-proclaimed prince pointing at us. Every head snapped in our direction, attention burning on us like a hot lamp. This was my nightmare, keeping my head tucked back as far as I could. "Do you have anything to say to your queen?" Iain motioned to us.

Ash kept his face turned away from Iain, his eyes on the ground, his shoulders taunt. Every breath moved his body, his hands rolling into fists.

"Apologize to your queen for this insult," Iain demanded, his chin raised with self-importance.

"She's not my queen," Ash muttered. Trees around the square started to crack and bend to his emotions.

"Excuse me, *subject*?"

My heart dropped as I watched Ash's self-control crumble.

"Nooo…" I tried to stop him, but it was too late.

Whirling to the prince, Ash threw off his hood, his shoulders rolling back.

"I *said*… she is not my fucking queen. Or a queen at all." Ash's voice boomed across the square, fury dripping off every word. "Nor are you a prince. You are a coward and *murderer*. All of you on the stage are." Ash reached for his gun.

253

The color drained from Iain's face, his mouth parting when he realized who was speaking, while Sonya stood emotionless, taking Ash in.

I saw recognition. Familiarity. A past.

"I'm here to avenge your own brother you murdered."

Boom! Ash's gun fired.

Everything happened in a moment, discharging the square into bedlam.

"Get him!" Shouts came from Lazar and Sergiu, ordering the guards to act, while other sentries shuffled the four of them off stage, getting them out of the line of fire.

"Ash!" I could see soldiers moving for us, closing in. He didn't move, his gun aimed at Sonya, trying to find an opening to shoot. "Come on!" I shoved him hard, forcing him to wake up, notice all the guards coming at us, their weapons pointed at us.

Bang! A shot whizzed by us, creating even more hysteria in the crowd.

"*Szar*," Ash hissed under his breath. "Go! Go!" Shoving through the throng of people, he became a battering ram, trying to make a path for us to get out.

A stream of guards pushed toward us, their faces expressionless, their eyes blank.

"This way!" I shouted at Ash, dragging him to an opening in the mob.

Pop! Pop!

Gunfire rang out, along with piercing screams in the air. Chaos and confusion had everyone running in all directions, knocking against my small frame and taking me to the ground.

"Raven!" Ash yelled, trying to help me up. "Don't let go." He took my hand, keeping low, and we darted through the swarm of people, the shouts from sentries breathing down my neck.

Adrenaline seared my nerves, turning my insides into a frenzy of violence, desperate to be let free.

You could kill them all. It would be so easy, the voice taunted me, rumbling power under my skin. *Stop denying who you are, what you are capable of.*

Bang!

A bullet seared close to my head, barely missing Ash's shoulder. Crouching even lower, we ran faster out of the square, men's boots and voices echoing after us.

All we seemed to be doing was running for our lives.

Sprinting at full speed, we snaked through the buildings, trying to lose our assailants, finding ourselves once again near the church.

Ash ripped open the doors and motioned for me to go in. "Have any confessions since yesterday?"

My mind went straight to images of us last night in that man's room, the things we did, how he made me feel.

The reverend's eyes widened when he saw us again, darting for the confession booth, needing sanctuary again.

Ash rushed me in, closing us into the small, dark cubicle and locking the door. His firm body once again pressed me into the wall, his heavy breathing trailing down my neck.

Last time we were here, I was still Scarlet. I didn't know the taste of him. The sounds he made when he was turned on. How his mouth felt on my skin. His tongue in my pussy. Sucking in, I closed my eyes, hearing boots clomp over the wood, spiking my heart rate. A few shouts volleyed off the high ceilings, the door to our compartment rattling.

"That is not in use," the clergyman stated. "And there are no weapons allowed in here. Please leave."

"I take orders from my queen," a strange voice snarled. "Not you, human."

Silence filled the room, tension lashing at me before I

heard the same one bark again. "Move out. They still have to be close by. We cannot fail her."

Boots treaded out of the church, the door slamming.

Peering up into Ash's eyes, I started to feel hurt and anger burn into the back of my throat, now able to think of what he almost did. How he almost forfeited everything, not caring about what happened to himself or me.

"Come out," the reverend's voice called to us. "They are gone."

Ash backed up, sensing the shift in my attitude, his jaw ticking as he unlocked the door.

"Well." The reverend sat down in a pew, his head wagging as we came out of the booth. "You two are very *wanted*."

"It's hard being this desirable." Ash's joke fell flat.

"Sit." The clergyman pointed to another bench.

"We'll pass. We're going to use the same tunnel we did last time." Ash started to turn for the stairs down.

"*Sit*." The man directed more firmly.

I strolled over to the pew and plunked down, my arms folding, wanting to do anything opposing Ash, my resentment growing. Plus, the man had helped us out twice now.

Ash looked at me, his hand running through his hair, annoyed, before he dropped to the bench in front of mine.

"Have anything to say about why you keep using this place as a refuge?"

"Nope," Ash huffed.

"Really?" I spouted, sitting up. "You have nothing to say about almost getting us killed? *Again*!"

"Again?" Ash's brows tempered, turning more to face me. "If you remember correctly, we were hiding in here because of *you* last time… *Scarlet*."

His dig only enraged me.

"And what about the time before that? And the one before that? You were about to shoot the prime minister and the queen in front of everyone."

"She is *not* a queen," he yelled, standing up. "And her twat of a son is not a prince. They are murderers."

"And you were about to be one in the middle of a crowded square with trained guards everywhere?"

"You have room to talk," he threw back at me. "Isn't that why the Mafia is after you?"

Oh, he didn't just say that. "Fuck you!" Shame and fury jumped me to my feet, matching his energy. "And I didn't mean to…" I cut off my claim, shaking my head. "You do!"

"Yes! It's the whole point of me being here. Why I never wanted you with me." He tossed out his arms. "And why do you care about their lives? Do you know what they have done? Those they have hurt and killed?"

"I don't care about them. I care about you," I shouted, wanting to suck back in the words I spilled. Ash's back straightened, his gaze making me feel raw and exposed, pushing more anger through me. "What the hell were you thinking?"

He tipped his head back.

"Tell me!"

"I wasn't thinking, okay?" he belted. "All I could see were the very people who took my soul from me. They deserve to die. To pay for what they did to Lucas and Kek, and most of all to *me*." He hit his chest. "Because I have to be the one who goes on… who has to keep living without them."

Tightness snarled in my chest and gut, a possessive jealousy I quickly shoved away.

"Maybe I wasn't thinking clearly, but it made me realize how much you have distracted me from my mission. The whole reason I am here." He put his hands on his hips with an accusatory tone. "And now they know I am here."

"And that's my fault?"

"Yes! You stopped me from fulfilling my promise. They could be dead now, but I ran away from the single thing that is important to me *for you*."

His statement struck me like a spiked mace.

"The only thing important to you?" I choked out. "Go fuck yourself, Ash. Go join your lovers…"

"Screw you!"

"Whoa!" The clergyman stepped closer, putting his hands out to us. "Let's calm down."

"What's stopping you?" I tossed out my arms. "Go." I motioned to the door. "Go get yourself killed for no reason."

"No. Reason?" he sputtered.

"You think they want you to die for them?" I continued, tears burning the back of my lids. "This is how they want you to live your life? Angry, resentful, and hard-hearted?"

"Don't act as if you know them or me," he snarled, leaning closer.

The reverend tried to push us apart again.

"You're right, I don't know them… but I doubt they'd want you miserable, basically begging for death so you don't have to feel pain anymore."

He jolted back, both of us panting.

"All right." The reverend's tone was low and calm. "Let's take a breath." He took one himself. "You two have some things to work out."

"No, we don't." I glowered at Ash.

He glared back. "Nope. All good."

"Yeah, I can see that." The man lifted a brow.

Shouts and feet hitting the ground right outside the church doors halted us. I waited for the door to swing back open, soldiers discovering us here.

"Come." He waved us to follow, hurrying through the abbey and entering a private door. We trailed closely behind as he took us down a hallway and to a back room. "It is better you stay hidden until it calms down." He nodded for us to enter. "You will be safe here. I promise."

"We need a way out of the city." Ash came up behind me. "We also need supplies."

The reverend dipped his head. "I will see what I can do."

"Thank you," I replied before he rushed us in, shutting the door and locking it behind him.

The room was dark and damp; the only light was from a window high above, the snow moving back in, fluttering against the glass. The tall stone walls and floor contained the chill seeping from outside. Glancing around, it looked like a hodgepodge of unused artwork, a table covered in old books and paperwork, damaged stained glass, some cleaning supplies, and a minuscule bathroom, which Ash probably couldn't even fit in if the door was shut. A single cot was stuffed in a corner, as if it might be used to sneak away for a nap.

Neither of us spoke, the silence dropping like icicles in the already freezing room. Moving around, I checked out the artifacts, distracting myself from the fact that we were locked in this small room together. Adrenaline and anger were slowing down in my veins while fatigue and pain nipped at the edges. Rubbing at my ribs, I flipped through a book. They were healing, but still a little sore.

Too aware of Ash's presence behind me, I traveled over to the cot, wanting to get away from him. Sitting down on the squeaky metal, I looked everywhere but at him.

"Ignoring me?" He huffed.

"Trying to."

His knuckles scrubbed at his thickening scuff, which of

259

course made him look even hotter. Pacing around the room, a few disgruntled noises rose from his throat before he finally spoke.

"I'm sorry, okay?" He moved his hand to the back of his neck, rubbing. "I'm sorry I put you in that kind of danger."

"I don't give a shit about me," I snapped. "I care that you are so blinded by your hate, needing revenge so badly, you're willing to make it a suicide mission." I tucked my legs into my chest as a protective barrier. "And that you didn't tell me this whole time it was the prime minister and this Queen Sonya you were after." They were different from just regular people who had killed his lovers; this upped the stakes a thousand percent. "Do you know how many soldiers they have guarding them at all times? How easy it would be to get killed before you even got close to them? I know how hard it is to get close to officials like that."

"And I almost had them!" Ash knocked his fists together. "They were so close."

"But you missed, and chances are you wouldn't have hit both in time. And now they know you're here." I tucked in tighter into myself. "What did you think would happen if you did kill them? You would've been caught and probably hung or shot right there."

He shrugged.

"You really don't care?" Sadness gripped my chest, burning my eyes. It hurt. It hurt because I realized how little I mattered to him. That staying alive for me was not something he even considered. "Right." I looked down, hiding the pain I couldn't deny. "Got it."

"Raven…"

"No. I get it," I replied curtly, wondering how I got here once again. Liking someone who did not feel the same about me. The old wound opened a crevice of anguish. My brain shut down, and I felt exhausted. "I'm tired," I muttered. Curling up on the cot, I turned away from him.

"Raven?" He said my name again, but I closed my lids and blocked him out, letting all the trauma I had buried deep lull me into a dark numbness.

Chapter 19

An old oil lamp on the table gave off a tiny bit of heat as the morning grew into late afternoon, the thick clouds darkening the already murky chamber.

I sat in a chair and watched her sleep. The chill in the room rolled her so tightly into a ball that I could barely see her under the wool blanket. The struggle of wanting to stay as far from her as I could fought against an inherent need to curl around her, letting my body heat hers. To feel her against me. Safe. With each passing minute, I felt the latter would win out.

Blowing out, I tipped my head back, scouring my face, my earlier actions playing in my head over and over, knotting up my chest and pissing me off more. I wasn't supposed to feel guilty. To be sick over what I did. It was the whole point of why I was in Romania.

Revenge.

Except right now, I not only failed in that, but I put her

in harm's way. And *that* was what was digging into my abdomen. If something had happened to her, her life taken in front of me because I was so hellbent on getting Sonya and Iain... she'd be another person I'd lose because of those two.

Staring over at her, the notion of her not being here shot me out of my seat. A growl tickled the back of my throat as I moved around the room, not able to sit still, a chasm in my chest.

You'd feel that way about anyone. You wouldn't want anyone to die.

I mean, she was a nice kid. She deserved a full, happy life, to find love and raise a family if it was what she wanted. Maybe the idiotic ex of hers would realize what he let go, or some smarter guy would come along, see what an amazing person she was, and never let her go.

My lip curled up at the thought of some *faszkalap* tasting her, hearing her moans, making her cry out *his* name. "Stop." I gritted my teeth, blood torching up the back of my neck. "You don't think of her like that."

I could hear the mocking laugh in my head as my cock pressed against my zipper. For almost a year, I barely got aroused. I was dead inside, and unless I was high and could forget for a moment, I hardly got an erection. So many times, I had a male prostitute fuck me until my dick was hard enough to push down a throat or slip into a pussy. It was all anger and anguish, needing to *experience* pain, to *cause* pain, to feel anything.

Something had changed along the way. I didn't know when it started, but I was afraid the reason was lying just feet from me.

"*Bazdmeg.*" *Fuck that*. I dug my fingers into the bridge of my nose right as the sound of a lock turned over. Instinctually, I grabbed for my gun just in case.

263

Raven scrambled up, waking instantly as the reverend came in.

"Just me." His arms were full of clothes and bags. The smell of food wafting out of one of them rumbled my stomach. "My apologies I was so long." He hauled some heavier coats onto the table. "It is not easy getting this stuff nowadays. And you two have caused quite a stir out there." He set the food down. "They are still searching around, but it has lightened up a bit. The rumor is you two were able to escape the city. They have set up blocks on all the major roads."

I muttered under my breath, opening the bag of food. The aroma of cabbage meat rolls hit my nose, causing my mouth to water. Ripping the bag, I placed the rolls out on the table, sliding them over to Raven. "Sit." I motioned for her to take the chair and eat, knowing she needed food. For once, she didn't fight me, taking a seat. I waited until she bit into the *sarmale*, groaning in bliss, my eyes transfixed with watching her eat. "So, we're trapped here?" I forced my head back to the reverend.

"Not necessarily." He clasped his hands.

Tipping my head in question, my attention jumped back to Raven when she moaned again, her eyes rolling back. I shifted on my feet, my body responding to her sounds.

"So good." She handed me a cabbage roll while she stuffed down another one before she even finished the first. Her manners had been tossed out the window, and I couldn't help but smile.

"What does that mean?" I chomped down on the *sarmale*, bursts of meat and spices filling my mouth, causing a noise to huff up. It probably wasn't even meat, nor good, but after days of living off oily tripe soup, it was amazing.

"I cannot help you past the walls of the city." The reverend touched the coats he laid on the table, his graying brows fusing together. "But I might know someone who can. A place you can hide out. Iacob is an old acquaintance who walked away from the church when we were seminarians and has taken his own *unique*, personal journey." His tone was slightly condescending, but I didn't call it out, not really caring. "He lives up in the mountains with a handful of individuals the same as him."

"Where in the mountains?" I asked. "I thought all roads were blocked."

"You wouldn't take normal roads to him."

"Where is he?"

"Iacob lives in the old ruins of *Bisericuţa Păgânilor*."

"The Pagans' Temple?" My body went still, knowing this place was very close to the Valea Cetatii caves.

"Yes." The reverend frowned. "He and his little commune have taken it over, practicing their rituals and magic."

"They're fae?"

"Some are human, some fae, and a Druid."

"What?" Raven's chair ground over the stone, a *sarmale* dropping from her hand, shock rounding her eyes on the reverend. "A Druid?"

Surprise swung me back to the reverend as well, biting back the ache at the loss of Tad. Druids were very rare. The old seelie queen had massacred them by the thousands, sending the ones who could escape into hiding. Very few remained and were a rarity to come across.

Tad was one of the only Druids I could say was a friend. Losing him still resonated deeply with my family, especially Brex. He had found a way to come back after his death, through a seer, and help Brexley with her powers, but since the battle with Istvan, there had been nothing from him.

"Yes, Iacob runs with an interesting group. They are

what I call free spirits." Reverend's tone rang with judgment. "But the land is spell-protected, and you will be able to hide out there."

Plus, it was a perfect jumping-off point to get to the caves.

"We can get supplies there?"

"Yes, the Râșnov Fortress is close, but they trade there."

"Great. Do you have a map?"

"Wait." Raven stood up. "I mean, we don't even know if we can trust them. Or him." She indicated the reverend. "This might be a trap."

"A trap?" The reverend looked insulted, as though because he wore a clergyman robe, we should believe him. I had lived too long and seen too much of the hypocrisy to know it wasn't true.

"Why would he bother?" I snorted. "He could just open the doors and call the guards in right now to get us."

Raven didn't look convinced, her teeth worrying her lip.

"Hey." Facing her, I lowered my voice, my hands cupping her face. "That temple is close to the caves. We can leave if you don't feel comfortable. But it might be a good place to hide out, get supplies. I won't let anything happen to you."

Her mouth opened to counter me, but I placed my thumb over her lips, gripping her chin with my fingers. "This is the best plan for us. We can't stay here any longer. It's very dangerous."

I felt a shiver go through her, her gaze meeting mine. The sudden impulse to kiss her slammed into me like an avalanche, making it hard to breathe and almost blinding me. Stepping back, I quickly dropped away from her before I acted on it, twisting back to the reverend.

"How do we get there?"

"I can take you as far as I can this evening. From there, you will have to hike up." He padded the coats again.

"Through heavy snow, but there shouldn't be any soldiers that way."

"Even if it's dark, how do we get out of this town without them seeing us? They're stopping everyone, right?"

"You become alms for the poor."

The wagon rocked roughly back and forth as the horse labored down the cobbled streets. My body spooned Raven's without fully touching her, our figures tucked in the corner, covered in heavy bags of grains, beans, flour, medicine, and clothing.

On the premise the reverend was visiting his poorer congregants to deliver provisions for the holidays, his one-horse wagon filled with supplies headed down the road carrying two criminals, unbeknownst to him if we were caught. It was the best plan we could come up with to escape the heavy eyes watching this city for us, though it could so easily fracture. Either by the guards or some do-gooder, thinking they were doing the right thing by turning us in.

Raven hadn't spoken since we gathered up what little we had and helped load the wagon. I could sense her nerves, the anxiety rising in her, reality finally sinking in, comprehending how dire this was.

The wagon wheel thudded over a pothole, slamming us against the board and almost tossing us across the bed.

"Fuck." I hissed to myself, instinctively grabbing for Raven. Yanking her into my frame, I tucked her head under my chin, an arm looping around her, the other holding the base of her throat to keep her pinned to me. Protected.

I felt her swallow a gasp, suddenly making me very

aware of her body against mine. The way her ass pushed into my cock, her natural smell wafting into my nose, which was dark and wild but held a sweetness, the curve of her throat against my palm. With her uneven breaths, her heart hammered in sync with mine, and all I could think of was what we were doing this time yesterday. My body marked the exact time I had been feasting on her and craved more.

My breath drifted down the back of her ear to her neck, and I felt her shiver. Her response was addictive, clouding my logic. This time I couldn't blame it on drugs, though I felt like I was on them. I adjusted slightly, my arm wrapped around her, and my palm grazed the patch of skin where her sweater pulled up. The heat of her soft skin went straight to my groin.

She pulled air through her nose, feeling how hard I was against her.

This was not the time or place. *At. All.* Yet, I couldn't seem to control my need. My fingers aching to push into her pants, greedy to feel her again, to see if she was as wet as I had a feeling she was.

It was so subtle, but I swear I felt her hips open, inviting me to do it, to sink inside her. Biting down on my lip, my hand vibrated, trying to hold back the overwhelming craving, but it was a losing battle.

"Hey!" A voice boomed in the dark, freezing the air and jarring me out of the moment. "Stop the wagon!"

Raven and I froze, dread cracking us like a whip. Fear pulsed in my ears as the reverend slowed the wagon to a stop.

"State your business," a guard barked in Romanian.

"I'm taking provisions to those in need," the reverend's throaty voice replied.

"Now?" another man asked. I could sense and hear at least a handful moving around the wagon in the darkness. "Kind of late, isn't it?"

"It's Christmas. And I have some who are very sick. They need medicine." I noticed how he never actually lied. There were people out there sick and in need. He just wasn't visiting them right at this time.

"Medicine?" a younger man's voice questioned, hearing him move to the side of the wagon, lifting something. "What do you have back here?"

"Medicine, supplies, food. It's for those *in need.*"

"I'm in need," the same young man snorted. "Especially being stuck out here in the freezing cold all night. Can't wait until I don't feel this kind of shit as much."

"Shut up, Jozef."

"What? Don't tell me you don't want to be like them? You're on the list too, Robert." I heard the rustling of a bag near my head. "Can't wait to have powers. Nothing will fuck with me then."

"You'll still be a little bitch." Another man chuckled, the smell of cigarette smoke drifting through the blankets to my nose.

"Search the wagon," the first man ordered.

The sound of boots hit the bed, the wagon sagging under the weight. I locked down even more around Raven. We were going to be discovered, and it was only a matter of seconds. I slowly reached for my gun, but Raven started to tremble against me. Her muscles spasmed, and a barely audible growl vibrated against my chest, reminding me of the time we hid under the floorboards at Anca and Vasile's place. The time she almost convulsed against the goblin metal's power, biting down on my neck to pinpoint her energy.

Fuck. Her shaking, even a little, would be noticed by them.

A soldier rummaged harshly through the inventory, getting closer and closer to us, his boots almost about to knock into mine.

269

Intuitively, I bit down on her neck this time, similar to the way you would subdue a wild animal, nipping down on her nerve.

Calm down, dziubuś. I demanded of her over and over in my head.

She went quiet under me, her muscles going still.

A hand grabbed the bag of corn next to my leg, my heart pulsing in my ears, my thumb squeezing over the trigger, ready for fingers to yank down the burlap bags we were hidden under.

"I really have to get moving before the next storm comes in," the reverend belted out. "Lives are on the line."

"Be better to let them die, Reverend," one of them responded. "More humane."

"Yeah, especially since they have no idea what is coming."

"Shut up, Jozef," the man above me barked. With a heavy sigh, I felt his weight head for the back of the wagon, jumping off. "Go! But next time, priest, we see you passing through here, you might not be so lucky. We *tax* these roads now."

The reins snapped in the air, the buggy jolting forward.

My pulse sputtered, releasing my mouth from Raven's throat as we swayed down the broken old road, breathing a relieved sigh into her neck.

"Stay down," the reverend muttered. "They might have scouts still watching us."

I planned to. "That was fucking close." I took another full inhale and exhale. Each time it felt closer and closer, and one of these days, our luck would run out.

"You okay?" I noticed Raven still hadn't moved, lying there like she was in shock. "Raven?"

"Fine," she said quietly, her voice rough. In the dark, I

could tell she wouldn't look at me, a strange wall building up between us again. Had she had enough of the danger I was putting her in and regretting her choice to be here with me?

A surge of panic clenched in my stomach, but I shoved it away, turning my senses out to the world around us, keeping on alert.

She should leave. It would be safer for her. Better for both of us.

Though the damn knot in my gut only moved up into my throat at the thought.

After hours of being knocked around, the wagon finally came to a halt.

"This is as far as I can take you." The reverend's voice was crisp in the night air.

Sitting up, I pushed the burlap off us, the icy weather snapping painfully at my warm skin. Standing, I peered around in the darkness. The wagon sat before a snow-covered bridge, a frosty river rumbling under. A few rundown houses sat quietly nearby, smoke billowing from the snow-capped rooftops.

"Cross this bridge, and there is a trail about a hundred meters down the road. The trail will take you up to the temple. Tell Iacob Reverend Baciu sent you."

Leaping down from the buggy, I reached up, taking Raven's hips and helping her down. I snatched up our bags and the heavy jackets we hid under. I strolled around to the front, slipping the coat on, feeling the loss of Raven's warmth against my skin.

"Thank you." I patted the horse down, nodding at the reverend.

"You were so kind to us, thank you." Raven yanked on her coat, dipping her head in gratitude to him.

"Stay safe, you two." He smiled warmly back.

About to turn away, I stopped myself, facing him again.

"We don't believe in your god or what you stand for, but you went out of your way and helped us anyway… twice."

The reverend pressed his lips together. "Kindness does not come from God. It's up to us. It should not depend on what religion you believe, nor what species, race, sex, or status you are. Compassion should exist between all life. Unconditionally."

A smile upped one side of my cheek, my head nodding in agreement. Giving the horse another pat, I put my hand on Raven's lower back and directed us across the bridge.

Heading into the unknown.

Temperatures plunged the higher we hiked, snow building up to our shins, filching energy with each forced step, the trail almost disappearing under the white flakes.

Clouds hid any moonlight, the deep foliage permeating the ground in opaque darkness. While my senses could feel nature, the trees guided me through. Raven seemed to move among it without hesitation, as if she was part of the darkness herself, leading the way.

It was odd for her to be this regal beauty with elite manners and entitled privilege, yet have something prowling underneath her skin that felt terrifying and wild. Like two people danced within her bones.

Snow crunched underfoot, accompanied by the sounds of our breathing, the forest speaking softly in its language around us. But my mind was anything but quiet.

"What are you?" My voice severed under the dark canopy.

She slowed her steps. "What?"

"What are you?" The first time, I hadn't really meant to let it slip out, but now that it had, I wanted to know.

"What do you mean?"

"You know exactly what I mean," I replied, my voice low and gruff.

She stopped, twisting her head back to me.

"You know it is rude to ask a very personal question like that."

My legs strode to her until our frames were only an inch apart, my gaze finding her bright green eyes. "My tongue was in your pussy last night… think we went way past personal."

Her gaze snapped up to mine, her lungs faltering at my brashness. She swallowed, her tongue sliding nervously over her bottom lip, drawing my attention to it.

Once again, I had an overwhelming need to kiss her, to feel her lips on mine, to know what her mouth tasted like as well.

My hands clasped her face, my voice so low it was almost on the ground. "What are you, Raven Scarlet?"

A puff came from her throat, her eyes searching mine with a strange fear, which almost hinted at pain. "I can't te—"

"Don't move," a man spoke. The sound of a gun clicked, a barrel pushing into the back of my head. "Not unless you want your brains and hers painting the snow."

I went still, watching Raven's eyes widen on the person behind me.

"Put your hands where I can see them," he ordered, patting me down, relieving me of the gun on my belt. "Slowly."

Inching my hands up, I kept my gaze on Raven, though I saw her head twitch to the side as if she heard something, her nose flaring.

There were others out here.

273

"You are trespassing." He finished patting me down.

Snow crunched when someone else circled around Raven, and I realized I hadn't heard the man approach us.

"You stole all our fun away." A younger woman with pale skin strolled up. Her hair, the color of bluebell wildflowers, lay like thin, soft petals down her back, her eyes the same purple-blue color. Small and delicate, the rifle in her hand looked out of place on her. "They were about to *a face dragoste.*" *Have sex.*

"Shut up, Viorica." The man behind me barked, but I saw her eyes flare with lust at his brutal tone. "We have a job to do, which I seem to be the only one who takes seriously."

"No one takes it as seriously as you, Vlad." Another man came up, broad and built, his dark brown skin blending him with the shadows until he looked at us. His eyes were a bright, glowing yellowish-brown. "And not nearly as much fun as watching him fuck her right here." He smirked, coming behind Raven. His eyes stayed on me as his hands moved down her frame, checking for weapons, sliding over her hips and up her stomach.

Snarling, I lowered my lids on him.

A smirk danced over his mouth, continuing his search, confiscating the knife and gun from her.

"Vlad?" Raven lifted her brows. The name was notorious all over the world, though in America, it was more linked to a storybook vampire and a ruthless leader who spiked his own people. In these parts, he was a cult hero, and many children were named after him.

"They call me that because I enjoy impaling trespassers." He stuffed my weapon into his belt, keeping his pointed at me. He was lean, with a mix of brown, black, and white feather-like hair, dark eyes, and a beak-like nose, reminding me of a goose.

"Or just impale Viorica and her cousin, Brânduşa, like you did last night." The man behind Raven chuckled. Viorica covered her mouth, her eyes dancing with humor and lust as she looked at Vlad.

"You can shut the hell up too, Codrin."

Codrin meant woods. Viorica and Brânduşa were flower names. I had no doubt we had found exactly the group we needed to.

"You know what we do to trespassers?" Vlad gritted at me.

"Invite them in for a warm meal and some brandy?" I replied dryly.

"No." He blinked at me, not getting my humor. "I kill them." His finger started to tug at the trigger.

"We're here to see Iacob." Raven stepped forward, putting herself more in front of me, as though she could protect me from getting shot.

"Raven," I growled, trying to move her behind me, but the silence of the other three took my focus.

"How do you know that name?" Vlad pointed the gun between us.

"Reverend Baciu sent us."

All three looked at each other, the name clearly meaning something to them.

"He told us we could find sanctuary here for a few days," Raven continued.

"Sanctuary from who?" Codrin asked.

"Your newfound queen and her men."

"She is *not* our queen," Vlad spat.

"See, we already have so much in common," I quipped.

Codrin lowered his gun, looking to Vlad to do the same. "We must take them to Iacob."

Vlad still glowered at us, his expression tight.

"Vlad…" Codrin expressed his name with a slight warning.

Vlad huffed, dropping his weapon. "Fine. Let's go then." He motioned for Raven and me to move. "But you pull anything, and I will gun you down where you stand."

"Ohhhh…" Viorica giggled, her shoulders shivering. "Don't you love when he gets all assertive and domineering?"

"You two." Codrin rolled his eyes, moving behind Raven and me. "Move."

Tracking behind Viorica and Vlad, we kept a steady pace up a steep path. Rock formations jetted out of the snowy earth, and I sensed thick magic thumping at my skin. I could taste the unique Druid powers swirling in it. It was telling me to turn around, to leave. Humans would feel this and stay clear, the spell keeping them out. Fighting against the instinct, I tangled my hand in with Raven's, knowing she felt it probably as much. Turning to look at her, I noted her face was white, her muscles tense. Squeezing her hand, I tried to give her comfort, but instead of confusion from the spell, I somehow sensed terror building inside her. Like her need to run had nothing to do with the enchantment.

"This way." Vlad steered us to the left, coming to what appeared to be a stone rock wall, a Pagan Temple sign displayed, when suddenly I felt the slam of magic. A *pop* cracked in my ear, energy sizzling over my form as we stepped from the woodsy, icy outdoors into a tepid hippie tent city.

Chapter 20
Raven

My mouth parted, my body twirling around to take in what was hidden behind the spell, guarding a community inside. Warm, humid air peppered sweat under my heavy layers. Men and women, dressed in a minimal boho style, smoked, chatted, and played instruments around a central bonfire. Tents, or what was more like igloo dome lodging, were spread across the terrain in intricate groupings. One large structure stood in the middle, framed from metal, a main community dwelling with a fire pit, seating, hammocks, blankets, and cushions—a giant living room where a lot of inhabitants congregated.

Lanterns flickered over the vibrantly colored blankets and pillows, sculpture art, paintings, and vegetable gardens dotting in between tents and throughout. At least fifty people, with a few kids, lolled around the spaces, talking, smoking, or playing games. Chickens strutted wherever they wanted, a few pigs and goats freely roaming around too. It seemed no one was abiding by the late hour, which humans deemed sleeping time. Even fae had given over to this in the new era.

The smell of herbs billowed thick in the air from those sitting around the fire, their attention barely lifting when we walked up, reminding me of a night I was at the Burning Man Festival, when everyone was coming down from their high early in the morning hours, still thrumming guitars and smoking weed.

"Brânduşa!" Viorica bounced in, calling to a woman near the fire.

A small, dainty woman turned her head. "Viorica?" Her velvety voice sounded like a soft breeze.

"Look what pretty bees we captured."

Brânduşa's bright yellow eyes widened as she looked to Ash and me. Dressed in a thin and loose purple cotton dress, her skin was darker, her hair a deeper purple, but I could see a likeness in their features.

Brânduşa glided up, appearing even more beautiful and delicate than Viorica. Drifting to us, her attention went straight to Ash, her eyes brightening like the sun, peering up at him as if he were a god. "I must be pollinated by you until I take all of your seed."

"Wha-at?" I choked out, surprise halting my feet, my brain slowly taking in the innocence of her voice and appearance and the bluntness of her words.

"I saw him first." Viorica tried to wiggle between her and Ash, her brow furrowing, and I picked up on a little jealousy. "He will pollinate me first."

"Like you two haven't shared before," Codrin mumbled with a snort, causing Vlad to glare at him.

Brânduşa continued to stare right at Ash, simpering through her thin petal lashes, not backing down to Viorica. "My pollen tube is ready to be fertilized."

My mouth dropped open, my head snapping to Ash. His one eyebrow quirked up, and the side of his mouth turned slightly up, finding this all amusing. "Trees and flowers don't pollinate well together."

"Oh, we're open to cross-pollination here. We don't like boundaries." Viorica bounced with a giggle. "We do not want to actually reproduce, so cross-pollinating with a different species is even better." She peered at both Codrin and Vlad with a lustful glance. "As much as we want."

"We don't live by society's rules." A short, beefy man with a beard and a booming voice stepped from one of the structures. Wearing butterfly boxers and a matching thin cotton robe with sandals, his expression was open and happy, though his dark hair, eyes, and facial features seemed familiar. "We follow our own."

The girls moved out of the way. The human man was only a few inches taller than me but held all the weight, making it clear he was the leader. His personality drew you in, putting you at ease, yet I could see his gaze took in everything, rolling quickly from his men to us, taking in the unspoken situation.

"It's a bit late and cold for a leisurely hike up a snowy mountain." The man clamped his hands together, his expression turning more serious. "And since you were close enough for my people to find you and you are not dead..." He eyed Vlad. "I am thinking you are here on purpose."

"Yes," Ash spoke. "We were sent here by Reverend Baciu."

The man tipped his head in slight surprise, his lips pinching.

"Told us to speak to Iacob."

"I am Iacob." The man confirmed what I had already figured. "And you are?"

279

"Rowan, and this is Scarlet," Ash quickly answered, gesturing to me.

I tried not to react to his fake name, my eye sliding over to him.

Iacob's cheek lifted, his eye squinting, skeptical of us.

"He said we might find sanctuary here for a few days," Ash continued.

"Sanctuary?" Iacob's bushy brows lifted. "From what?" Examining us again, he tipped his head. "He has never sent anyone here for sanctuary. That uptight bastard is not exactly a fan of what we stand for."

"Think he presumed we would fit in here better." Ash smirked. "And we had to get away from the city."

"It's more than that. He would not give my name if it wasn't life or death. What are you running from?"

"The new queen." Ash swallowed.

"Futu-i." *Fuck.* Iacob hissed, his happy features dropping into a scowl, reminding me more and more of someone. "Are you kidding me? And he brought you here? My brother is a real *măgar."* *Jackass.*

"Brother?" I sputtered, but instantly, the familiarity clicked in. The eyes and body structure were so akin to the reverend. "He said you were an old acquaintance."

"Not surprised." Iacob huffed. "He always was an insufferable, righteous asshole." He nodded for Vlad and Codrin to back down, our admittance passing some criteria. "We never got along, but it became worse the older we got. Being a clergyman was forced upon us by our father, to follow in the likes of him. Baciu, being the first son, wanted to please our father, no matter how fruitless it was. I learned quickly that kind of life was not for me, nor did I believe in any of it. I questioned too much, saw the hate, cruelty, fear, and hypocrisy inside the church and even in my own family.

I walked away, searching for my own path. Baciu has never forgiven me for turning my back on the church. On him." He shook his head with a frown, then peered at us. "So it says a lot that he sent you two here." He chuckled. "Either to drop this mess on me, put you right in the middle of the flame, or he actually wanted to protect you."

I wanted to believe it was the latter; Baciu had been kind to us. Saved our lives.

"Well…" he huffed, a tight smile returning to his face. "You're here now."

"We don't want to bring danger upon anyone." Ash motioned around. "It's only for a few days. We need to rest, get supplies in Râșnov, and then we will get out of your way."

"Râșnov?" Iacob wagged his head with a laugh. "That's the last place you should go."

"Your brother told us that was where the closest market was."

"It is, but he hasn't been there in a while. It's changed. A lot." I could hear a warning in Iacob's tone.

Ash adjusted his feet, his jaw ticking.

"It's now a military trading post," Iacob declared, my stomach dropping into my shoes. "They have procured residence in Bran, taking over Râșnov and Brașov. They seem to be multiplying every day throughout here."

"Seem to?" Vlad scoffed. "Their numbers doubled in only a week."

"Bringing in recruits?" I asked.

"No." Codrin wagged his head. "They're taking people from the villages."

"Forcing?"

"Or offering them money and land." Codrin raised one shoulder.

"When one of our own was killed in town getting

supplies, I put a stop to any more visits." A flicker of grief went over Iacob's eyes. "We depend mainly on the visits from Baciu for provisions, and what we can't get, we try to grow and make here." He motioned to the gardens of vegetables and herbs. "Produce our own medicine."

"Which still isn't enough," Vlad grumbled. "And we can't make our own bullets and guns."

"War." Iacob's nose wrinkled. "Such infantile actions of grown men."

"That's why we should have women in charge." I smiled thinly.

"I agree." Iacob nodded. "I may be the leader, but we worship our women here. They are the bearers of life, something men are deeply envious of, and why they chose to constantly put them down. Make them less. Afraid of their power."

"So being at a Pagan's temple isn't happenchance?" Ash's attention went over the space and people again, stopping on two little boys playing.

"I'd say we are closest to that, but we dislike labels. We all agree nature and love are sacred. And it should be given freely and without restrictions."

"Without restrictions? Even the children?" Ash's frame constricted, his throat bobbing as if it was hard to swallow, nodding over to the kids playing. I could feel tension coiling inside him, his childhood trauma seeping up, seeing himself and his sister in these adolescents. I had an urge to take his hand, let him know I was here, and ease his worry as if he meant something to me.

Like he was mine.

Iacob slanted his head, his lids narrowing. "Children should be raised to not fear showing or giving love, understanding how nature and this world work, but I think you are insinuating something else, which I find insulting. We protect and love our children."

"That's the same garbage they told me." Ash's teeth gritted, and I could see the tension between the two men rising.

"Ash," I seethed in his ear, stepping between them and giving a hard look to Ash. The few kids I could see were laughing and running around, appearing blissfully content. "We won't be in your way for long. Just a day or two before we continue on our journey."

Iacob nodded, his face relaxing into a smile, waving his arm. "Follow me. I'll introduce you to those awake, get you something to eat and a place to sleep."

"Thank you so much." I glanced back at Ash. *Behave.*

His eyes rolled up before he released a breath, nodding his compliance. He followed behind while Iacob took us toward the main dome tent.

Mainly fae, with a few humans sprinkled around, the assembly sprawled around the fire, laying on each other. This group appeared youthful, maybe in their early 20s, and barely dressed. They smoked a mix of herbs similar to sage and oregano. Their curiosity in us was piqued with a carnal sexual interest when we walked up.

"Celeste, can you find Dubthach? He can find them a place to sleep."

"How about with me?" A honey-blonde-haired girl with a thick Swedish accent sat up from a bench seat, her legs hitching over the shoulders of a man who sat below her on the floor. Her tank top drooped down, hardly covering her breasts. A sultry smile curled her lips as she continued to smoke, her eyes on Ash, not hiding what she would love to do with him.

"And she can stay with me." The half-lidded man

between her legs smiled at me. He was really pretty, his bare chest spotless of any tattoos or scars, which I found oddly unappealing.

"I don't think so," Ash replied dryly.

The man shrugged, looking up at the blonde, taking the smoke from her lips and putting it between his own.

"Celeste?" Iacob asked again.

"Fine." She kicked her legs off him, standing up, the tank just coming to her thighs. She had a tall, flawless, model-like frame, a stunning face, and watery blue eyes the color of a lake. Most likely a lake fairy. Her hungry gaze rolled over Ash again, her energy screaming sex.

A stab of jealousy prickled at my shoulders, a growl howling inside my bones.

Threat. Kill. Destroy.

The whisper was louder than normal, my hands rolling into knots as I tried to push back the words chanting in the back of my brain before they consumed me.

My body was still thrumming from where he bit my neck in the wagon. The reaction to it was so primal, so domineering. My pussy pulsed as my muscles went limp under his authority, not understanding how he knew that would subdue me instantly.

It turned me on and terrified the hell out of me that he had control over me. Yet, I was about to cut this blonde for the way she was looking at him.

A touch on my hand jerked my head to the left, like being snapped out of a coma. Ash's brows were furrowed at me, his fingers grazing mine, wordlessly dragging me from my dark thoughts. The fact he noticed, saw something in me change, twisted my jealousy to anxiety.

I dipped my head away from him, returning to Iacob as he pointed to each person, not hearing any of the names he rattled off. "And you already met Vlad, Viorica, and Codrin." He nodded as the two men sat down with the rest of the group.

Viorica instantly snuggled up to Vlad, though his expression stayed neutral. He watched Brândușa the entire time when she lowered herself next to the pretty fae guy.

A buzz of magic charged down my spine, drawing my eyes up as I noticed Celeste returning. Sauntering in, her hungry gaze was back on Ash. She dropped back down to her seat, giving way to the person behind her.

My lungs hitched, feeling his magic. It was different from everyone else here, and awareness of it shivered up my spine.

A tall, lean, young African man strolled up, wearing a dashiki-style shirt and cotton pants. The sides of his head were shaved, but his hair was left loose in curls on top. His penetrating brown eyes swept over Iacob and Ash, landing on me.

His magic charged over me like a stampede, picking at my defenses, pounding my heart in my chest.

I knew exactly what he was.

A Druid.

Chapter 21

Ash

The moment the man walked in, Druid magic hummed against my skin, feeling more like an intruder than familiar. Fae magic came in all types, variants, and strengths. Good or bad. It was something fae understood. Accepted.

The energy from a Druid sat differently, and it was always very clear to recognize, especially when you didn't come across a lot of them.

Being around Tad, I had grown more accustomed to it, to the relationship they had with Earth's magic. Different from mine, but still a connection. Tad was one of the oldest Druids, living centuries before I was even a thought. The older a Druid was, the more powerful they became. As the decades wore on, they absorbed more knowledge and magic.

This man was young, his power still a fledgling, though I could sense something about it that suggested he would someday be one of the greats.

He came in with a confident saunter, his eyes traveling

from Iacob to me with a nonchalant response, then his attention snapped to Raven. His feet came to a stop, his expression staying impassive, but his body stiffened, his gaze locking on her, his nose flaring. A sensation in my gut knotted, producing light perspiration to cover the back of my neck.

"Dubthach?" Dubthach, in Gaelic, meant "dark-skinned," sounding like Dew-aach. Iacob's forehead wrinkled, picking up on his reaction to her, peering between the two. "This is Rowan and Scarlet."

I reached out to shake his hand, wanting his attention off Raven. The Druid barely glanced at me, shaking my hand before he turned back to her. Raven's hand automatically lifted to follow the greeting. His fingers skimmed hers when a crackling sound hissed around us. Cold air swept through the encampment, with flakes of snow, the spelled barriers suddenly disappearing.

Dubthach yanked back, his shoulders going back in defense, the warmth curling back around us as if someone closed a door to the chilly outside. I'd almost thought her goblin bracelet stole his magic for a moment, siphoning magic as it does every time I get near it, but it wasn't possible. Druids weren't affected by that type of magic, nor any metal. The instance happened so fast I almost believed I imagined it.

"What the hell was that?" Iacob peered around, a frown tipping his lips, his hand rubbing at his arms. "Is something wrong with the barriers?"

"No." Dubthach peered at Raven in speculation while he spoke to Iacob. "I just strengthened them this morning."

"Odd." Iacob shook his head. "Well, as I was about to say, Rowan and Scarlet will be staying with us a few days. I thought you could get them something to eat and settle them in the healer's pod for the night. It's vacant right now, if I recall?"

He didn't let up his focus on Raven, as if trying to decipher her, something about her narrowing his brows and lining his forehead.

"Dubthach?" Iacob said his name again, touching his arm. The Druid finally swung his head to Iacob.

"Yes." He cleared his throat, his voice deep. His regard jumped to Raven again, his cheek twitching, his brow creased. "I will show you."

"Dubthach is our healer, teacher, and spiritual guide here." Iacob nodded for us to follow. "He will take care of whatever you need. We run mainly on the old fae hours here." Which meant they slept most of the day and were awake at night. "But some will be up with breakfast if you are on daytime hours." He started to walk away.

"Our weapons were taken..." I left off, knowing he understood my meaning.

"I'm sorry, we have a strict rule. No weapons in camp." He lifted his hands. "We are a peaceful place with children. You can get them when you leave."

Fuck. I hated being defenseless in a place I didn't know or trust.

"Now, go get some rest."

I nodded at Iacob, my hand going to Raven's back, prodding her forward.

She reluctantly moved, her hands tugging at the cuffs of her sweater, pulling it around her hands as if she wanted to keep the bracelet hidden from view. Probably a wise thing; we didn't need any questions or anyone to know she was weaker with it on.

Trailing after the Druid, I kept close to her, my hand still on her back. I noticed her body slightly trembling, her hair curtaining her face, hiding her expression, letting me take the lead. Glancing down, concern pinched my lips, wanting to ask her what was wrong, but I knew I needed to wait until we were alone.

Dubthach led us to a larger round dome tent. The walls were covered, but the ceiling was clear, letting the stars spark from above. Lamps flickered, illuminating the room in a soft glow. Several beds were lined up on the floor on one side, a curved wall of shelves with herbs and medicines lined the opposite, along with an exam table and even some dental equipment, which was probably for the humans living here.

"A washroom is through the door." He pointed to a door next to the exam table. "And you can sleep here." He motioned to the made-up mattresses on the floor. "If you are hungry—"

"No." I shook my head, noting Raven moving to the farthest point in the room, away from the Druid. His eyes watched her with intense curiosity as if she was a bug to inspect. The need to get him out of here rushed out my response. "We're fine. Just need some sleep."

Dubthach eyed me, his head dipping, turning for the door. "Breakfast will be in the canteen starting at 7." He observed us one more time, pausing on Raven, then stepped out.

Subtly watching her, I saw her shoulders lower, a breath leaving her lungs. "What the hell was that?"

Her head jerked toward me, noticing I was watching her with a frown. "What?" Her brows creased. "Nothing, except we are now in some Playboy bunny commune."

"Raven," I growled. "Don't even pretend with me. What's going on?"

"Nothing."

I wanted to tear my hair out.

"You were shaking. That Druid guy wouldn't stop

289

staring at you. Something weird was going on between you two." I stomped up to her. "And don't get me started on Playboy. The fairy was about to fuck you right there."

"Compared to Miss Legs and Tits, who descended from the heavens?" She rolled her eyes. "Or what about Ms. Fertilize My Pollen Tube and her horny cross-pollinating cousin," she spat back.

"Jealous?" I leaned into her, almost accusatory. We stared each other down, our chests huffing with anger, a tension that was constantly there now.

There was a line... and I sensed I was about to cross it. The need to kiss her burned through my body, wanting to grab her by the hair and bend her over the exam table. And I was a breath away from acting on it.

"Fuck off," she seethed, stepping back. Twisting away, fury wrung tight across her shoulders.

"Hey." I grabbed her arms, already regretting what I said. "I'm sorry." I breathed out, turning her to fully face me. "What happened? Why was the Druid staring at you like that? Why are you *still* shaking?"

She swallowed, not looking at me.

"Raven?" I held onto her biceps, trying to lower myself to look in her eyes.

"Do you really need a reason?" she huffed out. "We haven't been through enough in the last couple of days? And going from almost being caught by Lazar's men, freezing snow, to spring break in the Bahamas, to this horny fae camp edition?" She gestured around. "It's a lot." She pulled away from me, peeling off her heavy coat and tossing it on a chair.

"Yeah," I muttered, knowing what she said was true, but also it wasn't the full truth.

"Not going to tell me what was going on between you and Dubthach?"

"I have no idea."

"Raven…" I sighed.

"I don't!" She turned away from me, inspecting the room.

Too exhausted to fight her, I struggled out of my own coat, peeling down to my T-shirt.

"Let's get some rest and reconvene in the morning."

She snorted, her head shaking.

"What?"

"Reconvene?" She chuckled at my choice of grammar. "Okay, old man." She patted my shoulder, strolling past me toward the beds.

"Old?" I muttered with a snarl. To be fair, I was. I may look like I was only in my mid-twenties, but she *actually* was. And I needed to remember that. "At least when I was your age, we spoke in complete sentences, not this text talk."

"You know you're old when you use phrases like 'back in my day.'" She tried to mimic my voice.

"Think it's past your bedtime, young lady."

Laughing, she dropped onto one of the mattresses, leaning back on her hands, her smile lighting up her face under the glowing lanterns, her eyes glistening.

My throat went dry. Fuck. Raven was so beautiful, but her beauty went deeper than her skin.

What made me extremely uncomfortable was my response to the women offering me free, uncomplicated, and unbridled sex earlier. It should be a no-brainer since my cock seemed to be working again. I should walk out and take them up on it. Any of them. All of them.

It wasn't just that I felt nothing at their offers, but I glanced at Raven like I should feel guilty they were hitting on me. That I wasn't up for offer. But when that fae twat offered her his bed…

My hand went through my hair with frustrated anger. I strode away from her to the washroom. The thin door snapped behind me, firebulbs lighting up the simple room with a small stand-up shower, toilet, sink, and a cabinet with towels and extra toiletries.

I leaned over the sink, staring at myself in the mirror. For so long now, I felt as though I was staring at a shell of some guy. A husk that functioned only out of necessity. Now, my reflection held a man with flushed cheeks from the warm air, bright green eyes, and a verve I didn't expect. A few flakes of oats were still in my hair, and I looked tired and dirty.

But *alive*.

Maybe a soul was still in there somewhere.

My plan to come to Romania was never to leave it. To seek my revenge in killing Sonya and Iain and die contently avenging Kek and Lucas. To be with them. The only people I imagined I could ever love in that way.

With my friends, you'd never know finding a "mate" was extremely rare since they all found theirs. But for nature fairies, mates didn't exist. We weren't meant to ever be with one. So many nature fairies, even paired with someone, were with many others at the same time. My parents liked each other enough to "pair up" and have kids, but they weren't mates. Not even close. They were very open to others and sharing.

What I really learned when someone found their mate? Sex with any other wasn't even a question, and you'd kill if another touched your mate. Just watching Warwick and Brexley, not counting all my other friends who found their mate, it was clear how unique and strong the bond was. So, the way I loved Kek and Lucas was the deepest I could ever love. And they deserved my loyalty.

Turning on the water, I splashed water onto my face, taking several deep breaths before looking back up in the mirror.

I could see hesitation looming in my eyes, feel my resolve for revenge waning a bit.

No. I'm just tired.

I needed sleep, and I'd be good as new tomorrow. Reset and get back to my plan.

Taking a piss before I stepped back into the room, I finished up then found Raven was already curled up on a mattress, her eyes closed, the room lit only by the stars and moon above.

Sinking down on the mattress next to her, I tucked my arm under my head, staring up, listening for her steady breathing, which oddly calmed me.

Her head jerked up, glancing over at me as if she was making sure I was around.

"I'm here."

She rolled off her mattress, shoving it over until it hit mine.

"What are you doing?" I sat up, watching her crawl back down and scoot over to me, flipping a blanket over us.

"Shush," she ordered, grabbing my arm and pulling it across her.

"Raven?"

"I'm *trying* to get some sleep." She pulled tighter on my arm, curling me over on my side so I spooned her. "Close your eyes and be quiet."

I scoffed at her demand, but started to relax.

"So, Rowan, huh?"

"It's my middle name."

Her head turned back to me. "Ash Rowan?"

"Actually, Ash Hemlock Rowan."

293

"Really?" A huge smile curled her mouth, causing something to hitch in my chest.

"Yes, I know it's a lot of tree names."

"No, I love it," she muttered. "Ash Hemlock Rowan."

The way she said my name, the power of her knowing it, went straight into my veins, twisting a knot in my chest. Only two people knew my full name—Warwick and Kitty. I had never even told Lucas and Kek. But I told Raven.

"Ash Hemlock Rowan," she repeated, making it feel even more intimate.

"Go to sleep, Raven."

"Okay, old man." She took my arm, pulling it over her, tucking into her pillow. I didn't fight it, nor did I want to. The only time I seemed to sleep well was wrapped around her.

This alone should have kept me up all night.

The crow of a rooster bolted my eyes open, a rush of air streaming down the back of my throat, my body jerking awake.

Morning light shimmered through the top of the clear tent fabric, and it took me a moment to remember where I was. My brain rolled with fog from my deep slumber, wanting to sink back into it. Adrenaline jolted me awake, realizing I was alone, the bed next to me a jumble of blankets.

"Raven?" my raspy voice called out, searching the room. Rising, I tottered to the bathroom, pushing the door open. Empty.

I couldn't stop the tightening in my gut, the anxiety of waking up to her gone. We had no idea who these people really were. I trusted no one and hated her being out of my sight.

Shoving my feet into boots, I tied my hair back, striding out of the healer's pod.

Hazy sunshine washed down on the cocooned encampment. Snow piled up around the edges of the spell, leaning against it like it also wanted to absorb the warmth on the other side.

A handful of people moved around, doing chores. My fingers itched to join the woman in the garden, feeling the dirt slide through my hands, the smell of life growing. Getting closer, I noticed she was harvesting mushrooms. A quiet snort huffed from my nose, the fungi reminding me of Bitzy and Opie, the two sub-fae Brexley "adopted." I recalled the serene smile on that cranky imp's mouth when Bitzy was high. It was the only time you'd see her in a good mood, which was contrary to Opie. He always could turn anything into a good time. Especially when he was destroying centuries-old, one-of-a-kind fae books and making dresses out of the pages.

A stab of pain dropped the smile from my lips, and a deep hole ached in my chest that I hadn't let myself feel in a long time. I missed my friends. I even missed those two. Every time the hollowness crawled up into my chest, I snorted more fae powder, deadening my emotions, getting myself so addicted to the numbness I couldn't go a day without. Sometimes more.

My feet faltered, a notion hitting me. *When was the last time I got high?* I couldn't deny I craved it, wanted it badly, but it didn't feel like a necessity as it was before, an obsession I couldn't function without. It simmered underneath, yet it was something I could control, which of course made me want it more because, deep down, I knew I was healing. I didn't need to totally disappear into the void, and I was afraid of what caused that.

Who may have caused it.

Buckling down my straying thoughts, I glanced around, searching for the culprit of my annoyance. The spelled area held a quiet gentleness, as if the air didn't even want to speak above a whisper, knowing most were still sleeping.

Scanning the various areas, I hunted for Raven, letting the smells of food lure me toward a large white tent across the site. Pushing the flap to the side, I stepped in, scanning the space. The aroma of fresh coffee, eggs, and bread filled my nose, coming from a help-yourself kitchen area on one side with various breakfast foods on display: polenta, bread, eggs, fresh veggies, milk, juice, tea, and coffee. Mismatched tables and chairs were scattered around, filled with a fusion of human, fae, and bi-species—families, pairs, and single people sipping on their drinks and munching on breakfast in a happy cadence.

Kids running around laughing, acting like *kid*s. Ordinary. Normal.

It was a shift from the mood of the night hours. A more family-type atmosphere. Not like how I grew up.

My attention was pulled like a force field to a figure against the wall of the tent, sitting with a coffee, her expression solemn as she stared absently down at the table, lost in thought.

Relief slid out from my mouth.

Raven's dark hair was loose around her face, partially hiding it, trying to keep it as a barricade. She played with her ring as she always did when she was agitated. That uncomfortable feeling of knowing her, how she thought, and her behaviors gripped my lungs, twisting my relief into anger.

Striding over to her, I gritted my teeth.

"Don't ever leave me like that again," I seethed. Her head popped up, and I realized quickly what it sounded like. Vulnerable. Needy.

"Excuse me?"

Yanking out the chair across from her, I sat down, keeping my voice low. "We don't know these people. We can't trust anyone. So for now, you don't leave my side without me knowing."

For just a blink, I swore her green eyes turned a reddish color, her spine stiffening.

"And here I thought fae men weren't misogynistic."

"Misogynistic?" I sputtered. "It's called common sense. We don't know these people."

"I can handle myself," she stated firmly, the words bouncing off me like she shoved me. But, more than her anger, it was the walls she was placing around herself, putting me on the other side.

"I know, but not if they all came for you at once, and I didn't know... couldn't get—" I stopped, about to utter what I was most afraid of. I wouldn't be able to get to her.

She sat back, her expression between arrogant and condescending, a smirk playing on her lips. "You have no idea what I can handle."

"Not with that." I nodded to the bracelet she hid under her zip-up sweatshirt, the air warm enough for her to be without, but keeping it covered was smart. They didn't need to know she was at a disadvantage.

Her lips dropped to a scowl, sipping at her coffee, her fingers absently rubbing at it over the fabric.

It hit me again how she still seemed to come off unaffected by it, not like the rest of us seemed to. In prison, when they put it on me for punishment, my bones turned into lead, my energy lethargic. Killian almost died from the mix of iron and goblin metal daily around his neck. Yet, after weeks of knowing her, she seemed the same.

Critically, my awareness moved over her, recalling how

the Druid reacted to her. A hint of suspicion rubbed at the back of my mind, almost wanting to find a fault. A reason to push her away.

Was she some spy working for Sonya? Someone to play on my need to protect and help? Getting close to me while feigning to be some innocent bystander? Forcing her way into my life, finding out my plans, while I thought it was all coincidence?

Staring at her, the feeling in my gut rebuffed the notion. Even if she was, the metal would still affect her, still make her weak, blocking her powers, putting her at a handicap. Yet it might be the best cover to lure me in. My need to help others still was there, even when I thought it died with Lucas and Kek.

Reaching over the table, I wrapped my hand around hers, tugging it to me, feeling the goblin metal clawing for my powers near her wrist. I swept over the deep red jeweled ring, a metal insignia twisted around it.

"What are you doing?" Raven's forehead crunched.

"What's this?"

"A family heirloom." She tried to pull her hand away, but I gripped it tighter.

"And who is your family, *exactly*?" I tipped my head.

"Why do you care?" Her defenses slammed up. "I'm just the obstacle keeping you from your destiny to avenge, right? Why bother getting to know each other now?"

"I've tasted your pussy, Raven. Think we're past that."

Her cheeks flushed a deep crimson. I could practically taste heat moving up her body. A flicker crossed her gaze until she shut down her response.

"And why is it you are the only one who isn't distressed by goblin metal?"

"It hurts me."

My lips pinched, realizing how long I ignored this.

"Not as much as it should." My fingers slid under the cuff of her sweatshirt. She tried to jerk away again, inhaling sharply. Just grazing her wrist, the magic had my fingers coiling back. It wasn't fake, but it also had something unique about it. Different. Another energy source I couldn't place wrapping through it, almost like a buffer.

Odd.

"What is this?"

"What do you mean?" she snapped.

"It's not *only* goblin metal, is it?" I stared into her green eyes.

Her eyes danced between mine, seeing there was more to my questions, an accusatory ring to them. "You think I'm pretending? This isn't real?" She motioned to the cuff.

"I know it's real, but I also can sense there is more to it you're not telling me." *More to you, you're not telling me.* "By now, you should be barely able to stand. It should be sucking out your energy far more than it's doing. So tell me the truth, Raven. *All of it.*"

She watched me, and I swear I could feel her scraping through my sentiments and feelings, plucking out exactly my train of thought. "Are you accusing me of something?"

"Should I?"

"Wow." A harsh scoff pinched her lips as she yanked her arm from my grip.

"Then tell me." I leaned on my forearms. "Why do you have it on? Who put it on you? Does it still block your powers, or have you been lying to me?"

She glowered at me. "*Yes*, it blocks my powers."

"Why are you affected so little?"

She shifted in her seat, not looking at me. "It does affect me."

I glared at her. "Don't fucking lie to me, Raven."

"I'm not!"

"You should be almost incapacitated by now." I practically seethed out my allegation. "Why are you not? Don't you think I deserve the truth by now?"

She stared down at her arm folded on her lap, mulling over her thoughts. I could feel her lowering her guard as her mouth opened to speak.

A figure twisted a chair backward, dropping down at our table, slicing through our connection. Raven and I jolted at the intruder, bristling with defense.

Vlad leaned his arms over the back of the chair, a coffee in his hand, taking us in with his stoic expression.

"Have a seat." Derision dusted my tone. "You need something?"

Vlad peered around, setting his coffee down. "You want to go into the village for supplies? I will take you."

"Why?" Skepticism followed his gaze over the room in caution, wondering what trap he was leading us into.

"Iacob is being naïve to the threat around us." He scowled. "He doesn't believe in fighting or killing."

"But you do," I finished.

"I believe in protecting my property and my family," he stated, his black eyes challenging mine, his dark hair ruffling, resembling feathers. "And if being prepared without Iacob's knowledge saves them from harm, I'm willing to do that."

Geese were known to be exceptional guard dogs, territorial and aggressive to intruders coming into their home.

"Against what he thinks, the truth is we need more weapons to stand a chance. If I need to break the rules and have a gun on me to save my home." He shrugged. "So be it."

"You believe the threat will come here?" Raven questioned.

"It's only a matter of time," he stated firmly. "The military is growing every day, taking up more and more of this area. Invading the villages, building encampments up the other side of this mountain… without the consent of anyone living here." He sipped his coffee, a brow arched. "It won't be long until they come through this area. And we've already lost people. I won't let more die."

Honesty hung from his resolved tone, the determination locked in his frame.

"Okay." I dipped my chin, even more interested in getting Raven's cuff off, the need to peel it away, see what she was keeping from me. To do that, we needed supplies to get to the caves. "We'll need our weapons back."

"Not possible. They are held in Iacob's tent. So, my plan is"—he took the final sip of coffee, setting it down—"don't get caught." He rose from the chair. "We leave *now*."

"Now?" Raven repeated.

"Iacob sleeps until sundown, giving us only a few good hours to get there and back." He headed for the exit.

Raven blinked at me with surprise, our fight dissolving in the wake of this new mission.

Vlad stalled at the entrance, glaring back at us, flicking his head.

"Guess he means now, now." Raven got up from her chair, and I followed in her wake.

"Heading into enemy territory, both of us being hunted, with no weapons?" I muttered just enough for her to hear me. "What could possibly go wrong?"

Chapter 22

Ash

Bundled back up in our heavy jackets, condensation huffed from our mouths as we hiked toward Râşnov. The early morning sun glinted off the snow, enveloping the terrain in whiteness.

None of us said much, Vlad keeping an intense pace up and down the ranges to the citadel. My stomach protested its emptiness with sharp hunger pains, leaving me to wish I had eaten before we set off.

Turning a bend, all three of us came to a stop, taking in the magnificence of the fortified citadel perched on a hill. The lumbering fortress consumed the entire ridge with its creamy stone walls and towers, and brownish-red tile roofs. Built in the early twelfth century, the fortress was part of a defense system with other Transylvanian villages, also offering refuge for the villagers in times of invasion and war.

From here, I could see the gates with throngs of people, horses, wagons, and a few motorcycles clogging the artery of the entrance. Soldiers strolled the walls and held sentry at the gates.

"Keep your hood up and head down," Vlad instructed. "Stay to the middle of the crowd going through the gate. Don't do anything to bring any notice to yourself." He pulled up his hood, taking off for the gate. "And stay close to me."

Basically, be another blended body in the sea of people dressed in bland colors and heavy coats.

Tugging my hood, I burrowed deeper into my layers, herding Raven to go before me. My heart thumped faster the closer we got, the smells of horse manure, body odor, and mud overwhelming my senses. My ears droned with voices and babies crying while humans and fae moved through the gate.

Shuffling with the horde pushing against those wanting to get out, we slowly moved up to the guards. Glancing from below my hood, I held my breath as we pushed past them, the back of my neck prickling as I took in their stiff manner.

No emotion lay in their eyes as they watched villagers come and go, but I could see them searching, waiting for something to stand out. Their eyes dragged over me, my lungs clenching, feeling like they would see right through my layers, knowing I was the one they were searching for, but they slowly drifted past me, moving on to someone else. Air slipped from my lungs when we finally crossed the gates into the market.

The fortress grounds buzzed with activity. Stalls, wagons, and tables were set up in every available spot, with thin lanes in between for the customer to walk. Produce, meat, bread, grains, dairy, weapons, clothes, and black-market items were jumbled together with no structure or reason. The scents of roasting chestnuts, fried sausage, and burning fire from the blacksmiths coated the air in smoke.

"We have an hour. Get what you need and meet me by the gates," Vlad muttered to us. "And don't do anything stupid." He strode off.

"He's nice," Raven commented dryly.

"Come on." I led her into the tight cobbled pathways, aware of the guards watching from the wall above us, waiting for a thief to take his chance or someone to step out of line.

We weaved through the stalls, filling our backpacks with torches, rope, canteens, dried provisions, extra clothes, and new weapons. The money we got from the man in room 105 was starting to run low by the time we grabbed a sausage for lunch.

When our hour was up, the clouds had moved back in, dropping the temperature and our window of daylight for the walk back considerably. Devouring the last bit of my snack, I longed to consume about ten more to even take the edge off my hunger. That was another thing I noticed had returned. My appetite. The drugs and lack of caring about living had slimmed me down, but now I was ravenous. I wanted to consume everything I saw, And the way Raven bit into her food, her tongue licking up the sauce, made me crave more than a few sausages.

I was hungry for more than food, thirsty for more than drink. A bottomless pit for every sin.

"I don't know what's in this. I don't even care." She popped the last chunk into her mouth, her voice low, muttering through her bite. "I'm still hungry."

"Me too."

Her eyes darted up to mine, hearing something in my tone. Whatever she saw in my eyes made her swallow the piece down her throat roughly.

"You got some butter here." One hand cupped her face as my other hand skimmed over her lip, wiping it up. I didn't even consciously think before I sucked the butter off my thumb. When the realization hit me, a voice somewhere in my brain asked me what the hell I was doing.

We froze, staring at each other, my dick aching. The need to suddenly kiss her cracked down on me like a whip. I wanted to feel her lips against mine, taste the spices she just devoured against my tongue, hear her breathy groan, begging to slake her hunger as well.

Her eyes tracked mine as if she could see every thought going through my head, aware of how hard I was for under the jacket. Her teeth drove into her bottom lip, still covered in a slight sheen, drawing my attention to her mouth.

The hand holding her face slid further back, my fingers curling into the base of her neck, my mouth only inches from hers. So close I felt the heat of her breath, her heart racing against my chest. The pull to her was like a magnet, my lips barely grazing hers.

The pounding of hooves clattered over the cobbles, jerking my head up. A dozen black horses galloped into the courtyard, their riders wearing black uniforms trimmed in red and gold, only worn by private soldiers of the leader of Romania.

"Fuck," I hissed under my breath, yanking Raven against the wall with me, keeping my body slightly in front of hers, like two lovers conversing, hoping to blend in with the crowd.

The horses pranced in, each carrying a soldier, and each one ground against my spine. Something about them rushed air quicker in and out of my lungs. They weren't as stiff as the ones outside, but something was off, a smell or a familiar way they held themselves. And then my stomach bottomed out.

Iain rode in, his chin high in the air, his uniform cut to

fit him perfectly, his hair styled back under a hat. It was only a blink, a mere second, but for an instant, I saw someone else. My heart leaped into my chest and then dropped like it had been shot out of the sky.

From this angle, with his sharp, chiseled profile and blond hair... he looked like Lucas.

Pain pierced my heart, acid burning up my throat, and I felt his loss all over again. The disgrace over not honoring him yet. For even contemplating I could ever move on or find someone else, especially after only a year.

A hawk squawked overhead, tipping my head up, the bird circling the fortress, scanning for prey, the wings spanning larger than a normal hawk. A hawk-shifter. My chest halted, recognition dropping weight into my stomach.

The memory of that night, the battle booming around me. I laid in the blood of Kek and Lucas while Iain and Sonya escaped, along with Sergiu and...

Nyx.

The hawk-shifter who used to work for Killian, once a faithful soldier to him. But her vendetta against Warwick and Brexley for killing her lover changed her loyalty. When she tried to kill my friends, I shot her, thinking she was dead. She showed up at the battle, choosing to follow Sonya when they fled.

She hadn't crossed my mind since, forgetting about her, but now terror beat in my chest like her wings. Finding me, the man who left her for dead, whose family were the ones who took hers away, would be sweet vengeance.

Dipping deeper into my hood, away from her keen eyes, I hissed to Raven. "Keep your head down."

The neigh of horses twisted my head to the side. Riders came to a stop, dismounting from their horses, leaving Iain the central focus, Nyx swooping in for a closer perusal.

"There are dangerous criminals at large," Iain spoke to the assembly with a patronizing tone. "We are conducting mandatory checks from now on."

A low grumble of indignant voices muttered through the crowd.

"It is for your own safety as well."

I tried to hold back my snort. It had nothing to do with them and everything to do with the fragile, scared man on the horse.

"If you have your papers, you have nothing to worry about," Iain declared. "If you do not... I don't recommend running. You will not outrun her." He gestured to the sky. On cue, Nyx screeched above, chilling my bones. "Or my guards," he haughtily added, nodding to the men, giving them the signal to move out.

Awareness prickled at me as I watched Iain's smugness and the way the soldiers aggressively went for villagers, strange magic billowing off them, smelling like adrenaline, of fear in their last moments. A bitter copper taste laid on my tongue, memories surging up, plunging more terror into my system.

I knew what they were. Panic heaved through me, stealing my air, spinning my head as if I were caught in a wave.

Before he was killed, Istvan was able to improve his method of turning humans into fae. Most of his early research victims died horrible deaths, except a few like Hanna, who still struggled. Her shift into fae was unpredictable and dangerous.

He eventually achieved better results with his experiments, creating a new breed of fae from humans as he did with his son, Caden, who had been injected with Warwick's magic. It gave Caden powers similar to Warwick and a connection between them, which they both went out of their way to ignore.

Istvan's own son became the model subject, and Istvan opened up labs in Ukraine to produce more like Caden. Create an army of fae-humans who could easily fight and kill fae.

We destroyed the labs, but we knew a lot of test subjects had escaped. And I had a terrible feeling I knew where some were.

I observed the guards, the way they moved, the hints of fae they had taken on, and the shifter qualities their bodies were permanently intertwined with. One clearly was a gorilla-shifter, along with a tiger, bear, and wolf.

Iain surrounded himself with all animal-shifters who could intimidate and kill in a blink. They spread out, demanding papers from everyone.

"Where are your papers?" one growled, throwing a woman on the ground and grabbing her by her hair.

Her screams activated my need to protect and defend, my pulse pounding my ears.

"We have to get out of here," I mumbled into Raven's ear, trying to load my gun inside the backpack so they wouldn't notice.

"How?" Anxiety had her voice rising slightly. "They're blocking the gate."

I peered around, searching for another exit. There was usually more than one. I just needed to be certain where.

Two guards were moving our way, terror dancing on my nerves.

"Papers!" they demanded. Neither Raven nor I moved. "I asked you for your papers." The guard's booming voice drew Iain's head to us as though he could feel the blood of his enemy, the one hunting him down like he was a wild animal.

Our gazes locked. The color of his eyes differed from Lucas's, and in that moment, I saw the heartless shell, no longer seeing the things reminding me of the man I loved, but the man I detested.

Iain was right there. I could shoot him right between the eyes before they could stop me. But then my brain flashed to the after. The part where the guards came for us, shooting, killing Raven, or even worse, capturing her. What they would do to her because of me. The torture. The merciless brutality she would endure.

Vomit reached the back of my throat. *Fuck no.* I couldn't do that to her. Plus, when I killed Iain, I wanted him to suffer. Look in my eyes and know his life was about to end. Have Sonya watch her last son bleed out, understanding she would follow.

Iain's body jerked with awareness that it was me. "It's them!" His finger pointed toward me.

A hawk screeched from far above.

Terror fizzed in my muscles, needing to act, to protect Raven. Scanning the market, my gaze landed on a familiar figure. Vlad stood over by the blacksmith table, a huge fire blazing near where he was standing. His gaze went from Iain to me, and he gave me a tiny nod before he pretended someone knocked him over, stumbling into the fire pit and knocking it over. Burning coal and embers dumped onto the ground, the flames leaping for the fabric, igniting the tent with a whoosh.

Shouts and screams rang out, people scrambling out of the way of the flames, figures trying to retreat, run for the exit, the horses neighing and bucking as the fire lashed up the tent. It was complete chaos. A distraction. For us.

"No!" Iain yelled. "Get him. He's right there." But no one heard him above the commotion, his horse rearing back.

"Come on!" Clutching Raven's hand, I yanked her toward the exit, funneling through the mass of people trying to get out at once.

Gunfire shot in the air from the guards, but all it did was add to the hysteria. People stepped on others, pushing and shoving, emotion turning off anything but survival.

Kee-eeeee-arr. A hawk shrieked, claws skimming over my head.

"Faster!" I ducked into the crowd, yanking Raven harder.

"Ash!" Her cry was muffled when her petite frame got sucked into the swarm, my arms stretching back painfully to keep her with me.

"Raven!" My hand slid from hers, letting her recede into the throng like they were quicksand. "No!" I shoved back, trying to reach her, her frame ping-ponging off the masses. "Get off her!" I smashed my elbow into a man's side as I reached for her, pulling her up with me and rushing us through the gate.

Cries and more gunfire resounded like firecrackers, shoving people harder into my back. We spilled out of the fortress, the wider space giving us room to breathe.

The moment we exited, Nyx was right on me, squawking. Her claws dug into my scalp, her nails sinking in.

"Fuck!" I screamed, my hand rearing back, knocking the hawk hard. Her form tumbled into the mud and snow, which clung to her wings, taking her out for a moment. I didn't hesitate, hooking my hand with Raven's and taking off.

And like so many times since the day she walked into my life, we ran from danger, but this time, I never let go of her hand.

Trudging through the deep powder, our lungs fought to grasp the cold air. The threat of snow hung above us like a pendulum, ready to unleash its supremacy. A game of chance, and at any moment, our luck would run out.

A shrill, angry screech came from the distance, rushing me faster to the woods in a different direction than we came down, desperate for cover. We needed to get away from Nyx's sharp eyes. We couldn't let her follow us.

Raven didn't say one word, seeming in sync with my thoughts—get as far away as we could. Slipping into the protection of the trees, my tension eased being among them, but we still didn't stop. Along with the echoes of Iain's men, the shrieks of Nyx searching for us, hunting overhead, pushed us faster.

We couldn't go back to Iacob's camp. We'd only put them in danger, and we were so close to the caves here.

The thump of my heavy pack drummed with my breaths as we trudged uphill through the deepening snow. Nyx's cries grew further and further away until they bled into the noise of the forest, fading away. Still, I couldn't slow, driving us relentlessly forward.

"Shit," Raven hissed, tripping over a hidden log, her shorter legs struggling to keep up with mine, the snow inching up to our knees. Reaching back for her, I grabbed her arm, helping her up, brushing snow off her legs and jacket.

"I think we're safe now." Raking my gaze over the woods around us, the sounds of a living forest crackling softly in my ears. The trees felt like they were standing guard, protecting us. "We can rest for a moment."

She sucked in full pulls of air, her cheeks flushed pink.

"See?" She motioned to her wrist, out of breath. "It affects me."

My gaze went down to the bracelet hidden under her jacket, my lips pinching. In a moment, I went from thinking she was a spy about to betray me to almost kissing her. *Again.*

"Not as much as it should."

Her jaw tightened, tension weeding between us, wrapping around my chest.

"Well, we're gonna get it off you soon. This trail takes us to the caves."

She kept her attention to the side, her expression staying blank.

"Thought you'd be looking forward to getting it off?" I folded my arms, studying her features closer. "Aren't you?"

"Of course." She nodded, staring at me, but her tone prickled at me. I continued to watch her, trying to pry at her walls, peel all her responses back to the barest truth.

From a distance, a squawk pierced the skies, snapping me back into the protector role. Fear of being found, of her being captured, spurred me to move, the safety of the caves almost in reach.

Unrelentingly, I kept a steady pace for an hour, sweat dampening my back, my stomach rumbling for more food. The first sign of snowflakes floated down, scouts warning us of the militia coming behind, ready to dump on our heads.

My boots came to a flat area, the feel of pavement under my soles. Boarded-up stone huts with A-line roofs huddled near a snow path, blocked by a green gate. My attention went to the large marker indicating the location.

"Look." I pointed to a sign covered in ice and fresh flakes. *Valea Cetatii* was printed across the top, with chipped writing below stating it was closed. We both stood there, as if actually arriving was never something we believed would happen. We were battle-worn, exhausted, and so different from the people who started this journey.

The night we spent with Vasile and Anca seemed forever ago… the night he told me about the caves. About the Vâlve, Talyssa.

"They're spirits, so the metal has no real effect on them. And Vâlves have the power to take it away from you. Make all the gold and metals you acquired simply disappear."

Apprehension thickened the back of my throat, winding down to my stomach. The thrill of getting here mixed with the fear this wouldn't work.

"The caves are closed now. Been cleaned out for decades now. I don't know if she is still there."

If the Vâlve left the cave, we came for nothing.

"You ready?" I swallowed, nodding at the path.

Raven dipped her head, tracking with me down the lane, the trees quietly singing to me, trying to ebb the anxiety-causing mutiny in my chest.

The entrance to the cave came into view, gates blocking the access, but the door had been broken into a long time ago, rusting the hinges open. Yanking torches from my pack, I handed one to Raven.

"No turning back now." I winked down at her.

Her lips pressed together, her body tense as we stared into the cave.

"You okay?"

"Yeah." She feigned a tight smile.

"That was believable," I chuffed.

"I'm fine." Annoyance flickered her brow.

"Didn't believe it that time either."

"Don't like being confined." She shrugged. Why did it seem as if she was throwing out any excuse? "Go." She nodded at the entrance.

Something didn't settle with me. But as the daylight disappeared, the snow fell harder, and temperatures plummeted, I understood time was no longer on our side. Turning on my torch, I nodded for her to enter first. I peered back behind us as I slid through the gate.

The forest was quiet except for the snow hitting the leaves and branches and a slight breeze picking up. A shiver tickled the back of my neck like the trees were trying to warn me.

A storm was coming.

Chapter 23

Ash

The darkness was impenetrable, wrapping around me like it wanted to choke me. I didn't normally mind being underground, feeling Earth's heartbeat, but this was so impregnable it sat on my lungs and wouldn't let up.

Our torches lit a few yards ahead, bouncing over the white limestone formations of Mother Nature's molding art.

I shined my light on the dramatic formations. Stalactites impaled dramatically from the ceiling like spiked chandeliers. The stalagmites twisted and curved up from the floor, forming under thousands of years of the water's relentless attack. The vast space echoed with soft drips seeping from a river nearby, slicking the floor.

The temperate air made me peel off my jacket. The caves, oblivious to the weather outside, no matter what time of year it was, stayed a steady fifty degrees. In the summer, that might be chilly, but coming from the frigid winter outside, this was balmy.

"So?" Raven spoke low, her torch on the metal steps leading deeper into the caves. "How do we contact this thing?"

"Have no idea." I was afraid to even suggest it might not be here anymore. "Hoping it finds us."

"You think it will?"

"If we provoke it."

"What does that entail?"

"Pissing it off."

"You seem to be a master at that."

A soft scoff went through my nose, peering at her with a look that said, *No, dziubuś, that's you.*

Reaching for one of our purchases, I yanked the pick on the side of my pack from its holder. "We mine for gold or whatever we can find." I flipped the pick in my hand, heading down the steps.

"Why does it sound like a really bad idea?" Raven's boots pinged against the metal stairs, following me down to the next level. It was another massive space, designed to resemble some ice palace, a ballroom dripping in white diamonds. The smooth stone glittered in the light, the ground a graveyard of what was left. Overmined, leaving the place empty and hollow.

We walked along the slippery walkway for a bit before I took us off the path, climbing over boulders and venturing into another room.

"Shine your torch here." I pointed to a stone wall, something catching off our flashlight beams. The water wore down the rock until the mineral showed like veins under the skin. "Look there." I pointed to the tiny gemstones preserved in the rock streaming down the wall. "I'll start quarrying there."

"You sure you want to do this?" She bit her lip.

Doubt lined my stomach. I had never dealt with a Vâlve before, and Vasile warned me about their vindictive nature.

"Be careful. Vâlves are extremely emotional, and if you make them mad or hurt, they will come after you with everything they have. They will make you pay dearly."

"You have another idea?"

Raven shook her head. "No, but…"

"We have no other option than to at least try." I lifted the tool, and with a forceful exhale, I swung the pick down. The hit reverberated through my bones, the stone screaming out with a loud cry. Small chunks of rock crumbled when I yanked it out. Swinging up, I struck it again and again. The sharp edge gashed the rock surface, tearing through the skin to the raw bone underneath. Sweat dampened my back, lining my forehead after a dozen more strikes, my muscles burning and aching.

Crack!

A piece dropped next to my toes, cracking open like a broken watermelon, showing its guts. Instead of seeds, seams of gold threaded lightly through it. Not enough to make anyone rich, but I hoped it was enough to goad her.

Crouching down, I lifted a piece into my hand, my senses trying to pick up any kind of change, noise, magic, or shift in the air.

Nothing. "Fuck," I muttered to myself, standing up.

"Maybe it wasn't enough," Raven suggested.

"Or it's not even here anymore." I could hear the defeat in my tone. We had gone through so much to get here, and I never really let myself think about what we'd do if this spirit was no longer here. In my head, it worked out; all we sacrificed and experienced would not be for nothing.

This whole journey, my purpose for even being in Romania, felt as if it was crumbling under me. Every time I

317

had a chance to kill the very people I was here to destroy, I hesitated.

Every day since Lucas and Kek's death, I'd run a thousand scenarios in my head of tracking Sonya and Iain down, and in none of them did I falter. Not for a moment, even if it ended my life as well.

I was swallowed up in a sea of anger, confusion, guilt, and disappointment, and I could no longer tell what was up or down.

"*Szar.*" My fingers tightened around the stone until my joints popped. Fury boiled up until it slipped from my control. "FUCK!" I chucked the rock against a wall, splintering into dust. Picking up the other half, I hurled it at the same place, exploding more debris and minerals onto the ground.

"This was all for nothing," I bellowed, grappling for the pick and hurling it at the wall, watching the hit splinter more fragments, billowing grime into the air. *"Le van szarva!"* *Fuck it!* My hand ran through my hair, about to whirl around and find something else to throw when my eye caught a shimmering in the air.

"What the...?" I tapered off, seeing tiny pieces of minerals float in the air like fireflies, the dust becoming more solid instead of dissipating.

Raven gasped, her flashlight pointed at the hazy silhouette. It slowly shaped into a figure.

A woman.

Her figure was semitransparent, but her stunning features were sharp as if they were carved out of stone. Dressed in a layered sheath hanging off her shoulder, her frame was willowy and tall. Everything about her was gray, from her clothes to her skin, eyes, and hair, causing her to blend into the rocky surface.

Her eyes popped with fury, her gray lips pinching

together, the gold flecks twirling faster and faster, sparking off the light against her dull clothing. Her hand moved, and the gold pieces moved with it, showing they were at her command.

One swish of her hand and they could be used as bullets.

"Talyssa?" I spoke softly, taking a step. There was no point reaching for my weapon on my belt. It would be useless against a spirit. "That's your name, right?"

She jerked at my voice, her gray eyes staring at me, the minerals twirling, inching closer to us.

I held up my hands, shuffling slowly to Raven, wanting to get between her and the gold pellets. "We are not here to harm you."

"Just to steal from me." Her voice sounded like it was cut from the rock. "How do you know my name? That power is only given to those who are worthy."

I hesitated, recalling the curse she put on Vasile.

The metal darted within a foot of us in a threat.

"Vasile sent us."

"Vasile?" She heaved in anger. Her hazy silhouette faded, but her anger sharpened so vividly it slashed through the air, magic cracking at the walls, dropping more pebbles down on us. Her arms went out, freeing the gold pieces.

"Raven!" Shoving her behind me, I felt the gold graze past my head and body, the metal in the air kissing my skin as it whizzed by, but it never hit.

"How dare you utter his name," she seethed.

"I know he hurt you," I yelled, my hands up. "I know he is sorry." Of all things to say, it was the worst to utter.

A scream belted from her, the ground vibrating like an earthquake, and the deafening pitch boomed through me as if the earth had broken open. A rainstorm of rock showered down on us, scrambling me to Raven, pulling us against a bolder, covering her body with mine.

319

"How dare you enter here." Sharp rocks slashed at my skin, dumping down on us, my bones cracking under the weight of each hit. With a pained groan, I curled tighter around Raven. "Your bones will be nothing but dust. This is your burial ground." Blood dripped from the back of my head, my teeth gritting together, trying to ignore the pain.

A growl vibrated from under me, pulling my gaze to see Raven's nose flare as if she could smell my blood, her dirt-streaked face pinched with fury.

"No," Raven's guttural tone ground out, something flashing in her eyes. She pushed out from under me.

"Raven, no!"

"Stop!" Raven screamed, standing up, the power of her demand pulsing through the room, ramming into my chest, stealing my breath. *What the fuck?*

The Vâlve halted. She stared at Raven with incredulity, but I could see the anger building back behind her eyes.

"Stop it." Raven stepped toward her. "Do not let a man have this power over you."

Talyssa paused, blinking at Raven.

"Don't continue to live with this anger and hate when he's moved on. Living his life."

Talyssa's shoulders went back, her outline sharpening.

"You made him pay for what he did."

"Not enough," Talyssa sneered. "He said he loved me and he would never leave when all he did was use me, betray, and steal from me."

"Yes." Raven nodded in sympathy, her eyes sliding back to me. "Men suck."

"Hey," I huffed, slowly standing up and wiping the blood from my head.

"Why do you let him have such power over you?" Raven continued, ignoring me. "You get your power back when you no longer let him hold it."

Talyssa's form stiffened, though her outline stopped pulsing with angry energy. "He needs to be punished for the rest of his days."

"He will be." Raven swallowed. "You made sure of that. When she dies, he will feel the endless pain and ultimate agony of losing a mate, eventually succumbing to death himself." She spoke with authority, as if she knew what it felt like. "No one should have to go through that kind of agony."

Jealousy sank into my bones, painting my vision. My hand curled up into a ball with rage. Did she have that with her ex? Was he her mate? Was that why she couldn't get over him?

Talyssa's attention swiveled to me as if she could feel my temper change. Watching me closely, her gray eyes went straight through me as if *I* were the apparition.

Some spirits had the ability to perceive far more than what our eyes could, see deeper into us and the world. Things we might want to keep hidden.

I didn't want to know what she could see in me.

"You *didn't* come here to steal…" A realization tilted her head, her soundless steps floating closer to me. "You are here for *her*." She looked back at Raven. When her eyes turned to me, they had an awareness that twisted her lips, almost telling me *I see you. I see the truth.*

"We heard you have the power to influence metal." My feet shifted at her intensity, wanting to put up every barrier I could. "Even goblin metal. Make it disappear."

"Yes, I can."

I reached over to Raven, pushing up her sleeve, displaying the bracelet.

Talyssa inched back, her eyes locking on the spelled metal, her brow furrowing.

"Can you get it off?" Hope sped up my heart. "If you do, it's yours."

321

"Mine?" The spirit's eyes widened.

"All yours." I offered Raven's wrist to her. Gifts were a big deal to spirits. They were their weakness, yet she didn't react to my offer, her attention fully on the cuff. A sensation prickled at the back of my neck when Talyssa's translucent fingers stretched out slowly, hovering over the metal.

Raven jerked from my grip, stepping back at the same moment Talyssa withdrew from the metal, a strange hiss coming from her.

"What?" My head danced between them, but neither responded. I was nothing more than a spectator as the women squared off.

"Interesting," the spirit replied low, her focus dissecting Raven.

Raven's chin jerked up, her lids narrowing.

"What's going on?" No one seemed to hear me.

"You're afraid of what could happen," Talyssa stated. It was not a question, but a truth.

"Don't," Raven replied so low it sounded like a growl.

"Someone talk to me." The knot in my stomach expanded, dread making me feel as if I were about to walk off a cliff.

"You don't want it off," the spirit said to her. "You like it there."

"That's ridiculous," I scoffed. "It's goblin metal. Of course she wants it off." Doubt started to lace my throat. "Right?"

"It's much more than that." Talyssa's attention stayed on Raven.

"What?" My brows drew down, my head snapping to Raven. Her eyes were downcast, her throat struggling to swallow, not at all fighting Talyssa's claims. "Raven? What's going on?"

"Nothing." She shook her head. "Let's go."

"Go?" I sputtered, grabbing her arm. "What the hell are you talking about? We risked *everything* to get here."

"No, *you* did," she spat back, pulling away. "I never said I wanted to come here."

My mouth opened to rebuke her but stopped, my mind rolling back through our conversations, hearing my voice and not hers. I stepped back in shock, realizing not once had she ever stated her willingness to come here. She never pushed or even talked about getting the bracelet off. It was all me. I just assumed she did. It was a burden put upon her by those guards. Yet, I never saw them put it on her, never confirmed that was where she got the cuff.

"Who put that on you?" My voice was gruff and accusatory, my chin nodding at the element.

She tucked hair behind her ear, licking her lip.

"Raven?" My voice rose.

Her gaze was to the side, her jaw locking.

"TELL. ME. NOW!"

"My family did," she yelled back, her arms thrown out.

"Wh-What?" I shuddered, spitting out each word. "They put it on you? Purposely?" How could anyone do that to their child?

"I asked them to. They did it to protect me."

"Wait… what?" Disbelief rammed into me. "Why?" She shifted on her heels, not answering me. "Why would you do that, Raven?" I practically yelled.

"I had to, okay?"

"Had to?"

"Because I am a murderer!"

A barked laugh came up my throat. "That's why? Because you accidentally killed a guy during sex? I have known a lot of murderers in my time, and you are not one of them. It was an accident."

323

"It wasn't." Emotion flashed in her eyes.

"You are not capable of murdering someone."

"You have no idea what I am capable of. What I am."

"So you keep telling me," I shouted, getting an inch from her face. "Take it off. Let's see what you got." I knocked at my chest. "Show me who you really are."

"You don't want that," she insisted.

"Why?" I challenged, getting even closer. "What are you hiding?" I reached for her arm. "Why doesn't the goblin metal affect you as it does other fae?"

"Because it's not just goblin metal." The Vâlve spoke instead, wrenching my head to her and then back to Raven. "There's *more* you need to suppress."

Raven appeared ashen, terror stilling her in place.

"What?" I knew the ground under me was gone, but I had yet to fall. "What does she mean? What else are you hiding from me?" I gnashed my teeth at Raven, feeling like the girl I had spent so much time with was nothing but a stranger to me. "What the fuck are you?"

"Yes, Raven. Why don't you tell us *all* what type of murderous beast you are?" A woman's voice came from behind, spinning me around.

Fuck. I recognized the blonde woman pointing a gun at us. Eve. And the Russian Mafia was right behind her. My stomach dropped in my throat, my hand reaching for my weapon.

"I wouldn't do that." Eve wiggled her gun at me as the Russians spread out, their weapons on us. "Hands up."

Neither Raven nor I moved, my attention moving around, trying to see every player, every possible escape. I noticed Talyssa had disappeared; a spirit allows very few to see her real form.

"I said hands up," the blonde woman demanded, her gun clicking.

324

Slowly I let go of my weapon, not willing to put Raven's life in danger, my arms rising.

"Still ignoring my orders, Raven?" Eve moved in closer, a sneer centered on the girl behind me.

"I tend to disregard those who murder their own friends in cold blood," Raven snarled.

"There are always casualties in war. Reid sadly was a sacrifice which had to be made."

Three men circled me, stripping me of my weapons, the other two searching Raven.

"But really, it was your fault. If you just stuck to the approved plan that night, listened to me, things might have been different."

Approved plan? I peeked over my shoulder at Raven, wondering what else she had kept from me.

At one time, I had wanted to keep my distance from her, not get personal, know nothing about her. I thought I had her all figured out. A rich, bored, college coed, looking for a bit of an adventure. The joke was on me.

"Reid trusted you." Raven fumed with anger and betrayal. "My family and *I* trusted you. You've been with us for years." She shook her head in confusion. "How could you?"

"Gods, what a spoiled, privileged child you are. Unaware of true hardship out in the world." The woman sneered. "The mindless days I had to stand there while you shopped, had lunch at exclusive boutique restaurants, and cry about the same boy, over and over while getting texts from movie stars and models. Getting away with actual murder while everyone covers for you. Poor Raven..." She pushed out her lip mockingly. "Life was so cruel... while I was sold as a Russian child bride to some human in the States when I was ten. No one cared about those little girls, did they?"

325

Raven swallowed back sorrow and disgust. "You blame me for that?"

"No, but being on your protection detail, knowing the closer I got to you working as your bodyguard, earn the trust of your parents, the more I could bend them to their knees."

"But why?" Raven blinked back emotion. "What did they ever do to you?"

A deep laugh came from behind Eve, my blood turning cold at seeing who stepped out of the darkness.

Nikolay the Bloody.

"Oh *dorogoy.*" *Sweetheart.* The half-Vampir stepped to Eve, his nose brushing up her ear through her sleek ponytail, his hands on her hips, pulling her slightly back into him. A heated smile formed on her face, showing an intimacy between the two.

Lovers.

"What haven't they done? Your family has caused so much death and destruction. They are drowning in it, in their corruption." Nikolay's cruel smile was pointed at Raven. "But your hands are just as red now. And Mommy, Daddy, and your uncle just swept it all away, like his life didn't matter, like all our lives don't matter to you guys." He kissed Eve's neck, though his gaze never left Raven. He stepped around the blonde, a smirk on his lips. "And I think it's time you pay for your crimes. Have your family know how it feels to lose a child." He nodded at one of his minions. "To really feel despair."

"What?" Eve turned to him.

"Kill her," Nikolay ordered the men.

"No, please! Don't!" I tried to move my body in front of Raven's, ready to take the bullet. The three men around me grabbed me.

"Nik?" Eve frowned. "We are supposed to take her

back. *Vozhd* told us he would handle it." I knew that word had been once what Russians called Stalin. Chief, supreme leader.

"The *Vozhd* isn't here." Nikolay's vocals tightened, not liking her stepping in. "I am. And he told me to handle it."

"Nikolay." She blocked him, worry crinkling her brow. "He said nothing about killing her."

"Get out of my way." His lip curled, showing off his sharp canine teeth, his anger simmering under the seams. He was not someone you fucked with. "Or you will be next. I can find an easy fuck anywhere."

She jerked, hurt coloring her cheeks, and moved out of his way.

"You touch her—"

"You'll do what, tree fairy?" Nik folded his arms, a knowing grin hinting on his lips. "Yes, I know who you are, Ash. Your name back in the day, along with Warwick's, used to cause fear. Now look at you. A babysitter for a noble brat." He *tsked*, his head wagging. "Pathetic."

My jaw cracked under the pressure of my teeth. Nothing in this cave gave me any power; even tree roots were too far above me to feel.

"I don't particularly want to piss off *The Wolf*, but if you get in my way, I guess I'll have to."

"Fuck you."

"Your choice then." Nikolay shrugged, ordering his men. "Kill them both."

"No!" I bellowed. As a shot rang out, I wrenched from the men's grips and leaped for Raven. I felt it sink into my gut, the pain tearing through my abdomen, a grunt driving me to my knees. I lurched for one of the men holding me, taking him down with me, trying to grapple for his gun.

I heard Raven scream, calling for me, saying something

else in a fevered tone, but I could no longer hear her. Gunshots exploded off the cave walls, flashlights flickering around as pandemonium took my senses.

Metal clanked to the ground, my attention catching Raven's bracelet landing on the stone.

"No, Raven!" A woman's shrill tone pierced the air in an echo.

Everything felt like it stopped. The power coming off Raven halted the air in my lungs, freezing us all in fear with the warning that something even deadlier had entered the space.

"Raven! Don't!" Eve cried out again, as if she was the only one who knew what was coming.

A deep growl came from Raven, beams of light flickering over her.

She lifted her head, her hair sliding away from her face. My body jerked back, seeing her hair and skin turning black as night, her features slightly off, dark magic swirling around her.

A snarl lifted her lips, her teeth like daggers, her nails like scythes.

Her eyes flickered fire-red. Eyes I had seen before and recognized they only meant one thing.

Death.

Chapter 24
Raven

"Ash!" His name tore from my lips, his body lurching in front of me, dropping to his knees as the bullet ripped through his stomach. The sound of the gun rang in my ears, the intangible terror wrapping around my lungs while chaos danced around me, though I barely comprehended it.

I could smell his blood in my nose, taste it on my tongue, his life and energy bleeding from him while he still fought, trying to protect me.

They. Hurt. Him. Fury scorched my lungs, stilling me to the point time slowed down, incinerating everything but my need to protect. To kill what was hurting… *mine.*

I heard it growl in my throat. Possessive and deadly. My muscles vibrated with energy, magic pushing so hard against the cage of the bracelet that vomit pooled in the back of my throat.

Gunfire volleyed around me, ricocheting off the stone

walls and ground, zipping by me… and at any moment, one of those shells could take Ash away from me.

"Take it." My voice was low and lethal, commanding someone I could not see. But somehow, I knew she heard me. She was near. "Take it, Talyssa, I give it to you. *A gift.*" Gifts were a weakness to spirits. They could never turn away from a gift.

Energy buzzed next to me at my bequest, feeling the spirit's fingers touch my wrists, her energy skimming my skin, the Vâlve's magic coiling over my arm.

A bullet hit the dirt right at my feet, barely missing Ash.

I no longer cared or feared what I was letting loose. They would fear me.

"Now," I snarled and snapped.

Clink.

The spelled cuff loosened from my arm, dropping to the floor with a thud, freeing me of the heavy weight I carried. The creature I contained. Like a dam breaking, my magic flooded in, filling me with power, crashing into me like a storm.

"No! Raven!" Eve's cry snapped my head up to hers, her eyes widening in terror, knowing what was happening. She was the only one here who really knew what I was capable of. Had seen what I could do.

A stab of trepidation sizzled my veins at her terror, understanding I no longer had control of myself. Free from the cage I put myself in. Magic poured into my system, burning through my veins and searing up my vertebrae. Blades pushed out from my spine, tearing through my clothes like daggers.

A pull I couldn't even describe dragged my attention to the man on the ground, zeroing in on him. But then my nose picked up the scent of his blood, spilling out from his stomach and a cut across his cheek.

330

My brain shut off, my instincts taking over, wanting to destroy anything that harmed him.

"Raven! Don't!" Eve pleaded, her legs already retreating. She knew to run, to get far away, which only encouraged my nature.

Magic sparked behind my lids, my eyesight sharpening, allowing me to see through the darkness to better hunt my prey.

A deep growl came from my gut, my lip lifting, showing long canine teeth as dark energy swarmed around me, resembling thick fog.

My mouth parted in a hissed curse… and I no longer was me.

I was the monster of their nightmares.

Chapter 25

Ash

Eve's scream bounced off the ceilings and walls, her legs tripping up the stairs as a deep noise gurgled from Raven.

Raven.

The girl I had been with for weeks stood before me, capturing my full attention as I watched her hair and skin blend into the darkness, her teeth sharp as razors, coordinating with the ones on her back. I waited to see her fully shift, to become what I knew she was. Her form stayed human, but somehow even more frightening and formidable.

"_Ty che, blyad_?!" _What the fuck?_ Nikolay yelped, backpedaling and almost tripping up the stairs, his gun firing at Raven. "Kill her!" he ordered his men as he escaped after Eve.

A bullet grazed Raven's arm. Her lips parted, a growl rumbling through the cave, stopping the beat of my heart for a moment.

The gang of men shouted, shooting at her, their terror

332

thickening the air, making them more reckless while they ran for the escape.

A shot sank into Raven's arm.

"Raven!" I cried out, trying to push myself up, my wound hitching me over with a gasp, my teeth gritting. When I peered up again, she was gone.

A horrified scream came from the other side of the room.

It was her eyes, the glint of the blades on her back, her claws I saw through the dark. Red flames burned bright in her eyes before blood sprayed and a man's throat tore open. Death barely registered in his eyes before his body dropped.

"Run," another man cried out, pounding up the steps. The men shrieked in fear, racing up, their weapons firing back at her.

What the fuck? Nothing hit her, as if she was in some protective field.

My lids blinked through the darkness, noticing her lips moving, a sheen of energy circling her, repelling the bullets. Her magic was protecting her.

I could feel a unique energy; the power lacing through her muttered voice was not fae, though her body was. I couldn't fully hear what she was saying, but the few words I caught sounded similar to ancient Latin.

Like Druid spells.

Two men stalled before reaching the steps, their bodies going stiff. They turned to face her, dropping their weapons.

It was a moment before I understood—she was controlling them.

My attention went to her, her lips moving, her eyes glazed over as if she was no longer there. Thick liquid pooled from her nose and eyes.

Black blood.

Fear took over, pushing me to my feet and overriding the pain in my gut. "Raven?"

She did not respond. Her mouth moved in a continuous chant, the men's figures vibrating, a deep horror on their faces as blood started leaking from one of their eyes.

"Noooo! Please!" he screamed. A pop sounded, and his body dropped, red liquid gushing out of his ears, his eyes open, staring blankly. Dead.

The tracks of blood pooling from her nose oozed in heavy droplets, splattering to the ground. I could feel her energy draining as if her own power was killing her as well.

"Raven!" I bellowed, my hand reaching for hers. Magic slapped against my skin like a whip, wanting to shove me out. Gritting my teeth together, I forced it through the barrier she had around herself. "Raven, stop!" My fingers wrapped around hers. A bolt shot into my nerves, and my muscles quaked at the contact, feeling like fire was burning through me.

"*Dziubuś!*" My hand squeezed hers.

Her head snapped to me, her flaming red eyes narrowing. For a moment, I expected her wrath to strike out at me, adding me to the bloody mess of bodies strewn about. Her nose flared as if she smelled me, and in a blink, the flames in her eyes glimmered green, her features altering back to normal.

"Ash," she croaked, her eyes watering with blood. The bubble around her popped, her body crashing to the ground. The other man she controlled fell to the ground in a lifeless heap next to his buddy.

"Raven!" I dropped down next to her, ignoring the pain ripping through my gut, blood still leaking from my wound, adding to the slick mess on the ground. The moment I touched her, I sucked in sharply, sensing the hollowness in her, the absence of any magic. Even with the goblin metal, I could still feel magic within Raven. But now I felt none. She was an empty vessel. Magicless.

"Raven?" I swallowed, my voice shaking when I touched her again, rolling her over. A hiss of breath came from my lungs. Her body and face were back to normal, but black blood continued to leak from her nose and eyes, her skin so ashen I had to double check her pulse. A knot of dread formed in my throat when she didn't move, her chest barely rising.

"Raven?" I touched her face, feeling her sweaty skin cooling. She had no response to me. What if I lost her? What if she died here? All because I forced her to come. "Raven, wake up." No response. "Gods dammit, Raven," I roared. "You can't die on me now. Wake up!"

Her lids popped open, eyes burning red for a second before they dissipated into green, her lungs heaving in air. She blinked at me a few times, as if she didn't know where she was. She started to sit up, and I grabbed her, helping her. Her head twisted around, noticing the bloody, torn carcasses around us.

"Oh gods…" Her words were barely audible, her muscles quaking. "I killed them."

"Yes."

Struggling, she pushed to her feet, retreating from me. "You shouldn't be near me."

"You won't hurt me." I stood up, flinching as I tore the wound my body was trying to heal.

"You don't know that."

"I do." And I did. I had no idea why, but I did.

"I'm not good like you." She stepped back even farther, her gaze never meeting mine. "It's why I kept the bracelet on. To protect others from me. I am the monster you fear."

"I am not afraid of monsters." Regaining the space she put between us, I cradled her face, gripping it harder than I planned, needing her to look at me. I wiped the blood under her nose and eyes. "I surround myself with them."

335

Her eyes snapped to mine, her body trembling under my touch, weak with fatigue, but she held herself strong.

"Now, I think it's time you tell me the truth," I rumbled.

Raven swallowed, distress dancing in her green eyes.

"The whole truth," I gritted, gripping her chin harder. "What the fuck are you? What I just saw... none of it should be possible."

Her lips pinched.

"Tell. Me. Now. Raven."

Her expression shifted from trepidation to strength, her chin rising in my grip, her shoulders pushing back.

"I'm a dark dweller." She swallowed. "And a Druid."

Dark Dwellers were known as the assassins in the Otherworld, rare and greatly feared. If you saw one, you were already dead. I had actually met a few of them when we fought Istvan the year prior when the Dae Ember and her mate Eli helped us.

But to be that *and* a Druid. It should be impossible.

"Not just a Druid, but a natural Obscurer."

"What?" My hand dropped away from her, stumbling back, feeling the first twist of actual fear, no longer feeling the bullet embedded in my gut. "A natural Obscurer?"

They were unheard of. Natural Obscurers were powerful Druids born of *black* magic embedded into their DNA from their mothers. They went against everything in the Druid world of white magic.

Druids could train in black magic, but it was almost nonexistent to be born with it. It required an *extremely* powerful Druid to not "poison" her unborn child with black magic, killing them.

Druids had different magic than us, which fae already hated, but Druids mixing in black magic terrified us. They could control fae minds, bend us to their wills. And Obscurers were the darkest of Druids. The most rare and *deadly*.

336

"No." I swallowed, already knowing the truth but not wanting to believe it. There were rumors of two twins being born, but I heard nothing about them. "It's impossible to be both."

"Tell that to my parents and twin brother." She smiled coolly.

"No." I shook my head, putting the puzzle pieces together. I took another step back, dread pounding my heart. Seeing her in a new light, I realized why so many recognized her, why she held herself with such grace and poise. I could now see the resemblance, the mannerisms. The signs were all there for me, and I missed them.

Standing in a pool of blood and bodies she created, I stared at the pretty coed I had met in a bar over a month ago, by happenchance, not aware of the ties weaving around us, making our lives inevitably linked.

"You see it, don't you? Who my parents are?"

"I need to hear it from you," I muttered, requiring affirmation, though the truth was right before me.

"I am Raven Haley Scarlet Dragen," Raven stated, her chin rising with pride. "Twin sister to Rook Jared Raghnall." She pushed her shoulders back. "I am the daughter of Queen Kennedy and Lorcan Dragen."

She wasn't just some bored rich college girl… she was royalty.

An actual fucking princess.

"Well." I swallowed. "Fuck."

To be Continued…
Land of Monsters (Savage Lands #8)
Coming this summer!

About the Author

USA Today Best-Selling Author Stacey Marie Brown is a lover of hot fictional bad boys and sarcastic heroines who kick butt. She also enjoys books, travel, TV shows, hiking, writing, design, and archery. Stacey is lucky enough to live and travel all over the world.

She grew up in Northern California, where she ran around on her family's farm, raising animals, riding horses, playing flashlight tag, and turning hay bales into cool forts.

When she's not writing, she's out hiking, spending time with friends, and traveling. She also volunteers helping animals and is eco-friendly. She feels all animals, people, and the environment should be treated kindly.

**To learn more about Stacey
or her books, visit her at:**

Author website & Newsletter: ww.staceymariebrown.com

Linktree: https://linktr.ee/authorstaceymariebrown

Facebook Author page:
www.facebook.com/SMBauthorpage

Pinterest: www.pinterest.com/s.mariebrown

TikTok: @authorstaceymariebrown

Instagram: www.instagram.com/staceymariebrown/

Goodreads:
www.goodreads.com/author/show/6938728.StaceyMarie_B
rown

Stacey's Facebook group:
www.facebook.com/groups/1648368945376239/

Bookbub: www.bookbub.com/authors/stacey-marie-brown

Acknowledgments

I couldn't do this alone, so a massive thanks to:

Colleen - Thank you for being the I in "we" and always having my back. Couldn't do this without you.
Mo &Wendy - Thank you for making it readable! So lucky to have you both to make me sound intelligent!
Jay Aheer - So much beauty. I am in love with your work!
Judi Fennell - Always fast and always spot on!

To all the readers who have supported me - My gratitude is for all you do and how much you help indie authors out of the pure love of reading.

To all the indie/hybrid authors out there who inspire, challenge, support, and push me to be better: I love you!

And to anyone who has picked up an indie book and given an unknown author a chance. THANK YOU!

Contemporary Romance By S. Marie

Down for the Count

How the Heart Breaks

Buried Alive

Smug Bastard

The Unlucky Ones

Blinded Love Series
Shattered Love (#1)
Broken Love (#2)
Twisted Love (#3)

Royal Watch Series
Royal Watch (#1)
Royal Command (#2)

Foreign Translations

Italian Editions

L'oscurita Della Luce Serie (Darkness Vol. 1) (Darkness of Light)
Il fuoco nell'oscurità: serie (Darkness Vol. 2)
Gli abitanti dell'oscurità (Darkness Vol. 3)
Il sangue oltre le tenebre (Darkness Vol. 4)
Blood Beyond Darkness (Darkness Vol 5)
West (Darkness Vol 6)
City in Embers (Collectors Vol 1)
The Barrier Between (Collectors Vol 2)
Across the Divide (Collectors Vol 3)
From Burning Ashes (Collectors Vol 4)
The Crown of Light (Lightness Saga #1)
Lightness Falls (Lightness Saga #2)
The Fall of the King (Lightness Saga #3)
Rise from the Embers (Lightness Saga #4)
Savage Lands (Savage Lands Series #1)
Wild Lands (Savage Lands Series #2)
Dead Lands (Savage Lands Series #3)
Pezzi di me (Shattered Love) (Blinded Love Series #1)
Broken Love (Blinded Love Series #2)
Twisted Love (Blinded Love Series #3)
Descending into Madness (Winterland Series #1)
Ascending from Madness (Winterland Series #2)
Royal Watch (Royal Watch Series #1)
Royal Command (Royal Watch Series #2)
The Unlucky Ones
Buried Alive
How the Heart Breaks
Down for the Count

Portuguese Editions

Savage Lands (Savage Lands Series #1)
Wild Lands (Savage Lands Series #2)
Dead Lands (Savage Lands Series #3)
Bad Lands (Savage Lands Series #4)
Blood Lands (Savage Lands Series #5)
Shadow Lands (Savage Lands Series #6)
Silver Tongue Devil (Croygen Duet #1)
Devil in Boots (Croygen Duet #2)
Caindo na Loucura (Descending into Madness) (Winterland
Tales Livro 1)
Saindo da Loucura (Ascending into Madness)(Winterland
Tales Livro 2)
Beauty in Her Madness (Winterland Tales #3)
Beast in His Madness (Winterland Tales #4)
Má Sorte (The Unlucky Ones)
Sob a Guarda da Realeza (Royal Watch #1)
Royal Command (Royal Watch #2)
How the Heart Breaks
Down for the Count

Polish Editions

The Boy She Hates (Shattered Love #1)
(Broken Love #2)
(Twisted Love #3)

Czech Republic Editions

Divoká říše (Savage Lands #1)
Wild Lands #2
Dead Lands #3
Bad Lands #4
Shattered Love #1

French Editions

Savage Lands #1
Wild Lands #2
Dead Lands #3
Bad Lands #4

Israel (Modern Hebrew) Editions

Savage Lands #1
Wild Lands #2
Dead Lands #3
Bad Lands #4
Blood Lands #5
Shadow Lands #6
How the Heart Breaks
Down for the Count

Turkish Editions

Savage Lands #1
Wild Lands #2
Dead Lands #3

Russian Editions

Savage Lands #1
Wild Lands #2
Dead Lands #3
Bad Lands #4
Blood Lands #5
Shadow Lands #6

Made in the USA
Coppell, TX
01 November 2024

39472698R00195